A YEAR LESS A DAY

A YEAR LESS A DAY

An Inspector Bliss Mystery

James Hawkins

A Castle Street Mystery

THE DUNDURN GROUP
TORONTO · OXFORD

Copy-editor: Michael Hodge
Design: Jennifer Scott
Printer: Webcom

Canadian Cataloguing in Publication Data

Hawkins, D. James (Derek James), 1947-
    A year less a day / James Hawkins.

ISBN 1-55002-480-9

    I. Title.

PS8565.A848Y42 2003   C813'.6   C2003-903530-1

1   2   3   4   5   06   05   04   03   02

We acknowledge the support of the **Canada Council for the Arts** and the **Ontario Arts Council** for our publishing program. We also acknowledge the financial support of the **Government of Canada** through the **Book Publishing Industry Development Program** and The Association for the Export of Canadian Books, and the **Government of Ontario** through the **Ontario Book Publishers Tax Credit** program.

Care has been taken to trace the ownership of copyright material used in this book. The author and the publisher welcome any information enabling them to rectify any references or credit in subsequent editions.

                                    J. Kirk Howard, President

Printed and bound in Canada.
Printed on recycled paper.
www.dundurn.com

Dundurn Press	Dundurn Press	Dundurn Press
8 Market Street	73 Lime Walk	2250 Military Road
Suite 200	Headington, Oxford,	Tonawanda NY
Toronto, Ontario, Canada	England	U.S.A. 14150
M5E 1M6	OX3 7AD	

A YEAR LESS A DAY

acknowledgements

All characters depicted in this novel are fictitious and any resemblance they may have to any person living or dead is purely coincidental. However, I acknowledge that this work was inspired by the habitués of coffee shops around the world, including La Poet, Cannes, France; Perkins Coffee, Nanaimo, Vancouver Island, British Columbia — especially Sunnie and her staff; The Sunflower Café, Ladysmith, British Columbia; and most especially by the wonderful poets, musicians, writers, artists, patrons, and staff of The Corner Coffee House, Newmarket, Ontario, all of whom I have the privilege of calling friends.

Kathy the carer, John the engineer, Andrea the director, Carol the singer, Mabel the florist, Nancy the birder, Catherine the scrabbler, Mary the banker, Dave the mineralogist, George the superintendent, Kevin the librarian, Gillian the actress, Jesse the bird whisperer, Lynne the therapist, Mikaleena the fashion designer, Debbie the dairymaid, Lisa the herbalist, Innez the plivate eye [*sic*], Sandra the writer, Mike the builder, Pete the guitarist, Paul the photographer, Malcolm the novelist, Jenna the tot-teacher, Patrick the sailor, Ron the big guy, Paul the gemmologist, Katie the personal trainer, Lillian the sweetest woman in the world, Stanley the sweet and sour shrimp guy, Sharon the nurse, Patti and Donna — the mums, John and Cynthia — the greatest Brits, Diane the channel, Caroline and her caricatures, Ralph the barrista, Bob the musical director, Jim the cigar man, Sylvie-Anne le mademoiselle, Susan the lawyer, Tom the arranger, Rosie the hummingbird, Noreen the nightingale, Bernice the poet, Elaine the PI, Ted the accountant, Anna the hairdresser, Goldfinger Ron, Donna at the library, Roy the reporter, Angela and her fairies, Jim the market guy, Al and Kerry on the web, Rick the drummer, Tamara the bookseller, Jackie at the dead centre, Jeff the artist, Cara and Bene the Moonrakers, Carol the teacher, Kate at the kindergarten, Janice and her teens, Jim at Chapters, John the drycleaner, Peter the meteorologist, Artful Claire, Lara the songstress, Gord the storyteller, Ron the golfer, Mo the squirreller, Thor the constructor, Grant the plumber, Wendy the veterinarian, Elizabeth the jeweller, Diane the councillor, Leo the actor, Chris the Major, Jack the raconteur, Trish the entrepreneur, Tony the realtor, and the entire biker gang.

The staff: Cynthia, Brooke, Candace, Ann, Jessica, Debbie, Nancy, Lindsay, Jagger, Stephanie, Katherine, Kay, Cathy, Anouk, Chris, Robyn, Vilija, Sandra, Stefany, Mary Lou, Sunny, Christine, Philip, Kathryn, Megan, Anthony, Allison, Kristen and Sara.

Very special thanks to:

Michael Rowbottom for his many years of friendship and for his kind permission to quote his poem, "Trouble."

My greatest apologies go to all those I have missed and, above all, my greatest thanks goes to Sunshine, without whom none of this would have made any sense.

*This book is dedicated to
my younger daughter, Emmeline.
A golden heart who brings
light and laughter
to all who know her.*

chapter one

Life, love, lies, and lotteries are adventures so perilous that it is surprising anyone would willingly participate in any of them, but when all four coalesce and start ticking down in conjunction, the chance of a simultaneous joyous outcome is hardly worth a wager. Yet, the day Ruth and Jordan Jackson set such an escapade in motion, neither thought it at all risky.

Life was given to the couple nearly forty years ago by their respective parents with almost no consideration of the consequences, but their love had been more measured, though it had certainly taken friends and family by surprise — especially Ruth's. They may be of similar age, but that's where the resemblance ends. Jordan is tall enough to look arresting in uniform, and handsome enough to be a politician or a pilot, whereas Ruth had suffered plainness at birth and has gone downhill ever since.

"Oh, what a ..." but *lovely, beautiful* and *pretty* had stuck in crib-side throats.

"... nice baby," was as far as anyone had strayed from reality. "Lovely personality," friends and family would say as she grew dumpily through puberty, and Ruth's few friends who had shown up at their wedding had been more curious than congratulatory. However, life was not totally unfair to the dark-haired, plump young woman. Her premature pregnancy had been easily lost in the folds of flesh and the flow of her wedding gown, and Jordan continued loving her even after the stillbirth of their only child a few months later. Jordan's mother, on the other hand, had never loved her, and was very quick to assert that the loss of the child was clearly ordained by God.

As the years passed, Ruth's waistline inched apace; one inch per annum come feast and famine; binge and starve; high this, low that; quirky and quacky diets; blood, sweat, and tears — tears mainly. If only the tears had dissolved fat at the same rate as sweat does, Ruth would have found herself alongside Fergie in the tabloids, but, in the long run, the tears never helped.

The coffee house is her enemy. Lattés with whipped cream, double-chocolate explosions, and white-chocolate mousse bombs — death by chocolate. "Live by the sword ..." the maxim begins, and Ruth followed the maxim to the letter the day she and Jordan borrowed a fortune from his begrudging mother and opened the coffee house. "I'll expect interest with no excuses," Mrs. Jackson senior had said, and had turned up on the last day of each month to pursue the point. "This is just the interest, mind," she'd say with her hand in the till.

The day the fateful clock starts ticking begins a nanosecond after midnight, but only comes to life for Ruth at dawn, when crepuscular rays warm the curtains, and she wrestles against bedclothes and gravity to give Jordan a shake.

"I'll get the coffees going," she says, and hears the key in the lock downstairs as the baker's deliveryman lets himself in. "The baker's here," she carries on, as she struggles into a dressing gown. "Oh, come on, Jordan. Cindy'll be pounding on the door any minute."

"Damn woman," mutters Jordan, and Ruth wants to believe he's referring to Cindy, the part-time waitress.

"You haven't forgotten that I have to go to get those test results today," calls Jordan as Ruth's heavy footsteps on the wooden stairs vibrate through the old building. "Damn woman," he mutters again, and takes a chance on another thirty seconds before Ruth's voice shatters his dream.

"Jordan — Get up, now! Cindy's here."

Cindy is forty, but is stuck, like her name, in permanent adolescence. In her own mind she is barely out of college, the consequence of an unnaturally prolonged spinsterhood, and she still sports the ponytail, the obnoxious attitude, and the geeky glasses to prove her point.

The nauseating smell of stale coffee hits Ruth as she opens the door to the café. Cindy slips in the front door under the baker's nose and uses her wet coat to demonstrate her annoyance as she angrily fights it off.

"How come he gets a key an' I don't?" she moans. No, "Good morning, Ruth. How are you?" No pleasantries; just bitching.

"Because you lost the first three we gave you," snaps back Ruth. "Anyhow, you wouldn't need one if that lazy ..."

Jordan's footsteps on the stairs behind her cut her off. "I've gotta be at the hospital by ten," he says, seeking recognition of his suffering, hoping for a touch of sympathy, perhaps.

"You'll have to go by yourself," says Ruth. "Cindy and Coral can't manage lunch on their own. And knowing that place, you'll be there all day."

"Thanks," he mumbles as he shuffles into the kitchen to fire up the stove for breakfast.

Cindy is still bitching about "the crappy evening girls" who didn't wipe the tables properly — who never wipe the tables properly; her crappy landlord, crappy men, crappy life, crappy job ...

"If you don't like it ..." starts Ruth, then lets it go as she switches on the percolators. With Jordan shuffling around like a constipated duck, she doesn't need the hassle of trying to find a replacement for the woman. "I'll get dressed," she calls to Cindy as she heads back upstairs, then stops at the sound of tapping on the glass front door.

"We open at seven ..." screeches Cindy, then hardly drops a notch as she looks to Ruth. "It's crappy Tom."

"You'd better let him in," says Ruth, "Or the poor old guy will crap on the doorstep."

Tom rushes through like an express, scoops the daily paper, and hits the washroom at full speed. "Thanks, Cindy — I was bustin'," he calls in his wake.

"Shut the crappy door this time," shouts Cindy. "Nothing worse than some jerk fartin' in the morning."

"You haven't been married, have you?" chuckles Ruth, halfway up the stairs, and starts Cindy off again. "Nah. Crappy men ..."

The open front door is a magnet. "You open?" calls Trina Button, strolling in with wide-eyed innocence.

"Looks like it," laments Cindy, "but the coffee ain't ready yet."

"Herbal tea and horoscope is all I want," replies Trina as she drapes her jacket on one chair, her purse on another and sits on a third. "Can't do anything without my horoscope. Where's the paper?"

"It was here... Tom," Cindy calls, "you got the paper in there?"

"Yeah."

She turns to Trina and shrugs. "I would buy your own if I were you — God knows what he does with it in there."

"I'll wait," says Trina, "I'm not going back across that road again without checking my stars. It might say I'm gonna get hit by a bus."

"Not today," says a new arrival who's swept silently in, as if on skates. "You're safe today, Trina."

"Tomorrow, Raven. What about tomorrow?" demands Trina of the newcomer, as if she was looking forward to the experience.

"Ah. You'd have to consult me professionally about that," says Raven while fumbling in her purse for the key to her consulting room at the back of the café.

Raven is not the young woman's real name, but is so apropos of her startling appearance that no one challenges it. When Ruth had placed an ad for the small room in the window six months earlier, there were only two inquirers: the impossibly tall, sleek-bodied, black-haired psychic channel, who appeared from nowhere one suitably sultry morning; and someone equally dark who was exceedingly circumspect about his intended use. Raven got the room partly because she had held Ruth's nigrescent eyes in her gaze and announced, matter-of-factly, that as she could see the future, she wouldn't have bothered to apply unless the outcome was assured. It was a logic that Ruth had been unable to refute.

Raven, who may well have been hanged for her beliefs in less enlightened times, set up shop in the back of the café and lived on herbal tea and tofu while she read palms, auras, and fortunes for a pittance. However, her practice grew phenomenally when word leaked out that, for a more respectable fee, she would lay stark naked, inert, on a black velvet chaise-lounge, while spirits channelled through her. Why Serethusa, her spirit guide, would only speak to her when she was nude was a question no one had ever asked. It was the message, not the medium, that people came to hear; although quite a few — men and women alike — were happy to pay to see the medium.

"You're early ..." starts Cindy, but Raven is impatient.

"Where's Ruth?" she demands. "I've lost my damn key."

"Don't expect her to give you another ..." complains Cindy, but Ruth is back down, dressed, and cold-shoulders Cindy as she unlocks the office door for the incredibly slender woman.

"There you are. Take no notice... Man trouble."

"No it ain't. I ain't got a crappy man."

"That's what I mean, Cindy," says Ruth. "And I'm not surprised, the way you treat them."

"Harrumph!" Cindy exclaims, as she marches back to the counter and finds Trina using the phone to wake her kids for school. "You might have asked," Cindy moans. "Anyone would think you work here."

In the harsh light of a fluorescent tube, Raven's office is stark and cold, the chaise-lounge sleazy. The young woman hustles to light candles then, turning to Ruth, she stares as if she has sunk into a sudden trance.

"Do you ever buy lottery tickets, Ruth?"

"No. Just the government's way of taxing the stupid and the poor," she answers, then questions, "Why?"

"Buy one today Ruth ..."

"Ah. I don't think ..."

"I know you're not a believer. Just humour me. What have you got to lose?"

"But, I don't ..."

"Today's your day, Ruth. Everyone has a day."
Raven is earnest as she continues in a sing-song voice —
like an ersatz preacher hosting an evangelical television
show. "You mustn't waste your chance. The rest of your
life hinges on today, Ruth. I came in especially to tell
you ... I received a message from my channel. 'Tell Ruth
it's her day.' Serethusa said, as clear as ..."

Cindy barrels in. "Quick. Trina's had an accident
and crappy Coral's phoned in sick again. I'm pissed
off working ..."

"What d'ye mean, accident?" starts Ruth, but Trina
hobbles in with blood streaming down her leg and collapses on the chaise-lounge. "Fine bloody psychic you
are," she moans to Raven as she tries to stem the blood.

"Was it a bus?"

"No. A kid on a blasted bike. I was just going to the
7-Eleven for a paper. . ."

"See, I was right. Told ya you wouldn't get hit by
a bus."

"It's gonna be one of those days again," muses Ruth
as she grabs a handful of tissues and dabs at the blood.

"It will be if you don't get someone to help at
lunch," gripes Cindy as she storms off.

"Remember what I said," whispers Raven in Ruth's
ear. "Today."

"Yeah, OK. But first I gotta get someone to do
lunches. Jordan's going to the hospital ..."

"He'll be fine," cuts in Raven with a degree of
knowingness rare even for her.

"Good. Perhaps you could tell him that. Then he
wouldn't need to go."

"Don't listen to her," says Trina. "She said I wasn't
gonna have an accident."

"'Bus,' I said. And I was right ... It wasn't."

Ruth thinks her day has bottomed out an hour later when she calls in the coffee order and finds herself talking to a credit manager. "There has to be a mistake," she says, though she knows there is no error; knows that the baker had delivered without quibble — if his cheque hadn't bounced, whose had?

"Where the hell is Jordan when I need him?" mutters Ruth, then sinks with a pang of guilt. Hospital — suspicious streaks of blood in the toilet bowl; more to worry about than an unpaid bill for both of them.

"I need help out here," calls Cindy, sticking her head into the tiny office. "I haven't had a crappy break yet, and customers are walkin' out."

"All right."

"No, it's not all right, Ruth. Mouthy Dave just threw a crappy fit cuz I put sugar in his espresso ..."

"All right — I'll be there," Ruth yells, then promises that the coffee deliveryman will get cash.

"No cash, no coffee," says the credit manager, and Ruth knows she's over a barrel.

Raven is locking her office and leaving. It's barely eight-thirty. "Don't forget, Ruth," she calls over the counter as Ruth is already fogged up with information — was it three cappuccinos, two with sugar one with caramel and a vanilla latté with skim ... or was it ... "Forget what?" she queries testily.

"Your day," repeats Raven resolutely. "Today is your day. Serethusa said so."

"I'm quitting right now," bleats Cindy, tossing a pile of dirty cups in the sink — hoping one or two might break. "I've had enough of this crappy place. Dave just grabbed my fuckin' ass again."

"Yeah right," says Ruth to both of them, and puts double caramel in the latte as her head spins.

"I will quit, Ruth," Cindy carries on, but she snatches the coffees off the counter and heads to a table with a scowl that dares anyone to touch her or complain.

Ruth looks up from the espresso machine with an idea. "What are you doing today, Raven?"

Raven hesitates then grabs an apron off a hook on the side of the fridge. "Oh, all right — just this once. And only because Serethusa says it's your day."

Ruth smiles. "You must have known I was going to ask. Wouldn't want Serethusa to be wrong, would we?"

"Serethusa is never wrong."

"I really hope you're right, Raven," says Ruth, her mind chiefly on her husband.

Cindy is back with another order and a snarl for Raven. "Roped you in now, has she? I hope you know what you're doing." She drops her voice, though not far enough, "Make sure she pays you cash."

"I'll pay," insists Ruth, though she's wondering if the cash register will take the increasing load.

Ruth is right about the hospital. Jordan phones at four to say he's still awaiting test results. "Good luck," she says, but she is still flagging with the aftermath of lunch and her tone has an acerbic edge. The evening staff are in; two teenaged schoolgirls: Angela — who'll threaten death to anyone who calls her Angie — and Margaret, who has an opposing view and is universally called Marg. They are bubbly and enthusiastic — while Ruth is around — but will quickly droop until their boyfriends arrive at closing. At ten-to-eleven they'll fly around complaining about how busy they've been, and how they have to get up for school. Then they'll rush off, half done, to hit the bars and dance clubs 'til three a.m.

The phone rings as five o'clock approaches. Ruth grabs it, hoping it's Jordan; wanting to say, "Sorry — but I'm worried about you, that's all."

It's Raven with a final reminder. "Oh for Christ's sake — all right," mutters Ruth, then struggles out of her apron, grabs a dollar from the register, and heads for the convenience store across the road.

Jordan is parking the car as Ruth comes out of the store a few minutes later. He sits staring out of the windshield as if he's lost, and Ruth crosses back over the now-quiet road and approaches, wary of scaring him.

"Are you all right?" she asks, bending into the driver's window.

Jordan's hands are frozen to the wheel and his knuckles look close to bursting. "Cancer," he mouths, dropping a grenade with the pin pulled.

chapter two

The old Chevrolet sinks under Ruth's weight as she slumps into the passenger seat. They sit like accident victims waiting for the emergency services to show up, but no one calls 911. Theirs is an accident yet to occur, though the path is clearly set. The question, "How long?" remains unasked and unanswered, but holds them locked so powerfully on the road ahead that passing pedestrians stare worriedly.

Ruth breaks the silence eventually, conscious that the burgeoning feelings of loss and grief are trying to overwhelm her. "What did they say?"

"Six months, max," Jordan replies succinctly, and Ruth crashes.

"Sorry, sorry, sorry," she blubbers through the sobs. *Sorry I doubted you; sorry I nagged you; sorry it's happening to you.*

What about me? Someone inside her is asking as she tells Jordan, "There must be a mistake — they make mistakes, right? They're always making mistakes." She brightens momentarily. "Surely they can treat it — operate or something. They must be able to do something."

What about me? is screaming to get out as she waits for Jordan to get his thoughts together. *It's all right for you,* she tells herself as she watches him; waiting for his response. *You'll be dead. You won't have to deal with everything. The bills — all the fucking bills. Not just the bills we can't pay now — more bills — medical bills, the funeral.*

This is crazy — your husband is dying and all you worry about is money.

Jordan opens up a little, as if he's coming out of a coma. "Chemotherapy might help. They're gonna try."

Ruth isn't listening; her mind is spinning out of control. *Insurance — How many times have I told you we should take out life insurance?*

How the hell can we pay for insurance when we can't even pay the coffee supplier?

This is crazy — Stop worrying about yourself, bitch. Think of Jordan. What's going through his mind? Look at him; hug him; kiss him. Tell him everything will be all right.

"I don't know what to say," she says, doing her best.

Brilliant! Is that it? Is that the best you can do? But something holds her back; *This isn't happening,* insists the voice with a note of anger. *He can't die — he's not even forty. What about the holidays we never had? And kids; as soon as we have enough money — you promised.* "Don't worry," you said. "As soon as we can afford it we'll have more." *And if I can't?* "We'll adopt, foster — whatever it takes," *you said.*

"Jordan, there has to be something they can do," she says, finally bringing herself to lay a hand over his in an attempt to thaw him out.

"Chemotherapy and radiotherapy, they said. They gave me some booklets."

"So — they can cure it?"

Jordan shakes his head almost imperceptibly, but doesn't take his eyes off the road in front of him.

"I want to talk to them," insists Ruth. "They'll listen to me. They've got to do something. This isn't fair."

"They'll do their best."

"Raven," muses Ruth angrily. "Blasted witch. What does she know?"

Jordan looks at her, confused. "What?"

"Raven said you'd be OK."

Jordan snorts his derision, then says, "Dave — you know, the beer breath, triple-espresso, telephone engineer?"

"Cindy says he grabs her ass," says Ruth, momentarily distracted.

"She oughta be grateful," sneers Jordan. "Anyway, Dave thought his wife was seeing another guy. Then Raven says, 'Dave — stop worrying, she isn't.'"

"What happened?"

"He gets home and finds her in bed with a plumber."

"Raven's always bloody wrong."

"No. She was right. It wasn't a guy. The plumber was a dyke."

Their laughter is real, but fleeting, as the depressingly lonely road of widowhood quickly re-appears in Ruth's future. *Where now? What to do with the information — hide it in a Cadbury's chocolate bar or a litre of Häagen-Dazs Rocky Road?*

"I'm scared," she says.

"We'd better go in," suggests Jordan, trying to keep the conversation light. "It's poetry night — the girls'll be busy."

Ruth slumps back. "Oh, no. I don't think I can handle poetry night — they're such a depressing bunch. Why can't we just drive away and keep going forever? Maybe we can outrun it."

"We've got to carry on," says Jordan.

Ruth tries hard to keep her face up, but it crumples again. "I don't think I can."

Why bother? says someone inside. *Why not just go in there, fire the staff, fling out the customers, shut the doors, and open the fridge. You've eaten your way out of bad situations before.*

And look where it got me.

"Come on, Dear," says Jordan, easing her out. "We've got to be strong. We mustn't upset the customers."

"Customers!" explodes Ruth, "I don't give a ..." She pauses quizzically. "It's not contagious, is it?"

"No, of course not. Not directly. But if word gets out, it might as well be."

"I don't ..."

"Listen. I spoke to a counsellor ... people will avoid us — well, me, once they know. They don't want misery, Ruth. It's a coffee house. People come here to escape misery. We can't tell anyone, Ruth. Do you understand? We can't tell anyone at all."

"But they're our friends."

"Ruth, don't kid yourself. They're lonely, sad; holed up in one-room apartments, or holed up in a mansion with someone they can't stand. They're our friends because we're the only people they can rely on. They don't come for coffee — they can make coffee at home for peanuts. The coffee's just an excuse. They're escaping."

"I want to escape. Why can't I escape, Jordan? This is ridiculous. I don't give a shit about their sad little lives. This isn't happening to them, this is happening to us. Jordan, please tell me this isn't happening."

"We've got to face it ..."

"Why are you so calm? I want to scream. I want to kick something. It's a nightmare, right? Tell me I'll wake up." *Wake up somewhere else, as someone else — not trapped here in this horrible body with a husband who's going to leave me penniless.* "Jordan — tell me it's a nightmare."

The coffee house has taken on a new mantle by the time Ruth and Jordan are finally forced out of the car by the September evening's chill. The harsh fluorescents and muzak of the day have been extinguished, but it will take more than vanilla-scented candles and a mock-log fire to warm them. The stage is set with a single swivel chair in the soft glow of a pink spotlight. An eccentric collection of poets clusters around a table trying out their latest works on each other before braving the stage, while a cuddly bear of a man sneaks a chance to upstage his peers by slipping in a quickie while testing the microphone.

"Ask not for whom trouble comes a-knocking," begins Michel, a soft-voiced giant with the calloused grimy hands of a charcoal-maker. "It comes for thee."

Michel stops at the sight of the owners entering from the street. "Hi Jordan, Ruth," he calls, and all heads turn.

Jordan attempts a greeting smile, but Ruth's falls flat as the early poets acknowledge them. "Oh, God. The silly hat brigade," mutters Ruth with a contemptuous edge and she gets a nudge from Jordan.

"Shh ... They'll hear."

"Well, it's like a bloody religious uniform," whispers Ruth, and Michel reinforces her point by donning his wide-brimmed, aging fedora to signify that he is now starting in earnest.

"It's my latest poem, 'Trouble,'" continues the big man into the microphone, then he drops his voice an octave and takes on a poet's serious mien.

> Ask not for whom trouble comes a-knocking.
> It comes for thee.
> Don't answer the door
> Let misfortune meet you in the street
> At least you have a chance to run.

Ruth bursts into implacable sobs and dashes for the stairs to the apartment.

"Very touching, Michel," says Jordan, taking off after his wife, and the poet beams with pride.

"Thanks, Jordan."

As the voices drone in the café below, Jordan and Ruth run out of words and sink into the silence of over-bearing grief, their minds focussed so deeply on the hurt that they have no spirit for outward expression. Ruth cleans her glasses for the thousandth time and wishes she could smoke. There is a dried-out part-pack of Marlboros in her underwear drawer, a reminder of the day, a year earlier, that she smoked five in succession in a desperate effort to lose weight. It had worked — marginally and briefly — she'd vomited until the bile burned her throat. She hasn't smoked since, but now she desperately wants something to occupy her pudgy fingers. She knows they should be caressing and soothing Jordan, but something holds her back. She watches him, slumped pathetically into his favourite chair with his eyes boring into the carpet, and already sees a shadow.

"We could sell everything and live it up in Maui or Mexico for a few months," suggests Ruth, with more humour than sincerity as she attempts to bring life to the atmosphere, but Jordan harshly stomps on the idea.

Their assets wouldn't cover half of what they owe his mother, assuming they could find a buyer, and, with his condition diagnosed, he'd never get medical insurance — ever again.

I could eat, she thinks, *I could always eat*. But the insensitiveness of eating in front of Jordan while the malignancy develops in his intestines keeps her fastened to her chair. "If there's anything you want ..." she tries, and Jordan replies poignantly, "To live, that's all. I just want to live."

Ruth explodes in a gush of emotion and Jordan does his best to console her. They both want to hear the words, "Everything will be all right," but the words are wisely unspoken.

The café clears at eleven, and Ruth is happy to leave behind the gloom of the apartment while she goes downstairs to prevent the evening girls from escaping prematurely. The last thing she needs is a fight with Cindy in the morning.

The register appears to be a hundred dollars light when she cashes out, but with her brain already swamped, Ruth puts it down to miscalculation and turns her attention to the cake cooler.

How could you? demands her inner voice, and she slams the door, drops the knife and bursts into tears.

Jordan is asleep in his chair by the time Ruth returns with a black candle filched from Raven's consulting room. The flickering flame is warmly yellow, but it has a dark heart, and in it Ruth sees a dismal future. Not only will she have to run the coffee house without Jordan's help while the cancer and treatment take their toll, but she'll have to continue years after his death just to repay his mother and their other debts.

The night drags and periods of oppressive silence are interrupted by Jordan's snores, and the hum of the refrigerated display cabinets downstairs in the café — a nagging reminder to Ruth that a degree of solace is close at hand. Caramel crunch cake topped with Rolo ice-cream can be hers for the price of climbing down the stairs, but she worries that Jordan may wake and find himself abandoned, even momentarily, so she stays. Fearful that his final precious moments are already draining away, she studies his face and sees it aging under her gaze.

He's not forty for another five weeks, yet he has the drawn look of a prisoner — a lifer; his greasy wan skin the result of daily incarceration in the café's kitchen.

How can he sleep so soundly? Ruth wonders as the night air cools and she gently drapes him with a blanket. But hadn't it been her complaints about his lethargy that had driven him to the doctor in the first place? *If I hadn't kept on at him to work harder, this wouldn't have happened*, she tries telling herself, then shakes it off as she turns the spotlight on her husband, almost willing him to hear. "How could you do this to me?" she muses illogically. "Haven't I been through enough?"

Pull yourself together, she tells herself, realizing that the burgeoning anger is overwhelming her with a desire to smash him in the face. It's not his fault. He's not dying on purpose. And it's not your fault either.

"I bet the fucking old bat'll blame me," she whines to the air, knowing that somehow Jordan's mother will manage to twist the facts until her darling son's suffering can be laid at her daughter-in-law's feet.

It's not your fault, she tries again, but can't avoid the ridiculous feeling that she has somehow driven him into the arms of another, as if the tumor is a malignant third party with whom he is willingly flirting — a cancer that will ultimately win him away from her.

"Jordan, I love you. I'm not going to let you go," she whispers tenderly as she brings herself down and kisses him lightly on the forehead, but she knows that while a pair of frilly panties and a peek-a-boo bra may have worked in the past, it'll take more than that to break him away from this new mistress.

The flame of the exhausted candle is barely alive at dawn, and Ruth's tear-clouded eyes see Jordan through a fog as if he is already cloaked in a shroud when the sound of Cindy's crappy Ford pulling into the gravel parking lot reminds her that time has not stopped, despite her most fervent wishes. She is still dressed from the day before and rushes downstairs to the front door, waiting with a spare key in her hand, as Cindy arrives.

"Sorry. I should have given you this before," Ruth says, flooring Cindy. "Jordan's got a bit of a cold. I'll do the breakfasts," she adds and quickly turns back into the café.

"Are you all right?" queries Cindy, turning over the key in her hand. Ruth scurries away with her face to the kitchen. "I've asked Phil to come in early and I'll take on someone new if Jordan's not better in a few days," she calls over her shoulder, but has difficulty keeping her voice straight.

Ruth shivers as she turns on the bright kitchen lights. *It's the stainless steel appliances and ceramic tiles*, she tells herself, but knows it is Jordan's absence, and quickly fires up the gas stove. "I can't do this," she says, losing her nerve. Not that she can't cook — it isn't complicated. Eggs — "Any way you want" — bacon, sausage, hash browns, and bagels, mainly.

You can do it. You just need to eat first, says her inner voice. *You've got to keep up your strength.*

How can I eat when my husband's upstairs dying? she scolds herself.

Not today. He's not dying today, nags the voice, and she grabs a frying pan and opens the fridge. Three eggs or four, she is considering, when Cindy's shouts and the noise of a commotion in the café send her running. In an instant her mind conjures a terrifying scene, with Jordan writhing in death throes at Cindy's feet, and her heart is pounding as she plows through the door.

It's not Jordan, he's still asleep upstairs.

It's Trina, struggling to control a yapping yellow Labrador she has hauled in off the street, and Cindy appeals to Ruth for backup. "I told her not to bring her crappy dog in ..."

Trina cuts her off as she drags the animal around the room by its collar, looking for a tether. "It's all right, Ruth. It's not mine — it's a stray."

"Trina, this is a café!" remonstrates Ruth, but Trina's determination to rescue the animal makes her deaf, and she quickly fashions a leash out of an electrical extension cord attached to a floor lamp.

"No, Trina," screeches Ruth advancing the length of the room with the frying pan. The dog, sensing hostility, takes off with Trina and the lamp in tow. "Stop ... Stop," yells Trina as she is dragged toward the street, then she braces her feet against the door frame while the electrical cord streams through her grasp.

"Let it go," screams Ruth, racing to grab the lamp. Too late. The coloured glass lampshade explodes on the floor and the remnants of the lamp fly across the room to slam into Trina's back.

"Oh, shit!" exclaims Ruth.

"Don't worry, I'll pay," shouts Trina heroically, clearly enjoying the tug-of-war with the dog, and now, with the lamp's standard jammed across the doorway, the cord stops streaming and she begins reining in the reluctant animal.

"Don't you dare bring him back in here," barks Ruth as she stomps back to the kitchen, "And you fucking well will pay for the lamp."

Ruth is still in the kitchen, bawling into her apron, when Trina returns to the café and starts picking glass shards out of the carpet. "I put him in my husband's car," she tells Cindy triumphantly.

"Is he safe on his own?" queries Cindy.

"He's found my husband's lunch," laughs Trina, "Sushi and a low-fat strawberry yogurt."

"Trina!" exclaims Cindy, but Trina cuts her off as her face suddenly falls.

"Oh, Christ. I've left the kids' guinea pig in the oven."

"What?"

"Tell you later," yells Trina as she heads for the door and collides with Tom. "Sorry, Tom," she calls in her wake. "Family crisis — baked guinea pig."

Tom shakes his head and laughs to Cindy. "What the hell has she done this time?"

"Apart from wrecking ..." starts Cindy as she drops glass fragments into a dustpan.

"Hang on," says Tom, grabbing the morning paper. "Need the little boys' room first."

"Oh, crap," calls Cindy. "We're not even open yet."

Ruth's appetite for a fry up has vanished in the kafuffle, but it is no longer Jordan's condition that bothers her. One nagging voice has been supplanted by another — a voice of reason.

"You can't afford to eat the profits any longer," she

tells herself, and settles for a couple of carrots and a cup of tea while she cooks for the customers.

By eight-thirty the breakfast rush is winding down and Ruth has laboured upstairs and checked on Jordan four times. He wakes on the final occasion.

"Would you like some breakfast, dear?" Ruth coos.

Jordan pushes aside the blanket and struggles out of the chair. "What's the time? I should be cooking."

"Don't worry, we've coped," Ruth says, and bursts into tears with the instant realization that she's going to be coping for the rest of her life. That, short of a miracle, her life is heading for a wreck as fast as her husband's, but unlike him, she's the one who's going to have to deal with the bloody aftermath. "We'd better tell your mother," Ruth snivels as she reaches for the phone.

"She'll say it's God's punishment because we don't go to church anymore," says Jordan.

"And that's my fault?" shoots back Ruth, knowing well that her mother-in-law will blame her.

"He always used to go," she'll spit, "before he met you."

"Maybe we should start going again," says Jordan.

"Oh, that's brilliant," Ruth scoffs. "God gives you cancer, then you want to go to church and beg him to cure it." *Sanctimonious cow. Bet you'd be the first on your knees if you got it.* "I'm sorry," she pleads. "Don't take any notice of me. Of course we'll go to church if you want. We'll do anything you want. Tell me what you want, Jordan. Anything. From now on, anything you want."

"I don't want my mother to know," says Jordan coolly.

"Ruth!" Cindy yells up the stairs, "Are you doin' the crappy breakfasts or not?"

"We'll discuss it later," Ruth calls to Jordan, and she uses her apron to dab her eyes as she heads down the stairs.

Trina is back and is frustrating the crossword gang. Matt, Dot, and Maureen have wrestled the relevant page of the Vancouver Sun from Tom, and they studiously worry at each clue in succession.

Trina is like a butterfly as she flits ahead and robs the others of the easiest clues. "Trina! That doesn't fit," yells Maureen as Trina races across the page with "TANJIT," and collides with the "E" of "NUISANCE."

"You always do that," moans Matt, sotto voce. "You've ruined it now."

"Oops. Sorry," chuckles Trina insincerely. "It's not my day. I nearly cooked the kids' guinea pig."

"What?"

"Well, there was a frost last night."

"And?"

Robyn from the candle shop three doors away races in, close to tears, wanting to stick a hastily created poster in the window.

"Sure," says Cindy. "What is it?"

"Lost dog," says Robyn, showing Cindy a photocopied picture of a familiar Labrador. "I just let him out for a pee. He usually comes straight back."

"Trina," yells Cindy, "someone here to see you."

"Give Jordan a call, Cindy," demands Matt jovially. "We're stuck on 5-across."

"Only 'cos Trina made such a damn mess," moans Dot. "What is a Tanjit anyway?"

"I dunno," calls Trina as she glances at Robyn's poster, "But it's got six letters." Then she turns to Robyn for support. "It's only a crossword for chrissake ..."

"What about my dog?" snivels Robyn.

"He's at the pound. I'll take you. They know me there. I find two or three animals most weeks. You're really lucky I caught him ... Did you know he's fond of strawberry yogurt?"

"Yogurt?"

"Yeah, and sushi, though he spat up the wasabi on the dashboard."

Robyn takes the lead, saying, "Quick. We'll take my car," as she hustles Trina out.

"Jordan's sleeping-in this morning. Ruth's doing the cooking," Cindy calls to Matt once the commotion has died down. But Ruth isn't cooking. She's taken cover in the kitchen in the same way she's been hiding most of her life — using feigned busyness as an avoidance mechanism. Ten minutes later, as she angrily swats at a lump of dough with a rolling pin, she wishes she could disappear altogether when Cindy pokes her head around the door.

"Ruth. The coffee guy's here."

Ruth's empty stomach cramps and she stands quivering.

"What's the matter with you today?" asks Cindy.

"The till was short a hundred bucks last night," Ruth complains, though she knows that's not the reason her knuckles are blanching as she grips the pin.

"Yeah, I know," says Cindy. "I paid Raven. You promised her cash, remember?"

Ruth's grip doesn't relax. "Cindy. Do me a favour, would you? Tell the coffee guy I'm out ..."

Cindy shakes her head. "Won't work, Ruth. He already told me, 'No cash, no coffee.' He says you haven't paid in three weeks."

"Shit."

"I'd help, but ... How much d'ye need?"

"About five hundred."

"What about crappy Tom?"

Tom is an unremarkable little man in his late fifties who would be slowing down if he had anything to slow down from. His morning rush to the washroom, and the subsequent evacuation, are generally the most energetic motions of his day. In fact, the only other time Cindy has seen him move was the time two doubtful characters in raincoats walked in without the slightest intention of buying coffee and Tom shot out the back like a scorched rabbit.

"Had an important call from my Zurich office," he'd explained when Cindy cornered him the following morning.

Tom has two faces — both smiling: one that loans money to people without asking awkward questions, and the other that invests money for people who don't ask awkward questions. He lives on the edge, between penury and fantasy, and sees no point in waiting until he has made a fortune before plucking its fruits. His latest "Mercedes" is a twelve-year-old Toyota with peeling paintwork that he hides in a corner of the municipal parking lot. His second car, a "Rolls Royce Corniche," which "Only comes out on special occasions," bears an uncanny resemblance to the banged-up VW Beetle on blocks at the back of his apartment. But his one-room basement apartment is only a front — somewhere in the back of his mind it's an eight-bedroom mansion.

One thing is certain: Tom has an office. It's Ruth and Jordan's Corner Coffee Shoppe, where he hangs out every morning at the start of the week, then, at lunchtime on Thursdays, he'll loudly proclaim, "I won't be in the rest of the weekend," as if the weekend is already dripping away. "I'm popping over to the island for a bit of a sail."

No one scoffs. If anyone knows that Tom never goes further than his sister's bungalow in North Vancouver they keep it to themselves. As for sailing, the only yachts he's ever mastered are in the glossy boating magazines that he casually flips open when anyone impressionable is near. "I was thinking of this one," he'll say of a sleek fifty- footer. "What do you think?" he'll ask with a sigh of boredom.

"I think you need some new shoes first," would be an appropriate response, though no one ever says so.

Ruth's request for a five hundred dollar loan brings only a moment's thought, then Tom beams, "No problem at all, Ruth. Happy to help out."

Ruth catches her breath as Tom pulls a monster roll of fifties from his pocket. "Walking-around money," he says poker-faced as he tantalizingly peels off the first bill. Then he pauses. "Hold on, Ruth . . ."

He's changed his mind, thinks Ruth, and she visualizes the customers departing as the percolators run dry.

"Why don't I give you hundreds," continues Tom as if he has no idea of the torment. "Would that be all right with you?"

"Hundreds. Yes, of course," replies Ruth brightening, thinking *fives, tens, twenties, who cares?* "Hundreds will be fine if that's better for you."

"OK. Back in a moment," says Tom, quickly squirreling the roll back into his pocket, and he dashes out of the café before she can discover that his stash is a wad of carefully clipped newspapers ringed with a few photocopied fifties.

"Well?" questions the coffee guy with his hand out.

"He's ... He's just popped over to the bank for me," stalls Ruth, reddening, though her mind races as she tediously counts every bill from the till and adds it to the small bundle from her pocket.

"How much do I owe?" she inquires for the third time, seemingly confused, then starts counting all over again.

"Would you like a coffee?" she asks the delivery man with it half counted, then loses count as he scowls his frustration.

"Look, I'm in a bit of a hurry, lady."

"Sorry ... Lost count," she says starting at the beginning, knowing that the end offers no salvation.

He's caught on and counts with her now, "Twenty, forty, sixty ..."

Ruth stops. "Does that include today's delivery?" she asks innocently, but she's overstretching.

"Yes," he hisses. "That includes today."

"That's not fair ..." she starts, then backs off and takes a deep breath. "OK," she says, ready to confess, when Tom returns and slides five new hundred dollar bills into her hand.

"I promise to pay you at the end of the week," enthuses Ruth as soon as the delivery man has gone, but Tom is unconcerned.

"No rush, dear — pocket change. You just take your time. Six months if you want. You and Jordan aren't planning on running away, are you?"

Ruth runs, tears streaming over her cheeks, and slams herself into the washroom where she sits staring deeply into the mirror, wishing she could liberate herself from reality as easily as Alice. But the mirror is cold-hearted and reflects the truth.

"Who'd wanna look at a fat lump like you," she had often mused to the mirror as a teenager, before consoling herself with a box of Oreos and a good cry over a chick flick, while her peers were out screwing in the back of the family Ford. But, by then, she'd had years of practice in vanishing, especially at school where her baby fat had been solidified by the misery of being the universal punching bag. Weakened and slowed by her lumpiness and hampered by poor vision — once her glasses had been snatched she was easy prey — her only defense was inconspicuousness. Not easy for someone her size.

"You're early, Phil," says Cindy as Phillipa dashes in trailing her coat and shaking the rain out of her hair.

"Shh. Where's Ruth? She wanted me in at nine, but what with the kids an' my mother, then I heard the news and had to check the lottery."

"Did you win?"

"Nah. Some lucky sod has though. Five mil' and it's someone around here, according to the radio."

"More chance of getting hit by a crappy bus ..." starts Cindy, but Raven appears from nowhere and cuts her off.

"Not today, Cindy. Today I'd put my money on the lottery. Would you let Ruth know I won't be in for a few weeks?" she adds breezily. "Something unexpected has come up."

"Fine crappy psychic you are," mutters Cindy, but Raven has already taken off.

"Ruth's blubbering in the washroom," Cindy tells Phillipa, "God knows what's going on. It's like a bloody madhouse in here today, and look at the crappy fuckin' weather."

"You want crappy, move to Newfoundland," says Phillipa.

"I might just do that, Phil," replies Cindy as Trina rushes in and shivers in front of the fire while a puddle grows around her feet.

"Robyn is mad at me 'cuz I saved her dog's life," Trina explains to the crossword gang. "I sometimes wonder why I do favours for people."

"Why?" asks Maureen.

"He might have got run over."

"No. Why is she mad at you?"

Trina's tears turn to a giggle. "It cost her fifty

bucks to get him out of the pound, another thirty for a rabies shot, twenty-five for a licence — which she should have had anyway, and then she got a ticket for another two hundred for letting him loose on the street in the first place."

"Oh, shit ..." mutters Maureen, but Trina isn't finished. "She wouldn't bring me back from the pound. I had to walk. Now I'm late for work."

"You'd better get going then," says Matt with his arms folded over the nearly completed puzzle, then he remembers the guinea pig.

"He's fine now," calls Trina over her shoulder. "I shoved him in the freezer for a couple of minutes to cool off."

The café fills with the mid-morning office crush demanding cappuccinos and lattes faster than man or machine can make them. Ruth is back in the kitchen, warming up the fryers and griddles as she prepares for lunch, when Jordan shuffles in.

"You shouldn't be up," she begins kindly, then she slams a stainless steel spatula onto the metal table. "This is crazy. What's the point in doing this? What's the fucking point in doing anything anymore?"

Jordan recoils at the venom, but Ruth drops her voice and starts to snivel again. "I'm sorry, but we should be together every moment. I shouldn't be stuck here cooking for a load of ungrateful pigs, and I can't go out there and pretend nothing's happened. I want to be upstairs with you ..."

"Because you are dying," hangs unspoken, as it will at the end of almost every sentence in Ruth's immediate future. "We must do this because you are dying. We can't do that because you are dying. I must say this because ... Don't say that because ... Take this because ... Don't cry because ... Don't shout because, don't scream, don't make a fuss, don't argue, don't demand, don't force, don't yell, don't tell. Don't . . . don't . . . don't."

Ruth's future is filled with the caregiver's burden of don'ts as she asks Jordan, "Why don't we hire a cook so I can be with you all day?"

"Because I'd get on your nerves and you'd be happy to see me go."

"Stop that, Jordan. Please stop. I know we can't afford it."

"That's why we mustn't tell my mother — not yet anyway. Once she catches on, she'll probably want her money back."

"Tell her she can't have it," says Ruth, though she knows the suggestion is going nowhere.

Jordan's mother was English, before she emigrated, a grouchy northerner from Newcastle-on-tyne. She's a Geordie with the dialect, the arms, and the determination of a Sunderland steelworker. If she wants her money, only God might stand in her way.

"Ruth, I hate to ask ..." Jordan hesitates.

"What is it, love?" Ruth queries, lightly dusting him with flour as she enfolds him.

"I'm going to need money for drugs and stuff."

"Don't worry. We'll be al right. Just take what you want," she says, thinking, *Tom will have to wait.*

"Then there'll be other things: travel, special food. How will you manage?"

"Jordan, I said, 'Don't worry.'" She says, then floods into tears as she realizes that the man dying in her arms is more concerned for her future than his own. "You needn't worry," she reiterates softly, realizing that truth has become an early casualty.

"Don't worry about me. I'll be all right," she carries on, but what is she supposed to say? *"Sorry, Jordan, but we simply can't afford for you to have cancer right now."*

"I'm sure it will be OK," she adds, still praying for a misdiagnosis or a spontaneous remission. *It could happen*, she tries convincing herself, and now, more than ever, wants that to be the case as she comforts him — a man about to be overtaken by mortality who finally seems to care.

Not that he hadn't been a good husband, in his own way, for seven years. And if he had found more enjoyment in the pages of *Hustler* and *Playboy* she would accept her share of the blame. The bigger she had grown, the more he turned to the stack of magazines by the bed.

"Look at this," he'd say, pointing enthusiastically to a couple of stick insects with digitally enhanced pudenda in some impossibly contorted pose. "We should try that."

Jordan had usually ended up seeking satisfaction from the image on his own, while Ruth had shuffled, embarrassed, to hide out in the kitchen.

A new world had opened up to Jordan when they had subscribed to the Internet, and his interest in Ruth had flagged entirely as he surfed porn sites and dating agencies.

"I can't sleep," he'd complain to Ruth as she crashed after an exhausting day. "I think I'll send some emails," he'd add, stealing quietly out of the bedroom and softly closing the door.

Ruth caught him eventually, the morning he fell asleep at the monitor with his hand in his pants and a live sex show streaming across the screen. She had promptly stopped the monthly cheques.

"Sorry Jordan, we can't afford it," she had explained when his screen died.

"You can't do that. We need it for business," he had insisted. "Everybody's on the Net now."

But Ruth knew which bodies on the Net he was most interested in, and held firm. "We managed all right before."

Ruth weeps quietly as she continues holding Jordan in the kitchen. "It's not going to happen," she whispers in his ear. "You're going to be all right."

"But what about you, Ruth? I worry about you."

Ruth collapses to the floor, sobbing uncontrollably, unable to deal with the knowledge that her dying husband is burdened by a future that he will not be party to. But her grief is deeper. For the first time in her life someone actually cares. No one has ever cared before. Not even her parents. On the contrary, apart from fleeting satisfaction at the moment of her conception, neither her mother nor her father had taken any pleasure in their daughter.

To her father, Ruth does not exist and has never existed. The few minutes it took to inseminate her mother, a seventeen-year-old devotee of the Fab Four, when she was high on their music and pot, is a distant hazy memory in his mind.

"I'm one of the Beatles, luv," he had claimed to the young Canadian woman, and had the Liverpudlian accent and a guitar case to prove it.

"He's a famous English musician," Ruth's spaced-out mother confessed to ten-year-old Ruth one night — but when wasn't she spaced-out? In fact, had she not been high the night of the Beatles concert, she probably wouldn't have splayed herself to a complete stranger in the middle of "Hard Day's Night" when he was supposedly banging away on his guitar with his cohorts on stage.

"It was dark in his dressing room," her mother had continued to the confused ten-year-old who was demanding to know why all the other girls in her class had fathers. "But there was a star on the door and he definitely said his name was George."

To the tormented offspring of a single mother in a rural Canadian community in the sixties, the probability, however bizarre, that her surname was Harrison was gold. Armed with the first bit of good news in her short life, Ruth had gone to school the next day full of vengeful thoughts. "You can't play with us, you haven't got a dad," the other kids had frequently taunted, but it wasn't them talking, it was their mothers, well aware that Ruth's mother had a certain reputation.

Word spread and, despite the scoffing of a jealous few, was widely believed. That April day in 1975, and only that day, Ruth had shone in the glow of her supposed father. But, by the following morning, a dark cloud had descended and left her in a deeper gloom than she could ever have imagined.

"Liar, liar, pants on fire," chanted the entire school, fuelled by the scornful skepticism of their parents, and then they had thrown rocks at her — schoolyard gravel in truth, but the cuts went much deeper than the scratches bathed and tended by the school secretary.

"Double home burger with super-size fries," yells Cindy through the intercom, and Ruth drags herself up and pulls herself together.

"What are we going to do, Jordan?" she asks, not expecting a resolution.

"We'll just have to carry on," he replies, offering none.

It's only eleven-thirty, but lunches have started and Ruth will be trapped in the kitchen until three. The café is starting to fill with regulars, but there is an interloper. Detective Sergeant Mike Phillips of the Royal Canadian Mounted Police is new to the area, though he has quickly sniffed out a coffee shop. Tom, with his roll of fake fifties bulging in his jacket, has a nose for the law and has eyed the newcomer guardedly from the moment he entered, but he's trapped as Phillips sits directly across from him and starts a conversation.

"It's still raining," says Phillips.

"Vancouver," says Tom in explanation, then he downs half his coffee.

"I'm from Toronto," says Phillips and is mentally preparing a potted biography when Tom drains his cup and slides out.

"See ya," says Tom. "Gotta check on my investments."

"Weird," mutters Phillips as he sits back with his Caffe Americano and looks forward to an upcoming visit to England.

chapter three

"Detective Inspector David Bliss," cries a London Guildhall usher, running down a list on a clipboard.

"That's you, Dad," says Samantha Bliss as she prepares to help her father to his feet. "Can you manage," she asks, "or should I come with you?"

"I can manage, luv," Bliss says, though he wobbles alarmingly as he tries to rise from the deeply-cushioned chair. Bliss's prospective son-in-law, D.C.I. Peter Bryan, steps in and steadies him. "I've got you, Dave."

Daphne Lovelace, a sparky and spry septuagenarian who has lied about her years so often she's forgotten her true age, holds out a pair of crutches to her old friend, saying, "You really ought to be in a wheelchair, Dave."

"I'll be fine, Daphne. You and Sam should go on in. The show will be starting in a minute. I guess Sergeant Phillips isn't going to make it."

"We'll be in the middle of the front row," says Samantha proudly as she gives her father's tie a final tweak; then she takes Daphne's arm and leads her toward the Grand Reception Hall with Peter Bryan at her side. Bliss barely controls a laugh at the sight of Daphne's giant polka-dot hat as the crowd parts to let it through. "Made it myself, 'specially for the occasion," Daphne had beamed when she arrived, but Bliss felt that the word *constructed* or *erected* would be a more accurate description of the process.

Bliss takes a final look around the Guildhall's opulent foyer and is disappointed that RCMP Sergeant Phillips is not amongst the fast-thinning crowd. Then he takes up his crutches and slowly heads for the antechamber where the Commissioner, dignitaries, and the other award recipients are assembling for their grand entrance to the award ceremony.

"Hey, Dave," calls a cheery Canadian voice as Bliss nears the small side door.

Bliss spins and winces as his injured leg scrapes the ground, then he beams at the sight of the Canadian Sergeant in his ceremonial dress uniform. "You made it, Mike."

"Sure. Wouldn't miss your big day," says Phillips. "Where am I supposed to sit?"

"Front row. Samantha and Peter Bryan are keeping a seat for you."

"Detective Inspector David Anthony Bliss is hereby awarded the Commendation of the Commissioner of the Grand Metropolitan Police Force," reads Samantha from the vellum scroll, as the five of them await the hors d'oeuvres in the main dining room of the Dorchester Hotel two hours later.

"That was quite a ceremony," says Phillips.

"For service above and beyond the call of duty," adds Daphne, reading over Samantha's shoulder.

"It's hardly an OBE though, Daphne," says Bliss, knowing that the somewhat reckless Canadian adventure that brought him the award pales in comparison to her wartime heroics in Europe and Asia. Bliss ignores Daphne's black look and sloughs off the praise as he encompasses his daughter, his boss, and the Canadian officer with a gesture. "You three deserve this more than me. I would have been dead if you hadn't rescued me."

"It all sounds jolly exiting," carries on Daphne. "I read it in the *Times* — how you'd been shot and left for dead on an island. How the Natives attacked ..."

"They didn't attack," protests Bliss. "The newspaper got it wrong." They just pointed their guns at me when they realized I threatened their dodgy little exploit."

"But the bear attacked you. That bit was right, wasn't it?"

"Yeah," cuts in Phillips. "It sure is, Daphne. Biggest damn bear I've ever seen. Took a dozen shots to scare him off."

"That's why I'm glad you could make it," says Bliss. "I wasn't in a fit state to thank you properly before I left Canada."

"My pleasure," says Phillips. "Anyway, I always wanted to take a look at London. But, how are you doing now?"

Bliss's head goes down. "It's going to take quite awhile — nearly lost the leg — infected wound, a lot of nerve damage. Good job I've got my daughter to take care of me. Sam's been great."

"The stairs at your little place must be a nightmare," says Daphne to Samantha — forever practical — then she turns to Bliss. "Why don't you come and stay with me for awhile? The country air will do you good, and I could make you up a bed in the study."

"Hmm ... Westchester," muses Bliss, with memories of a previous secondment when he'd first encountered Daphne — the police station's cleaning lady.

"That sounds like a great idea, Dad," jumps in Samantha just a fraction over-enthusiastically.

Bliss catches on immediately. "I smell a conspiracy," he says, looking from Daphne to his daughter. "Are you two ganging up on me?"

"No ..." starts Samantha, but can't get her expression to agree.

"It's a waste of time lying to me, Sam," says Bliss with a smile. "I guess you've had enough of me under your feet all day."

"Oh, Dad ..."

The arrival of the waiter gives Samantha thinking space and Peter Bryan comes to her aid. "Actually, Dave, I think it would be a great idea. In fact, I'm pretty sure that admin will actually pay Miss Lovelace to take care of you ..."

"I don't expect ..." protests Daphne, but Samantha stems the dissent with a warning look.

"I'm not going to argue," says Bliss, catching them all by surprise. "Daphne makes the best treacle pudding I've ever had. Anyway I haven't seen the old General for a year or so."

Daphne slumps at the thought of her old tomcat. "The poor thing died of old age back in the summer," she tells Bliss, and he knows her pain.

"That's a coincidence," he says. "Balderdash, my old cat, died as well."

"Oh, dear," sympathizes Daphne; then she perks up a little. "Actually, I'm getting a kitten next week. She's the fluffiest little thing, and her fur looks almost red at times. I was going to call her Madam Rouge but I thought that made her sound a bit like a Parisian street walker, so I'm calling her Missie Rouge instead. What do you think?"

"I think I'm looking forward to meeting her," says Bliss.

Now it's Daphne's turn to smile, though Bliss holds up a hand in caution. "But it won't be for a few weeks. I've got my physio to finish first."

"Anytime you're ready, Dave, and I've got room for you as well, Mike, if you'd like."

"Thanks Daph," replies Phillips. "But I've gotta get back to Vancouver in a day or so. The place might fall apart without me."

chapter four

Vancouver may still be standing, but Ruth's world is crumbling by the time Jordan's fortieth birthday approaches, though a new-found purpose has bolstered her through the darkest moments.

A month of intense therapy has taken its toll on both of them, and Ruth tries hard to hold back the tears each time she sees him off with his neatly packed overnight bag, hoping it will be the last time he'll have to go. But hope cuts both ways, and she vacillates between hoping he'll suffer little and die quickly, and hoping he'll outlive his prognosis, despite the misery he may endure in the meantime.

"I'll be fine," he'd assured her the first morning as she desperately clung to him at the curbside in the thin dawn light.

They really couldn't afford the cab, but Jordan wouldn't hear of her leaving the café to drive him into the heart of the city at rush hour. "Cindy can't do breakfast on her own," he'd said, "and you'd barely get back in time for lunch."

"I'll visit you this evening," she'd promised, perking herself up as she'd helped him into the taxi.

Jordan's face had dropped. "It'll just make things harder for me, Ruth. You'll come all that way and I'll be asleep, or you'll get upset."

"I don't mind ..."

"I do, Ruth ... I mind. I don't want you remembering me hooked up to a machine. Besides, the evening girls will have their boyfriends in and turn the place into a rave joint if you're not watching them. I'll phone, OK? And it's only a few days."

"But, I can't ..." she'd started.

He'd shushed her with a finger to her lips, and she hadn't asked again. Each week thereafter he had quietly slipped out of the apartment's rear door when her back was turned, like a womanizer on a date.

"I didn't want you getting upset," he would tell her when he'd phoned as promised, as he had done each week, his watery voice trying to lighten their short conversation with a "doctor" joke. "The doctor said I had to drink plenty of liquids," he'd laughed one night, "and I asked him if that meant I had to give up drinking solids." Then, after two or three days, he'd arrive back, struggle up the stairs, and barely hit the bed before falling asleep.

The nights without Jordan's comforting presence are an awful prelude to the future, but during the day, Ruth has found new zeal. Trina started it. She's a home care nurse whose patients always die, though only once was it her fault. Generally, by the time she gets them, they've been hacked about and patched up beyond endurance and are simply awaiting the inevitable. Trina's greatest contribution to their well-being is her unintentional ability to make them laugh as she changes incontinence pads and colostomy bags, and her only culpable failure occurred when she dropped the contents of a fully loaded bag on the aging patient's cat. "Oh, crap!" she'd cried, and the bag's owner had laughed himself to death at the sight of the shit-covered creature racing around the room like a greased pig, with Trina in hot pursuit.

It was Trina who'd brought light into Ruth's dark world. She knows about Jordan; she'd guessed — not the specifics, but enough to force Ruth's hand one morning when Jordan was away, getting his "fix," as he called it.

Trina had blustered into the café's kitchen in search of a condom for Cindy, and found Ruth in tears. Ruth's snivelled claim of "onions," as she wiped her nose and gestured to her baking table lacked credibility. Trina's culinary creations may have included such unlikely exotics as "creamed cabbage cheesecake with oyster sauce," but even she knew that cherry tarts rarely contained onions.

"It's Jordan, isn't it?" Trina had correctly surmised as she threw her arm partway around Ruth's shoulders.

Ruth had easily capitulated. The crushing weight of dealing with Jordan's illness without family assistance was overpowering. In any case, she'd told herself, it was just a matter of time before Trina would be calling professionally.

"Please don't tell anyone," she had begged Trina, before tearfully explaining Jordan's condition.

Trina had cheerfully leapt to Ruth's aid — here was someone to rescue who wouldn't defecate all over the bedsheets or drop dead at her feet — and she started immediately.

"Just take a look at you," she'd fussed, dabbing at Ruth's swollen eyes with a tea towel, and taking out her makeup. "You're going to have to pep yourself up and give Jordan something to live for."

"I know, Trina."

"And you need to take care of yourself. It's no good you getting sick as well."

"I will, Trina."

"And look at your clothes. There's room for me in there as well. You look like my husband's blow-up doll did when I got jealous and stuck her with a hypodermic."

Ruth had laughed for the first time in more than a month, and her new found mentor laughed with her, then Trina stopped and pulled a face at the clock. "Shit. I'm late for work again," she'd said, heading for the door. "I'll be back. You're taking this evening off."

"Wait a minute," Ruth had called. "Why the hell does Cindy want a condom?"

"Don't worry," Trina had shouted, "it's probably too late now."

It's two days to Jordan's birthday and he returns from his treatment to be met by a new woman. Trina has worked a miracle, thanks to Marcie, her next-door neighbour. Marcie is a large woman who suffers from a compulsive possessive disorder, and she plunders over-sized-fashion houses with as much abandon as a welfare mom in a thrift store giveaway. But, like all addicts, Marcie has remorseful periods, and it hadn't taken much for Trina to trigger a guilt attack and help her clear some closet space.

"You look nice," says Jordan returning from his latest "fix," and Ruth smiles as she helps him up the stairs to his bedroom. She has long since moved her bed into the apartment's sitting room, so as not to disturb him morning and night, and even reinstated the Internet subscription, though she is careful not to catch sight of the screen in his room.

"Thanks, Trina," says Ruth, when she has skipped back downstairs to the waiting woman. "I think he liked it," she adds, pirouetting in her new size sixteen Alfred Sung from the Marcie collection.

"Great! And we haven't even started yet."

"What do you mean?"

"See what I've got for you," Trina says, holding out a complimentary pass to Fitness World. "Three months' free trial," she adds enthusiastically. "We're going to have you looking absolutely great. I've even gotten you an appointment with my manicurist."

But Ruth breaks down again. "Why, Trina? What's the point?"

"Look. If Jordan sees you're upbeat and looking forward to the future it'll give him more optimism. Believe me, Ruth, determination is everything. If he loses the will to carry on ..."

Jordan's birthday seems more of a stumbling block than the final milestone in his life, as he props himself up in bed and forces himself to open the few birthday cards. Sentiments such as, "Happy 40th and many more of them," leave Ruth blubbering again, but Jordan takes her hand.

"It's all right, Ruth. I understand."

Ruth's carefully chosen card accompanies a bottle of Jordan's favourite whisky — the only gift she could find that didn't have "Guaranteed for life," stamped on it. She had sought something really special; something that he would cherish for the rest of his time, but as she cruised the stores in search of the perfect gift, she became more and more despondent. The thought of Jordan saying, "Thanks. It'll come in handy after I've gone," only heightened her melancholy. She'd finally given up and bought the whisky when she'd found herself reflecting on the irony of Jordan being outlived by a set of plastic handled screwdrivers made in China.

The digital camera was another matter. Its purpose was so disturbingly evident that she had twice carted it back to the store. In their nine years together, Jordan has avoided being photographed with as much fervour as an aborigine worried about the theft of his soul. Even their wedding album has vanished. "I think mom's got it," Jordan had claimed vaguely when Ruth was turning the apartment inside out, but he had never asked for it back.

Jordan's final birthday may be Ruth's only remaining chance to obtain a lasting impression, and she imagines herself peppering a wall with his images, much as she did with the man she idolized as her progenitor. Until her marriage to Jordan, the belief that George Harrison was her father was the only solid ground in her life and, as a teen, she'd lain on her bed for hours studying the features and creases of his sharply chiselled face with the fervour of an evangelist facing Christ, planning for the joyous day they would finally meet.

In Ruth's childhood reveries, George would dash out of one of the many posters on her wall, gather her into his arms, and lavish on her everything due to a newly discovered daughter — her own suite of furnished rooms in each of his mansions; a red Ferrari; a personal chef, perhaps; and, above all, a bodyguard.

"You just wait," she'd hiss to her tormentors at school recess, though she wisely never completed the sentence.

Like all children, Ruth sometimes doubted her parentage, though never once imagined that she was adopted or fathered by the mailman. Her misgivings centred solely around whether George Harrison would be prepared to admit his culpability. But, at such moments, she would peer deeply into his eyes and convince herself that all she needed to do was to cross the Atlantic and present herself at his front door.

Photographing Jordan turns out to be easier than Ruth could have imagined. In fact, once he's toyed with the camera, he appears quite keen, even showing her how to paste pictures directly onto the computer monitor. Nevertheless, Ruth has qualms as she quickly clicks off a few shots, feeling that she is forcing him to acknowledge the inevitability of his demise when she should be giving him hope.

"We should invite your mother over for tea, Jordan," she suggests lightly, taking advantage of his tractable mood, and hoping to offload some of her burden.

"I don't think so."

But Ruth has been winding herself up for this moment, hoping to cheer Jordan with a little afternoon celebration in the café. "I really think you should to tell your mother," she says determinedly, as she reaches for the phone.

Jordan stays her hand. "Please ... Not yet," he says. "You know what she's like — she'll worry."

"Why shouldn't she worry ..." starts Ruth, but stops herself with the realization she is uncharitably thinking her mother-in-law will be more worried about losing her investment in the café than losing her son. "Oh, it's up to you. She's your bloody mother," she says, letting Jordan take the phone. "I just wish I had a mother."

"Not if she was like mine," spits Jordan, and Ruth steams.

"You ought to be grateful that you've got a mother. You don't realize how lucky you are. You even had a father ..." Ruth pauses and pulls herself together as she sees the hurt in Jordan's eyes. "Sorry, Jordan," she says, knowing how much his father had meant to him, but she'd lost her father too — a father she'd never even seen. George Harrison's death had meant more than the end of her dream — it had forever slammed the lid on the possibility that she could prove her heritage.

While growing up fatherless may have been difficult, she was barely fifteen when she had found herself entirely alone. "I've just lost my mother," she'd tell concerned adults, and they had always jumped to the same conclusion. But Ruth's words were not some carefully parsed euphemism. She really did lose her mother and, despite the fact that it has been more than twenty years since she vanished, her mother's name has never been logged in police records as a missing person. In fact, if fifteen-year-old Ruth had been able to come up with the rent at the end of that month, no one else might have known that her mother simply went out one night and never returned.

"Mom will come back eventually," the teenager had convinced herself as she hid out in their dingy basement and tried to eat her way to happiness; after all, her mother had always returned before — to let the swellings subside and the bruises heal.

"You're a good girl, Ruthie," her mother would tell the young girl as she bathed the battle scars. "You're not gonna be like me. You're gonna get an education like your dad."

But Ruth had already quit school. Handicapped by her size, she was never able to outrun the mob of girls streaming out of the school at the end of the day.

With careful timing she might latch on to a departing teacher, but an ambush usually awaited somewhere on the route.

"My dad's bigger than your dad," never helped Ruth either.

"You ain't got a dad."

"I have so."

"Yeah, he's a fuckin' insect."

"A Beatle ... He's a Beatle."

"Well, this is what we do to beetles ..."

By lunchtime, Ruth has abandoned any hope of persuading Jordan to call his mother, and she is in the kitchen when Trina struggles into the busy café with a wheelchair.

"I brought Mr. Jenson ..." Trina calls to Cindy.

"Johnson," says a thin voice from under a battered panama.

"He gets very befuddled," whispers Trina, then she questions herself and takes a quick peep under the hat. "Oh, you're right. It is Mr. Johnson. How did that happen?"

"You said you were gonna buy me lunch," complains the ancient man as Trina explains to Cindy, "He's from the home. I'm always mixing them up. Is Ruth in the kitchen? I've got a book for her."

"Don't give me nothing to chew," comes the voice from under the hat. "I didn't bring my teeth."

"He likes rice pudding," says Trina as she dumps her charge and heads to the kitchen.

"You can't leave him there," calls Cindy, but Trina is on a mission. The book, liberated from Marcie's extensive library of unopened digests, is called *"Fight Cancer with Food and Live Forever,"* and Trina figures the sooner Jordan starts, the better.

"It's gotta be worth a try," she is telling Ruth when Cindy breaks through on the intercom.

"Trina. There's a very funny smell out here."

"Oh shit! ... Colostomy bag," exclaims Trina and takes off at a run.

By the time Trina arrives the following morning, the café has turned upside down and, according to Cindy, Ruth has lost her mind. "Look at this," she complains to Trina, stabbing angrily at the cooler filled with salads. "It looks like a cow has thrown up in there. Where's all the cakes?"

"Where's Ruth?" asks Trina, and Cindy nods toward the kitchen.

"I've been up all night," gushes Ruth as Trina dashes in. "Look," she adds, sweeping her hand across the opened book and around the bare shelves.

"Trans fats, saturated fats, and hydrogenated oils — all gone," she says, ticking off her checklist as she points to a packed garbage bin, then she turns to the next bin and plucks at bottles, cans, and packages as she sings out: "White flour, refined sugar, nitrates, sodium, modified starch, unpronounceable something-or-other, more unpronounceable stuff, chemicals, chemicals ... more chemicals."

Ruth stops to jab at Marcie's book and recites, "'Golden rule number one,' Trina: 'Never eat anything you can't pronounce.'"

"You can't throw all that away ..." starts Trina, but Ruth's on a roll as she turns to the third bin. "Burgers, bacon, wieners ..."

"But I could take it to the women's shelter," says Trina starting to haul out the still packaged food.

"No you don't," says Ruth, ripping it from Trina's hands and dropping it back in the bin. "Those poor devils have enough problems without you poisoning them."

"Poison?"

"Yes. It's a wonder no one ever sued us for making them fat."

"They couldn't ..."

"They can in the States," says Ruth, flipping through the book. "And I haven't even started yet. Here it says, 'broccoli and garlic,'" Ruth pauses to look up, sensing a certain lack of enthusiasm from Trina. "Thanks, Trina. You've no idea what a difference this will make."

"Ruth. You've got to be sensible."

"I am. That's exactly what I'm doing from now on."

"What I mean is, you've got to be realistic. There's a lot we don't know about cancer. How is Jordan doing anyway?"

Ruth's fervour wanes at the thought of her husband. "He doesn't say much. He's on the Internet quite a bit."

"That's good. He might come across some coping strategies, maybe even some new therapeutic procedures."

Ruth doesn't answer. If Jordan has found coping strategies online they are not medically related.

The intercom buzzes to life. "Tom's usual please, Ruth," calls Cindy. "Two eggs, sunny-side up, bacon, and sausage."

Ruth gives a sly smile as she puts her finger on the button. "Check the new breakfast menu please, Cindy."

"Shit," mutters the waitress after a few seconds and races to the kitchen.

"What's happening, Ruth? What about breakfast?"

Ruth shrugs. "Nothing fried, Cindy — no bacon, burgers, or hash browns. I mean, look at those people out there. Look what they're doing to themselves."

"But that's the point, Ruth — they're doing it, not you."

"Aiding and abetting, Cindy. We're aiding and abetting, and we're not going to do it anymore."

"But we'll lose all our customers."

"Better than poisoning them."

"This is ridiculous, Ruth. That's why they come here: to get a fat fix."

"OK. So what are you saying? If we sold guns and a guy comes in and says he wants to blow his brains out, we'd sell him one?"

"No, of course not."

"Right," she says, walking away. "We've sold our last gun, and if they don't like it they can try McBurgers'. I am not helping anyone else to kill themselves."

"Ruth," yells Cindy, "they're not stupid. They know they shouldn't be eating this stuff — that's why they do it. People eat properly at home, they come here for everything else. We can't afford to lose them."

Cindy is right. They can't afford to lose customers; in fact, if it hadn't been for Tom, the padlocks would already have been on. Tom has been terrific; cheerfully keeping Ruth afloat for weeks after the phone guy and the frozen food guy had followed the coffee guy, then Jordan's mother had turned up on schedule with her hand out. She'd arrived on one of Jordan's treatment days and the temptation for Ruth to inform her of her son's affliction was almost overwhelming. But the old woman's mind was so focussed on her money that she hadn't asked about her son until she was preparing to leave.

"Getting his hair done," replied Ruth curtly, then stopped and smiled thankfully at the realization that, despite several weeks of treatment, Jordan had lost relatively little hair.

Ruth had never tallied her borrowings from Tom — if he didn't worry, why should she? Jordan was the only importance in her life, and if Jordan needed money for medicines and extras, she could rely on Tom. Neither did she begrudge Jordan a bottle or two of liquor; indeed, according to some of her research, alcohol could actually be beneficial. It was certainly a view that Jordan held.

The marijuana was a different matter and had initially been a source of serious discord. Jordan had the evidence on his side: numerous reports gleaned from the Net that exalted the modest weed to the level of a super-drug, a modern day penicillin or insulin.

"It's medicinal marijuana, Ruth," he'd insisted the first evening she'd been hit by a toxic cloud as she walked into his room. "It's government approved."

"I know what it is," she'd spat, ready to fly at him. "My mom was a hippie, for chrissake." Then she'd stopped and scuttled out of the apartment, driven by childhood ghosts.

Ruth had walked the labyrinth of neighbourhood streets that night with her eyes on the sidewalk like a rat in a maze, blindly taking turn after turn without any hope of finding the way out — other than by luck. And as she walked, her young self walked by her side, reminding her of the times her mother had dragged her from street to street, with their possessions in a supermarket cart, and of the ignominy of being turned away by relatives and past friends despite the tears of her young daughter. "Cry harder next time," her mother had shouted, slapping her around the head until her ears sang. She'd cried, but often to no avail, and they had frequently ended up sleeping in a car, or couch surfing in mildewed mobile homes; traipsing from the welfare office to shelters, falling lower and lower, yet never quite hitting the street. Sometimes there would be an "uncle" willing to take them in for awhile, until her mother started pawning the furniture for her dope, then they'd be back pounding the streets again. But, all the time, Ruth had clung to her roll of posters, together with the beaded purse her mother had stolen for her for Christmas 1977, and dreamt of the day her father would rescue her. In the purse was Ruth's most prized possession — her birth certificate; incontrovertible proof of her heredity. It wasn't the fictitious name on the document that gave her hope. "I just said John Kennedy for a lark," her mother had told her, but the date of her birth could not be fudged so lightly: the twenty-second of May, 1965. Nine calendar months to the day after the Beatles' sold-out concert at Vancouver's Empire Stadium.

With a degree of arm-twisting from the authorities, Ruth's aunt and uncle had finally taken her in following her mother's disappearance. Her mother's elder sister had some compassion for the young girl who spent most of her time hiding in her room, morosely staring at a wall of Harrison posters with a mirror in her hand as she tried to spot a likeness. With George crooning "I Need You" and "Love You To" on a garage sale record player, Ruth had attempted to pull her flabby face into the hungry features of the man, but a terrible hollowness grew inside her as the probable truth slowly sank in. But if George Harrison wasn't her father, who was?

England holds the key to her heritage, and she planned the search for her father from the moment of her mother's confession. She even wrote to Paul McCartney, before his knighthood, although, even then he had seemingly been too aloof to respond — just a standard thank you letter, inviting her to join his fan club — for a fee. She would have written to George himself, but the fear of rejection held her back and drove her to eat. But without parents to reassure and comfort her, everything drove her eat.

Now, twenty years later, the prospect of ever reaching England dwindles daily, but so does Ruth. Under the crushing weight of Jordan's illness, the responsibility of running the café without him, and the mushrooming debts, a lesser woman might have shrivelled away entirely, but Ruth glosses over the cracks and stumbles on. However, Cindy sees beneath the surface and pauses at the door as she leaves one day.

"Are you all right, Ruth? You've lost a ton of weight recently."

"You're supposed to say congratulations."

"Oh. I didn't mean ..."

"It's all right, Cindy. Thanks for noticing, but I'm fine."

"Only, Jordan's been sick for weeks. I'm just worried you're gonna catch the same bug."

It has been months, not weeks, but if Jordan's bug has caused him to lose any weight it isn't evident. If anything he's a little bloated.

"It's the cancer growing inside me," he explains sourly when Ruth rags him about his expanding gut one evening, and she throws herself at his feet in remorse.

"I'm so sorry, Jordan. Forgive me please," she begs, wondering how she could be so insensitive.

"Anger," suggested Trina in the café the following morning, "and it's perfectly natural, Ruth. You're angry that this is happening, and subconsciously you see him as being responsible."

"But it's not his fault."

"I know what you need," says Trina, already heading for the door, and she's back twenty minutes later with a loaded sports bag.

"Kick boxing?" questions Ruth, digging through the bag.

Trina leaps around the café flinging out her legs at the studious crossword gang and punching air. "Yeah. You gotta work off the anger, Ruth."

"Oh, Trina!" yells Maureen. "We're trying to concentrate ..."

"Sorry," she whoops, and flings herself back to Ruth. "Marcie and I started lessons together, but she quit," she says as she continues limbering up.

Marcie had ordered the custom designed lime-green Lycra ensemble, with matching boots and gloves, from a celebrity sportswear outfitter on the Internet, while Trina had picked up a second-hand kit for fifty bucks at Cash Converters.

The instructor had been late for their first lesson at the gym, and Trina's impatience had quickly gotten the better of her.

"Come on, Marcie. Kick me," she had cajoled, as she'd ducked and weaved in front of her friend, and Marcie had eventually made a half-hearted stab.

"No. Like this," enthused Trina, and Marcie had burst into tears and rushed to the change room, ripping off her pricey gear.

"What's the matter?" asked Trina in her wake.

Marcie had slumped to the bench, crying, "You never said people were going to kick back."

"I've booked us for a class this evening," Trina tells Ruth, but Ruth's face clouds.

"I can't leave Jordan tonight."

"Why not?" says Trina. "He doesn't know you're there half the time."

It is true, though Ruth is generally careful to avoid the admission; unwilling to acknowledge, even to herself, that Jordan has become addicted to the Internet; addicted to sites that she doesn't even want to think about.

"I'll ask him," says Ruth, noncommittally.

Since his return from England, DS Phillips is becoming a regular at the Corner Coffee Shoppe, and Cindy begins making his caffé americano without asking as he seeks a seat near the back of the café.

Tom, near the door, is poring over a new yachting magazine with Matt, and is seriously debating whether or not to upgrade to a sixty-footer when he spots the officer. "I'd better give my people in New York a call to sort out the financing," says Tom as he quickly folds the publication and sneaks out.

"You're new around here, aren't you?" Ruth says to Phillips as she delivers his drink.

"Couple of months," he nods. "RCMP. On secondment from Ontario."

Attempting to bust the biker gangs, though he doesn't admit it.

"Oh. You're a cop?"

Phillips sweeps his hand over the unoccupied adjoining chairs. "I assumed everyone knew. One little guy scoots out every time I come in. God knows what he thinks he's done; early sixties — needs new shoes."

"Tom?" queries Ruth, looking around. "I wanted to speak to him."

"I hope I'm not driving customers away."

"No. Please keep coming. It's reassuring to have you here."

Trina has her head in the sports bag, pretending to check out the equipment, but she looks up as Ruth passes and says cheekily. "I saw that."

"What?"

"The way you were looking at him over there."

"How could you?" snaps Ruth, and stomps back to the kitchen close to tears.

It's the end of November, more than two months since Jordan's bombshell. Raven still hasn't returned, and word around the coffee counter is that Serethusa had channelled her the winning lottery numbers. Ruth has too much on her mind to be concerned. "She paid three months in advance," she shrugs one day when Cindy wonders aloud if the statuesque woman will ever come back.

The Corner Coffee Shoppe has never been more popular. The original clientele has largely remained loyal, though many have started losing weight, and the spreading word has drawn fat-fighters from around the neighbourhood. But Jordan's face falls unexpectedly as Ruth tallies the books at the end of the month and declares in delight, "We made nearly two thousand."

"That's good," he says, like someone making a point with an antonym.

Ruth picks up on Jordan's lack of enthusiasm, but gets it wrong and assumes he is upset that he won't be around to share in the success. What to say? *It'll help pay for your funeral!*

"I've paid your mother and all the bills," she carries on, with nowhere else to go, though she doesn't mention the money she owes Tom. But Jordan's downcast eyes finally get to her and she questions, "What's the matter?"

"I wasn't going to tell you," says Jordan.

"Tell me what?"

Jordan turns away. "No. This isn't fair. You keep the money. You'll need it when I'm gone."

"What? Tell me what," she demands.

Jordan plays the computer keyboard for a few seconds as he weighs his options, then, with his eyes firmly on the floor, he lays out the situation. The radiotherapy and chemotherapy have had no effect, and despite his outward appearance, the cancer has metastasized throughout his body, eating away at his organs and his mind.

"I feel like killing myself right now," he angrily admits. "Why should I wait? What have I got to wait for?"

"But I thought you were doing better," protests Ruth.

"It's the drugs, Ruth. Without the drugs I'd be finished."

Ruth stifles the sobs as she sits back thinking, *Please wait 'til Christmas. It's only a few weeks away.* But there's a gremlin inside her saying, *That's right. Tell him to hang on 'til Christmas so you can go through the gift nightmare again, and just think of all the happy Christmases you'll have in the future.*

"There is something I've been meaning to ask," she says, finally plucking up the courage. "I'd like to try for another baby."

"Ruth ..." he starts, but she persists.

"I know you'll say it's stupid, but when you're gone I'll have nothing left. If it was a boy I'd call him Jordan, and I'd tell him what a wonderful dad you would have been: a proud and caring man who would have loved him and cherished ..."

"Ruth ..." he tries again.

"And if it was a girl, I'd tell her all about you, how kind you were, and ... and ..." she pauses, then bursts into tears. "You've no idea what it's like growing up thinking your father's a man in a poster. But you're not just a picture. You're real, and If I had your baby he'd be real ..."

"Ruth," he says gently as she winds down, "it's too late. That's one of the side effects. I can't, Ruth, it's too late. Although there is ..." Then he stops as she looks at him questioningly and stifles her sobs.

"There is what?"

"Nothing," he says, looking away, but she grasps his chin and turns him back, demanding. "There is what?"

Jordan takes a few seconds, then tells her about an experimental program with a ninety percent success rate that he's found on the Internet — two weeks' intense therapy requiring total isolation as the body is cleansed of toxins with special herbs and minerals.

"Trina was right," Ruth yells delightedly. "She said you'd find a cure on the Web."

"Calm down, Ruth," says Jordan. "It may not work. Anyway, there's a big problem."

"What problem? Do it — you must do it. Why won't you do it?"

"Because it costs ten thousand dollars and I'd have to go Los Angeles, that's why."

"How dare you?" Ruth shouts, "How could do this to me? I don't care what it costs. If you think money is more important to me than your life, you must be crazy. When? When can they do it?"

"It's not that easy ..."

"What do you mean?"

Jordan takes a few seconds to arrange his thoughts, but Ruth is unrelenting.

"Jordan. I'm asking you what you mean."

"There's selection tests and things. They don't take everybody," he says, "Then there's the money ..."

"I'll get the money; stop worrying. Get on the computer, or whatever you have to do, and tell them you want to try."

"If you're sure ..."

Ruth buttonholes Tom in the middle of his morning dash and has him dancing up and down in the middle of the café.

"That's a lot of money for you, Ruth," he says sagely.

"I know. I know. But it's really important. And the café is making good money now. I'll easily pay it back. Can you lend it to me? Please."

"I'll have to talk to my people in London," he says in all seriousness and even consults his watch before declaring that, with an eight-hour time difference, he just might catch them before they leave the city. "As long as I can get to the little boys' room first," he says pointedly, and Ruth blushes as she steps aside.

"Oh yes, of course. Sorry."

It is a little after three p.m. in the city of London and Samantha Bliss is driving her father past the Bank of England on their way to Daphne's home in Westchester. If Tom does have any people in London, they're not amongst the bowler-hatted bunch scuttling out of the building and struggling with recalcitrant umbrellas as they battle the weather and head for Bank tube station.

"Look at this fucking weather," complains Samantha as she wipes at the condensation on the windshield.

"At least Daphne won't swear at me all the time," rebukes Bliss, but Samantha cuts back quickly. "Careful, Dad, or you'll be walking."

"Sorry," he laughs, adding, "I'm looking forward to a few weeks with her, actually — especially Christmas — she's such a game old bird."

"I hope no one shoots her then."

"Very droll, Sam ... Oh. Watch the lights."

"I can't see a fucking thing," she moans as they slide to a halt; then she gives her father a sly look. "Just don't get up to any mischief with her, that's all."

"Sam! She's old enough to be my grandmother."

"I didn't mean that kind of mischief, Dad. You know what I mean."

chapter five

Trina is brimming with mischievousness and hiding behind oversized shades as she sidles up to Ruth in the café's kitchen a week later. "I've got you into the cancer support group. Tonight at seven," she says, darkening her voice.

"Only you could make it sound like a fucking adventure," snaps Ruth, though she's not ungrateful. "You didn't give them my name did you?" she asks quickly.

"Nope. Just said you were a friend."

Ruth climbs down a notch. "Jordan will kill me if he finds out."

"I dunno why."

Ruth tries to fix Trina's eyes through the dark glasses — desperate to convey the delicacy of her situation. "Jordan borrowed some money, and if the lender discovered he was ..." she pauses, but the word "dying" is too much for her.

Trina finishes the sentence, sneering, "I suppose the bastard would want it back."

Ruth nods, though she has no intention of explaining that the bastard is Jordan's mother.

"It's not Tom, is it?" asks Trina as she takes off her glasses to stare quizzically at Ruth.

"Tom?" Ruth questions in surprise. "The Tom who comes in every morning? Why him?"

Trina freezes. "That's three questions, Ruth."

"So?"

"Golden rule, Ruth. If you ask someone a direct question and they come back with three or more in return, you've got your answer."

"You could be wrong ..." starts Ruth, but Trina isn't listening as she rants about Tom.

"The greasy little turd's a shark. 'Borrow as much as you like,' he says, but he never tells you he charges, like, a gazillion percent interest a week."

"How much?"

"A gazillion. Plus the arranging fee he tacks on the first week so you get hammered with the interest on that as well."

Ruth pales. "I didn't know ..."

"Oh yeah. He's a skunk."

"What happens if people can't pay?"

"He doesn't care. It's not his own money — he hasn't got any." Trina drops her voice. "He's just a front man."

"For who?"

Trina shrugs. "I don't know. But you can bet it's not the sort of person you'd ever invite to a Tupperware party."

Ruth had spent the rest of the day cowering in the kitchen, trying to keep her hands off the sharpest knives, and by the time she arrives at the group meeting she needs all the support she can get. Trina takes her, and Erica — the soft-haired, soft-bodied coordinator — welcomes them with a face-splitting smile as a group of wretched women shuffle morosely in.

"You wouldn't believe how difficult it is to get men here," says Erica. and Trina takes a quick look around at the slump-shouldered matrons and unthinkingly mutters, "I'm not surprised."

There's an edge to Erica's tone as she looks at Trina and explains, "We don't usually allow visitors, but if you're quiet you can stay."

The semicircle of dejected participants introduce themselves, reciting their husband's afflictions mechanically, like addicts at Alcoholics Anonymous. "My name is Joy. My husband has stage-two, grade-four, prostate cancer," says one woman, her face now permanently fixed in anguish. "He's had a bilateral orchiectomy, but his legs are swelling and he's down to a hundred and ten pounds. But I'm strong. I will survive."

It's Ruth's turn, and Trina gives her a nudge. But Ruth's stuck to the chair. Her mind is whirling. Jordan's cancer is somewhere, but where precisely? He's never told her. "Cancer," is all he's ever said and she's never pushed for more ... never wanted more. His cancer is the other woman — the one tearing them both apart and taking him away, and it's not something easily discussed over dinner — it's more a topic for a surprise breakfast attack when the offender is too bleary to defend himself after a night's partying. But Ruth and Jordan haven't partied for a very long time.

Erica encourages her. "Just tell us where the cancer is, Ruth; how aggressive; how advanced; some symptoms — weight loss, hair loss, etcetera."

"He's usually tired," says Ruth under pressure. "He just lies around."

"Huh ... Men!" utters Trina and catches a warning look from Erica.

The disclosure that Jordan is going to Los Angeles for the experimental treatment brings a skeptical look from Erica and censure from Trina.

"You never told me that," Trina complains, but Erica shushes her and turns to Ruth. "Maybe you should keep a journal. Something we can work through together. Questions, fears, the good things and the bad."

"Something cheery to read later on," mutters Trina, risking eviction.

"The main thing is to keep your spirits up." Erica pauses with a grin that looks like a grimace. "And try to be positive, Ruth. Look on the bright side."

"Yep. You'll soon have your own bedroom back," murmurs Trina *sotto voce* with her head in her purse.

The meeting slowly falls apart as weary participants head back to their nightmares, while Trina drags Ruth into a pub.

"Keeping up your spirits," insists Trina ordering large gins, and she gives Ruth a playful shove as a man at the bar takes his time looking her over.

"Could be your lucky night," whispers Trina irreverently and Ruth looks up, startled.

"Did you see that?" she says, as the man gives her an obvious wink.

"Well, you're a good looking woman, Ruth."

"Rubbish. It's the dress."

The dress wasn't from Marcie's collection. The continual strain and the demands of running the café single-handedly have reduced Ruth to a point where she can fit into some of Trina's baggier outfits. Ruth may still fill the full woollen skirt and ballooning blouse with wholesome curves, but virtually all the curves are now in the right places.

As their drinks arrive, Ruth's concern over money bubbles to the surface and she starts, "You know you said that Tom's a shark ..."

"I knew it," spits Trina. "He's hooked you hasn't he?"

"Just a bit," Ruth admits ruefully.

"Pay him back, the moment you see him." says Trina earnestly, "Before you get too deep."

Ruth is already sinking, and Tom circles for a few days, trying to catch sight of her as he moves around the café flourishing his flashy magazines like a badge of honour. Ruth busies herself in the kitchen with the door closed and prays he won't knock.

I thought you'd stopped hiding, mocks the voice inside, and she doesn't disagree, but what to do? You could ask him how much you owe, but what then? Whatever his answer she has no means to pay — even the interest. A quick calculation brings her close to fifteen thousand dollars, though that doesn't include the arranging fee or accumulated interest, and Jordan still needs more than they make each month.

The approach of Detective Sergeant Phillips' robust figure has saved Ruth from Tom on several occasions.

"Hi, Mike. You're getting to be quite a regular," she tells him one day, and he smiles and gives her hand an affectionate squeeze. "It's like 'Cheers,'" he says. "Everybody knows my name."

Ruth turns peach, drops her eyes, and slides back to the kitchen. Trina is shoulder-surfing the crossword gang as they scrunch tightly around a small table in a corner, but Ruth's hurried departure catches her eye; so does the policeman's satisfied glow.

"I think he likes you," she tells Ruth a few minutes later, but Ruth feigns deafness as she pummels some whole-grain dough and slaps it into baking pans. "Have you paid Tom yet?" Trina continues as she helps herself to an apple. Ruth's affirmative nod is a lie. Trina knows, but doesn't push the point.

It's over a week since Trina's warning, but Tom's meter is still running. Ruth knows there will be a judgment day — the day after Jordan's funeral, when she stands to survey the wreckage of her life — then the greasy little man will pop up with his hand out.

You could run. You've done it before, Ruth tells herself, thinking of the times her mother had forced her out of basement windows and dragged her from motel rooms before dawn, and she keeps it as an option. But there is an alternative. The date of the Los Angeles experiment has not yet been finalized. Could she beg Jordan to give up his hopes and reclaim the enrolment fee?

The need for action comes sooner than expected when Tom nails Ruth the following morning.

"*How* much?" she shrieks, though knew it was coming.

"Over eighteen thousand," Tom repeats. "I'm not worried personally, Ruth, but my people in London ... I'm sure you understand."

It's only a few weeks to Christmas, and Jordan seems to be responding well to the relentless regime of treatment. He's away three or four days a week, and even appears somewhat rejuvenated on his return.

"You're looking good," says Ruth and, burying her guilty conscience, she brings up the Los Angeles experiment. "I want you to go if you're absolutely certain it will help," she tells him, hoping to trigger a question mark. She certainly has reservations herself, particularly after the skeptical response she'd been given at the support group.

"I've never heard of it," Erica had admitted, "but there's a lot of quackery out there."

However, Ruth's hopes crash as Jordan announces that he is actually deteriorating, despite outward appearances, and his only remaining prospect is the experiment.

Ruth immerses herself in work as she tries to blot out the future and, despite Trina's encouragement, spends her days hiding in the kitchen and sinking under the weight of her loneliness and grief. But the loneliness is not confined to the days Jordan is absent; it is with her every day. Erica at the support group had warned her: "The problem with cancer is that you can lose the person long before they die." And Ruth has lost Jordan. In-between his weekly treatment sessions, he hibernates in his smoke-filled room. Now she knocks and waits. Sometimes he'll answer and call her in, but more often she is forced to creep quietly away.

"Depression," says Erica at the next meeting. "He's trying to come to terms with it. You'll just have to give him time."

"He doesn't have time," blubbers Ruth.

Downstairs, in the café, Ruth smiles and makes light of inquiries about Jordan's health as she tries to keep a sheen on their shattered life, while upstairs the chasm between them has become almost insurmountable. Only during Jordan's weekly treatment sessions is Ruth able to enter his room to clean and change the linen, but it is becoming increasingly painful for her to look at his empty bed. Feeling like a visitor to a mausoleum, she tiptoes around, touching Jordan's possessions with reverence — and she never pries.

The accidental discovery of a box of pills doesn't initially bother her, but as she goes to replace them in the drawer, she notices that the box is clearly date-stamped. "September the twenty-first," she reads aloud and, intrigued, she opens the box, but finds nothing other than a full blister-pack.

A few minutes later she is downstairs in the café's kitchen, shoving the box in Trina's face, yelling, "He's not taking them! He thinks we can't afford them and he's trying to kill himself!"

Trina takes a look, seeking the reference number on the label, but it has been torn off. "Give me his health card number and I'll check," she says. "Though don't tell anyone, or I'll lose my job."

Jordan phones that evening, his muffled voice sounding more distant than usual, and Ruth is taciturn as she fights to keep back news of her find.

"I asked the doctor how I could avoid falling hair, and he told me to jump out of the way," jokes Jordan, as he tries to cheer her up, but her mind is elsewhere and she forgets to laugh.

"Well, I thought it was funny," he says, but senses tension and cuts the call short. "You'd better get some sleep, Ruth. I'll call you tomorrow."

Subconsciously, Ruth knows that sleep is just another nightmare waiting to torment her, and avoids the torture by staying awake in a chair. She succumbs eventually, and the nightmare morphs to reality when the phone rings and she leaps up, convinced that Jordan has died during treatment. But it's Trina, whispering hoarsely, "Ruth, is that you?"

"It's nearly three o'clock," Ruth groans.

"I know," says Trina excitedly, as if they are on a

sleepover. "I'm on night shift at the old-folks' place. I'm checking the ministry computer, but Jordan hasn't bought any drugs in the past month." She pauses to scroll down. "Hold on," she whispers. "There has to be a mistake. He's not on the system at all. This can't be right ... Oh, gotta go. Someone's coming."

Ruth makes some coffee and fights to stay awake as she tries to make sense of the information. *Trina must be wrong*, she thinks, but then has another thought. *Maybe Jordan has used a nom-de-plume in his determination to prevent his mother from discovering his ailment and reclaiming her money.*

Cindy opens the door at seven, and Tom hits the washroom at full speed. Trina, in his wake, veers off and heads straight for the kitchen.

"Then why didn't he take the pills?" Trina wants to know, when Ruth lays out her suspicions about an alias.

"He's given up. I knew it," says Ruth as the truth sinks in. "He's so sure of this thing in Los Angeles that he's just not trying anything else."

"But these pills are from September," says Trina. "Jordan didn't know about the Los Angeles experiment back then, did he?"

Ruth takes a moment, then bursts into tears. "He's worried about the money. It must be the money."

Ruth's financial lows hit bottom when Tom finally corners her as she makes a crunchy-cashew salad. He has a dark look as he tells her, "My people need some money now, Ruth."

"But I can't ... Not yet," she says, dicing carrots and celery. "I'll soon be able to pay. This place is making money. I've just got a few things ..."

"Ruth ... When my people say 'now,' they kinda mean now."

"But, Tom. You said ..."

Tom stops her with his hand. "Ruth. You don't understand. Now means now."

"I can't pay," Ruth says boldly, as she fiercely attacks a cucumber. "What can they do, take me to court?"

Tom laughs wryly. "Ruth. These people don't use courts — they use bricks and razors."

Ruth freezes and weighs up the carving knife in her hand, wondering if it might be easier in the long run to slit Tom's throat and plead insanity.

"I thought they were in London," she scoffs, but, in truth knows that semantics won't help. "If I could do anything about it I would," she says. "I just can't give you any money."

"There might be something ..." says Tom, eyeing Ruth's fulsome physique.

"What? Anything," she replies, throwing in the cashews and drizzling vinaigrette, though she could never have imagined what she was agreeing to.

Ruth is back hiding in the kitchen again. She's been there for three days with hardly a break, but this time she is avoiding Trina. "Tell her I'm at the cash and carry," she warns Cindy. It's nothing that Trina has done, she just has a way of wheedling the truth out of people, and Ruth doesn't want to take the chance.

Trina revolts eventually and slips past Cindy, calling, "Just checking the kitchen. I think I left my tampons there the other day."

Ruth is teasing her hair in the burnished stainless steel range hood as Trina hustles in.

"Oh, you are here," says Trina as Cindy breaks through on the intercom.

"Sorry Ruth. Trina just ..."

"I'm here," shouts Trina, slamming her hand on the "Talk" button.

Ruth turns from the mirror, guessing she's been found out, and fluffs her lines. "I was just ... You know ... just ... um."

"You've got a date," breathes Trina, taking in the heavy lipstick and indigo eye shadow. "Is it Mike, that nice policeman?"

"No ..." starts Ruth, then changes her mind and apparently confesses. "Yes. All right. If you must know. But I don't want you telling a soul. Absolutely no one, do you understand?"

"Don't worry, Ruth. I don't blame you, really ... although others might."

"I was doing all right up 'til now. I knew I should've locked that door. I knew you'd ruin it," cries Ruth.

"Sorry," coos Trina, sweeping the tearful woman into her arms. "Come on upstairs. Let's do that makeup properly. You look as though you've had an accident."

An hour later Trina stands Ruth in front of a mirror and proudly exclaims, "Ta-dah."

"Where's my glasses?" says Ruth squinting.

Trina picks up the glasses from the table, hesitates for a moment, then races for the door. "Don't move," she calls. "I'll be back in a minute."

"I can't move," yells Ruth. "I can't see without them."

Twenty minutes later Trina re-appears, out of breath.

"You said a minute," moans Ruth, still standing.

"Sorry about that," gushes Trina, "but look."

"What? I can't see ..."

"Oops, sorry," says Trina, and she hands Ruth a funky pair of octagonal glasses with opal highlights.

"Mine are special ..." begins Ruth, but Trina stops her.

"Just try them."

The overall effect is magical and Ruth peers disbelievingly into the mirror. She even pokes out her tongue a little just to make sure it isn't a trick. Silent tears slowly appear like dewdrops on rosebuds, and Trina dashes to mop them with a tissue. "Hey, stop that," she says, "You'll ruin the mascara."

"Sorry," mumbles Ruth, but she takes off the glasses and hands them back. "Trina, I can't afford these. How much do they cost, for chrissake?"

"Nothing," lies Trina. "A friend makes them."

"Are you sure?"

"Yeah. It's still your old glasses — it's an optical illusion. He just puts new frames over the old ones. He's a sweetheart."

Ruth's "date" is still an hour away as she sits on Jordan's empty bed trying to rationalize her planned exploit. *You could've waited until he was in Los Angeles,* she tries telling herself, though she knows that is just a delaying tactic. *There's got to be other ways ... Go on then — name one.*

Ruth switches on Jordan's computer and pulls up his last few sites. *It can't be that bad,* she's convinced herself, but as she scrolls through page after page of pornography she has to force herself to watch, and her heart sinks as she thinks of the loss Jordan has endured, and his pathetic attempt to regain his manhood through images on the Internet.

"You have thirty-seven new messages — Hard Drive," pops up on the screen and she quickly turns it off, feeling she has already violated his final moments.

Ruth's edginess has her dancing around the apartment like a teen before the prom, inspecting her face and hair again and again, until, with a quick check to make sure the alley is clear, she slips out the back door and walks three blocks before picking up a cruising cab.

The driver seems particularly familiar with the downtown address and drops Ruth at the side door. "Good luck," he says, and gives her an appreciative whistle as he drives off.

Ruth stands back, surveys the old industrial building, and takes a deep breath. Running is still an option. It's nippy under the clear evening sky, but walking to the aquabus terminal might sharpen her mind and enable her to find a better solution.

She inches forward. There's a number on the door, but no name. She manages to ring the bell on her third attempt, and jumps at the sharp buzz of the intercom. The latch clicks open. "Come up — second floor," says a man without query, and it takes her a second to spot the overhead security camera.

Ruth's footsteps are slow as she clangs her way up the bare metal staircase. *It's not too late*, she tells herself at each landing. *Going down is much easier than going up*.

"Ms. Jackson?" confirms the same man as she finally reaches the top. She nods and he waves her into a room with a couch and a couple of cameras on tripods. "I'm Dave," he says, using his forefinger to click an imaginary camera in front of his face.

"Ruth," she responds as she sizes him up: early twenties, pimply, with straggly hair, and the start of a cameraman's hunched-back. Her pulse is racing and her hands won't stop, but Dave looks harmless and she takes some steadying breaths, fights back the feeling that she is going to vomit, and asks, "Have you been here long?"

A door slams open and a tattooed English gorilla in studded leather ambles in.

"Jessica," he booms, giving Ruth a cursory sweep.

"Jessica?" she echoes.

"Yeah. You gotta have a name — know what I mean? You look like a Jessica. I'm Mort."

"Hi, Mort," Ruth starts conversationally, holding out her hand, but he cuts her off, and she shrinks at the realization that he has nothing to shake with.

"First time?"

"Yes," she mumbles, unable to take her mind off the shrivelled stump that should have been a right hand.

"Thought so. Well, take off your clothes, Jessica. Time's money — know what I mean?"

Ruth is slow as she peels off her sweater and blouse, and Mort watches impatiently as he massages the truncated wrist with his good hand.

"C'mon lady. We're on a schedule — know what I mean?"

"Yes. Sorry ... Should I take my bra off as well?"

"Everything, lady. Dave ain't in kindergarten, even if he looks like a kid."

Ruth stops with her bra in her hand, "I didn't ..."

"Look lady, excuse the pun, but jugs aren't as big today as they used to be — know what I mean? Guys want the whole juice machine today. That's the only thing that sells — know what I mean?"

"Yes, but ..."

"Did you bring something to work with?"

"Tom didn't say ..."

Mort waves her to stop with the stump and calls to Dave. "Get out a couple of dildos for the lady, Dave."

Sweat's running off her brow as Ruth starts to rise. "Tom only mentioned breasts."

Mort throws up his arms. "Lady, please. Listen to me. This ain't a debating contest. Do you need the money or not?"

"Yes, but ..."

"Good girl. Now take 'em off, jump up on the bed and give Dave some smiley wide shots for your portfolio — know what I mean?"

Two hours later Ruth is still trembling as she climbs the stairs to an empty apartment. Jordan will be back tomorrow and, while she would almost prefer to die than ask, she has no choice — he will have to get the money back from Los Angeles.

Tom crashes through the door at seven the following morning and heads straight for the kitchen.

"You screwed up, you silly bitch," he hisses at Ruth, "Mort's f'kin furious you wasted his time. All you had to do was take your f'kin clothes off. What's so hard about that?"

Ruth still has a carving knife in her hand, but figures he's not worth the effort; anyway, she has made up her mind. "Don't worry, I'm getting the money back — well, ten thousand, anyway."

"My people don't like being messed around, Ruth."

"Your people?" laughs Ruth as she peers into the weasely little man's eyes and sees right through him. "You don't have people, Tom," she spits. "You don't even have a pot to crap in; that's why you use ours every morning. And somebody's been stealing the toilet paper. Is that you?"

"No ..."

Something snaps, and Ruth suddenly finds all her

suffering, fears, and worries enveloped in a roll of toilet paper. "I said, 'Is that you,' Tom?" she shouts and backs him against a fridge with the knife. "Is that you?" she screams into his face.

"Ruth," he pleads as the knife presses at his throat.

"I said, 'Is that you' taking the toilet paper?" she hisses as the knife starts to cut.

"Ruth, please."

A bead of blood oozes from Tom's neck. "Have you been stealing the toilet paper?" she demands.

"You don't know what they're like," Tom bleats, and Ruth realizes that his head is on the block alongside hers.

"The toilet paper, Tom. What about the toilet paper?" she yells as the crimson welt begins a slow leak.

"Yes ... Alright, alright. I took a roll of toilet paper."

"Rolls," she hisses through clenched teeth. "Rolls of toilet paper."

"Yes. OK. Rolls of toilet paper."

"Thank you," she says calmly, and slowly withdraws the knife. Tom's hand goes to his throat and he takes a breath of relief and starts to say, "Sorry," when she slams her knee into his groin with enough force to lift him off the ground, and he drops to the floor with eyes full of tears.

"That's for the toilet paper, Tom. Now tell your people to wait a few days, OK?"

"Oh, my balls!" Tom cries, writhing in agony on the kitchen floor, but she sneers, "You're lucky I didn't cut them off after what you set me up for. Now get up and get out."

Ruth is still pumped as she waits in the apartment to confront Jordan. She has disconnected the phone line to his computer and mentally practices her tactics for over an hour before she hears his footsteps up the back stairs.

"I'm tired," he says, his voice dragging the ground as he slumps into the room.

"The computer's not working at the moment," she tells him firmly as he heads to bed. "I need to talk to you first."

He drops into a chair, asking, "What is it, Ruth?"

Ruth brings out the box of pills and carefully places it on the table between them, like an exhibit. "Why haven't you been taking your pills?" she inquires.

"They're expensive ..." he starts, but she's ahead of him.

"If you needed more money you could have asked, but that doesn't answer the question. Why didn't you take these? You'd paid for them."

"They upset me, so I got something else."

An alarm bell is ringing in the depths of Ruth's mind, but she forges on. "I spoke to the support counsellor. She says that Los Angeles thing is probably a scam."

"What does she know? My doctor really thinks it will work."

Ruth brightens momentarily at the news, then folds as she sees her plan to repay the money coming apart. "Is he sure?"

"Pretty sure. He wants me to go as soon as possible."

"Just before Christmas?"

"Probably."

Ruth sits back, her future full of open-crotch photo shoots, and she hits on an idea. "Who's your doctor?"

"Benson ... Why?"

"I'm going to talk to him tomorrow."

"I don't think you can," says Jordan. "I don't think they're allowed to discuss my case with anyone else."

"They can if you give me permission," she says, then grumbles, "I always feel like such an idiot at the support group when I don't even know the type of cancer, or what you're taking. I am going to see Dr. Benson tomorrow to get some answers. And I'll find out more about Los Angeles while I'm at it, all right?"

Jordan starts, "I'm not sure ..." but she shushes him.

"No arguments, Jordan. I'll reconnect your computer, but first I want your signed consent ... Deal?"

Ruth's plans start unravelling in the early hours of the morning when Jordan begins a prolonged bout of sickness. "I must be getting worse," he explains weakly, his voice hoarse from retching. "Will you stay with me, Ruth? I'm frightened," he adds, and she spends most of the night sitting at his bedside listening to the reassuring sound of his snores. She creeps away before dawn and has most of the lunch menu prepared before Cindy and the new girl, Marilyn, arrive at seven.

Jordan wakes early, and his thumps on the floor above the kitchen send Ruth scurrying upstairs.

"Don't leave me, Ruth. I'm really scared."

"You'd better come with me back to the hospital," she suggests, but he shakes his head. "I'll be OK in a day or so. It might be the chemo."

With her mission on hold, Ruth has the coffees made by seven when the staff and Mike Phillips arrive. Ruth smiles as Tom U-turns on the threshold and heads to Donut Delight with his head down.

"Thought I'd pick up a coffee on my way to the city," Phillips tells Ruth. "But I'm not in a rush."

"I was going this morning, but Jordan's not well," says Ruth as Trina turns up.

"Pity. I could've given you a ride," says Phillips.

Trina catches on and quickly jumps in. "I'll look after Jordan, Ruth. That's my job. You go — everything will be fine" Then she drops her voice. "Another date already?"

"Trina ..." warns Ruth with a trace of amusement.

"I hope your husband doesn't mind me taking you," says Phillips as he opens the car door for Ruth.

"Not at all," she replies, failing to mention that Jordan doesn't know. She would have told him, but feared he would freak out when he discovered that she'd taken Trina into her confidence. In any case, as she'd told Trina, he'll probably sleep all day. "Just put your ear to the door every so often," she had said. "Don't go in unless he calls."

It's more than an hour's drive, and Ruth's tenseness comes through as she fiddles with her purse and stares stolidly ahead.

"You OK, Ruth?" Phillips asks. "You look as though you're going to snap something."

"Going to the doctor," she tells him truthfully, though he gets the wrong impression and looks concerned.

"Nothing too serious, I hope."

"Oh, no," she says, thinking that it will be if Dr. Benson insists Jordan should go to Los Angeles.

"So what do you actually do, Mike?" she asks to change the subject.

Phillips gives her a sideways glance. "You're not in league with the Hell's Angels are you?"

"No. Of course not."

"Just joking, Ruth," he laughs. "I'm on the anti-gang squad: money laundering, drugs, pornography, gambling, prostitution — you name it."

It actually had taken them an hour-and-a-half, battling the morning traffic, but Mike Phillips had dropped Ruth at the front door of Vancouver General.

"I'll be fine," she'd assured him when he'd wished her luck, but she had quickly found that she was in the wrong building. "The oncology department is way over on West 10th," a helpful nurse had told her, and she ended up two blocks away after walking a maze of corridors with scary signs and frightening smells.

An hour later, Ruth sits in the soothingly decorated waiting room of the Cancer Agency surrounded by a dozen equally anguished relatives and wipes tears from her eyes.

"Mrs. Jackson ..." calls the receptionist, and Ruth leaps to her feet.

"Yes?"

"The administrator will see you now."

Martin Dingwall has had years of experience delivering devastating news and has switched off his computer, blocked incoming calls, and turned down his smile. "Come in, please," he greets Ruth at the door, and solicitously guides her to a chair.

Ruth sits with the anxiety of a convict waiting for the switch to be thrown as Dingwall deliberately settles himself behind his desk and picks up a single sheet.

"I really don't know what to tell you, Mrs. Jackson," he begins solemnly, looking deeply into her eyes. "We simply have no record of anybody named Jordan Jackson fitting your husband's profile."

"I know that," she cries. "The receptionist told me that ages ago. But there has to be a mistake. He's been coming here for months."

"Not according to our records."

"But what about Dr. Benson? He'd know surely."

"Mrs. Jackson ... May I call you Ruth?"

She nods.

"Ruth. We have no Dr. Benson registered here."

"I might have got it wrong. Jenson — What about Jenson?"

"Ruth. We've checked all of our records; we've even had someone phone all the other hospitals in the region. Nobody has any record of your husband whatsoever."

"Wait," says Ruth, with an idea. "He's probably using a different name. He didn't want anyone knowing he had cancer."

The administrator's face lights up in hope. "OK. What name? We'll check."

Ruth's face falls. "I don't know ..." Then she brightens, "But Dr. Benson will know."

"Ruth. There is no Dr. Benson," says the administrator with more than a hint of exasperation.

"I could give you a description of Jordan," enthuses Ruth.

"We have thousands of patients," says Dingwall shaking his head. "Though a photograph might help," he adds doubtfully.

Ruth bites her lip and doesn't bother to look in her purse. She has no photographs. The ones she had taken with the new camera had vanished into cyberspace.

"Sorry Ruth. The computer crashed," Jordan had sheepishly explained a few days after his birthday when she was anxious to view them. "It seems to have mucked up the camera as well," he'd claimed, though insisted that he'd be able to fix it when he was better.

"Do you have any other information?" continues the administrator. "What type of cancer? What treatment he was receiving? Are you sure he has cancer?"

"Of course I'm sure. I've been going to the support group. They would have known."

Dingwall shakes his head again as he puts down the single sheet bearing only Jordan's name, address and date of birth. "I can only suggest that you go home and ask your husband," he says with a tone of finality. "But I have to warn you, this isn't the first case like this that I've dealt with."

"What do you mean?"

"Sometimes people have delusions about illnesses, Ruth. They may even believe something is seriously wrong with them ..."

Ruth's mind has been racing out of control from the moment she arrived, but suddenly everything is clear. "I know what you're doing. You're lying to protect Jordan's privacy, aren't you?"

"No ..." he tries, but Ruth angrily flourishes Jordan's authority.

"I've got permission ... Here — that's his signature. You can check."

"I know. You've already shown it to me. Believe me, Ruth, that is not the problem. I'm trying to help. Even if I couldn't give you specifics, I could certainly confirm that he was a patient. Why don't you just phone him? You're welcome to use my phone."

Ruth can't explain her reluctance to phone Jordan, even to herself, but decides to take action. "I'm going to the other hospitals," she declares. "Your computers must be wrong. I know he's been treated somewhere. He had pills ..."

"OK. What was the name of the drug?" asks Dingwall with a final ray of hope. "We might be able to track the prescription."

"Zofran," says Ruth remembering the name Trina had found on the pack.

Dingwall sits back, shaking his head again. "I was afraid of that."

"What?"

"It's too common. Most of our cancer patients take it to quell nausea. We'd never trace an individual dose."

Three hours and nearly two hundred dollars in cab fares later, Ruth is back at Vancouver General, admitting defeat. There is no record of her husband, or a Dr. Benson, in any of the Vancouver area hospitals, and if Jordan has used an alias there is no way of tracing him. Bewildered, and destitute of ideas, she finally seeks a payphone.

Trina picks up on the first ring, and sighs in relief. "Ruth. Thank God it's you. Jordan's gone missing — he's not with you, is he?"

"No, of course ... What do you mean, 'missing'?"

"I couldn't hear anything from his room, so I had a quick look in to make sure he was all right ..."

"I told you not to."

"I know, I know. But it was lunchtime, and I thought he might like some of my cauliflower–banana soup. Honest, Ruth, he's not here."

"Banana soup?"

"I ran out of cauliflower, but banana's the same colour. Anyway, he's not here, Ruth. We've looked everywhere. Cindy hasn't seen him either. He's gone."

"Stay there. I'm coming back."

"I gotta get the kids from school — the guinea pig's having babies — but Jordan's mother's on her way over. I found her number ..."

"Oh, for fuck's sake, Trina. Did you have to? Why couldn't you just do what you're asked for once?"

chapter six

For the second time in two days, Ruth Jackson finds herself crying as she undresses in front of strangers.

"Everything?" she asks, trying to hang on to her panties.

"Everything," says the police matron as she holds out a one-piece prisoner's suit. "Put this on, then sit over there and look straight into the camera."

"But I haven't done anything," blubbers Ruth, as another female officer sweeps up her clothes and carefully seals them in an evidence bag.

"Tell the judge, dear, not me. Just hold that board up under your chin and give us a wide smile."

The camera's flash makes Ruth blink, but at least the picture won't end up as a centrefold in *Bazoomerama*.

"What happens now?" she snivels.

"More inquiries, Ruth," says the officer with the bag. "But it's not my case. You'll have to ask the detectives in the morning."

"Do you mean I have to stay here all night?"

"Yup."

"But what about my husband? I should be out looking for him. He's dying. Why aren't you looking for him?"

"We are, Ruth. Believe me, we are."

The officer is wrong — no one is actively searching for Jordan. However, his description is circulating around the city's press offices as the morning's headlines are decided. "Dying man disappears," gets the most votes at the *Sun*, while the *Province* goes with "Police baffled."

The *Province*, encompassing a more global view of law enforcers, has hit the nail on the head in this case, and a group of detectives sit around a table strewn with coffee cups, cellphones and dossiers, scratching their heads.

Inspector Bob Wilson, Sergeant Dave Brougham, and Constable Gunn, known universally as BB, are trying to stay alert after ten hours on the case. They had started with Jordan's mother on their backs, before Ruth had arrived home, but their investigations had stalled. With no sign of a struggle, and no scent of a body, there are few immediate leads.

"Let's see what we have, and we'll make a fresh start in the morning," says Wilson, seeing the clock nearing midnight. "Give us the basics, Dave."

"Jordan Artemus Jackson," starts Brougham from his notes. "Male; forty years; five-eleven-and-a-half; owns a café in the 'burbs with wife, Ruth, thirty-seven. She's clean as far as we can see, though I ran her mother: string of petty thefts, drugs, soliciting — but absolutely nothing after 1980."

"Maybe she's done her mother in as well," says BB.

"Doubt it ... She was only fifteen," snaps back Brougham.

"What about you, BB?" asks Wilson, "What did you get from the staff?"

BB scans a statement on the table and paraphrases, "Cindy Cloud. Worked for them for a year or so. Here she says: 'I haven't seen Mr. Jackson for months. I thought he was upstairs in the apartment.'

'What about her?' I asked. 'Any odd behaviour?' Now this is interesting. She writes: 'Back in September, Ruth suddenly said that all the food in the place was poisonous and she chucked it all away.' 'Was that before or after you last saw her husband,' I asked. 'Just after,' she said, quite positively. Then she says, 'Ruth told me Jordan was ill.'"

BB looks up, making sure he has the floor, then continues, "I asked her if Mrs. Jackson had told her it was cancer, and she said, 'No, Ruth never mentioned cancer. She said he had a cold at first. I thought it was just a bad bug.'"

BB pauses while he skips ahead, then carries on. "This bit's interesting as well. 'Did they ever fight?' I asked, and she said, 'Yesterday morning there was a big commotion in the kitchen. I was busy and it stopped before I had a chance to investigate.' 'And that was Mr. and Mrs. Jackson, was it?' I said. And she replied, 'I suppose it was, although Ruth's usually pretty soft, so I was surprised.'"

"Interesting," says the Inspector, but Sergeant Brougham jumps in, "Mrs. Jackson told me about that. Says she had a run-in with a money man over a loan."

"OK," says the inspector, "we'll get forensics to do the kitchen for poison residues first thing, and if there was a fight we should find something. Do we know if the guy will corroborate?"

"Working on that," says Brougham.

"That's about all from the Cloud woman," says BB, "She seems pretty straight — even remembered the last day she saw him for sure. She says here, 'It was the day Ruth said he was going for a hospital check-up in September.'" BB looks up to add a final touch. "I told her I found it strange she hadn't said anything to anyone about not seeing him around, but she said, 'I just assumed he used the back door.'"

"Thanks, BB," says Inspector Wilson before turning to Brougham. "What did you get from his mother, Dave?"

"An earful, sir," he laughs. "God! Is she a strip of moose hide or what? I bet she would have lynched his wife if we hadn't been there. 'Arrest her — she's a bloody murderer,' she was screaming up and down the street."

"But what does she say in her statement, Dave? Stick to the facts."

"The facts, according to her, are that her daughter-in-law murdered her son and fed his body to the macerator. The problem is, there isn't a macerator; I checked. She hasn't seen him since September either, and she's been there three times since.

'First the fat bitch says he's getting his hair done,' Gwenda Jackson had bleated. 'Then she told me he was at the wholesalers, and finally she tells me he's gone fishing.'

"The trouble is," continues Brougham, "Ruth insists her husband was having treatment for his cancer and didn't want to worry his mother, so she had lied about where he was."

"That would certainly make sense," says Wilson, "If there was the slightest evidence that he had cancer."

"And even she admits that there isn't," pipes up BB.

Brougham carries on where he left off. "Most of the time his mother ranted on about how it was a plot to steal her money, then she came up with something really interesting. The night before last she was visiting a friend not far from the café. 'I was playing euchre with

Mr. Ashbourne when he looked out the window,'"
Brougham reads.

"Isn't that your Ruth?" Ashbourne had asked as
he'd squinted into the shadows of the streetlights.

"I don't think so," Gwenda had replied, not immediately recognizing the well-dressed woman.

"She was sort of disguised, her hair was all different,
and she had funny glasses on," she had told Brougham.
"She looked like a tart — all dolled up. And her weight!
She was a bloody ton before — then in September it starts
falling off her. She didn't see me. She was getting into a
cab, looking around, making sure no one saw her."

"Do you remember the cab company?" Brougham
had asked.

"We think we've traced the cab," continues
Brougham to his colleagues, "but the driver's in Hawaii
until after Christmas."

"I should be a cab driver," mutters BB.

"Anyway," says Brougham, "Mrs. Jackson doesn't
deny getting a cab. She just won't say where she was
going. Said it was private."

Looking for more information, Brougham picks up
Gwenda Jackson's hefty statement and zips through it.
'She wouldn't let him phone me — too expensive ... she
only married him for my money ... God knows what he
saw in the fat bitch.'"

"Who else have we got?" asks Wilson, shuffling
through the growing file.

"Erica, the cancer support woman," says BB. "She
didn't buy Ruth's story at all. Here she says, 'I was suspicious because her husband didn't seem to have symptoms consistent with most cancers. I could only go on
what Mrs. Jackson told me.'"

"The best we've got so far is the woman who discovered him missing," says Brougham picking up Trina's

statement. "She's a case. She thinks he's just playing a joke on her. Mind you, she thinks everything's a bit of a joke. When I said I was having a hard time swallowing Mrs. Jackson's story, she offered to give me a laxative to clear out some room for it."

"Trina Button," he carries on as the laughter dies. "She's a home care nurse who was supposed to be looking after him, but it turns out she hasn't seen him since September either." Brougham stops to chuckle to himself at the memory of their meeting.

The interview of Trina had taken a farcical turn because she had insisted on popping out of her chair at every opportunity to act out her story.

"I listened like this," she had said, rushing to stick her ear to the interview room door, "But I didn't hear anything," she'd continued, pulling a blank face.

"You don't have to show me ..." he'd started, but she had grabbed his phone and pretended to dial, "Then I called his mother, and she said straightaway that Ruth had murdered him."

"Put the phone ..."

Trina had dropped the phone and rushed to peer worriedly out of the window. "I was scared. I didn't know how long Ruth would be. She was out with her new boyfriend ..."

Brougham looks meaningfully at his colleagues as he takes up Trina's story. "She claims Mrs. Jackson has been dating a policeman."

"His name is Mike," Trina had told him. "He must live around here. He's a regular ... He's strong, tall, handsome ..."

"That would apply to most of us ma'am," Brougham had told her, though doesn't repeat it as he continues to the others. "Apparently they'd only been out a couple of times. Mrs. Jackson denies it, but Trina Button says they were out together the night her mother-in-law saw her getting into the cab."

"No wonder she didn't want to be seen," says BB.

"That's what I said to Ms. Button."

"It doesn't sound very good, does it?" Trina had agreed. "But her husband wasn't particularly nice to her — he never took her anywhere."

"Could that be because he was in bed dying of cancer?" Brougham had suggested.

"Perhaps the most significant thing was Ruth Jackson's reaction when Trina Button told her that her husband was missing," Brougham carries on. "Apparently she flew off the handle at the woman."

"She was really angry at me for going in to his room," Trina had admitted to Brougham. "She even swore at me on the phone, which wasn't like her at all."

"She'd never sworn at you before?"

Trina had put on her thinking face in an effort to prove her voracity, then said, "Possibly. Only, most people swear at me, so I don't always take much notice ... Anyway, all I did was take a peek and she just erupted. Mind you, I'm sure that had nothing to do with him being missing. She was probably just upset because she'd found out he didn't have cancer."

"Are you saying that she wanted him to die of cancer?"

"No. Not dragging on like that. She wanted it to be quick."

"More like poison, perhaps?"

Wilson takes a final shuffle through the statements then says. "I guess that just leaves the suspect herself. What did she say, Dave?"

Ruth had been oblivious to her own perilous circumstances as she'd cried her way through the entire interview. "He's dead. I know he his," she had wailed repeatedly. "I should never have left him."

"Do you want a lawyer?" Brougham had asked, offering her a tissue.

"I haven't done anything," she'd insisted.

"Is that a 'no'?"

"I haven't done anything, but I can't afford one anyway. Why won't you just find my husband?"

"What about your mother, Ruth. Could she help you out with some cash? You really do need a lawyer."

"I don't have a mother. I lost her when I was fifteen."

"Oh. Sorry ... Your father?"

"Lost him recently," she'd said, though had been careful not to confuse the situation by explaining.

"And now your husband. That's more than careless, Ruth. Have you got any living relatives?"

"Only my mother, I suppose."

"You just said she was dead."

"No. I said I'd lost her."

Brougham had pulled back, wondering if she should be hiring a psychiatrist in place of the lawyer. Ruth had seen the skepticism and explained. "She just took off one day and I never heard from her since."

"And you didn't try to find her?"

"She wasn't worth finding."

"I see. What about your father? Didn't he leave you anything?"

A lasting distrust of Liverpudlians with guitar cases, she thinks, but merely shakes her head. "No."

"She's still claiming he's got cancer," Brougham carries on. "She thinks it has finally affected his brain and he's out there wandering around somewhere. "Who else knew he had cancer?" I asked her, but apart from the Button woman and Erica at the support group, she hadn't told anyone. "Well, where do you think he is then?" I wanted to know, and she gave me some story about a place in Los Angeles where he might have gone for a cure."

"Have we checked it out?"

"There's nothing to check out. According to her, he'd paid ten grand to some outfit on the Internet, but there's no record of it."

"What about his computer?"

"Clean; nothing on the memory at all. It looks like someone's reformatted the hard drive."

"Getting rid of the evidence?" suggests BB.

"Maybe."

"What did she say about her boyfriend?" Wilson wants to know.

"Categorically denied it," replies Brougham, "and I kinda believe her, despite what Trina Button says."

"What about motive?" asks Wilson. "Any ideas yet?"

"Usual thing. Trying to escape from a lousy existence," replies Brougham. "She admits borrowing eighteen grand in the last few weeks; she's dropped sixty pounds in three months; gussied herself up and got some sexy glasses. I bet she looked around the place one day and thought, 'I can do better than this.'"

"Then what?"

"Get rid of her husband and take off for new life in the tropics like a new person."

"Christ. Is everyone going to Hawaii but me?" jokes BB, but Wilson is serious as he says, "That works for me, Dave. But where is the money now?"

"Don't know," admits Brougham, recalling the closing stages of the interview when he'd asked if she would try for bail.

"I haven't got any money," Ruth had told him.

"But the business made money," he'd suggested.

"Recently, yes."

"So — you have some money."

"You might as well know. I borrowed a lot of money, but I paid for Jordan to go to Los Angeles. It was a special treatment. His doctor said it could cure him."

"Then we'll talk to the doctor ..."

Ruth had collapsed in grief. "I don't know who he is. I got the names muddled up. But Jordan will know."

"If you'd tell me where he is I could ask him," Brougham had shot back brusquely, then he'd brought out the unused box of Zofran that had been found in Ruth's purse, and placed them squarely on the table in front of her, demanding, "What about these?"

"Jordan didn't take them," she'd replied innocently. "He said they upset him, so he switched ..."

"But the box is full, Mrs. Jackson. How could they have upset him if he hadn't taken any?"

Brougham raised his eyebrows, and the alarm that Ruth had heard when she'd originally found the box now had a source. But she'd had no answer for the officer.

"You don't know anything do you?" he'd said in frustration.

"Not anymore, no."

"Either you're very stupid or you're very clever," he'd said. But there was a third alternative. She could see it in his face. "You might just be very dangerous."

chapter seven

Despite her years, Daphne Lovelace, OBE, of Westchester, an ancient city of buttery limestone nestled in the lush countryside near the coast of southern England, still throws herself into Christmas with the enthusiasm of a store Santa. The great day may be weeks off, but the decorations are already up, apart from the tree, which is still rooted to its pot outside the back door awaiting the annual holiday.

"I've had some of these close to fifty years," Daphne had told David Bliss as she'd pinned up festive chains and paper bells, and she'd given him a sour look when he'd offered to buy new ones. "These will see me out," she'd replied a bit testily, and she'd violently snapped open a concertina'd ball to make her point.

"I should be doing that," Bliss had replied, frantically hanging onto the wobbly stepladder under her, but she had been adamant, saying, "Not in your condition, David. You're here to recuperate."

But the shine of recuperation is beginning to tarnish a week later as the thought of one more day surfing the TV or the Web while rural life rambles past the window has Bliss fuming, "I wish this damn leg would heal."

"It probably would if you did what you were told and stayed off it," admonishes Daphne as she adds a dollop of molasses to her pudding mixture.

"Here. You needn't get up. Give it a stir for luck."

"Have you got a spoon?"

"Roll up your sleeves — get your hands in there and do it properly," Daphne orders. "Only sissies use spoons in Christmas puddings."

"You expecting a lot of people?"

Daphne gives it a moment's thought. "No. Just you and Samantha, really. And her fiancé, of course. He seemed such a nice man at the ceremony."

"So. Just the four ..."

"And the Joneses and the Elliotts of course, but they come every year, so I hardly notice them. Not one of them is over ninety, but the way they carry on you'd think they're ready to pop their clogs. Then there's Phil and Maggie Morgan from next door — he's been on his deathbed for the past fifteen years. I guess St. Peter's got enough boring old farts without having him as well."

"So. Just me and Samantha ..."

"And I expect Minnie Dennon will accidentally stop by, saying, 'Oh, I didn't realize you had guests, Daphne.' Hah! If all accidents were as predictable as Minnie's, we'd never have any."

"So. Just us four," laughs Bliss, and Daphne smiles.

"Well. Everybody wants to meet my celebrated guest."

"I'm not celebrated ..."

The phone interrupts and Daphne glances at the stove's clock. "Who would call at this time?"

"Mike. How are you?" gushes Bliss a few seconds later as Daphne holds the phone to his ear.

"Helloo ... Sergeant Phillips," yells Daphne at the phone, making Bliss wince.

"Hold on," says Bliss, "I'll wipe my hands."

It is nearly twenty-four hours since Ruth's arrest — lunchtime in Vancouver — and Phillips is calling from his office. "Police baffled" had caught his eye in the *Province* that morning, though he'd not taken any notice until Inspector Wilson had slipped in and carefully shut the door behind him.

"You're not bugged are you?" Wilson had asked, poking under Phillip's desk and upending his phone.

"No. Why?"

"This could be a bit awkward, Mike. What do you know about a Ruth Jackson?"

The name Jackson had left Phillips looking blank and he'd reached for his computer keyboard. "What does she do? Dope, porn ..."

"Ruth Jackson," Wilson had pointedly repeated. "Runs a coffee shop out your way."

"Oh, that Ruth. Yes, I took her to the hospital yesterday ... Why?"

"Dave, a friend of mine has gotten herself into a bit of trouble," Phillips tells Bliss once the English detective has wrestled the phone from Daphne.

"I was just about to give him my brandy sauce recipe," Daphne huffs, as Bliss tunes into Phillips and volunteers to assist if he can.

"It's a bit of a long shot, but it might help her if we can trace her father. He's English."

"No problem, Mike. Let me grab a pen, and I'll get the details."

"It's a bit vague," he'd started, though "vague" would not adequately describe the meagre information he had gleaned from the distraught woman. Ruth had burst into sobs of relief the moment he'd walked into her cell, and hadn't stopped crying throughout his visit. Wilson had kept a cold eye on the RCMP sergeant, watching for signs to back Trina's claim, and the way that Ruth had rushed to fling her arms around Phillips hadn't eased his mind entirely.

"Mike. Thank God you've come," she'd sobbed, until Phillips had finally peeled her off and asked her if he could help.

"I haven't done anything, Mike," she'd wailed. "Why are they keeping me here? Why aren't they looking for Jordan?"

"I can't talk about your case, Ruth," Phillips had said, as instructed. "But you need a lawyer. You told the detective that your father was in England. Do you know where?"

"This is ridiculous," Ruth had mumbled through the tears. "They can't find my dying husband in Vancouver but they want to find my father."

"Look. Your dad might ..."

"He's not a dad. Dads don't do what he did," she'd bawled, and through a barrage of tears she had poured out her mother's version of her conception.

"It's not strictly police business, Dave," Phillips continues as Bliss returns to the phone with a notebook. "But she's got no one else to turn to. And I thought you might be fidgety with so much time on your hands."

"You're right. What's she done?"

"Murdered her husband. I don't buy it myself, although I have to admit it doesn't look good."

"What's she saying?"

"She can't believe he's gone. Keeps insisting he was dying of cancer."

"And he wasn't?"

The answer is as puzzling to Phillips as it is to his comrades in the Vancouver force. The Zofran was certainly for cancer sufferers, but beyond that, there wasn't the slightest evidence that Jordan had ever been tested or treated for the illness.

"She might have got bail, but we found traces of blood on a knife," continues Phillips after explaining the cancer dilemma.

"Have you looked under the floorboards?" inquires Bliss.

"There's a forensic team pulling the place to pieces right now."

The forensic team had started at nine, after a briefing in the café. "Blood, body fluids, unusual stains, weapons, and ideally a stiff or two," Inspector Wilson had told them. "Concentrate on the apartment and the kitchen first — I expect the customers would have noticed a cadaver on the floor out here. And have a special look for poisons, though it sounds like she made sure she'd got rid of them."

"What about fingerprints?" asked a dactylographer, readying her brushes.

"If you find a bottle or weapon — otherwise it won't give us anything. We already know it's an inside job. Her dabs will be everywhere."

"They'll probably be there for a week or more," Phillips continues to Bliss. "Unless they turn something up."

"And you don't think they will?"

"I was gonna say that she doesn't seem the type, but they all say that don't they?"

"They do over here, Mike."

"Anyway. It's a real long shot, Dave, but I'd like to help her if I can. She's got no relatives she knows of in Canada and wants to trace her father."

Daphne is dividing the pudding mix into three greased bowls as Bliss takes the sketchy details of Ruth's father, and she has them in the steamers by the time he puts down the phone.

"Here you are," says Daphne draining the remains of the rum into two glasses and handing one to Bliss. "It seems a shame to waste it."

"Thanks, Daphne," he laughs, then shakes his head. "God knows how Mike thinks I'm going to trace this bloke."

"What have you got?" she asks, sliding alongside him.

"Male; white; with a Liverpudlian accent. Apparently the woman's mother told her that he'd said his name was George, and he had a guitar case."

"Where was this?"

"Vancouver. August 22, 1964, at a Beatles concert."

"Oh, *that* George. Well it should be easy enough to find him, unless he was cremated."

"I don't expect it was him," says Bliss. "Probably some fan with a matching haircut."

"Wasn't that about the time of the FLQ crisis in Quebec?" asks Daphne, deep in thought.

Bliss shakes his head, laughing. "I've no idea Daphne. They didn't teach international political science in my kindergarten."

"I keep forgetting you're just a boy, really," laughs Daphne as she heads to a bookcase in search of some long forgotten facts.

"I'll try to get more information from her when she's calmed down," Phillips had concluded on the phone to Bliss, adding, "The problem is that most of what she says doesn't pan out, so I'm not sure if this is just another of her fantasies."

Ruth's mind is in a tailspin as she spirals deeper into an abyss of misery, and she is still bawling when Inspector Wilson appeals to Phillips to have another talk with her. "See if you can do anything with her, Mike," he says. "I'm worried she'll blow a boiler the way she's carrying on."

A friendly face warms Ruth a fraction, but her bloodshot eyes plead for help as she blubbers, "Mike, please make them let me out so I can help find him."

"Just tell me where he is, and I'll make sure he's looked after."

"I don't know. I keep telling you. Please let me out."

"You'll have to apply to a judge for bail."

"Why would I need bail? I haven't done anything."

"Are you sure you can't afford a lawyer?"

"I haven't got any money."

"She's not telling the truth," says Wilson, shaking his head at Phillips a few minutes later. "She admits borrowing eighteen thousand over the past few weeks and there is several thousand unaccounted for in the business, according to her mother-in-law."

"What about hard evidence, sir? What have we got?"

"I'm not sure I should be discussing this with you, Mike. You're aware of the allegation that you have a personal interest?"

"That's garbage."

"OK. Well, bottom line ... As you know, forensics have found human blood on a kitchen knife; the cab company that supposedly took him for his treatment didn't; her apartment is full of pot, and we've got a video from the drug squad showing her buying on the street; her mother was a mainliner, judging by her record; and, to top it off, her husband's been missing for three months while she pretended to everyone that he was upstairs with a touch of the flu. Not looking good for your friend, Mike."

Phillips takes a breath and weighs in, "I thought something wasn't right, just the way she trimmed herself up and started taking care of herself, wearing lipstick and eyeshadow, getting her hair done."

"As if she was on the lookout for a replacement," suggests Wilson. "Although that doesn't make really sense. From what I've heard, he was the one who might have been on the prowl."

"Do we know what her husband looks like? I never saw him."

Jordan's appearance arises again half an hour later when the detectives and crime scene officers hold a progress meeting.

"She says she hasn't got any pictures of him at all," Brougham tells the group of detectives and forensic officers."

"That's kinda suspicious," chimes in BB. "Particularly as she claims he was on his death bed."

"She said that there were some on the computer, but he lost them."

"Hah! That's convenient," snorts BB.

"There's no sign of a passport, health card, or driver's licence," one of the forensic officers adds. "Although we

should be able to get replicas from the various ministries
— if the pen-pushers don't invoke the privacy act."

"What about credit cards?" inquires Inspector
Wilson, and BB lights up.

"You might find this interesting, sir. I checked. He
hasn't used a credit card since early September."

"I asked her about that yesterday," Brougham says,
rifling through his notes. "When she said he called her
from a payphone at the hospital, I said, quote: 'Did he
pay with a credit card? Does he have credit cards?'

'Not any longer,' she said. 'I cut his up last summer
because he kept buying things we couldn't afford.'"

"She's thought of everything," says BB, his impli-
cation clear.

"What's the situation with the knife?" asks Wilson.

"It's positive for human blood," a forensic officer
tells them while checking his notes. "Fourteen-inch
stainless steel with a single edge."

Brougham looks up, "I've spoken to her about that,
and we're having all the hospitals, walk-in clinics, and
morgues checked for a white male, late fifties, goes by
the name of Tom."

"What did she tell you?" asks Wilson.

Brougham stops in momentary thought as he casts his
thoughts back to the interview, when he had stood over
the snivelling woman with the carving knife on the table
in front of her, saying, "This knife's got blood on it."

"It's a kitchen knife," she'd sniffed.

"So — Beef, pork, lamb? Whose blood is that Ruth?
And don't bother lying anymore — it will be tested."

"I wasn't lying," she'd started fiercely, then sobbed
her way through the story of Tom and his loan business.

"And you expect us to believe that this Tom,
whose name and address you can't remember, lent you
eighteen thousand dollars with no paperwork, not

even a signature, and then you cut his throat?"
Brougham had said.

"She claims it was only a scratch, but until we turn
up a body we have no way of knowing," continues
Brougham to his colleagues, then laughs as he says,
"You'll never guess why she did it: She says he was stealing her toilet paper."

"That's taking capital punishment a bit far isn't it?"
laughs BB.

Another part of Ruth's story that has quickly sprung a
leak concerns the cab that Jordan took each week for his
treatment sessions. The cab company has no record —
not even for the first trip when Ruth had tearfully seen
her husband off.

"It was definitely Bakers," Ruth had told Brougham.
"We always use Bakers."

"The first alleged treatment session was just over
three months ago," Brougham tells the others, "but
Bakers only keeps records for three months, so we
can't verify it one way or the other. But all the other
trips she claims he made should have been recorded,
and they are not."

"He'd have a cab pick him up at the back door so he
didn't have to go through the café," Ruth had explained
to Brougham. "I only saw him off the first time. Usually,
I'd say goodbye to him upstairs and he'd call a cab when
he was ready and slip out the back."

It wasn't a total shock when Brougham had informed
Ruth that Bakers had no record of picking Jordan
up after the first treatment session in September. But
it would no longer be a total shock if they told her

that Jordan had been abducted by aliens in a little green spaceship.

"He must have used a different cab company ..." Ruth had started, but Brougham had shaken his head. "Nope. I checked them all." Then he tried a different angle. "What about yesterday, Ruth? When you say you went to the hospital to talk about Jordan's cancer?"

"I did."

"So why did you lie to the nice man who gave you a ride?"

"I didn't."

"Sergeant Phillips said you were very nervous in the car; that you hardly mentioned your husband and you claimed you were going for a check-up."

"That's not true. I said I was going to the hospital, but I didn't tell him why."

"Why not?"

"He didn't ask."

"What about the evening you went out with him?"

"I've never been out with him."

Brougham knew he was trawling the bottom when he'd continued, "Your friend, Trina Button, claims you'd had a few dates with him."

"He's just a friendly customer, that's all," Ruth had retorted angrily and had left Brougham at a dead end.

"So where were you going in the cab that evening that you didn't want to be seen?" Brougham had persisted, although he already knew the answer, he was just pushing buttons.

BB had tracked the cab driver in Hawaii and the man had easily remembered Ruth and her destination.

"She didn't look the sort that usually goes there," the vacationer had told BB over the phone. "She was quite classy. Nice looking too — groovy glasses, nervous as hell."

"What sort usually goes there?" BB had wanted to know.

"Well, you know what the place is, don't you?"

BB had not known of the porn movie studio on his beat, though the Mountie's organized-crime squad certainly did. Mike Phillips had quickly filled him in.

"A gang of bikers led by a crazy English toad runs the place. We think the porn is a bit of a front. It's mainly a clearing house for dope. They've got a small pot grow-op in the basement, but most of the supply comes in from other growers."

"You seem to know a lot about it, Sergeant," BB had queried.

"My job, kid," Phillips had replied, asking, "What's your interest?"

BB's declaration that Ruth is a part-time porno queen leaves Phillips with a bad taste, but there is a simple way for him to establish the facts, and he scoots back to his office, shuts the door, and pages a field-operative with an urgent message.

Two hours later, as the forensic team is finishing for the day at Ruth's coffee shop, Phillips is across town reading a newspaper with his back to the wall of an unwholesome greasy spoon.

The RCMP sergeant doesn't look up, but he sees the café door opening and Vernon McLeod, the young photographer from the porn studio, walk to the counter for a coffee. There are only a handful of customers, all seeking refuge — some from the rain, but most from life — and McLeod carefully checks each one out before settling himself at the table next to Phillips. The young photographer has his eyes on the far wall and his cup covering his mouth as he questions to the air. "What's the panic, Mike? I haven't been burnt have I?"

"No. You're in the clear, Vern," says Phillips, with his head down in the paper. "But we need a quick ID in a murder case. Ask me for the sports."

McLeod puts down his cup and turns. "Can I see the sports page, Buddy?" he asks loudly, and Phillips reaches over with the pages.

"Recognize her?" asks Phillips once McLeod has studied Ruth's features for a few seconds.

"I don't take much notice of their faces ..." he begins, then pauses with a look of recognition. "Oh, yeah. She was in for a tryout. She the victim?"

"No, suspect. Was she any good?"

McLeod gives Phillips a leery glance. "Do you think it's fun watching women perform all day?"

"It beats taking mug shots of women with split lips and black eyes."

"Don't you believe it, Mike. There ain't much difference. Anyway, she wasn't the type."

"So, what happened?"

"The creep who runs the place pulls out a foot-long dildo and she heads for the hills."

"You didn't get any pictures?"

"Sorry to disappoint you," says McLeod, shaking his head. "Though I have got her on video." Phillips' face instantly picks up and McLeod reads it wrongly, as he adds, "Door surveillance, Mike. Nothing to get excited about."

"I just don't know why she would even consider doing it."

"Same as the rest of them — the money," says McLeod, handing back the paper.

By the time Phillips returns to the police office, Brougham is having another go at Ruth in the interview room. Brougham thinks he's dug up a bone and he's not letting go easily as he questions, "We have information that you disposed of a quantity of contaminated food in September, Mrs. Jackson. Why?"

"Contaminated? What food?"

"The food you said was too poisonous to be taken to the women's shelter."

"It wasn't poisonous ..."

"Trina Button says ..."

"She doesn't know what she's talking about."

"I kind of agree with you there," Brougham says, recalling his interview of Trina following her arrest at the café earlier that morning.

Trina, wearing her nurse's whites, had stopped by the café with the intention of liberating some of Ruth's clothes — so that she would look nice for her first court appearance that afternoon. It simply hadn't crossed Trina's mind that the crime scene tapes across the doorways applied to her, so she had given the police officer on guard duty a friendly wave and slipped underneath as if it were an everyday occurrence.

With a cheery, "Hi," to a couple of forensic officers helping themselves to coffee and cookies in the café, she'd confidently walked upstairs to the apartment, selected a decent-sized suitcase, and started to pack.

"Excuse me," she'd said, nudging the fingerprint officer aside as she bustled around, selecting suitable items from the closet; trying a few things against herself in the mirror; avoiding everything with even a trace of stripes.

She had worked her way quietly around the forensic team for several minutes, and had the suitcase half-filled, before she had spotted Ruth's treasured purse, together with the George Harrison posters, atop a cupboard.

"Could you just reach that bag for me, please?" she'd asked one of the officers.

"Sure," he'd said, handing it to her; then he'd pulled a puzzled look.

"I just got arrested for attempting to pervert the course of justice," Trina had laughed as she caught up with the crossword gang temporarily re-housed in Donut Delight.

"What happened?" Maureen had asked when no one else seemed willing.

"I was just picking up a few things for Ruth when they grabbed me. 'You can't arrest me,' I shouted. 'I promised my next client an enema.'"

"And they still let you go?" inquired Darcey.

"Yeah. And they didn't even search me."

"You sound disappointed."

"Well, they were all wearing surgical gloves."

"Trina!" exclaims Matt in disgust, then he leans forward. "This place stinks. I hope Ruth's not gonna be long."

"I'll be bringing you in a wheelchair by the time she gets out. If the sergeant's right."

Sergeant Brougham is still laughing about the incident at the start of a progress meeting late that afternoon.

"I reckon she's got a moose loose in the top paddock," Brougham tells Wilson after explaining that he had recovered the suitcase of clothes and let Trina off with a warning.

"You got something against moose, Dave?" laughs Wilson.

"Yeah. I totalled my Chevy under one in Alaska last year. Stupid animals. No moose is good moose as far as I'm concerned."

"What have we got, then?" asks Wilson, motioning Brougham, BB, and a couple of forensic officers to sit.

Speculation outweighs factual evidence as the officers flip through their notes and make the most of slim pickings.

"There was absolutely no trace of poisons, not even domestic stuff like fly killer, drain cleaner, or rat poison. Everything we found was totally non-toxic," begins one of the crime-scene officers.

"That's interesting," says Wilson. "You'd expect some poisons."

"She got rid of 'em in September," suggests BB. "Cleaned out everything just like the Cloud woman told me."

"Maybe. But where's the body?"

"I bet she cleared out a freezer to make room and dumped him later," suggests Brougham, then lays out his theory. "She might not have meant to kill him — it happens, right? Abused woman, smacks him over the head with a frying pan and 'Boomph!' he's dead."

"Was she abused?" asks Wilson. "I don't remember anyone saying that."

"No," admits Brougham, "Though God knows what goes on behind closed doors. I'm just speculating that if it was a spur-of-the-moment thing she would have had no money to run with, and no way of disposing of the body. So she cleans out the freezer, claiming the stuff is poisonous, and slips him in. Then she spends a few months collecting enough money to get away. Cindy, the girl who works there, said that once her husband vanished in September, Jackson had gotten really tight. Apparently, before that, she'd graze her way through the cake cooler and dip into the ice cream all day long; then suddenly it all stopped. And they were much busier as well after he'd gone. I bet she's stashed some cash somewhere."

"But where's the body, Dave?" demands Wilson, and Brougham shrugs.

"She had three months. A few bits in the garbage every day ..."

"Then why cause the commotion at the hospital yesterday?"

"Double bluff," pipes up BB. "Remember — she wouldn't phone her husband. The administrator offered. She wouldn't phone because she knew he wasn't at home."

"But she phoned eventually," reminds Brougham.

"Yes. When she was alone at a payphone, and that was just to let the Button woman know that she could leave because she was on her way home."

"I still don't get it," admits Wilson. "Unless she claims that her husband must have been in his room because Button had looked after him all day."

"That woman is driving me nuts," says Brougham. "If she's not snooping around the café, she's on the phone demanding to know what we're doing to help her friend. She's phoned at least six times today and she's been in twice."

Trina has actually been in to see Ruth three times, and sent away twice, but now she is waiting in the interview room with a large plastic garbage bag.

"You've got a visitor if you can stop crying long enough to see her," the matron tells Ruth. "She's brought you some clothes for your remand hearing."

"Trina?" she queries hopefully.

"Dry your eyes and you'll find out."

"Hi, Ruth. How are you doing?" asks Trina as Ruth crashes into her arms. "Not good, eh?"

"Sit down," orders the matron, dragging the tearful woman off, and Ruth falls into a chair.

"Who's running the café today?" snivels Ruth.

"The Gestapo," says Trina, recalling her adventure.

Ruth has a fearful look as she queries, "Not Jordan's mother?"

"No. But I got arrested. It was quite a lark. I was just trying to get some of your clothes ..."

"Getting arrested isn't a lark, Trina."

"Yeah, but I hadn't done anything wrong."

"Neither have I, Trina," she cries. "Neither have I."

"Look what I brought," says Trina, anxious to change the subject, and she opens the bag like it's a birthday present. "I had to bring you some of my clothes," she says, pulling out some snazzy pants. "They wouldn't let me have yours. But I expect these will fit you now. You're beginning to look like an Easter snowman. You should eat."

"Eat, eat, eat," spits Ruth. "Why does everyone tell me to eat? All my life people said, 'Stop eating, fatso,' and now it's, 'Eat, eat, eat.' How can I eat; how can I sleep or even think, knowing he's out there, cold and starving?"

"But you'll get sick if you don't eat, Ruth."

Ruth isn't listening. "Trina," she implores, looking for support in her friend's eyes. "Tell me honestly. You do believe that Jordan was there don't you?"

"Well ... I did think it strange that I never saw him."

"Trina," Ruth bawls. "Even you don't believe me."

"Of course I do ... Though you did lie to me. If you'd told me he wasn't in his bedroom, I wouldn't have gone in."

"He was there. I didn't lie ..." starts Ruth, then gives up.

Several minutes of awkward silence is punctuated by Ruth's constant sniffing, until Trina sneaks a peek at her watch. "I can stay another two minutes," she says, and that gives her just enough time for an idea she's been working on.

"OK, Ruth. If Jordan really had cancer ..." she starts.

"He did, Trina. I know he did."

"All right. I'm agreeing with you. I'm saying that if he did, and he was using a false name, what would happen when you killed him?"

"I didn't kill him," whines Ruth. "Why won't anyone believe me?"

"Well, the police have got a lot of evidence."

"But, I didn't."

"I know ... Although the police are pretty sure that you did."

"I did not."

"OK. But let's just assume that you did for the moment. What happened to his alien?"

"What alien?"

"The one Jordan was pretending to be."

"Do you mean his alias?"

"Whatever. All I'm suggesting is that if we wait and see who doesn't turn up for treatment in the next month or so, then we'll know who to look for."

"A month," cries Ruth, losing it again as Trina is escorted out. "I can't wait a month in here. I have to find him now."

Ruth's ability to search for her husband, and her psyche, take a serious blow mid-afternoon when a crusty old battleaxe in a judge's gown yells, "Stop snivelling in my court you stupid woman," and remands her in police custody for a further forty-eight hours.

The certainty that Jordan was alone and dying somewhere on the street, and the agony of her powerlessness to help him, had gripped Ruth's chest with an iron hand, and she had fainted in the prisoner's box. "Shove her head between her knees," the judge had ordered from the bench, and Ruth had quickly regained consciousness, though her mind had closed off to the outside world, and she had sunk into torpor.

Ruth had been led back to her cell like a zombie and, as the matron and guards watch her on the cell-block surveillance camera later that evening, there is growing concern about her catatonic state.

"The scout hasn't moved in over an hour," says one as he taps the screen. "Just stares at the door like she's trying to bore a hole in it."

Ruth is frozen in a trance, bolt upright and motionless, keening with a high pitched whine as tears stream down her cheeks. She is determined to stay awake for a second night — and every night — until Jordan is found, and she cries constantly, catching the salty tears on her tongue and sniffing back the snot. But behind her immobile face is a sharp mind focussed on every aspect of Jordan's battle with ill health. She relives every one of his pain-filled expressions and every anxiety drawn word, counting the number of times he'd said, "What's the point in carrying on?" and the occasions he'd wished aloud that he had been struck by a truck and saved the benefit of a leisurely penitence. "It's like jumping off a cliff in slow motion," he'd claimed one day, asking in a child-like tone, "Will the rocks hurt, Ruth?"

It is Jordan's pain more than her own that drives Ruth's incessant tears and, as the evening wears on, her constant bawling starts rattling nerves.

"Shut up. You're upsetting the other prisoners," shouts one of the evening staff as she hands over her charges to the night crew. "She hasn't quit all evening," the outgoing officer complains to Dawn and Jean as they sign in.

"Well I won't stand for it," says Dawn grabbing the cell keys and shouting, "Jackson you shit-rat. Shut up now before I make you."

"Oh great," moans Jean as Ruth wails even louder, crying, "I haven't done anything. I haven't done anything."

By midnight, Ruth is under attack from all sides as prisoners and officers alike try to sleep.

"Can't you shut her up?" yells one of the male guards from the adjacent block, and Dawn grabs the keys. "Right. That's enough Jackson."

Dawn's first slap sends Ruth reeling to the floor, but the crying intensifies until hysteria sets in.

"Shut up; shut up; shut up!" screams Dawn, an inch from her face; but the howling won't stop, and Ruth is turning beet-red through the strain.

A couple of kicks go unnoticed in Ruth's agonized mind as she seeks a way out of purgatory, and a voice inside is begging, *please hit me, hurt me, wake me up and end this nightmare.*

They hit and they kick, but the nightmare doesn't end, and ten minutes later Ruth is still screaming as an uncaring doctor "tut-tuts" at the red contusions on her face. "Been knocking yourself about have you, dearie? I'm going to give you something to calm you down."

Ruth's trembling hand takes hold of the doctor's wrist and she peers into his eyes with every ounce of will. "I don't want anything. My husband is out there dying in the rain, and they won't believe me."

"Let go of my hand dear."

"They're keeping me prisoner here."

"I know ... Now be a good girl and let go."

"Why are they doing this to me?" she screams into his face as her nails dig deep.

"Let go. You're hurting me," he tries calmly.

Ruth snaps. "Why won't you believe me? Why won't you believe me? My husband is dying on the street."

"Let go; please let go!"

"This is a set-up. You're in on it. His fucking mother's set me up."

"Guard ... Help! Help!"

The shrill shriek of a panic alarm sends guards running, and a wall of uniforms pound down the corridor and crash through the door. Ruth sinks under the deluge as the terrified doctor is dragged away. "Leave her to us," screams one of the guards, wound up from an evening of Ruth's wailing, and fists fly.

A few minutes later the doctor is brought back, armed with a hypodermic needle. Inspector Wilson has arrived and the yelling has stopped, but one of the male guards is hobbling around clutching his chin, moaning, "The f'kin bitch kicked me. The f'kin bitch kicked me."

Ruth is still swamped in a sea of flesh, but she manages to get her teeth into the pudgy hand covering her mouth, and she shouts, "you should take up kick boxing — it's good for anger." Then a fist lands straight in her face and she flops as the doctor jabs in the needle.

"This is very serious for you," says Wilson as he helps ease the subdued woman from the floor a few minutes later.

"I don't fucking care. Why don't you listen? I haven't done anything."

"You realize that you will also be charged with assaulting a doctor and two guards ..." starts Wilson, but Ruth is still snivelling.

"I don't care what you do to me. It doesn't matter anymore. All I tried to do was save his life."

chapter eight

The lights had gone out for Ruth a few minutes after the loaded needle had been shot into her arm, and have stayed out all night. Morning dawns in darkness, as Ruth's swollen and pus-encrusted eyes refuse to open. Her sobs salt her wounds and sting her eyes until she bursts into another wail.

"Shut up, for fuck's sake, Jackson," yells a warden, and Ruth tries, but fails.

"You don't want me to come in there, Jackson. Now shut the fuck up!"

At home, Ruth would have buried her head in the pillow, as she had most nights for the past three months, but here there is no pillow. Stripped to her underwear, "for her own protection," she lies on a wooden bench with only a thin blanket for warmth and nothing for comfort, and continues bawling loudly.

Keys rattle and a chair's leg scrapes on a tiled floor. "This is your last warning, Jackson ..."

Holding her breath, Ruth cries as silently as she is able, while the morning matrons, inured to her suffering by years of experience, relax back and sit at the end of the corridor discussing her as if she is tabloid trash. Noreen, the mouthy one, is a flabby blond in her fifties who gets a kick out of the job, while her partner, Annie, just wants to put her kid through university.

"It says here that they haven't found her husband's body yet," says Annie as she reads the article on the font page of the *Province*.

Noreen pours herself a coffee. "No. And they haven't found the one whose throat she slit either. Then there's her mother."

"I heard about that. Apparently she just vanished, and no one ever reported her missing."

"There's a lot of that going on — makes you wonder about going out at night."

"But she was only a kid."

"Teenager — wouldn't be the first."

Nothing has missed the rumour mill: Ruth's explorations into the underworld of pornography and drugs, even the suggestion that she was running a coven in Raven's back room.

"They found black candles and a black leather settee, one of the guys was saying," says Noreen, dropping her voice. "Witchcraft, I bet. Human sacrifice in the suburbs. Did you hear what she did to the doctor?"

The way the night staff had portrayed the melee, Ruth had fought with demonic strength, and her nails had clawed so deeply into the doctor's wrist that she might even be a vampire.

"Bled like crazy," one of the night matrons had said as she gave her the keys and handed over at six that morning. "She got her nails right into his vein."

But Ruth won't be doing it again. When she finally

pries open her ballooning eyes she'll discover the root of the pain in her hands — all her nails have been trimmed to the quick.

"You try to bring your kids up right and there's shit-rats like that around," moans Noreen as Inspector Wilson arrives.

"So, how is our client this morning?" asks Wilson, nodding to Ruth's cell.

Annie looks up. "Someone's going to throttle her if she doesn't shut up."

"She's no fool; she's working on an insanity defence." says Wilson.

"If she doesn't shut up soon, I'll plead insanity as well," cracks Noreen. "You heard she attacked the doctor?"

Wilson nods. "One of the reasons I'm here."

The sickly taste of blood and bile still cloys at the back of Ruth's throat and makes her retch as Annie gives her a poke. "Visitor," she says. "Will you behave if we give you your clothes?"

Dressing takes Ruth an eternity, while Noreen and Annie stand over her and make a point of staring. Her new clothes are ripped and filthy from the fight, and the sting of her raw fingertips on fabric makes her whimper as she tries to do her buttons up, but no one helps. And all the while, the swelling over her right eye pulses like the discordant din of hip-hop and threatens to drive her insane.

"I've got some good news, Ruth," says Wilson, with an edge to his voice, as she is blindly led, in handcuffs, into the interview room ten minutes later.

"What?" she snivels, though is barely able to speak through swollen lips.

"We've found your friend Tom."

Ruth catches her breath and looks up. "He'll tell you ..."

"It's good news for us," continues Wilson, talking over her. "Bad for you, I'm afraid. He denies any knowledge; says he never lent you any money."

"What about his neck? I cut ..."

"Says he nicked himself shaving. He swears that you don't owe him a cent."

Momentary relief turns to apprehension. *That's what he says now,* she thinks, *but he'll change his mind as soon as I get out.* "He got me into porn," she whimpers.

"We know all about that ... But what about the drugs?"

"They're for my husband's cancer."

"Not that kind of drug, Ruth. We're not stupid. We know what's happening. We've even got you on surveillance videos, buying on the street."

A brick might have hit harder, although the hurt wouldn't have been so deep, and she slumps in tears as her worst fears come true.

"Don't get upset, don't cry, don't argue," she had told herself on the occasions when Jordan had been unable to get out of bed, and she had buddied-up to a bunch of denim-clad sub-humans outside the youth club and walked back to the café with dirt on her hands.

"From the amount found in your apartment, you'll certainly be charged with possession — possibly trafficking," continues Wilson.

"But it was Jordan's medicinal marijuana," she tries lamely.

"And that's why you bought it from a pusher on Queen Street?"

The pain in her fingers and face can't compete with the pain within as she fights with images of her broken mother and recalls all the promises she made to herself that she would never, ever, end up on the same road.

"What's happening to the café?" she asks eventually, when she sees no other path.

The spark of life that Ruth and her husband had kindled has gone, and the café is now as cold and clinical as a mortuary. Sheets of white paper plaster the windows, shielding the forensic team from the lenses of press photographers. And the tropical aromas from Ethiopia, Columbia, and Costa Rica are lost in a welter of dust motes as floorboards and ceilings are pried and probed. Halogen spotlights turn December's gloom into glacial brilliance, but the light is as frosty as the winter's sun on the distant Rockies.

The gaggle of reporters who'd hung around outside the café the first day have already moved on; so have most of the rubber-neckers and displaced customers. Donut Delight is bursting with the overflow, and the crossword gang is crammed into a tight spot. There is only one topic of conversation.

"Sends a shiver up your spine doesn't it?" says Darcey, without looking up at the others. Matt and Maureen nod while trying to concentrate on 10-down. *"A cheap place to stay in Ireland."*

"You don't think she did it, do you?" asks Matt, but nobody answers as Trina pushes through the crowd and plops, "INNOCENT," in the spot before anyone can stop her.

"Of course she didn't do it," says Trina, jamming herself between the other two women, with her eyes on 31-across.

"Have you been to see her?" asks Matt.

"I'm on my way now. I took her some really nice clothes yesterday to cheer her up."

"How is she?"

"She seemed happy when I told her that I'd find Jordan."

Darcey and Maureen look up and say, "How?" in unison, but Trina clams up. She has a plan, but she doesn't want anyone poking holes in it — and she knows there are holes.

"Oh, look. There's Cindy over there," she says, loping off.

Cindy looks out of place as she sits on her own in Donut Delight, with her resume in her purse and her eye on the front door of the Corner Coffee Shoppe at the other end of the street.

The crime-scene tape has been reinforced by a second strand since Trina's incursion, and the uniformed policeman now has a critical glance at every visitor's badge — even those with whom he had breakfasted an hour earlier at the briefing.

"The scout's got quite a violent streak," Sergeant Brougham had told the small group as they had sat around the café waiting for a plumber to begin dismantling the sewer system. "I wouldn't be surprised to find something gruesome in the drains."

"Do you still want us to do the floorboards, Sarge?" asked one of the men.

"Yeah, Pete; as soon as the truck arrives and we get the carpets out of the way."

The rolled carpets, enveloped in plastic sheeting, are being carried out and piled into a large blue van as Trina slides into the seat opposite Cindy, asking, "What's happening at Ruth's place?"

"They're taking the crappy carpets now. There won't be much left soon."

"What else have they taken?"

"They've got a dumpster around the back. Jordan's crappy mother is there telling them what's his and what's hers and what to chuck out."

"Oh, no," sighs Trina and takes off at a run.

"What's going on at the coffee shop, Cindy?" asks a voice from above, and Cindy snaps back her head.

"Raven!" exclaims Cindy. "Where have you been? I didn't think you were ever coming back."

Raven's face falls. "Neither did I." Then she laughs, "You were right, Cindy. All men are crappy. But what's going on? They wouldn't let me in."

Cindy drops her tone. "It's like the kitchen-sink version of psycho. I heard it all — the yelling and shouting." She stops and looks around before dragging Raven down into a conspiracy. "I told the police I was too busy to look, but to tell the truth, I didn't wanna get involved. I know what men can be like when you get between them and their crappy wives. Been there, done that."

"Jordan killed her?" Raven asks incredulously.

"Other way around. She killed him."

Raven's face screws-up in confusion. "Are you sure?"

"Yeah. She's in jail. It's in all the papers."

"I don't believe it," says Raven firmly, but Cindy checks around again then whispers in her ear. "I'm not supposed to know this, but I've got a friend who says Ruth's pretending to be insane."

"No ... That's not ..." starts Raven, but Cindy is still whispering. "She even attacked a doctor and the guards. I heard they put her in a straitjacket. I knew something was up when she went overboard with all that crappy rabbit food."

"I have to contact Serethusa," says Raven, as she slides out of her seat; then she pauses. "Where's all my furniture and stuff?"

"I should have thought you could afford new," says Cindy, but stops as Raven gives her a confused look. Then she queries, "You did win the lottery, didn't you?"

Raven's chaise-lounge is in the dumpster with many of Ruth's clothes and a load of rotting food from the closed café, together with a furious Trina Button.

"You can't throw this away," Trina is yelling to Jordan's mother as she wades through the garbage, pulling out Ruth's possessions.

"Leave it alone you stupid woman," Gwenda Jackson shouts as she tries to grab the stomping woman. But Trina is too fast for her and has her hands full by the time Sergeant Brougham appears.

"Not you again ... Get out of there."

"She's throwing all Ruth's stuff away," bleats Trina.

"Well, she won't need it where she's going," shoots back the older woman. "And I'm damned if I'm having it in my place after what's she's done."

"She hasn't done anything ..." screams Trina, but gives up when she feels wetness on her foot and realizes she is standing in something messy.

"Come on. Leave that stuff and get out," orders Brougham, and Trina relinquishes everything apart from Ruth's roll of posters, her bead bag, and what feels like a pound of squashed tomatoes on one foot.

"Put those back," says Jordan's mother, tussling with Trina over Ruth's posters, but Brougham steps in.

"She might as well take them. They're allowed posters in jail these days." Then he turns to Trina sternly. "Now stay out of there and leave it alone or I'll arrest you again."

"I'm telling Ruth what you're doing," Trina spits at Gwenda Jackson as she squelches away, trailing pureed tomato.

But telling Ruth is not as easy as Trina had hoped. A bureaucratic roadblock awaits her at the police station. "You're only allowed one visit, and you saw her yesterday," Noreen tells Trina, anxious to keep Ruth's injuries from public scrutiny, then spends twenty minutes trying to come up with the relevant regulation.

"I'm not leaving 'til I see it in black and white," says Trina crossing her arms, and she laughs when Noreen threatens to arrest her for trespassing.

"Go on then," says Trina, holding out her hands with her wrists together. "Then I'll get to see Ruth."

"This isn't a joke," says Noreen sternly. "Your friend is in very serious trouble."

"So will you be if you're lying to me," shoots back Trina. "Now where does it say that I can't visit my friend again?"

Ten minutes later, with Ruth tidied up a bit and her hair brushed, Trina walks into the interview room bubbling with excitement, laughing, "I nearly got arrested ..." then she stops in horror. "What happened to your face? And look at your fingers. What happened to your nails?"

Noreen and Annie stand, arms folded, and stare at the ceiling as Trina carries on. "And what about your clothes? They were nearly new. And where's your glasses?"

"I fell over," sobs Ruth, and she carries on crying as Trina gives the guards a dirty look and tries to cheer her up with a cuddle. "Never mind. I'll bring you some more clothes. You'll just have to be careful, that's all. You'll soon be out of here."

"How?" whimpers Ruth.

"I've started a campaign to get you released," says Trina with new-found bounce.

"Tell me it doesn't involve dynamite, Trina."

"No. It's a publicity campaign. I put it on the Internet last night. You've already got supporters in Moscow, Senegal, Sydney, and a couple of places I can't pronounce.

I've even got half a dozen American lawyers offering to take your case to the UN Human Rights commission."

Ruth painfully raises her eyebrows. "How much will that cost, Trina?"

"Oh ... I hadn't thought of that. I thought they were just being helpful."

"Lawyers?" queries Ruth.

"OK. But the *Sun* is going to do an interview with me this afternoon. Don't worry. Jordan will turn up and tell them it's all been a mistake, then you'll be out."

The thought of getting out overwhelms Ruth, but then every thought overwhelms her, and the tears flow again.

"Your mother-in-law is tidying the place up for you, and she gave me some of your things to take care of," says Trina, landing another punch, then she finds herself crying alongside her friend. "Cheer up, Ruth," she implores through the tears. "Mike says that his friend in England is going to find your father for you."

Trina, as always, has erred on the side of optimism and, in truth, David Bliss has virtually given up any hope of tracing the man on the sketchy information supplied by Mike Phillips. However, in a last ditch effort, he has decided to visit Liverpool and is nearing the Beatles' Merseyside home with Daphne Lovelace as navigator. It's early evening in England and the wintry drizzle contrasts sharply with the bright morning sun that still shines in Canada. Vancouver, nestling under the Coastal Range, is still cool and crisp in the mountain air, but Inspector Wilson is rapidly warming up as Trina Button tears into him.

"She's been beaten up," Trina yells into Wilson's face, once Ruth has been led back to her cell.

"She fell ..."

"Don't fucking lie to me. I'm a nurse. I can see when someone's been smacked around."

"She attacked the doctor," Wilson protests.

"No more beatings," orders Trina. "You keep your hands off her. She's getting a lawyer right now."

"She hasn't got any money. She'll have to apply to a judge for legal aid."

"I said, 'she's getting a lawyer,'" snaps Trina as she storms out.

Liverpool's cramped back streets of terraced houses are gleaming under a fresh glaze of sleet as David Bliss gingerly navigates in search of a hotel. The Beatles are pumping out "Day Tripper" on the car's CD player — "It'll put us in the right mood," Daphne had insisted — while Bliss's injured leg is throbbing in time.

"I'll have to stop soon," says Bliss, as he furiously kneads his thigh.

"I'm sure it was around here somewhere," says Daphne, peering determinedly through the gloom to spot the Norbury, a hotel she has eulogized as a gem among gems for the past two hundred miles. "I distinctly remember it; they did a wonderful lobster bisque."

"But that was ten years ago," moans Bliss testily as the pain from his leg shoots up his spine.

"More like twenty," replies Daphne, and Bliss hits the brakes.

"This will have to do," he says as he slides into the driveway of The Royal Hotel ten seconds later. "My leg is killing me. I can't drive another inch."

"Are you sure you can drive all right with that leg?" Daphne had asked as he'd rented the car in Westchester that morning and, although he'd been emphatic, he had been forced to halt every fifteen or twenty minutes to shake out the cramps. "You should let me drive," she had offered several times, but he had convinced himself that the pain was therapeutic and soldiered on.

"Maybe you can drive back," he'd told her eventually, with little intent.

Inspector Wilson is still in his office, smarting over Trina's attack, and is praying for something concrete to bolster his case. The possibility that Ruth could be telling the truth doesn't cross his mind, but the possibility that Trina Button might come back with some high-priced reinforcements does. *We just need a break,* he is thinking, when a phone call sends him flying back to the Corner Coffee Shoppe.

"You might want to take a look at this," enthuses Sergeant Brougham as he meets Wilson at the café's front door and guides him across a floor of splintered boards.

"I need some good news. I've just had that Button woman ripping into me."

"I'm gonna screw her if she doesn't back off," agrees Brougham, then points to an area where a force cameraman is rigging a spotlight.

"It's under the floorboards just there," says Brougham, "You can see it quite clearly."

Wilson kneels to peer into the hole and his face lights up. "Gotcha," he says under his breath, then calls, "Well done," to the officers standing around.

An hour later, Noreen stands over Ruth as she slumps snivelling at a desk in the interview room, while Wilson is in the next room watching her on a video screen and combing his hair in preparation for his performance. "Right, Dave," he tells Brougham, "keep the camera rolling. Let's see what the lovely lady has to say about this."

The interview room door opens and Ruth cringes at the sound. Noreen has softened under the heat of the camera and is soothing, "Don't worry, Ruth. No one's going to hurt you," but Ruth is so infused with fear that she cowers like a wounded animal in a leg trap as Wilson enters and towers over her.

"Good morning, Mrs. Jackson," he begins solicitously as he hams for a future audience of twelve. "I am going to show you something, and I want you to tell me what it is."

Ruth's eyes go the floor. She knows what's coming. From the moment Trina told her she'd been arrested for stepping on the toes of the forensic officers at the café, she knew her luck would give out and they would unearth her secret.

"What is this, Mrs. Jackson?" Wilson asks as he lays a folded document on the table in front of her.

Ruth's eyes stay down, though her whimper turns into a continuous pitiable whine.

Wilson has no pity and shrewdly lets the moment build before he takes a breath and tries again. "Mrs. Jackson. I'm asking you to explain what it is that I've placed on the table in front of you. Would you please do that?"

"Insurance," she mumbles without lifting her head.

"Sorry," he says. "I missed that. Would you speak up, please?"

Ruth can't speak up. The nightmare she has endured for two days has turned into reality and casts a pall over the rest of her life. "It's insurance," she mumbles again.

"What kind of insurance?"

"Life insurance."

"And this insurance was on whose life?" carries on Wilson, leading Ruth by a nose-ring through an interrogation maze for the benefit of tidiness. The answers are all printed in bold black and white on the insurance policy on the table, but Wilson wants blood. "Whose life?" he repeats, but Ruth can't bring herself to answer.

"Jordan Artemus Jackson, it says here," prompts Wilson. "Who is Jordan, Mrs. Jackson?"

"My husband."

"Correct. Now I want you to look carefully at ..."

And so it goes, detail after pointless detail, page after page — a dripping tap that threatens to drown Ruth in anguish and remorse. There can be no dispute. Ruth Jackson took out a life insurance policy on her husband's life to the tune of one hundred thousand dollars just days after he slipped from the Coffee Shoppe's radar screen.

"Look at the date please, Mrs. Jackson," continues Wilson, the scent of victory lifting his voice. "What is that date?"

"September nineteenth."

"Yes. September the nineteenth of this year. Just over three months ago — but only just."

"I know what you're thinking ..." sobs Ruth, but Wilson cuts her off.

"Just one more question, Mrs. Jackson, and I want you to think very carefully before you answer. Ready?"

Ruth nods, but she already knows the question, and knows that she has no satisfactory response.

Wilson pauses for a second to give the camera an opportunity to savour the moment, then he gloats, "Wasn't the nineteenth of September almost a week after you claim that your husband tested positive for cancer?"

"Yes, but ..."

"And wasn't the nineteenth of September almost a week after your husband was last seen by anyone but you?"

"But ..."

"One second, Mrs. Jackson," says Wilson, holding up his hand while he prepares for his big finish. "Would you please read this line for me?"

Ruth knows the line well enough to recite it from memory, but she stutters and sniffles her way through it in a small voice. "This policy shall not take effect until ninety days following its acceptance."

The trap has shut and Ruth gives in. "I knew I'd get caught," she is crying as Wilson informs her that, in addition to drug trafficking and various assaults, she will also be charged with fraudulently obtaining life insurance; then Sergeant Brougham scuttles in, sidles up to Wilson, and whispers in his ear.

"Oh, shit," mutters Wilson and switches off the microphone as he turns to Ruth.

"Well, apparently you now have a lawyer, Mrs. Jackson."

Ruth Jackson doesn't have just any lawyer. Trina has hired Wilson Hammett, known as "The Hammer" to constables and crooks alike — for good reason. He may be small and prematurely balding, but he sits on a throne above the Vancouver underworld and skims the scum off the top. Common murderers and everyday rapists rarely interest him, or can afford his fees, and he seeks out the headline grabbers. Nothing gets him off the golf course faster than a bent politician, a kiddie-porn merchant, or a whiff of heavy-handed police tactics.

"They've beaten her to a pulp," Trina had exaggerated, as she'd handed over the first instalment of a thousand dollars.

"This could get very expensive," Hammett had warned with a heavy lisp, as he took the cheque. "Are you quite sure about this?"

"Quite sure. It's my fault. If I hadn't peeked I would never have known he'd gone, and she wouldn't be in this mess."

"Well, I'm not sure ..."

"Plus, I was the one who took her to kick boxing class."

"Well, I don't know if you should blame ..."

"But I do. And if I hadn't put the guinea pig in the oven ... Oh, never mind. You probably wouldn't understand."

Ten minutes later, Ruth is still crying as she is led into the visiting room, surrounded by a posse. Noreen and Annie have been reinforced by a male officer, and as Ruth sits, the three fold their arms and make a wall. "Stop snivelling," barks Noreen. "You're not a kid."

"I can't afford a lawyer," Ruth whimpers as Hammett enters with his young assistant and sits opposite her.

"It's legal aid," he says, exactly as Trina had suggested, then he turns to the officers. "I'll call you if I need anything."

"She's very violent ..." starts Noreen, but Hammett waves her off.

"Mrs. Jackson will be fine, I'm sure."

"What happened to your face?" he asks as she sits, but Ruth waits for the "click" of the door behind her before saying, "I couldn't stop crying. Nobody believes me. The doctor thinks I'm crazy."

"Miss Dawson will just take a few photos of you," says Hammett and he has a sly glance at the room's surveillance camera as his assistant takes out a miniature digital camera. As expected, Noreen blusters back in with her sidekicks and starts bleating about photographic regulations. Miss Dawson swings the lens to catch the enraged matron and has the camera snatched from her hand. Hammett slowly stands and fills the room with his energy as his lisping voice angrily sibilates, "I suggest you give my assistant that back immediately, unless you wish to add a further assault charge to those we are already contemplating."

Noreen backs off, but Hammett hasn't finished, "And tell your Inspector that I am entitled to a private conversation with my client; that means I expect that surveillance camera turned off immediately."

"I've spoken to Inspector Wilson," Hammett tells Ruth, once he's listened attentively to her side of the story. "They'll point to the insurance policy, and they'll say, 'Why did you hide it under the floorboards?'"

"I didn't want Jordan to think I was trying to make money off of his death."

"Fair enough, but it seems that everyone has a problem with Jordan's cancer."

"My husband had only a few weeks to live. Why won't anyone believe me?"

"I want to believe you, but you've got to give me something to go on. Who was his doctor? Which hospital? What kind of cancer?"

"I don't know," she whimpers.

"Ruth, It's not the most credible defence I've come across, and what's your explanation for his disappearance?"

"I didn't kill him."

"Ruth. I'm your lawyer. No one knows better than me that you didn't kill him. I'd stake my own life on that. But the judge might think I have a vested interest."

"What's going to happen to me?" she whimpers.

"As it stands, all they've really got is a little blood on a knife and the fact that you took out a hefty insurance policy on someone who's vanished. Your next court appearance is tomorrow. I'll demand bail, but I may as well warn you," he shakes his head, "I don't see it happening."

"But I've got to get out. Jordan needs me."

As Ruth cries her way back to the cell, Wilson and Brougham are watching on the bank of surveillance screens in the jailer's office.

"What do you think of her, Dave?" asks Wilson.

"If my wife blubbered that much I'd probably take out life insurance on her."

"I spoke to the insurance broker," continues Wilson, ignoring the quip. "She didn't mention any cancer — even signed a form saying there was nothing wrong with him. The broker said the only thing that bothered her was that she couldn't claim if he died in the first three months."

"So you think it was premeditated?"

"Nah. Probably got into a fight over money or another woman. I think he was already dead by the time she took out the policy, then she realized that she had to keep him alive for three months before she could claim. Look at the way she'd hidden it. If that Button woman hadn't noticed his bed was empty she would've waited until his body was found and neatly buried, then dragged the policy out and laughed at us."

"But where's the body?"

Wilson has a grandstand view of the mountains from his windows and he peers thoughtfully into the snowy peaks as they blush in the setting sun. "He's probably up there somewhere, in the forest or under the snow. A hiker will probably find what's left of him in the spring, unless she comes clean."

There is no view from Ruth's barred window, and the dark shadow of a high brick wall leans in on her, turning day to dusk.

"My eyes hurt," she whimpers to the evening officer. "Would you turn off the light, please?"

As the light dims, Ruth lays in the quiet gloom surrounded by the shards of her life, and she stares at the remnants of her nails and prays for salvation from a god that she doesn't have any faith in. *Why is this happening to me?* she wants to know. *What did I do to deserve this?*

The sins of the father shall be visited on the son, replies the god inside her mind — her only god; the god who had turned her from her mother's course; the god who had steered her resolutely along the path of honesty and integrity, until the day she had veered off track and fraudulently taken out life insurance on her husband.

Why did you do it? her god challenges. *You knew you'd be caught.*

Why me? she questions, demanding an individual answer to a universal question. But her god has no answer; has never had an answer. The answers have always come from outside, even in childhood. If she'd never actually heard anyone say, "Poor little devil. She doesn't stand a chance," she'd seen it in their faces as she'd lined up with her mother at food banks and welfare offices. And she'd seen it in the faces of relatives and friends as her mother used her as a bargaining chip for a bed. And, most often, she'd seen it in the angered faces of her cohorts at school as they'd punched and kicked; "fat ugly people wearing glasses deserve to be squashed like slugs," their prissy, perfect little faces had sneered.

Why me? she continues to ask as her mind spins in a turmoil of anguish. *Why does everything go wrong for me?*

What about Jordan, bitch? Do you think he's enjoying this?

What's happened to him? Where is he?

Don't pretend you don't know.

He's slunk away to die like a wounded cat.

You know that's not true. Who are you trying to kid? Think; when did you last see him?

I can't remember. You're confusing me.

He wasn't there in the apartment, was he?

Yes. He was.

So when did you last touch him; feel him; make love to him?

I can't remember.

"Jackson. Are you all right, Jackson?" A voice from outside tries breaking through, but Ruth blots it out as her mind whirls with a notion that finally threatens to drag her under.

Had he been there? she asks herself, as hands gently prod and a voice calls, "Mrs. Jackson — Ruth. Are you all right?"

What if he had been merely a mirage? An apparition of his former self still lingering in his room? His spirit still haunting me?

"Ruth. Come on. Wake up, Ruth," continues the voice, worriedly.

Nobody else ever saw him — in three months.

He always went out the back door to the taxi.

Did you see him?

No ...

Neither did the taxi driver. Don't you find
that strange?

He was going for treatment.

"Mrs. Jackson. Wake up now!" shouts another voice.

What treatment? Which doctor? Which hospital?

I don't know. You're confusing me.

Do you see him now?

No.

Are you sure? Look deep; look really deep in the
darkest corner. What do you see?

"Quick. Call an ambulance. I think she's having
a seizure."

chapter nine

The drizzle has stopped overnight in Liverpool, but the pain in Bliss's leg is still dragging him down as he and Daphne head to the Beatles museum from their hotel in the morning. They had been late to bed and late rising, thanks to Daphne's desire to visit the hotel's nightclub, where a Beatles tribute band had knocked out passable impressions of Fab-Four favourites. Daphne, showing more knee than most, had bopped her way through "Twist and Shout," "Hippy Hippy Shake," and most of the other chart-toppers until after one a.m., while Bliss had been forced to sit on the sidelines nursing his throbbing leg.

"A good walk should get the knots out," Bliss had told Daphne as they'd left the hotel after breakfast, although he'd added, "This is probably a complete waste of time. I'm not even sure what I'm looking for."

"We won't know unless we try," says Daphne, picking up the pace and gaily swinging her pink, plastic "I love the Beatles" handbag that she'd insisted on digging out of the attic for the occasion. "I was thinking of wearing my 'Love Me Do' baseball cap," she'd had told him before they'd left Westchester. "But the bloomin' moths have got at it."

"Oh dear. What a shame," he'd said, stone-faced.

The foyer of the Beatles museum, a pasty recreation of the Cavern club, is packed by a flock of elderly Japanese tourists, all topped with pudding-basin haircuts and tagged with huge nameplates, emblazoned "Kyoto's 40th Anniversary Worship the Beatles Tour." However, there is clearly consternation amongst the congregation and, as Bliss and Daphne join the crush, the young attendant from the tiny souvenir shop polishes his English to loudly apologize for the fact that the museum, and the archives, are being refurbished, and won't be reopening until mid-January. "But," he carries on, as if it's an accomplishment, "we have managed to keep the Beatles souvenir and memorabilia shop open for your enjoyment today."

"Show them your badge and tell them it's official," suggests Daphne, giving Bliss a dig.

"Are you trying to get me sacked, Daphne? I'm off duty, on foreign turf, with a personal inquiry. I can't do that."

"Leave it to me then," she says slipping his grasp, and she elbows her way to the inquiry desk before he can stop her.

"Hello young man," Daphne starts, dragging the attendant away from a furious interpreter who is loudly complaining that they had come all the way from Japan. Then she seemingly spots his souvenir Beatles tie. "Is that the Rolling Stones?" she queries, straight-faced.

"No ... It's the Beatles, ma'am," he says in nasal Liverpudlian. "This here's the Beatles museum."

Daphne laughs, "I know. I was just pulling your leg. You can do that when you're my age — I'm eighty-five you know."

"Well, congratulations madam. Now how ..."

A Yoko Ono doppelganger forces her way to the front, pulls out a tuning fork, and announces, "My swee' lor'," and, as the ensemble bursts into their protest song, a coach load of German fans pour through the doors and line up behind Daphne.

"Is that your real name?" Daphne asks, poking the attendant's name tag.

"Ringo — yeah. Me pa was a great fan of his."

"Fascinating," says Daphne, well aware of the Teutonic tension building behind her. "I was in the war, you know," she says, leaning forward a notch.

"Yes. Good. But ..."

"We won."

"I know. But, how can ..."

"Oh, sorry. Silly of me, rabbitting on like that. Well, to cut a long story short, my neighbour and very good friend, Mavis Longbottom — you probably don't know her — she used to be the cook at the Mitre hotel." Daphne catches the end of Ringo's tie and pulls him gently down to her level. "Terrible food. I'd stay at the Westway if I were you. Anyway ... Have you ever been to Westchester?"

"No, madam ... but there's a queue ..."

"Oh. I know, you're so busy, and this close to Christmas. Anyway — did I tell you I was eighty-five?"

"Yes, I think ..."

"Thought so." Daphne grabs his tie again, wrenches a little harder, and whispers, "I lied. I'm actually eighty-nine. Wouldn't think so, would you?"

"No ..." he replies, easing his tie from her grasp with an eye on the increasingly restless lineup. "But what exactly did you want, madam?"

Daphne straightens herself up and pronounces, "That's what I like in a young man. Decisiveness." Then she leans in, really tight. "The thing is, Mavis Longbottom's husband was a Scouser from around here somewhere, and he always reckoned he was a close friend of your boys, even went on tour with them. Now Freddie died a few weeks ago, and poor old Mavis thought it would nice to get all his old pals together ..."

It works, and two minutes later Daphne and Bliss are alone in the archives with Ringo telling them to take all the time they want while he fends off the onslaught at the front desk.

"1964 North American tour," says Bliss as he opens a battered steel filing cabinet. "This is it Daphne," he calls, and quickly finds a group photograph.

"Did you know Ringo's real name was Richard Starkey?" inquires Daphne as she glances at the posed picture. "OK, next stop the newspaper office," she adds, opening her gargantuan handbag and popping the photograph in.

"Daphne — that's theft!" exclaims Bliss.

Daphne hesitates for a second then snaps shut her bag. "Yes, David. I do believe you're right." Then she marches to the door, saying, "We'll mail it back anonymously. Anyway, what are you going to do, arrest an eighty-nine-year-old spinster?"

"You're not eighty-nine," he breathes, but she's gone.

For Daphne, getting the picture printed in a newspaper is child's play, as she re-runs her "Freddie Longbottom" routine with the features editor of the Merseyside Mail.

"I don't know which was Mavis's husband," she prattles, concentrating deeply on the group of twenty or so musicians and staff in the picture, "but I'm sure that one of your readers will be able to put names to them." Then her voice slowly grinds to a stop and a look of consternation comes over her face.

"What's up, Daphne?" asks Bliss.

"Oh, nothing ... Just a shiver up the spine," she says, adding, "Do you realize that half these people are probably dead already?"

"Scary, isn't it," says the editor. "Anyway, Miss Lovelace, let's see if we can commune with the living ones — I do like a challenge."

"Daphne, you are outrageous," laughs Bliss as they make their way back to the hotel.

"I am, aren't I," she admits, adding, "It all comes back, you know."

Bliss knows well what she means; knows of her background with the special forces and French resistance during the war, and her exploits with the secret service afterwards. Then he stops in thought. "Wait a minute," he says. "You weren't in Vancouver in the sixties, were you, by any chance?"

"What makes you think that?" she says with a twinkle in her voice.

"You were!" he exclaims.

"Shh. It's a secret. But not Vancouver. I went to the Beatles' concert in Montreal."

In Vancouver, it's only three days to Christmas, and Ruth Jackson has slipped off the front page of the *Sun* and ended up at the bottom of page two, where she is easily missed. "Prisoner collapses in cell," reads the column heading, and continues, "An unnamed prisoner was taken by ambulance ..." However, it's the large, seasonally-correct photo of Trina Button on the front page, with snowflakes the size of poppy petals falling around her, that holds the attention of the crossword gang.

"I can't believe she'd do that," says Matt, shaking his head.

"I can," jumps in Darcey without hesitation.

Maureen just snorts her disdain. "I don't think we should let her do the crossword anymore."

"We've never let her," says Darcey. "Hasn't stopped her though, has it? Oh, look out."

"I've been arrested again," roars Trina gleefully as she bursts into Donut Delight.

"We saw," mutters Maureen under her breath.

"Look. Look," says Trina grappling the paper from Matt. "I made the front page."

The gang are forced to look again. Trina, wearing only the bottom half of a bright red, slinky bikini, together with a velvet Santa hat, is standing in the middle of the Lion's Gate bridge with traffic at a standstill as two policemen try to wrestle away a huge placard that is just barely covering her breasts.

"Did they airbrush your nipples out?" queries Darcey, taking a close look.

"Don't think so," says Trina, peering at the picture.

"There was a time when they didn't allow bare tits in the *Sun*," Matt says nostalgically as he focuses on Trina's placard.

"Jordan Jackson. Call 569-3425," the sign pleads, and under the picture is a caption reading: "Woman bares all to get her man."

Trina's cellphone rings. "Hold on," she calls as she presses it to her ear. "Trina Button, how can I help you?" she answers as if she's working at a call centre, then she listens for a few seconds before saying, "Sorry, but no thanks." Cutting off the caller, she turns triumphantly to the gang. "That's thirty-nine already."

"Thirty-nine sightings of Jordan?" asks Maureen hopefully.

"No. Only two were Jordan Jacksons," replies Trina, "and neither of them the right one." Though she neglects to add that the other thirty-seven were men offering a variety of dubious services and activities. The phone rings again. "Trina Button. How can I help you?" she says, and she listens intently for a few seconds before grabbing Darcey's pen. Matt sees what's coming and is a fraction too late as Trina makes a dive for the crossword. "Where?" she says, and fills in 27-, 28-, and 29-across with a seventeen-letter suburban address. "1465 Newport Avenue," she muses as Maureen rolls her eyes.

"Oh, sorry," says Trina, tearing a chunk out of the paper. "I mucked up your crossword. Hang on. I've got some more in the car."

"More?" queries Matt.

"Yeah. I bought fifty copies. It's not every day I get on the front page."

Trina's phone rings again as she heads out the door. "Trina Button ..."

By the time Trina has reached her car she has taken two more crank calls and has completely forgotten about the crossword as she heads to the police station, bursting with news.

"What do you want now?" demands Inspector Wilson after the desk officer has talked himself red trying to get someone to speak to Trina.

"What's going on?" asks Trina. "I asked to see Ruth and anybody would think I'd trodden in dog poo from the look on his face."

"Didn't you see the paper this morning?"

"Yeah. I'm on the front page. Oh, is this about the arrest? I'm not complaining, I nearly froze my boobs off, but it worked. And your men didn't hurt me, although one of them had very cold hands. Maybe they should wear gloves ..."

"It is not about the arrest. It's about Ruth," cuts in Wilson, putting on a concerned mien, and Trina slumps in the chair listening in disbelief as he explains. "She confessed; then after she'd spoken to her lawyer, she had a kind of stroke."

"Confessed ... ?"

"Yeah, 'fraid so, and I probably shouldn't tell you this, but she took out a big life insurance policy on Jordan just about the time he disappeared."

"Where is she?" demands Trina, already at the door.

Mike Phillips is on his way in and Trina barrels into him in the doorway.

"You're Ruth's friend aren't you?" he says.

"Mike," she howls. "Did you know about Ruth?"

"I heard," he says. "I was just going to the hospital."

In the parking lot outside the police station, Trina hops into Phillips' car uninvited. "I'm too shaky to drive," she explains, then babbles non-stop all the way to the hospital. "She didn't do it, Mike. I don't care what they say. She didn't do it."

Ruth lays inert at the centre of a web of life support paraphernalia as they are ushered into her room by the policeman guarding the door, and Trina pulls up short as tears threaten to overwhelm her. It's not the deathly pallor of Ruth's face that alarms her so much as the purple bruises. "Look what they did," she cries softly as she tenderly reaches out to touch Ruth's discoloured cheek.

Phillips is keeping very quiet as a young nurse arrives and bustles around.

"Malnutrition, dehydration, and she's got some burst blood vessels in her brain that've given her stroke-like symptoms," she tells them as she checks the monitors, adding, "Hypertension — probably caused by severe stress."

"Having her head smacked on the floor probably didn't help," mutters Trina, but Phillips quickly steps in with a frown of concern. "Can she hear us?" he whispers.

"Possibly," says the nurse. "It's a job to know." Then she leans in and gently takes Ruth's hand. "Can you hear me, Ruth?"

Ruth can hear, but the individual words are lost in the gentle burbling of a pebbly stream as her brainwaves randomly race around.

Move your hand! a voice deep in Ruth's mind tells her. *Move your hand so they know you're alive.*

I'm moving it, I'm moving it, she tells herself, but the babble of unintelligible sounds continues, just beyond her reach.

"Has she moved at all?" Trina is asking the nurse, but the young woman shakes her head. "Have a try if you like. I certainly can't feel anything."

"How long?" asks Phillips quietly.

"You'd have to ask the doctors, but they won't know the full extent of the damage for some time. By the way, would either of you know her next of kin? We haven't been able to contact anyone."

"Someone's trying to find her father right now," Phillips tells her, with his fingers crossed.

Bliss and Daphne have done their best, and, after priming the press, are returning to Westchester, but they've taken to the countryside rather than racing on the highway. "I prefer this," Daphne had told him as they'd ambled along the gently weaving sideroads. "It reminds me of my courting days."

Courting is the last thing on Bliss's mind. His leg hasn't stopped throbbing since leaving Westchester yesterday. Painkillers have helped, but he was wary of overdosing and blurring his judgment, so he talks to keep his mind occupied.

"I still have no idea how we're going to get someone to admit the dirty deed," he says. "Even if we get the names."

"You'll think of something, David. You always do," replies Daphne, patting his good leg.

"Not if her father really was George Harrison," he says. "It's too late for him."

"The tabloids would have fun with that," laughs Daphne. "But how could you prove it?"

"DNA, I suppose. He had cancer for a long time; I bet there are some blood samples in a lab somewhere."

"They are more likely in somebody's safety deposit box waiting for a Sotheby's memorabilia auction," says Daphne, just as Bliss's leg makes him grimace. "I'm going to have to stop and stretch again."

Daphne fumbles in her giant "Beatles" bag for her driving glasses. "No problem," she says. "I'll take over."

"I don't know ..." Bliss starts, but takes a look at the near-deserted road and concedes. "Just for awhile, then."

A few minutes later, Daphne perches on the edge of the driver's seat with her face rammed into the windshield. "Don't worry. I was driving before your dad bought his first Playboy," she says as she peers over the top of the wheel and hits the gas. "I'd forgotten just how much fun it was," she says, screeching the car around the first bend at sixty kilometres an hour as Bliss grips his seat.

"There's no rush, Daphne."

"Sorry, David. But I don't get the chance very often."

She slows a touch and concentrates furiously as she zips along the twisty road, but Bliss is more tense than ever and is about to suggest that he should take back the reins when he spots a warning sign in the gloom. "Daphne. Speed!" he cautions, and a second later the flash of a radar camera dazzles them. Bliss grabs the wheel as Daphne heads for an oak tree and he shouts, "Slow down, Daphne. Slow down."

"Stupid place to take pictures," bitches Daphne, temporarily blinded.

"It's a speed trap," says Bliss.

"That could cause accidents. I jolly well hope they catch people."

"They just caught you."

"Oh. I didn't realize," says Daphne, then she cheers up. "Never mind, I can afford it. You wouldn't believe how much the force is paying me to take care of you."

"Mind the truck!" Bliss yells as she lets her concentration wander again.

"Oops. Not very good in this light I'm afraid."

"Pull over Daphne. My leg's better now."

"Only if you're sure."

"Westchester," announces the city sign not a moment too soon for Bliss, and he stretches thankfully as he exits the car. "I only hope you don't lose your license," he says as Daphne opens the front door for him.

"Oh, no. Don't worry, that won't happen;" then she drops her voice, "I probably shouldn't tell you this, but I've never had one."

"What?"

"Well it always seemed such a lot of bother ..."

"Daphne ..."

The blinking light on Daphne's answering machine in the front hallway gives her cover as she rushes to press 'play,' saying, "I expect it's for you, David."

"How d'ye know ..." he starts as Mike Phillip's voice fills the hall. "Hi, David. I was just wondering if you'd got anywhere on the Beatles' case. Only it's kinda urgent now."

"I wonder what's happened," queries Bliss.

"I sure hope we can trace her father," Phillips says, as he and Trina stand, sad-faced, over Ruth's motionless body.

"I'd rather find Jordan," Trina replies, then remembers the phone call she'd taken at Donut Delight. "It's probably nothing," she continues, pulling out the crossword puzzle, "but some guy phoned and said that a Jordan Jackson rented an apartment from him three months ago."

Phillips scans the address, and is saying, "It's worth a try," when Trina notices his watch.

"Oh, look at the time. I've got to go to work." Then she grabs Ruth's hand and softly calls, "Don't worry. Mike and I will take care of you."

"What about the address?" queries Phillips as Trina heads out.

"I'll meet you there at three this afternoon," she calls over her shoulder and Phillips turns to sit by the bed, telling Ruth, "Hang in there. If anyone can sort this out, she will."

"Mike," shouts Trina dashing back into the room a minute later. "I need a ride."

It's long past four and DS Phillips checks his watch again. If it hadn't been for a procession of interestingly shady characters ebbing and flowing through the front doors of the decrepit apartment block in front of him, he would have quit earlier, on the assumption Trina had given him the wrong address.

"Sorry. Guinea pig escaped," Trina blurts, dashing up to his car just as he turns the ignition. "Have you been here before?" she asks, as she slips into the passenger seat holding a copy of the *Sun*.

"What are you doing?" he puzzles, as she holds the paper in front of her face and peeps through the hole torn in the middle of her picture on the front page.

"Stakeout," she whispers, squinting through her own navel.

"Put it down," laughs Phillips. "You'll get us arrested."

"I don't mind," she says. "I'm getting used to it."

"Trina ..."

"All right," she says, then asks again, "Do you know this place?"

"Yes and no," answers Phillips watching two tight-skirted women steadying a grinning john as he staggers into the lobby with them. "Lamb to the slaughter," chuckles Phillips. "He might make it to the elevator, but that's the only ride he's gonna be getting from those two today."

The women are back out, divvying up the contents of the man's wallet before Phillips finishes. "See what I mean?" he says. "Now what the hell am I supposed to do?"

"I'm more worried about Ruth," says Trina, urging him out. "Come on. Let's talk to the super."

"Come up. I'm in 201," the man tells them through the intercom, but as they head for the elevator, the smell knocks them back.

"Oh my God," mutters Phillips, as his hand goes to his nose.

"You should have my job," says Trina cheerfully, as she pushes the elevator button, but when the door opens she shrinks back. The drunkard is there, standing in the corner that he has mistaken for a toilet.

"Oh, shit," moans Trina, and they take the stairs.

"I phoned 'cuz I noticed your picture in the paper," says the superintendent with a leer, and Trina is grateful that she has Phillips standing behind her as she faces the wispy little man who seems to be the source of much of the stink. "Jordan Jackson rented a unit here, apartment twenty-four," he tells them, and the description he gives certainly matches Ruth's recollections: tall, in his forties, with mousy hair. As for his illness, "It's an apartment building, lady, not a fancy nursing home. We ain't equipped to look after sick people. He'd get visitors — I'd see people coming and going."

"Who?"

"Asking questions like that around here ain't very sensible, if you follow."

"But he was definitely sick?"

"Oh yeah. Some guy from health services came in during the week, but most of the time he was on his own. Slept a lot, I expect. Had cancer you know."

"And you're sure his name was Jordan Jackson?"

"Yeah. It's in my book. Here — have a look," he offers, and Mike Phillips takes the opportunity to scan the page for familiar names.

"How did he pay?" asks Phillips.

"Cash."

"Where is he now?"

"What are ya? Cops or something?"

"No. We're just Jordan's friends ..."

"Then you oughta know," he says, slamming his book.

"Know what?" asks Trina.

"Know he's dead, of course."

"It has to be a different Jordan Jackson," resolves Trina as she sits with Phillips in a nearby coffee house mulling over the information, but the problem they face is that the tenant had paid cash for three months in advance, and the superintendent hadn't taken any other details. "Money talks," he'd told them. "And Mr. Jackson certainly had that. So I'm fucked if I know why he'd wanna die in a dump like this."

"To start with, this guy's been dead for over a month," continues Trina as she tries to untangle the two Jordans, but Phillips wants straight facts.

"According to Inspector Wilson, no one has seen Ruth's husband since early September. He could have died anytime between then and now."

"But where was he being treated?" shoots back Trina. "Who was the doctor? No, it must be another guy with the same name."

"Of the same height, same description, suffering from the same disease?" queries Phillips skeptically.

"But he couldn't have been living here and at the café ..." Trina is protesting when she slowly dries up and allows Phillips to ask the obvious.

"OK, then. So who, apart from Ruth, will swear he was at the café during that time?"

"What are we going to do, Mike?"

"Dig up some evidence," says Phillips. "If he died, there has to be a death certificate and a buried body somewhere."

"But where?" asks Trina, knowing that the superintendent had been of no help when Phillips had inquired about a funeral.

"Who would've gone?" the old man had shrugged. "I don't think he had relatives or friends. I just got a phone call from the hospital saying that he'd passed on and they'd make the funeral arrangements."

Trina had seemed surprised, saying, "I didn't know they'd do that," but the man had shaken his head solemnly, and said, "Well, no one else wanted him."

"Would you recognize him?" Phillips had asked as they'd prepared to leave.

"I doubt it. Like I said, he sort of kept out of the way. Have you got a picture?"

They'd had no picture of Jordan Jackson to show the old superintendent, but, in England, Bliss is having much more luck. While the Beatles' group photo had not made it into that day's paper, it had bounced back on the editor's desk with a complete list of names within a few hours.

"It's a copy of one from our photographic department," he explains to Bliss on the phone the following morning. "One of the reporters thought he recognized it and pulled the original from the archives. We never published it at the time, but whoever took it wrote all the names on the back. Now who were you looking for again?"

Bliss would be surprised if Freddie Longbottom made the list, although, knowing Daphne, he wouldn't be totally stunned. "Any chance you could email it to me?" he asks, without mentioning Freddie. "I expect Mrs. Longbottom will recognize the names."

"Sure. And I'll get someone to check records. We might have something current that will help you track some of them down."

"Thanks," says Bliss, giving his email address as Daphne stands over him.

"We could be in luck," he tells her as he puts down the phone.

"I knew you'd do it," she beams, full of admiration. "You are such a clever man."

Trina is having less luck in Vancouver. No further credible news of Jordan Jackson has surfaced overnight and, while Ruth's condition has remained stable, she's no nearer consciousness. The police are stepping up inquiries, believing that the best defence is a good offence — and there is no better offence than murder for keeping the public's mind off the odd black eye in the cells.

Hammer Hammett, on the other hand, is milking Ruth's injuries as he prepares a flurry of lawsuits, and Trina has been trying to warm up the *Sun* to campaign for a public inquest. But it's the weekend before Christmas, only two days of mayhem before the annual round of disenchantments, recriminations, family arguments, and suicides begin. Everyone has more weighty things on their minds than a touch of police brutality.

"If she had a handful of kids it would be a different story," the Saturday journalist at the *Sun* had told Trina. "Something very serious like, 'Father of five missing as mother fights for life,' would probably make the front page."

"Or another picture of me with my boobs out," she'd added pointedly, and he'd slunk off saying he would see what could be done.

"I don't know why we don't have Christmas in July like the Australians," Trina is complaining to the crossword gang mid-morning in Donut Delight. "Most people would be away at the beach, and the stores wouldn't be half as busy. Plus, it wouldn't be snowing or raining."

"Well, it's almost over. Only tomorrow, and that's a Sunday, so most places will be closed," says Darcey.

"Tomorrow?" puzzles Trina, checking the date on the paper and exclaiming, "Shit!"

"What?" chant Maureen and Matt in unison.

"Christmas shopping," shouts Trina, already on the move. "I knew I'd missed something."

"What did you forget?" calls Darcey, with a suggestion or two in mind.

"Christmas," she yells, tearing for the door. "I forgot Christmas."

"Can you believe that?" says Maureen, as Trina hits the street at a run. "She didn't touch the crossword."

A black BMW with ominously tinted windows purrs to life as Trina rushes out of the donut shop, then follows her as she races to the parking lot for her car.

Trina drives as scatterbrained as she thinks, and the BMW on her tail raises the ire of numerous seasonally-challenged motorists as the driver flits from lane to lane to keep up with her zippy Volkswagen.

The two leather-jacketed figures that emerge from the BMW to stalk Trina into the mall are too large to be shadowy, and they stand out amid the desperate throngs anxiously seeking the perfect Christmas icon among the piles of glittering trash.

Trina scurries from store to store, losing her escort in the maelstrom, as she grabs gifts for her husband, two teenagers, and two sets of parents. "Make sure the receipt's in the bag," she calls, knowing that most of the stuff is for her two teenagers and is only on loan until Boxing Day: "Yuk! It's: Pink! ... Green! ... Shiny! ... Greasy! ... Dorky! ... Dweeby! ... Yuk! Mother, how could you?"

"Take it back and exchange it, then."

Trina has the VW almost full by the time she hits the garden centre, then heads for the supermarket, with the BMW still in tow.

Filling buggies on the run and dumping them at strategic spots, Trina darts around the supermarket like the winner of a monster-grab competition.

"All four buggies ma'am?" says the guy on cash, and she scratches her head.

"I thought I had five," she says, and is threatening to dash back into the aisles to search when the mumbling of an insurrection in the ranks behind her changes her mind. "Don't worry. As long as there's at least one turkey, that'll do."

Trina's car was already sprouting gifts, with a tree and an ornamental concrete birdbath tied to the roof rack, but by the time two bag boys have helped her to empty the second cart, the small Volkswagen is completely full. "If you get in, we could pack it in around you," suggests one of the youths, but Trina has a better idea. "Taxi," she yells, and five minutes later she has a convoy snaking behind her as the black BMW follows the cab.

"She's f'kin bonkers," says the BMW's driver, Mort, the one-handed English creep from the porn studio, as Trina scorches her way through intersections and past patiently waiting traffic jams, with the cab racing to keep up. The two goons in the back of the Beemer snort agreement, while Tom sits in the front passenger seat concentrating on the fleeing VW as they weave through Vancouver's maze of one-way streets.

"Leave her to me, Mort," says Tom, puffing himself up. "It should be easy enough to get her to back off."

"I don't wanna see no more stunts," warns Mort.

"'Course not."

"No more titties on the front page of the dailies. Know what I mean?"

"Don't worry, Mort. I can handle her."

"You'd better."

"We could always pull the plug on Ruth," suggests one of the goons in the back.

"Be subtle, my boy. Be subtle," says Mort. "Tom here is gonna take care of everything, aren't you?"

"Sure, Mort. You can trust me."

"We'll just see where she lives," says Mort, ignoring an angry horn blast as he runs a red light. "Maybe she's got kiddies at home. It's always useful to have a backup plan. Know what I mean, boys?"

"Sure, Mort. Whatever you say, Mort," says Tom, mindful of the loaded pistol by the side of Mort's seat.

"Hi, guys — where's your dad?" shouts Trina as she opens the front door into the spacious hall. The taxi driver is anxious to unload, and already has his hands full of groceries as Trina rushes back to the car to help.

"Hi, Mom," comes the delayed response, but Trina is temporarily distracted by the black BMW that is slowly cruising by.

"Ma'am?" says the cab driver, holding the bags out for her.

"Oh, sorry," she says, getting her mind back in gear and giving the driver her sweetest smile. "Put that straight in the freezer, would you?" Then she rushes back inside to yell up the stairs. "I said, 'where's your dad?'"

"It's not really my job ..." the driver tries as he staggers past her with a month's supply of meat, but Trina bolts back to her car muttering, "Teenagers," as she wrenches a boxed bicycle and a snowboard from the trunk.

"Grab this," she says, handing the cab driver the bike. "Stick it in the garage will you?" Then she races for the front door with half a dozen food bags and a DVD player.

"I still don't know where your dad is," she yells, as she rushes up the hallway and trips over a pair of frozen turkeys.

"Where is the freezer ..." the driver starts as he struggles in with the bike.

"Basement," she shouts, then backs off. "Sorry. Thought you were one of the kids. Freezer's in the basement. You can't miss it."

Dumping her bags on the kitchen table, Trina is shouting, "We could use a hand here, kids," as she sprints back to the car and starts piling boxes onto the driver.

"This isn't my job really ..." he's protesting, and Trina has nothing but empathy. "I know it isn't. This is really kind of you." Then she yells past him. "Rob and Kylie will you please help? And where is your father?"

"Thanks ever so much," she says, as the driver staggers into the house with boxes of assorted slippers and a Christmas tree. "Just put the tree in the family room," she adds, then shrieks, "Rob ... Kylie. Santa won't come if you don't help."

"Do you want me to decorate it as well?" the driver snarls as he dumps the tree in the hallway.

"Oh, you needn't ..." Then she pauses. "You were joking, right?"

"Yes ma'am, but ..."

"OK. One more load," she calls, undeterred, and scurries back to the cab to dig out the rest of the food.

Plastic grocery bags slice into her fingers as she gallops back into the house, with the driver running behind her, but she stops at the bottom of the stairs to shriek, "Rob and Kylie. This is your last chance. Where is your father?"

"I already told you twice," yells Kylie, putting her friend on hold.

"I didn't hear," screeches Trina.

"Where does this go, Ma'am?" asks the driver, toting a guinea pig cage.

"Just drop it round the back and plop him into it, would you sweetheart? Where did you say, Kylie?"

Kylie gives up with a sigh, saying, "I'll call you back Deirdre. Mom's having a fit," as she puts down the phone. Then she appears at the top of the stairs. "I'm here, mom."

"Oh. There you are, love," says Trina. "I just said, 'Where's your dad?'"

"Mom, will you please just stand still and listen? I already told you twice. He's gone Christmas shopping 'cuz he says you forgot again."

chapter ten

Half a world away, the experience of Christmas in the Lovelace household is the antithesis of the Buttons'. Daphne has orchestrated the event with military precision and, by the time the turkey is nicely sizzling, she is putting on the final touches.

"Dinner's at one o'clock, so I told the old fogies to come at about twelve," she tells Bliss as she blows on a table knife and gives it a shine. "By the time they get their coats off, their slippers on, and their teeth in, you'll be ready to carve."

"Me — carve?" queries Bliss.

"Of course, David. I may not look it, but I'm old enough to remember the days when every self-respecting man could wield a knife at the table."

"Usually in Agatha Christie's novels," chuckles Bliss as he stabs himself in the chest with a pen and expires histrionically, exclaiming, "Murder in the dining room."

"Oh David, you are funny," she says as she heads for the kitchen. "By the way, I invited Mavis Longbottom. I thought it was only fair after the way you've been using her and Freddie."

"Didn't you invite Freddie as well?" calls Bliss, seeing an opportunity to shove a copy of the Beatles' picture under his nose, asking, "D'ye recognize anyone, lad?" just for kicks.

"No. I told you, he's dead."

"Oh," says Bliss, disappointed. "I thought you'd made that up."

"Freddie was her first," Daphne explains as she bustles in with a table decoration. "But she's been through a couple more since him. None of 'em lived very long. Can't say I blame them."

"Daphne," laughs Bliss, and he takes another look at the email from Liverpool. In addition to the four broody-looking men in black at the front of the photograph, the remaining seventeen faces now have names, although, according to the accompanying letter from the newspaper editor, eight are believed dead and four are women.

"At least that cuts the odds to one in five, if he's one of the lucky ones," Bliss had told Daphne when he'd printed it out from his laptop, though he still has no plan of action to find Ruth's father.

"I've a feeling we're going to be distinctly out of place with all these oldies," natters Daphne as she starts setting the table. "It's a pity Samantha and Peter couldn't make it. They really should get flu shots like me, then they wouldn't have this trouble."

Bliss keeps his eye on the picture, knowing that Samantha had been working on an exit strategy from the moment she'd been invited.

"Daphne's really with it," his daughter had told him. "But I'm fucked if I want to sit around all afternoon with the rest of 'em and talk about the war and the price of incontinence pads."

"Oh, Sam ..."

"And you needn't bother with the guilt thing, Dad. Anyway, we're going to Peter's. His parents want to give me the once-over."

"OK," he'd said, giving in without a fight, knowing that every argument he believed he had won in his daughter's twenty-six years had generally been an exercise in self-deception.

The Joneses and the Elliotts, sharing a cab, arrive at eleven-thirty, but spend five minutes digging through pockets and purses for precisely ten percent of three pounds fifty-seven.

"He would have been lucky to get tuppence in my day, the way he drives," bitches Blossom Jones as the taxi speeds off.

"You're early," says Daphne opening the front door.

"Didn't want to be late meeting our famous detective," whinnies Beattie Elliott, and all four stand in the hallway staring at Bliss as if expecting him to spontaneously combust.

"You'd better start taking your coats off," says Daphne, breaking the spell. "Dinner will be ready in an hour."

Phil and Maggie Morgan, the next-door neighbours, arrive on time, on foot, and are exhausted. "That bloomin' garden path gets longer every year," moans Phil. "Still, it won't be long before they're carrying me down it, I s'pose."

"I hope someone shoots me if I ever get like that," mutters Daphne in Bliss's ear as she scuttles around, collecting coats and shoes.

Mavis Longbottom's arrival is a surprise for Bliss, as she nimbly jumps out of a sporty little Fiat and drags her "latest" toward the house. "Come along, Gino," she says, pulling an elderly shrew as if he were a recalcitrant child.

"I'll be surprised if he lasts very long," Daphne mordantly mumbles to Bliss as she prepares a welcoming smile for the couple.

Minnie Dennon is the final arrival, stumbling over the doorstep, and flinging herself into Bliss's arms as he stands in the hallway readying a handshake. "Oh, sorry. Didn't know you had guests, Daphne," says Minnie, wearing more makeup and jewellery than Elizabeth Taylor, and Bliss laughs as Daphne quickly drags her off. "You did that on purpose, Minnie," mutters Daphne under her breath.

"I did not ..." protests Minnie, but Daphne drives her toward the kitchen. "You can help me with dinner, if you wouldn't mind."

"I was just going to talk to ..."

"Later, dear. I want your opinion on the Brussels sprouts first."

"So, David," says Phil Morgan, as the remaining guests crowd in on him with their sherries in hand. "Daphne tells us you got the Commissioner's commendation for solving murders."

Murders, robberies, frauds, and rapes ... Daphne's friends may look fragile, but they suck up the gore of London's underworld with relish, as Bliss of the Yard fills them in on some of his more interesting cases. "It's pretty gruesome," he warns several times, and they grimace with glee as they urge him on.

"Dinner," calls Daphne, on time to the minute. "Find your seats." Then she whispers to Bliss. "I put you at the end, next to me, David."

The table, replete with a holly centrepiece topped with slender white candles in a silver candelabra, is a picture that would be welcome in the pages of *Victorian Dining*. Daphne has even inscribed place names in calligraphy on hand-laid vellum and, as Bliss sits, Minnie slips into the dining room with the final steaming plates of vegetables and plumps herself into Daphne's seat.

"I put you over there, Minnie," scowls Daphne as she makes an entrance with the bird.

"Oh. I'm here now," Minnie says, hanging on to Bliss's arm. "Unless David minds me sitting next to him, of course."

"Minnie," snaps Daphne, using the turkey as a weapon. "I have to sit next to David to help him carve."

"I suppose you're used to slicing up bodies," says Don Elliot as Minnie moves, but Daphne cuts him down. "David's a police inspector, not a mortician, Don. He leaves the gory stuff to others."

Turkey, ham, stuffing, sprouts, and four varieties of root vegetables are garnished with clove-scented bread sauce, chipolatas, bacon rolls, cranberry jelly, and the thickest gravy Bliss has ever spooned out of a gravy boat.

"Minnie made the gravy," announces Daphne like a schoolyard snitch. "I think she did it quite well, considering. Don't you?"

Daphne's assertion that the oldies would eat little proves entirely wrong as the gang stuff themselves, but later, when Bliss mentions the point over the washing up, Daphne scoffs, "They're like a bunch of toddlers. They were just showing off because you were here."

"David made the pudding," Daphne insists volubly once the dinner plates are cleared, and, despite Bliss's protestations that he merely stirred, she declares that everyone must try some.

"Oh, I'd do anything for a man who cooks," grovels Minnie from the other end of the table. "You simply must give me the recipe, David."

"It's a secret. Isn't it, David?" snaps Daphne before he can respond, and Bliss is forced to accept everyone's congratulations as Daphne douses the candles while he flames the brandy.

"I think we should hold a seance," suggests Mavis in the eerie blue light. "They always do that in the presence of great detectives."

"Back to Agatha Christie again," moans Bliss, but Daphne seems keen. "Maybe we could solve one of your mysteries for you, David."

"As long as we don't have to take off our clothes this time. I'm getting past that now," moans Beattie Elliott.

"It's a seance, not a witches' coven, Beattie," scoffs Mavis. "You never have to take off clothes for a seance."

"Really?" says Beattie, and Don Elliott turns scarlet as his wife gives him a dirty look.

"But we need an intriguing question," enthuses Minnie, now back on Bliss's arm. "What's the mystery, Mr. Inspector, sir?"

Daphne has an idea as she relights the candles. "Get your picture out, David. Let's ask who Ruth's father is."

"No ..." he laughs.

"Spoilsport," says Minnie, patting his injured thigh, and he quickly gives in.

With the table cleared, and chairs set around, Bliss brings out the photograph and numbers the five living suspects, explaining, "One of these men may have fathered a child in Vancouver, Canada, in August 1964."

"Oh, David. Such precision. Most men are so wishy-washy," fawns Minnie squeezing into the seat next to him, but Daphne is on her back in a flash.

"You'd better sit over there, Minnie," says Daphne, putting her next to the door. "We need someone frisky to pop up and down to put the lights out."

"Are you quite sure we don't have to take off our clothes?" fusses Beattie, and Daphne retorts, "Yes. We're sure," a touch heavy-handedly.

The lights go out, and the moonlight streaming through the window casts deep blue shadows. "This is spooky," whines Blossom. "I'm scared of ghosts."

"It's only a game," snorts Daphne. "Now ... Everyone put your hands flat on the table, and no cheating."

Mavis waits for a few seconds, until movement stills, then, feeling justified in taking the lead as it was her suggestion, she intones, "Is there anybody there? Is there anybody there?"

"What's supposed to happen?" whispers Beattie in the dark.

"In the movies, there's always a knocking sound," says Don.

"Yes, but in the movies there's always a dead body when the light comes back on," adds Minnie.

"Are you all right, Gino?" calls Bliss, suddenly fearful the shrivelled geriatric, who's hardly spoken all afternoon, may have passed over in the gloom.

"Yes," replies Gino, and Bliss lets out a sigh of relief as Mavis shushes them before repeating. "Is there anybody there? Is there anybody there?"

"That was a knock," exclaims Don. "I distinctly heard a knock."

"Knock once for yes and twice for no," intones Mavis. "Is anybody there?"

"One," counts Daphne at the sound of a sharp tap. "Somebody is there."

A slight movement in the shadows at the far end of the table catches Bliss eye, and he's deliberating whether or not to speak up, when Beattie lets out an electrifying scream.

"Lights, lights," yells Bliss, and as Don leaps out of his chair he collides with Minnie and they end up in a heap.

Daphne eventually hits the switch and all eyes are on Beattie as the lights come up. "There was a hand round my throat," she shrieks. "My pearls ... My pearls have gone."

"Minnie," says Bliss, sternly and immediately. "Please give Beattie her pearls back."

"Oh, David," says Minnie, her voice dripping with admiration as she pulls herself up from the floor and takes a string of pearls from her purse. "You are a brilliant detective. How did you know it was me?"

"Why did you do that?" wails Beattie, snatching back her pearls.

"Minnie thought it would be fun to give me a real mystery to solve, didn't you?" says Bliss.

"Of course," replies Minnie, smoothing Beattie down. "It was only a lark, dear. I wasn't going to keep them."

"I wouldn't put it past her," mutters Daphne, but Mavis is anxious to continue. "Quiet everybody. Put the lights out again, Minnie. Someone was calling from the other side."

It takes a few seconds for the atmosphere to darken, then Mavis starts again. "Is there anybody there?"

A single sharp knock echoes eerily in the stillness and Bliss watches for movement, though he sees none.

"Have you passed over?" continues Mavis, solemnly.
Knock!

"Will you answer a question?"
Knock!

"I see five male faces in the photograph I am holding. Do you see them?"

Knock!

"Which face is the one that we seek?"

If a spirit has been summoned, it seems confused for a few seconds while the silence builds.

"Ask again," whispers Minnie, and Mavis starts, "Do you see the face?"

"One," counts Daphne under her breath, then the knocks continue. "Two, three, four, five."

"Number five," pronounces Minnie enthusiastically as she leaps up and switches the light on.

"Which one is that, David?" asks Daphne, squinting at the photo as the others crowd around.

"This one," he says with his finger on a youngish man in the second row, and he consults the accompanying list. "His name's Geoffrey Sanderson apparently and, according to this, his present whereabouts are unknown."

"I ... I um ... I'd better make some coffee," stutters Daphne as she heads to the kitchen.

"Oh, Daphne. I meant to tell you," calls Minnie in her wake, "young Jeremy Maxwell is back in town."

"Jeremy Maxwell," breathes Daphne, and she is stopped in the doorway by the news.

"Yeah. Didn't you know his parents quite well?" adds Minnie, and Mavis Longbottom furiously kicks her under the table.

"Oh, Mavis. Be careful, dear. You kicked me," bitches Minnie. But the damage is done. Daphne is clearly flummoxed, and she hovers in the doorway while all eyes are on her. Bliss wants to help her out, but has no idea what's happening.

"Are you all right?" he asks, and Daphne unfreezes enough to stammer, "Yes ... Yes. I'm fine. And yes, Minnie, you are correct. I did know them." Then she scuttles into the kitchen mumbling, "I'll make the coffee."

"Why did you say that?" hisses Mavis with her sights firmly on Minnie.

"I don't know what you mean," professes Minnie, though Bliss sees a hint of culpability on her face and slides into the kitchen.

"Can I help?" he asks, as Daphne busies herself with the percolator, then she turns questioningly. "Do you know what true love really is, David?"

"I think so."

"I was sure at one time. Absolutely certain. So certain that I would have given my life ... But the price was too high in the end," she says, then she slams around the kitchen with such aggravation that Bliss backs off.

"I'll ask who wants cream," he mutters and leaves her taking out her frustration on the cupboard doors as she searches for the demerara.

The atmosphere has chilled to such a degree by the time Daphne returns with the coffee that most are searching for their coats and shoes. "That was a wonderful Christmas, thank you," says Gino, taking everybody by surprise and, as the guests leave, Daphne is at the door hanging fiercely onto Bliss's arm as if fearing that he's about to be carried off.

"Can you believe that woman?" she snorts as Minnie trips away into the night. "She couldn't keep her hands off you for a minute, and she seventy-five if she's a day."

"Never mind," says Bliss, giving Daphne's hand a comforting squeeze.

Daphne quickly shuts the door as if hoping to keep out the ghosts of the night, but she can't shut out the ghost in her mind; the one that has been quiescent for many years; the one that has suddenly been re-awoken by the mention of Jeremy Maxwell, and she stands in the hallway with so many unanswered questions on her mind that she runs. "I think I'll go straight to bed," she says as she makes for the stairs. "It's been a long day and I like to get up early Boxing Morning for the hunt."

"You hunt?" asks Bliss, though he has no great difficulty imagining Daphne riding to hounds.

"Of course not," she protests. "I'm a sort of saboteur."

Boxing Day morning dawns cold and dark for Trina as she stops for a coffee on her way to her first patient in Vancouver.

"I hate Boxing Day," she'd moaned to Rick as she'd leaned out of bed and smacked off the alarm. "I always find at least one of my patients dead."

"Don't go then," he'd said, playfully pulling her back under the sheets, but she'd reluctantly struggled free.

"If I don't go today, I'll have three bodies to deal with tomorrow. Anyway, I promised them all turkey."

"We could feed most of Vancouver with what we've got left," he'd joked. "Take everybody turkey."

Frost crystals dust the sidewalk like a skim of snow, and Trina's footsteps crunch in the stillness of the holiday morning as she makes for Donut Delight. Then a light on the street corner catches her eye and pulls her off course.

"Under new management," declares the sign in the window of the Corner Coffee Shoppe, and Trina tentatively tests the door.

"Hi, Trina. I'm running the place now," calls Cindy cheerfully, as the door opens into a new world. "Mrs. Jackson has put me in charge."

"What about when Ruth comes back?" asks Trina, feeling somewhat traitorous as she enters the refurbished and re-carpeted café.

"After what she did?"

"Cindy. Ruth didn't do anything."

"So, how come she took out life insurance on him, eh? And how come there was blood all over a carving knife? And what about the poison?"

"Who told you ..." begins Trina, but sees the answer as Jordan's mother emerges from the kitchen in an apron.

"What do you want?" snaps Gwenda Jackson, remembering Trina from her escapade in the dumpster.

"Just a herbal tea, I think," starts Trina, turning up her nose at the cholesterol-filled cakes crammed into the cooler and the smell of frying bacon in the air. But Jordan's mother has other ideas.

"You wanna keep your nose out of other peoples' affairs lady," she warns, then adds, "I don't want you in here spreading your lies about my boy. You're barred. Now get out."

Trina's tears are not for herself as she leaves empty handed — they're for Ruth. The speed at which her ailing friend's authority has been usurped has her so wrapped up in rage that she walks blindly toward her car and doesn't immediately notice Tom, sneaking out of the shadows, until he's forced her into a corner.

"What do you want? I'll scream," she shouts, not recognizing him in the pre-dawn gloom.

"It's OK," he says, stepping closer. "Don't worry. Nothing's gonna happen."

"It will if you come any nearer," Trina warns as she readies a kick.

"OK," says Tom slacking off a fraction, but he's got pressure at his back. Mort, the Brit from the porn studio, is at the wheel of his BMW, and watches through the deeply tinted windows from across the street.

"You know who I am, Trina," continues Tom and she finally catches on.

"What do you want, Tom?"

"I just want a word about our friend Ruth," he says, but the creepiness in his voice has Trina on edge.

"What about Ruth?"

Tom warily inches forward and darkens his tone. "My people have told me to tell you to just leave it alone, lady. That's all I'm saying."

"I'm not bothered about you and your silly games, I'm just trying to find her husband."

"He's taken off, and that's all there is to it."

"And you expect me to believe that?"

Tom shrugs. "If you know what's good for you, you'll just leave it."

"Am I supposed to be scared?" Trina asks, close to laughing.

"Lady, this ain't no joke."

"Are you smoking something, Tom? Isn't it time you grew up?"

"Just leave it alone and I'll get my people to back off."

"Get stuffed," she spits in his face then stalks off, scoffing over her shoulder. "Worms like you don't have people, Tom. People like you have worms."

Trina has a busy morning, but her mind is distracted by Tom's warning as she cleans up the aftermath of her patients' Christmas excesses, although, thankfully, she has no bodies to pick up. It's mid-afternoon by the time Ruth gets a visit, and Trina is surprised to find Mike Phillips already there, sitting quietly by the bed. "My family are all back east in Ontario," he explains, quickly releasing Ruth's hand. "I just thought I'd see if there was any improvement."

"No change?" queries Trina, checking out Ruth's lifeless features and the array of equipment.

Phillips shakes his head sadly. "No. Although the chief has ordered an internal investigation, and Wilson's pulled the guard off the door."

"I'm not sure that's such a good idea," says Trina, and goes on to outline her early morning confrontation with Tom. "I just don't get it," she confesses to Phillips. "Ruth's in debt up to her armpits, so he ought to be happy that I'm trying to get her freed."

"I definitely shouldn't be telling you this," says Mike, and swears Trina to silence before explaining. "I smelt him the first time I saw him. He's a bottom-feeding money launderer. I bet he doesn't want you, or anyone else, poking around in his cesspit in case we wonder where the stink's coming from."

"I warned Ruth about him," fumes Trina. "I told her he was dangerous."

"He's slimy, but I'm not sure how dangerous he is. Although, I wouldn't say the same for the people he works for."

"Who ..." starts Trina, then sees from the look on Phillips' face that she's not going to get an answer. "Never mind," she says, then explains excitedly that she's had all the records checked and discovered that no registered health care worker had visited Jordan Jackson in the dingy apartment building within the past three months. "He's not in the system anywhere, and neither is that address — not for a Jackson anyway."

"How did you find that out?" puzzles Phillips. "I thought health records were supposed to be confidential."

"I just lied to the admin clerk," declares Trina with a degree of pride, and Phillips can't help smiling as she adds, "I've been doing it so long they just assume I'm authorized."

"So what was Jackson doing at the apartment?"

"The other woman," pronounces Trina unhesitatingly. "I bet he'd set himself up with a bimbo on the Internet, and he'd spend half the week with Ruth and the other half horizontal jogging in the downtown eastside. No wonder Ruth said he was always worn out by the time he got home. I bet he's run off with her, whoever she is."

"Slight problem," says Phillips as he digs into his briefcase and comes out with a photocopy of a death certificate. "I've been pulling favours as well."

"Jordan Artemus Jackson," Trina reads aloud. "Cause of death: Metastasized carcinoma."

"Twenty-second of November," Phillips adds, saving her the trouble.

"Cancer," she breathes. "But I don't understand ..."

The solution, when it unfolds, is so obvious that Trina runs with it while Phillips nods agreement. "Jordan wasn't being treated," she muses aloud. "He saw his own doctor, found out his chances, and decided to die. Ruth would never have agreed, he knew that, so he even bought a box of Zofran and left them where she'd find them to add weight to his story."

"That's what I suspect," continues Phillips, picking up the plot. "And each week he'd spend a few days at the apartment while he pretended to be at the hospital."

"Where is he buried?" asks Trina.

"He was cremated a couple of days later."

Trina sits back digesting the information, then she leaps in delight. "That's great. She's off the hook. He died of natural causes."

Phillips is less enthusiastic. "There's a couple of minor problems," he says, dragging her back down. "First — Ruth maintained he was alive until the day you discovered him missing so that she could claim on the life insurance policy — not exactly kosher."

"And thousands of others would have done the same in the circumstances."

"That doesn't make it legal though."

Maybe not, but she never tried to cash in on the policy."

"Only because she was in jail."

"You don't know that was the reason," says Trina fiercely. "She might never have gone through with it."

"It doesn't make any difference. She broke the law when she fraudulently took the policy out, and she wasn't in jail then," says Phillips, then drops his eyes sheepishly.

"What's that face about?" questions Trina, and Phillips opens up.

"You didn't hear this from me, but I've seen it happen before. The only way to justify what happened in the cells will be to throw the book at her — attempted fraud, several assaults, possession, and trafficking. Most of it won't stick in court if she has a good lawyer, but it will destroy her credibility."

"That's terrible ..." complains Trina.

"It's a tough life," admits Phillips as the door opens and Raven glides in like a black wraith. Trina looks up in delight.

"Hi, Raven. Where've you been? I heard you won the lottery."

"No. I just got the booby prize," she says, though she isn't interested in giving details until she has found out about Ruth's condition.

"Her husband's dead," explains Trina as if that somehow accounts for her comatose condition.

"I heard," muses Raven as she lovingly strokes Ruth's forehead, "and I'd told her that I saw great things in her future. I don't understand it — Serethusa is usually so right."

"Like she said I wasn't going to have an accident," teases Trina.

"Bus ... I said quite clearly that you weren't going to get hit by a bus, and I was right. Anyway, what's happened to Ruth?"

Trina and Mike Phillips start to lay out the case for Raven as they sit either side of the bed, each holding a hand, but she stops them with a gesture.

"Wait," says Raven, with a close eye on Ruth. "She can hear. I saw her aura change when you started speaking."

"Her what!" exclaims Phillips with naked skepticism, but Raven shushes him. "Just keep hold of her," she continues as she glides her hands in the air above Ruth's face and stares off into another world.

"What the ..." starts Phillips, but Raven and Trina silence him simultaneously. "Shhhh ..."

"Ruth ... Ruth," calls Raven in a barely recognizable voice. "Ruth, it's time to wake up now."

The noises in Ruth's head quiet to a murmur as Raven's words penetrate, like a pinpoint of light in the blackness, and as Raven's hands float over her body Ruth battles dreamily with the possibility that her spirit is struggling to flee.

Heaven is waiting for you, says a muffled voice somewhere so deep in Ruth's head that it could be God, but Ruth knows that it is the Devil, and she fights against the growing spotlight.

"Her aura's changing again," enthuses Raven without opening her eyes as she wills Ruth to the surface. "I can feel her chi returning and her chakras opening to allow the life-force back in."

"Come again?" queries Phillips but Trina, with her hand on Ruth's pulse, suddenly shrieks, "Yes!" in delight as she feels the slightest twitch of Ruth's wrist under her fingers. "She moved. I felt it. She moved. She moved."

A nurse barrels into the room at the sound of Trina's

cry, runs her eyes over the monitors and immediately assesses the situation. "Ruth," she coos, gently brushing the sleeping woman's forehead, "can you hear me?"

A slight flutter of Ruth's eyelids signals the beginning of a long, steep climb, but the nurse, and the trio of friends around Ruth's bed, whoop in delight at the spectacle and Trina kisses everyone.

"Thank you, Raven," yells Trina, with tears in her eyes. "You're terrific."

"Thank Serethusa, not me," says Raven, beaming. "But now we have to find Jordan's spirit so they can be reunited."

"But he's dead!" exclaims Trina. "Mike's got the death certificate."

"Trina," says Raven, patiently, "what you call death is only another step in life. Jordan's earthly body was just the shell that enabled his spirit to experience what we call life. He's still alive, he's just in another world, that's all."

"Ruth's in luck if the judge believes that," mutters Phillips, but Raven hasn't finished.

"I must contact Serethusa again. I was wrong about Jordan. I even told Ruth he was going to be fine. What will she think of me? I'm usually so right."

Trina gives Raven skeptical look, but keeps her thoughts to herself as the lanky seer unwinds herself and heads for the door. "I'm going to have to consult Serethusa and my books again," she says. "Something's wrong; I couldn't focus on his aura the last time I saw him — something dark and shadowy was blocking me, but I didn't see him passing over so soon."

"Yeah, well, you didn't see my accident coming either, did you?" reminds Trina, and Raven explodes.

"I said 'bus,' Trina. Not a fucking kid on a bike."

chapter eleven

Vancouver is a low-rise city, dwarfed by a coronet of snow-capped mountains and encircled by verdant foothills crowded with cypresses, cedars, and firs. "Beautiful British Columbia," scream the licence plates of a million gas-guzzlers that cram its streets and smog its skies, but, on a rare winter's day, when the clouds have been pushed over the Rockies to Alberta, and the fog has lifted off the Pacific Ocean and melted in the warming sun, Vancouver's glassy towers shimmer like golden nuggets in a river bed.

It's the last day of January, nearly six weeks since Ruth Jackson collapsed in the cells, and in the mid-afternoon sunshine, Trina Button watches the traffic on Oak Street from Ruth's window in the Women's Hospital until she spies Mike Phillips pulling into the entranceway.

"OK. He's here," she bubbles excitedly as she pushes a wheelchair up to Ruth's bed. "We're taking you to the park, Ruth," she prattles, as a nurse helps her lift

Ruth's willowy remains into a wheelchair. "Would you like that?"

"Yeah," replies Ruth with difficulty. "I'd like that."

"Mike has borrowed a van, so we can just shove you in," carries on Trina as she tucks a blanket around her friend, then she heads off at full speed for the elevator like a kid with a doll's carriage. "Wheee ..." she calls, and she hears Ruth chuckling at the thrill.

It has taken more than a month, but, thanks to Raven, Ruth has finally drifted out of the fog of unconsciousness, and is climbing back into the full light of day. Any cloudy patches in her future can wait, and her face lights up at the sight of Mike Phillips in the parking lot.

"Hello, Mike," she pronounces, syllable by syllable, and he bends to gently stroke her pallid face.

"Hi, Ruth. Trina says we're going to the park."

"I know."

Stanley Park is a remnant of temperate rainforest that somehow ducked the pioneers' axes as they cleared the Fraser valley. But now it clings precariously to the edge of the cliffs, in constant fear of being toppled into the estuary by the burgeoning city at its back.

"What would you like to do first, Ruth?" asks Trina once they've arrived and unloaded her.

"I want to go home," she croaks painfully and Trina chokes back the tears as she says, "Soon, Ruth. You'll soon be home. But today we'll go to the forest and the beach and watch the ducks and gulls, shall we? Hey, we might even see an eagle."

"I want to go home."

Ruth's home, together with her husband and her livelihood, has vaporized into history, but her future is not totally bleak; at least the Crown Prosecutor no longer objects to her being granted bail. Faced with a tide of civil suits from Hammer Hammett, and an urn full of ashes accompanied by a valid death certificate, the Vancouver Police have backed off a tad — though, just as Phillips had predicted, they are determined to press ahead with the assault and fraud charges.

"OK. Beach it is, then," chirps Trina. "Then the duck ponds. Mike's brought a load of bread, though I bet the seagulls will snap most of it up."

"Then we'll find somewhere nice for tea — if you're not worn out," adds Phillips.

Ruth faintly smiles as they push her toward the sandy shore. "Thank you, Mike," she says under her breath.

Ruth Jackson is not the only person with an urge to go home. The dreariness of January in Westchester is beginning to weigh on Bliss, and he has his sights set on the brighter lights of London. The weather has been generally gloomy since Christmas, but so has Daphne. Not that she would admit it. Indeed, every time Bliss has even hinted at her melancholy she has primped herself up, saying, "Rubbish. I'm fine." But she has not been her usual irrepressible self, and "Doctor" Bliss has diagnosed that she is suffering from an increasing sense of impending doom. For someone racing through life with their foot on the floor like Daphne, the possibility of running out of gas must be daunting, he believes.

Bliss is no closer to finding Ruth's father, although he has eliminated two of the surviving suspects. Having tracked down the last known addresses of the five young men in the photograph, he has written to each. Only two have replied, now old-age pensioners. They had kicked off the Beatles' 1964 North American tour as young roadies, but had jumped ship in the casinos of Las Vegas and never made it as far as Vancouver. Neither the spirit's choice, Geoffrey Sanderson, nor the other two, have replied, and Bliss is sitting on the case while he considers his next course. He had planned to post a plea in the *Merseyside Mail,* but he had backed off in the middle of January when the seemingly innocuous Freddie Longbottom legend had misfired.

A scruffy young reporter from the *Westchester Gazette* had turned up on Daphne's doorstop one day, having been tipped off about the impending reunion by his counterpart in Liverpool. "My editor wants me to do an obituary piece about Freddie Longbottom and his connection to the Beatles," he'd told Bliss, as he'd scratched his scalp with his pen. "But I can't find any record of his death. Not in the past year or so. Do you know anything about him?"

"Ms. Lovelace isn't here at present," Bliss had truthfully replied. "I expect she'll know. I'll get her to give you a call when she gets home."

"Now let's see you get out of this one," he'd laughed as he gave Daphne the reporter's card when she'd returned from the butchers'.

"Oh, you worry too much, David," she had snapped, and seconds later she'd been on the phone to the reporter, explaining that he was undoubtedly very confused, and was clearly thinking of the wrong Freddie Longbottom. "My Freddie hasn't lived in Westchester for forty years or more," she had explained with absolute sincerity. "I think they said he died in Rangoon or Kathmandu, but you know what these foreign telephones are like. Anyway, you'll be the first to know if I get any more information."

"You are terrible," Bliss had exploded as Daphne put the phone down, but she had sloughed it off. "Why shouldn't I lie to the press? They usually lie to me."

Now, as the snowdrops and crocuses begin to force their heads into the lengthening daylight, Daphne has brightened as she bustles in from an afternoon's assignation that she'd purposefully kept from her lodger.

"We thought you'd got lost," Bliss jokes, stroking the kitten on his lap, although he had been more than a little concerned when he'd awoken from a post-prandial nap to discover that she'd sneaked out without even leaving a note.

"I'll just put the kettle on ..." Daphne begins, then changes her mind and blurts out that she has been to visit Jeremy Maxwell at Thraxton Manor.

"Who?" asks Bliss

"Don't you remember, Millie ..."

"Oh, yes. Christmas Day. You said you knew his parents."

"I think I will make that tea," she says as if a shadow has suddenly veiled the sun again, and she slips into the kitchen.

"Did you ever fall in love with the wrong person, David?" she calls from the kitchen's sanctuary after a couple of minutes, and Bliss asks cynically, "Is there ever a right person?" before realizing that Daphne's question was rhetorical.

"You mean ... You and Jeremy Maxwell?" he questions as he pokes his head into the kitchen.

"No," she says testily. "Of course not. He's only a boy."

"Oh. His father, then?"

Daphne nods, though she keeps her eyes on the can of Whiskas she is opening for Missie Rouge. "Nobody would take much notice today. Even prime ministers have little indulgences amongst the prettier backbenchers, but forty years ago ..."

"What are you saying?"

"Monty Maxwell was our member of parliament. Nothing fancy. He didn't have his own portfolio — he had too many enemies for that. He was a bag carrier for the minister of defence."

"And you fell in love with him?" breathes Bliss, but immediately sees in Daphne's sheepish face that there is more — much more.

Daphne strokes the purring kitten as she seeks the past and the future simultaneously, while trying to work out the ramifications of revealing the painful details of a long-lost relationship. The whistling kettle shocks her into action eventually but, as she switches it off, she finds in its shiny façade a pair of young eyes sparkling with happy memories, and her thoughts take her back to Buckingham Palace, May 1963.

"By order of Her Majesty, Queen Elizabeth II, Ophelia Daphne Lovelace is hereby awarded the Order of the British Empire for services rendered in the security of the Nation, its Commonwealth and Dominions," the master of ceremonies had trumpeted on that occasion, and Monty Maxwell had been waiting with his chauffeured Rolls Royce to take her and her parents to dinner at the Ritz afterwards.

"It's not every day that one of my constituents is elevated to the aristocracy," he had insisted, and Daphne had been so light-headed with joy that she'd flung herself at him — body and soul.

"He was married, of course," Daphne tells Bliss as she snaps herself back to the present, but he's already guessed that much.

"And did he love you?" asks Bliss.

"Love is a mystery, David," muses Daphne as she pours the boiling water over the tea leaves. "This is Keemun tea," she adds, trying to break the spell. "It's the Queen's favourite. Did you know?"

"No," he admits, but he won't let her off the hook. "So, tell me about Monsieur Maxwell."

Daphne loses herself in the aroma of Keemun — the sweet dry scents of the Mediterranean — and contemplates the intensity of illicit love and the gravity that draws two bodies together to form a union stronger than any that can be forged at the altar.

Monty had brought sunshine into her life with such passion that, for the year that their affair lasted, she had swum in Nirvana's perfumed waters from Monday to Thursday almost every week. But every Friday, when Monty left London to go home to his wife and young son on their country estate in Westchester, the waters had muddied and cooled.

"Do you have to go?" Daphne would plead as they breakfasted together on Friday mornings, but she always knew the answer. "One day, Daph," Monty would say as he kissed away her tears. "One day soon it will be just you and me."

"You know, David," Daphne says as she fills Bliss's cup. "In so many ways, love can be like a pot of tea. It's comforting, warming, dependable. Something to look forward to as you take the bus home in the rain. There's nothing worse than coming home to a cold empty house in the middle of winter, but a cup of tea makes all the difference."

"So does a lover," pushes Bliss, seeing which way she is headed, but she stalls as she inhales her tea meditatively.

"A fresh pot of Keemun always makes me think of a honeymoon in Provence. I can smell the oleanders, the hibiscus, and lavender, and it even has a hint of dryness, like eucalyptus leaves chattering in the Mediterranean breeze. Mind, after awhile, when it gets stewed and stale, it leaves a stubborn brown stain."

"Like a marriage," Bliss suggests, and he gets a nod of agreement from her.

"Yes. Like marriage." But the marriage she has in mind is Monty's, not hers.

"My marriage is a thing of the past," Monty had repeatedly assured her, yet, every weekend and every public holiday, and especially Christmas, she'd been alone in her London apartment waiting to rush to the phone. And how many times had it rang just to annoy her?

"Oh. It's you, mother ... What am I doing? Nothing much." *Now, I'm waiting for the phone to ring again.*

"All right?... Yes, I'm all right." *But I'll be better when I hear his voice.*

"Lunch? ... No. Not today, mother. I'm expecting a call." *Please, Monty. Please call.*

"Tomorrow? ... Maybe, Mum. I'll let you know." *But only if he calls. But will he call?*

Why doesn't he call? she had asked herself a thousand times each and every Saturday and Sunday as she'd passed on parties and suitors to sit by the phone. But she knew why, and even felt satisfaction from the sacrifice. *See — This is how much I love him*, she would tell herself, while he was dining and dancing away the weekend with his wife in Westchester.

"Monty Maxwell and his wife opened the fete on Saturday," Daphne's mother would rattle on, oblivious to her daughter's involvement. "They make such a lovely couple, don't you think?"

"I don't know ..."

"Silly of me. Of course you don't, now that you're stuck in London all the time."

Daphne didn't have to stay in London on the weekends — there was always a bed for her at her mother's in Westchester; always a roast leg of lamb or a rib of beef for Sunday lunch. But Monty Maxwell would never be far away — in body or in mind — and the thought of being dragged to Communion by her mother on Sunday morning made her cringe further.

"Oh, look. It's little Ophelia," the church's nattering spinsters would chirrup, unable to grasp the fact that Mrs. Lovelace's little daughter was nearing forty, and had long ago ditched Ophelia in preference to Daphne. "Ophelia sounds more like a bloody opera singer or ballerina," she had bitched to the other girls in her billet. It was the day she had started her wartime training to infiltrate France and aid the Resistance against the Nazis, and she had dug out a dictionary to prove her point. "Ophelia means 'help,'" she'd read aloud, though neither she, nor the other young women, could decide whether that meant she was supposed to help, or she needed help. But she had no such dilemma over Daphne. "It means 'a laurel leaf,'" she had proclaimed triumphantly, and had ended up being suitably crowned for her heroism. As Daphne Lovelace she had left Ophelia, her prissy counterpart, far behind as she'd parachuted into the path of the enemy and fought her way to Paris after D-Day. And, after the war, she had used a dozen other names as she'd finessed the escape of defectors through the Iron Curtain before battling alongside the French at Suez.

The thought of her mother's churchy friends addressing her as Ophelia was enough to deter her from seeking the Sacrament, but a much stronger deterrent was sure to be proudly sitting in his family pew at the front of the nave. And Daphne would have to force a look of indifference as the fawning vicar would make a point of bowing in Monty's direction and throwing in a special blessing for "Our honourable and most noble member of parliament and his beloved wife and son."

The term "honourable" was a paradox that Daphne had never comfortably reconciled in relation to Monty; however, the noble visions of Sir Lancelot on his charger sweeping her off her feet and carrying her to his lair were wholly consistent with the situation in her mind.

"Have you ever loved so fiercely that nothing else in the world mattered?" Daphne asks Bliss as she sips her tea by the fire.

"Yes," says Bliss, "I have."

"I mean, loved someone so much that you would actually be prepared to sacrifice yourself to save them?"

"Yes, I think I did. But it ended in disaster."

"It always does, David. It always does," says Daphne despondently.

"So what happened to Monty?" prods Bliss, but the dancing blue flames of an oak log grab Daphne and she sinks into the past — to a warm Sunday in late June, 1964.

The tragic day had started off well enough, with Daphne's phone ringing at eight in the morning. "I'm just taking the dog for a walk," Monty had said as he'd fed coins into the payphone in Westchester's marketplace, and he'd ended, as always, by declaring, "I love you, Daph. You know that. We'll soon be together for always, I promise."

Monty's words would have been reassuring had she not heard them so often and, as she'd left her apartment to seek distraction among the pigeons in St. James's Park, all she could do was hum the Beatles' "Eleanor Rigby," over and over again.

"When? When? When?" she had mumbled to herself, as she had paced alone around the park before enviously watching a newlywed couple posing for photos in front of Buckingham Palace. Behind them, in the Palace grounds, the flamboyantly costumed band of the Coldstream Guards had struck up "When I'm Sixty-Four," and the crowd was still cheering as Daphne choked back a tear and headed towards the river.

Lunch at a depressingly dingy tourist trap on the south bank had dragged her spirits even lower, until she had taken the subway to Berkeley Square, where she had been convinced that she had heard a nightingale singing — though it may have been nothing more than a common sparrow or even a squeaky bicycle wheel.

"Everyone who knew about us said there was no future in loving a married man," Daphne explains to Bliss, as the flames of the fire gradually flicker out and leave only a smoulder. "But I suppose I wanted to believe it would somehow work. I thought she would finally understand and let him go."

"And she didn't?"

"If only it had been that simple."

Daphne's shoes had developed a mind of their own that June Sunday and, as she'd traipsed the sights of London from St. Paul's to Westminster Abbey, she had tortured her mind for a solution. *I could wait for him*, she'd told herself for the thousandth time. *Wait until he's out of politics and young Jeremy has gone to university.*

But she and Monty had walked that field before, and had waded through a stockpile of mines. "We'll never be able to keep it secret for fifteen years ... You'll get fed up ... Imagine the ruckus if we're caught ... Marylyn will take me to the cleaners ... What happens if I'm offered the PM's job?"

"You could turn it down. King Edward abdicated for Mrs. Simpson," Daphne had insisted.

"And look what happened to him. Anyway, slipping out from under a crown is kid's stuff compared to Marylyn's ball and chain."

Five-year-old Jeremy was the major problem in Daphne's opinion, and she had often worried aloud about the trauma that a divorce would inflict on him. Maxwell had seemed less concerned. "He hardly knows me," he had protested more than once. "He probably thinks I'm the bloke who just comes to cut the grass on Saturdays."

"Stop worrying, Daphne," Maxwell had told her at breakfast that Friday before he had headed home. "I'll think of something."

There was an inexplicable sense of unease in her mind as that fateful Sunday evening dragged on, but the more she was pulled toward her empty apartment, the more she resisted. Another evening alone staring at "Sunday Night at the London Palladium" on television was more than she could bear.

Monty Maxwell was ever-present in her mind, and the moments without him were excruciating, but as she traced and re-traced her steps along the Thames embankment in the late-night sunshine of the summer solstice, she finally saw an answer. Ahead of her lay London's most renowned picture postcard — Tower Bridge, with its magnificent stone portals linked by lofty walkways high above the traffic's roar and the sluggish river.

Could she? Was he worth it? Was any man worth it?

But I'd be doing it to set him free — my last great act of martyrdom, she had tried persuading herself as she had stopped midway across the bridge and peered down at the torpid murky water far below.

But whether or not Daphne's death would liberate Monty would never be put to the test.

"What are you doing, Madam?" a voice had demanded out of the blue and she had spun to find an enormous policeman at her shoulder.

"Just looking, officer."

"As long as that's all," he'd responded with a knowing eye, and Daphne had quickly backed away.

"Yes, of course. What did you think?"

"I'm not paid to think madam," he had replied pompously. "I'm just paid to protect life and property."

Then he'd softened, "Take it from me, luv. No man is worth that. And I should know, I am one."

Daphne had laughed just enough to bring her to her senses. "Don't worry, officer. I know that," she'd said and, as the sun set under Westminster Bridge, she'd headed home with a clear mind. Monty Maxwell's extramarital shenanigans had come to an abrupt end.

"I'd finally decided to dump him," Daphne tells Bliss as she stokes up the embers and sets another log ablaze. "But Monty had other ideas. Though it didn't turn out the way he had planned."

"What happened?" Bliss asks quietly as he helps himself to more tea.

"I may as well tell you. You'd only dig up his file if I didn't."

"His file?"

"A murder file, Dave. I assume central records at Scotland Yard keeps them forever."

"Murder?"

Daphne uses the poker as a delaying tactic and viciously prods at the log as if it is somehow blocking her way. "I knew something was wrong the moment I got back to my apartment," she tells Bliss eventually. "The front door was ajar. It was either a burglar or Monty. He was the only one with a key, but he wasn't due back from Westchester until Monday afternoon."

The apartment's open door had drawn Daphne inquisitively, and it simply hadn't occurred to her to call the police. However, she had quietly slipped a needle-sharp steel hatpin out of her purse and loosened her legs before entering. "A sweet smile and a swift kick in the bollocks will drop any man to his knees," her unarmed-combat instructor had taught her as she'd prepared for war more than twenty years earlier, and it was a tactic that had never let her down. Though, on this occasion, she had needed neither. Monty Maxwell was the intruder, and he was already on his knees. In fact, as Daphne silently crept into the room, she was fearful of disturbing her ex-lover, thinking that he was praying as he knelt on the floor with his head buried in the seat of an upholstered chair.

"Monty," she had called softly, but he hadn't moved.

"He was dead." Daphne says as she puts the poker down and faces Bliss. "He took the honourable way out — a single bullet in the brain."

"Suicide," muses Bliss, now understanding the reason for Daphne's paroxysm when Millie had mentioned the Maxwells on Christmas Day.

"There was a note," says Daphne and she rummages through her writing cabinet to find the forty-year-old scrap of sepia-edged paper.

"I wanted to take you with me, my beloved, but I couldn't wait for you any longer," reads Bliss. "They will know where to find me. I love you with all my heart. Take care of Jeremy for me ... MM."

"But you said, 'murder,'" queries Bliss as he hands back the precious note.

"Marylyn," Daphne replies. "Apparently Monty had visions of the three of us being together in the afterlife, so he sent Marylyn off with an earful of lead and came for me."

"But you were out."

"I was. Although I don't know why. Any other weekend I would have been there, in suspended animation, waiting for Monday when I'd spring back to life."

"Subliminal messaging," suggests Bliss. "Something in his manner or tone probably reflected what he was planning, and you subconsciously picked up on it."

"That's very clever of you, David. Though at the time it just seemed ironic that at the very moment I was thinking of chucking myself into the Thames, Monty was getting ready to bump me off."

"So, what happened?"

"I got the blame of course. I suppose I should have known that would happen, but I guess that if loving him was wrong, then I didn't want to be right. But it wasn't fair. Everyone was devastated about poor old Marylyn, but I was the one whose heart had been torn to shreds, and I was the one who had to live with it. I didn't get any sympathy. Nobody said to me, 'Oh, you must miss him, you poor thing,' like they would have done to his wife, if she'd lived. Nobody blamed her for being a miserable money-grubbing social climber who drove him away."

As Daphne takes the suicide note back from Bliss, she pauses for a few seconds while the horrors of the ill-fated day replay in her mind. Yet it is the image of the other woman, Marylyn Maxwell, and her supercilious grin that still irks her the most.

Daphne had met Monty's wife a few times, when her mother had put her foot down and insisted that she spend the odd weekend in Westchester for a family occasion.

"Ah, it's Daphne Lovelace, OBE," Monty would exclaim convincingly whenever they had bumped into each other in public. "Haven't seen you for ages," he'd add for the benefit of anyone listening. And if Marylyn was close at hand he'd always made a point of presenting her. "You've met my wife haven't you ..." he'd say, though it was never a question. "This is Daphne Lovelace from the Ministry, dear," he'd explain to Marylyn, and she would immediately find someone of greater consequence in the crowd. "Oh, look, Monty, dearest. There's Lord Westbourne over there," she'd simper, then she'd drag her husband away, calling over her shoulder. "Nice meeting you, Dorothy."

"Young Jeremy was away for the day," Daphne tells Bliss as she returns Monty's suicide note to the cabinet. "He'd gone to the beach with the church Sunday school and the nanny had been given the day off. From what they could piece together, Monty sneaked up on Marylyn and just let her have it, then he came for me."

"What happened to the boy?"

"No one in the family wanted him. I guess they worried he might turn out like his father, so I offered to bring him up. Well, you can imagine what his mother's folks thought of that, so they persuaded Marylyn Maxwell's sister in Vancouver to take him in. The problem was that Jeremy had never met her and he'd got very attached to me after his parents' deaths. He used to call me Auntie Daffodil — you know the way kids get things muddled up — so I thought the least I could do was escort him as far as Montreal."

"August 1964," says Bliss. "That's why you were in Montreal when you saw the Beatles."

"Brilliant, Dr. Watson," laughs Daphne, though her face clouds at the memory of Jeremy's aunt. "She was a nasty bit o'work," Daphne tells Bliss, then confesses that once she'd met the woman she had been tempted to hang on to Jeremy and slip out of Canada, to head south through the States to Mexico or South America.

"She was probably grouchy at birth," continues Daphne, as she recalls her meeting with Jeremy's maiden aunt to hand over the boy. "She could have been a driving examiner, from the way she carried on, and she was only thirty or so."

"What do you know about driving examiners?" queries Bliss, and Daphne's face burns.

"You fibbed to me," he says triumphantly. "You failed your test, didn't you?"

"Yes," she snaps. "All right, I did. But only because the car wouldn't start halfway through."

"That wasn't very fair," sympathizes Bliss, but Daphne looks up with a sheepish grin and decides to come clean. "It wouldn't start because I'd crashed into a lamppost."

"Oh, dear," whistles Bliss, then quickly changes the subject. "Did Jeremy remember you today?"

"Well he was only five at the time," Daphne says, excusing her erstwhile charge for the puzzlement he'd shown when she'd loudly knocked on his front door.

"Hi. Can I help you?" he'd asked in a strong Canadian accent, and Daphne had momentarily frozen in surprise.

"I think I was still expecting a young boy," she explains to Bliss. "It was a bit of shock to see a middle-aged man standing there. Mind you, I recognized him straight away. He's got his father's eyes, and he's tall and handsome. Much like you in many ways, David. I can quite see why I was so drawn to him."

"Oh, Daphne ..."

"Anyway, Jeremy was thrilled to see me, once he knew who I was, and he even remembered sailing the Atlantic with me. We took the *Franconia*, one of the old Cunard steamers, from Southampton to Montreal, and Jeremy was so excited I think he forgot all about his mother and father by the time we'd crossed the channel to pick up passengers in France. I taught him to say 'Bonjour,' and he danced along the Le Havre cobblestones, running up to complete strangers and shouting, 'Bonjour. Bonjour.' He was so funny." Daphne pauses and her eyes go back to the flames as the seriousness of the voyage sinks in. "His little life had been torn apart worse than mine, but he didn't understand. You don't at that age. 'Mummy, and Daddy have gone to heaven,' he would tell anyone interested, as if they'd taken a cruise on the Nile; then he'd cheerfully add, 'I'm going to live with my auntie in 'Couver with the bears.'"

"Did he remember calling you Auntie Daffodil?" asks Bliss as he sees the delight in Daphne's eyes.

"I think so," she says, adding, "We had tea and he took me on a tour. The old house itself is in an awful state. His uncle would have been the last one to live there, though he died more than twenty years ago. Jeffrey says that he's got big plans for the whole estate, and the stable conversion that he's had done is very nice. Of course, he's just like his father — dirty dishes and laundry everywhere."

"He's not married then?"

"No — never has been."

"Figures."

"Anyway. I told him that I'd go round a few times to help him straighten up and do a bit of cleaning, if you don't mind being on your own a bit."

"Daphne, I don't mind at all. In fact, I was thinking that it was time I got out from under your feet, to be honest."

"Actually I did wonder if you were missing the high life," says Daphne, adding, "Jeremy was worried about me neglecting you, but I said you wouldn't object. It is the least I can do in the circumstances. Of course, you're welcome to stay as long as you like."

"Another week, perhaps," says Bliss. "I was thinking I might take another trip to Liverpool to check out those addresses. My leg's much better now."

Daphne takes another poke at the fire as she runs something else through her mind, then she opens up. "Actually, I've been meaning to tell you something. It was a very long time ago, but I'm fairly certain that one of the young men in the Beatles' photo tried the same trick on me in Montreal."

"Geoffrey Sanderson?" queries Bliss immediately, recalling the way that she had reacted at the sight of his face and mention of his name on Christmas day.

"He tried to tell me he was George Harrison," scoffs Daphne. "But I didn't believe him for a minute."

"What did you do?"

"The old knee definitely came in handy that time," she admits with a giggle, then she groans as she bends to put another log on the fire. "There's a bad winter coming; I can feel it in my bones," she says, straightening herself with difficulty.

chapter twelve

The bears have long-since disappeared from downtown Vancouver, forced into the surrounding mountains along with the elk and the cougars by the city's sprawl. But raccoons and squirrels will still snatch food from an outstretched hand in Stanley Park, while feral pigeons and gulls still brazenly whisk sandwiches and snacks from the fingers of startled picnickers on Granville Island.

Ruth's improvement has been spectacular. It's her third outing to the park in ten days, and she chuckles in delight as Mike Phillips throws a hunk of bread onto the beach, while Trina tries to chase it down before the ducks and gulls can grab it.

"Oh, Trina," rebukes Phillips mildly, as she faces off with an overstuffed mallard.

"They get fat and lazy if they don't have to work for it," yells Trina breathlessly as she scampers around the beach to the squawks of startled birds.

Ruth is still in the wheelchair, but it's no longer a necessity, and she spends more time each day peering out of her window at a world that looks the same, but has changed beyond all recognition. Her daily visits from Mike and Trina cheer and encourage her, though there is an artificiality about their conversations as everyone studiously avoids mentioning Jordan, coffee houses, or criminal charges.

"A catastrophic relapse is quite possible if she is upset," Ruth's doctor had warned them more than once. "Her blood pressure is still much higher than we would like to see."

Raven has visited a few times to relay a spiritually uplifting message from Serethusa. "Tell Ruth not to worry," her spirit guide had said, "she will soon be led out of darkness into the light."

"Does that mean I'll be going home soon?" Ruth had asked; but that was a question that no one was willing to answer.

"When can I go home, Trina?" Ruth wants to know once they have loaded her back into the van and are heading for a tea shop, and Trina looks to Phillips for inspiration. But she's on her own as Phillips shrugs his shoulders and keeps his eyes on the road.

"Thanks a bunch," Trina snorts, then she turns to Ruth. "The truth is ..." she begins, then freezes as she searches for humane words to convey the inhumanity of her friend's predicament. Homeless, penniless, unemployed, destitute, and soon to be a convicted felon, are not words she wants to use. "The truth is ..." she tries again and can see the tears already welling in Ruth's eyes.

"The truth is, Ruth," she says, finally spitting it out as she crosses her fingers. "That my husband and I would like you to come and stay with us for awhile. Until you get back on your feet. If you'd like to, that is."

The tears come anyway, trickling joyfully down Ruth's cheeks, but she's not the only one choked up at the good news.

"You've got a great husband, Trina," Phillips tells her with a wobble in his voice as he pats her shoulder.

"Yeah, I know," replies Trina. "He's very supportive."

Three days later, Ruth's hospital bed has clean sheets and Rick Button arrives home from work, parks in the underground garage, and walks into his kitchen as his wife prepares dinner. "I've just found a strange woman watching television in the basement suite, Trina," he says with a confused expression.

"Yeah, I told you," explains Trina, as Kylie rushes in yelling, "What's for dinner, Mom?"

"Tuna Bourguignon with cabbage fritters," she says nonchalantly, adding, without changing tone, "It's only Ruth. She's had a traumatic experience."

"Oh, great," spits Kylie, while pretending to vomit. "I guess I'm eating out again, then."

"OK, dear. See you later," carries on Trina as she lightly dances around the kitchen in search of condiments, but Rick grabs her arm and eases her to a standstill.

"Tuna Bourguignon?"

"Yeah. Low fat, high protein. Ruth needs a wholesome diet."

"I realize you're a home care nurse, Trina," Rick says, peering deeply into his wife's eyes. "But I don't think you're expected to bring work home with you."

"Shh ... Ruth will hear," cautions Trina, wrenching her arm free. "Anyway, she's not one of my patients. She's just a friend who needs help. And you didn't complain when I told you."

"When did you tell me?"

"The other night in bed."

"I thought so. And was I asleep?"

"You can't blame me for that. You're always falling asleep when I'm telling you things."

"'No more strays,' I said, after the last one you brought home."

"No," Trina insists sharply. "You said, 'no more stray goats.' *That's* what you said."

"Trina. Nobody but you could find a stray goat in the middle of Vancouver, so when I said no more strays, I meant ... Oh, never mind. How long is she staying?"

"Not long," Trina says as she bounds into his arms and kisses him lusciously. "Just until she goes back to jail."

Jail is not in Ruth's immediate future if Hammer Hammett has his way and, in spite of Gwenda Jackson's insistence that Ruth be charged with murder, Inspector Wilson of the Vancouver police is floundering in his efforts to prop up the case against her. Ruth's apparent confession, on closer examination, has sprung a number of leaks, not least amongst them being the fact that the emergency room doctor had clearly diagnosed physical abuse in police custody as being a contributing cause of her condition. "That's called obtaining a statement of culpability under duress," Hammett had smugly announced amid a further flurry of writs.

The discovery of a white Carrara marble urn inscribed, "Jordan A. Jackson Aged 40 years," in the mausoleum of a funeral home by Mike Phillips and Trina had further bolstered Ruth's defence, although Jordan's mother had not been at all convinced, and insisted that her son's ashes should be put under the microscope.

"But what do you want us to look for?" Inspector Wilson had inquired, knowing that, short of a bullet or the blade of a dagger, it was unlikely that any evidence survived the furnace.

"Poison, of course. It's obvious — the bitch poisoned him for the money. Why won't you do anything?"

"Because two doctors certified he died of cancer, and we didn't find any evidence to the contrary."

"What about the bloody knife?"

"We've checked that out, Mrs. Jackson. And the fact is that the DNA doesn't match Jordan's."

Jordan's DNA had been obtained from his doctor, once Mike Phillips had tracked him down from the death certificate and passed the information on to Inspector Wilson.

"We ran a few tests and took a few samples when I first saw him," Doctor Fitzpatrick had explained to Wilson. "Though, from his symptoms, it was obvious to me that his cancer was already well advanced. He was HIV positive as well, so he didn't stand a hope."

"Why did he leave it so late?"

"Typical male bravado, Inspector," said the doctor, looking Wilson up and down. "Most men assume it won't happen to them, and by the time they wake up, it's too late."

According to Fitzpatrick, it was much too late by the time Jordan had sought diagnosis and, once he knew the situation, he had refused any treatment, saying that he didn't want to prolong his family's suffering any more than necessary. All he wanted to know was how long he had to live.

"I explained to him that there was a possibly that he might recover," the doctor had told Wilson, though when the inspector asked if that was realistic prognosis, the medic had shaken his head sadly. "No. Not unless you believe in miracles."

"Not me," Wilson had retorted. "I'm a cop. I don't even believe in the Easter Bunny."

"Nor me," the doctor had laughed, though he was willing to speculate why Ruth had continued to maintain that Jordan was alive after his death.

"There was no body," he'd explained to Wilson. "He'd obviously slunk off like a dying cat so she wouldn't have to face his death. And that's why she didn't come to terms with it. He wasn't dead — not in her mind. It happens all the time when ships sink or buildings are bombed. Some relatives never accept the inevitable and spend years searching mental institutions and the streets, convinced that their loved ones have just lost their memories."

Inspector Wilson may have nodded his concurrence with the doctor's view, though he couldn't get his mind off the fact that Ruth had a hundred thousand very good reasons to want Jordan to outlive the ninety-day qualifying period on the life policy.

The warm afternoon sun is turning the sky rose-pink as it sinks into the Pacific Ocean and Gwenda Jackson eulogizes her son in a Vancouver church.

"God always takes the best ones young," Jordan's mother says at the memorial service, now that his ashes have been turned over to her.

There is a sparse congregation: Darcey and Maureen from the crossword gang, Cindy and a few members of the staff, and Trina Button — recording the event on a mini tape recorder linked to a microphone disguised as a pen in her breast pocket.

"Just in case the old witch says anything defamatory against Ruth," she had explained to Mike

Phillips, showing him the equipment she'd bought at a spy store.

"Good for you," Phillips had said, and he had volunteered to spend the afternoon looking after Ruth, knowing that she had not been invited to attend and would not have been welcomed.

Across the Atlantic, in England, the sun had set without ceremony nearly six hours ago, just as a winter storm marched in from the west coast. Black clouds darken an already leaden sky as David Bliss drives back to Westchester from Liverpool, but at least he has eliminated all the surviving members of the Beatles' ensemble except for Geoffrey Sanderson. Daphne's Beatles' CD has somehow stuck on two tracks and will not eject itself from the car's player, so Bliss has listened to "The Long and Winding Road," and "Drive My Car," until he can stand it no longer, and he switches on the radio in time to catch news of the impending depression.

Thank God the snow has held off, thinks Bliss, as he gingerly snakes the car around the unsalted roads on his way back to Daphne's, and as he parks in the street, he is surprised to find her house in complete darkness.

An icy blast tears at Bliss's clothes as he tries to find the right door key in the shadows. He is tempted to ring the doorbell, miffed that Daphne has gone to bed without leaving the porch light on, but decides not to. He gets the message. Daphne had thrown a huffy little snit the previous day when he'd said that he was planning to return to Liverpool on his own this time.

"Suit yourself," Daphne had spat. "I've probably got plans anyway."

"You can come if you want to, Daphne," he'd said, backing down and attempting to console her. "But I just thought it would be a long day for you, that's all."

"No, I understand perfectly, David," she'd snapped. "As long as you realize that if your leg gives out, you won't have me to drive you this time."

Bliss shouldn't have laughed, but he did, and is apparently paying the price as his frozen fingers fumble with the key in the darkness.

The front hallway is frosty and unwelcoming as he kicks off his shoes, and he shivers with a feeling of déjà vu, though he is unable to finger the cause. The hearth in the sitting room is cold and, unusually, Daphne has already laid the fire for the morning. *That's very strange*, he thinks, knowing that she generally leaves the embers to cool overnight.

"Daphne," he calls, gently tapping on her bedroom door a few seconds later, with Missie Rouge noisily begging for food at his feet.

"What's the matter?" Bliss asks, lifting the crying kitten, and he's tempted to creep back downstairs to find the animal some food rather than wake his host. It's close to midnight, and she is obviously still angry with him but, as he stands on the cold landing, Bliss has a sudden feeling of dread that forces him to knock again, louder — much louder. "Daphne, are you all right?"

Twenty minutes later, with every light in the house burning brightly, Bliss is accompanied by Inspector Graves, the senior night-duty officer from Westchester Police Station, as they pore over Daphne's empty bedroom, seeking clues.

"It isn't like her at all," says Bliss, pointing to the neatly made bed. "This hasn't been slept in, and it doesn't appear as though she's taken anything with her. Something serious has happened."

Inspector Graves is unconvinced. "Well, there's no sign of a break-in, Dave. She's probably just gone out with a friend."

"It's past one, and it's bloody freezing outside," Bliss explains forcefully. "And they're forecasting a snowstorm on the radio. Where would she be in Westchester at this time of night?"

"There's a couple of nightclubs," jokes Graves, though Bliss hasn't forgotten the sight of her bopping to the Beatles with an aging beatnik in Liverpool, and he asks Graves to send a couple of lads to check the clubs, adding, "You never know with Daphne."

"Yeah. She's a feisty old bird all right," reminisces the inspector, recalling the time when, as housekeeper at the police station, she'd torn a strip off the chief superintendent for washing his muddy golf shoes in the kitchen sink. "But there's probably a rational explanation. I think we can safely give her until the morning to show up."

Bliss shakes his head and puts his foot down. "No. She wouldn't have gone anywhere without feeding the cat. Plus, she knew I was coming back tonight. She would have left a note. Something has happened to her."

The search for Daphne starts with her friends, and Minnie Dennon doesn't waste a second. "I'll get a cab," she'd cried as soon as Bliss had phoned, and she's standing on Daphne's doorstep fifteen minutes later — fully made-up and ready to roll. By three a.m., the rest of Daphne's friends have been roused out of bed by the phone, or by a constable pounding on the door, but none of them admit to harbouring the missing woman or have any useful suggestions.

Alzheimer's, dementia, depression, dipsomania, and domestic violence are all easily discounted in Daphne's case. "She was absolutely fine yesterday," insists Bliss, tiring from constantly having to excuse Daphne for her failure to conform to the norms of octogenarianism. However, amnesia is not a condition that he can so easily discount. "She could have fallen in the street and hit her head," he concedes, "but surely someone would have found her and taken her to a hospital."

The hospitals have been checked as a priority, but have proven negative, and the local officers have seemingly exhausted all possibilities when Bliss has an idea.

"What if she's fallen asleep on a late-night bus?" he suggests, knowing that it's not unheard of for heavy-eyed passengers to nod off and be woken by the depot's cleaning staff in the early dawn.

It takes half a dozen policeman twenty minutes banging on bus doors and shining flashlights into the frosted windows to write-off that theory, and once the town's parks and public places have been checked, they have run out of ideas.

A canine unit and some reinforcements turn up a little after four, when the entire street is alive with activity as Daphne's worried neighbours huddle under heavy coats and blankets as they check their gardens, garages, and outhouses with flashlights and hurricane lamps.

The suddenness of the storm catches Bliss off balance and threatens to send him skidding along the icy pavement as he listens to Graves giving instructions to the dog handlers while they sit in the warmth of their vans. Then the snow begins and forces him back into the shelter of the house.

"That's all we need," moans Bliss, already frustrated at the lack of progress and the repeated assurance by his country cousin that Daphne is safely tucked up in bed somewhere.

"Don't worry, Dave," Inspector Graves has said at least ten times. "She'll be fine."

The snowstorm begins in earnest just as the dog teams set their noses toward the woodland footpath at the end of Daphne's road. "It's like a scene from *Scott of the Antarctic*," mumbles the inspector as the four men and two dogs are engulfed in the horizontally blowing wall of whiteness.

Ten minutes later, one dog team returns empty handed. "It's useless trying in this, guv," the handler explains as he peels a layer of snow off his dog's snout. "It's a f'kin blizzard, and it's blowing right in his face."

The other dog team is not far behind. The two men in blue and their black Labrador are barely visible in the solid white curtain of snow as they return with their heads down against the storm. "You'd need a Pyrenean in this," says one of the men as he shakes a pile of snow onto Daphne's hall carpet.

As the flakes fall, so does Bliss's spirit. "If she's taken a tumble in the woods, she won't last long in this," he says, anxiously peering out of the window into the frigid miasma of snow and ice, but there seems little anyone can do other than fill out a missing person report and wait for the storm to abate and the daylight to return.

"Date of birth?" asks the inspector, once he's taken her name and general description, but neither Bliss nor Minnie has any idea.

"It should be in her file at the police station," Bliss suggests, though he doubts she was overly honest when she applied for the job. "But she doesn't look a day over sixty and sometimes I wonder if she's still a teenager."

"Next of kin?" asks the inspector, and Bliss has to admit that he doesn't know that either.

"She never had children," he is able to say with certainty, though as for other relatives, he has no idea.

Minnie has taken over the kitchen and is supplying ten officers and two dogs with Daphne's Keemun tea and chocolate cookies with a little more gusto than the situation demands, and Bliss frowns his disapproval. "Minnie," he calls as she hands around a loaded platter, "those are very expensive biscuits."

"Oh, Daphne won't mind," she chirps lightly, though the officers take the hint and back away.

"Do you know if Daphne has any relatives?" Bliss asks, but Minnie shakes her head. "She never mentioned anyone."

"Acquaintances?" asks Graves, and Minnie brings up Jeremy Maxwell.

"The son of an old friend of hers," explains Bliss. "She's been helping him to move in."

"His father was Monty Maxwell, the member of parliament," says Minnie with an air of smugness that makes Bliss think that she is on the point of hanging out Daphne's dirty laundry, but she contents herself with adding that Jeremy is the new resident at Thraxton Manor."

"I thought that old place had fallen down years ago," exclaims Graves.

"It has," says Bliss, based on information from Daphne. "Apparently he's furnishing the quarters over the stables, though he says he's got plans for the old mansion itself."

The new occupant of the Maxwell estate drowsily answers the phone after several rings, but has no idea where Daphne could be. "Let me know when you find her, eh," he adds, and, as Graves puts down the phone he turns to Bliss. "He sounds American."

"Canadian," replies Bliss. "He's lived with his aunt in Vancouver since he was a kid."

"So, where do we go from here?" asks Graves, but he knows the answer — file the paperwork, put out a missing person alert and pray that she shows up unharmed. "We can't do much more until it's light and the storm eases," he tells Bliss. "You look all-in, Dave. You could do with a spot of shut-eye."

"I've been up since this time yesterday morning," admits Bliss without checking his watch, "but I'm damned if I'm going to bed 'til we find her."

It is nearing five o'clock, and Inspector Graves' radio is alive with reports of accidents and emergencies all across the city as the storm begins to bite.

"We're going to have to go, Dave," he apologizes as catastrophes mount. "Why don't you give her a few hours, and if she doesn't show up by nine, come down to the station. Things should be a bit quieter by then."

"They've put her on the back burner," Bliss complains to his daughter when he phones her at seven. He knows there is nothing Samantha can do to assist, but he feels responsible for Daphne and needs to talk. Minnie Dennon is still at the house, but she's helped herself to a large cognac and has been curled up, asleep, in front of the fire since the officers left.

"Something dreadful must have happened to her," Bliss continues to Samantha, then lays out his fears that someone will trip over a pathetic little bundle in the snow as they struggle to work through the blizzard.

"It's only just started here," Samantha tells him as she peers into the wintry scene outside her window, then she piles on the bad news. "They say it might last a couple of days. I do hope the poor old soul's inside somewhere."

"We're predicting the heaviest snowfall in two decades," says the glum-voiced meteorological officer when Bliss phones for confirmation a few minutes later.

"So much for global warming," Bliss snorts as he drops the phone and grabs his coat.

There is an uncommon air of cordiality among the few officers and civilians who have fought their way into Westchester police station by eight a.m. Men and women who usually guard their little fiefdoms with bared fangs are suddenly affable and welcoming to those who have struggled through the tempest with them.

"I've made a fresh pot of tea if you'd like some," calls the lost property officer to the inquiry desk clerk, and they sit and chat like old friends. But tomorrow, once the novelty has worn off, they'll be back at each other's throats.

The everyday business of policing has been suspended while all efforts focus on the storm. Crime technicians and secretaries find themselves manning emergency phones as the catalogue of traffic accidents, fallen trees, collapsed roofs, and flooded buildings continues to mount. The crime rate is also soaring, sparked by a series of early morning power failures, when some opportunists had used the blackout to loot a tobacconist, a couple of jewellers, and the drug cabinet of a pharmacy.

Bliss is completely despondent as he wanders the deserted halls, hoping to find anyone available to search for Daphne, but he knows that the situation is rapidly deteriorating and he pauses in the main foyer to wipe the condensation off the window and peer into the street. In the pre-dawn darkness, the streetlights struggle to penetrate the snow and add a touch of glitter to the arctic vista, and Bliss spies a familiar figure stumbling out of the whiteness and making for the police station's front door.

"I had to walk," complains Superintendent Donaldson as he crashes into the foyer and shakes off an overcoat of snow. "All the bloody roads are blocked." Then he looks up. "Oh, hello, Dave. What are you doing here? I thought we'd sent you back to The Smoke long ago."

"Daphne Lovelace is missing, sir," replies Bliss, his mind unwilling to waste time on niceties.

"They called me at home," nods Donaldson with a serious face. "She was something of a fixture around here."

"I know, sir."

"I sometimes wonder if the men took more notice of her than they did of me," chuckles Donaldson; then he straightens his face. "You'd better come up to my office and fill me in."

Daphne's duty as Westchester's police station cleaner had spanned more years than anyone could remember, but no one would forget the fact that she had solved almost as many cases as some of the tardier detectives.

"Have you thought of interviewing old so-and-so?" she had been known to hint as she'd delivered the detective inspector's tea, and rarely had the tip proved worthless.

"Make yourself at home here," Superintendent Donaldson tells Bliss as they reach his office. "I expect you know your way around," then he opens the office safe and slips out a package of chocolate digestive cookies. "Breakfast?" he offers, but Bliss shakes his head. "There's got to be something we can do, sir."

"We've got every possible man out there, Dave. I mean — look at it, it's thicker than my wife's tapioca pudding, and that's saying something."

"I'm worried sick about her."

"I can see that, but what can I do? All the men are out on patrol, and it's not as though I can open a new box of them. Anyway, we've no idea where to start looking. If I had five hundred blokes, I still wouldn't know where to send them."

"I know, sir," says Bliss. "I just feel so useless. I'll get out there as soon as it's properly light."

"Dave — find a bed somewhere and get some rest. We'll call you the minute it stops or we find her, OK?"

By mid-morning, Bliss can stand the tension no longer. If anything, the sky has darkened since dawn and the visibility has worsened. Even the police cars have been pulled off the narrow streets, now clogged with abandoned vehicles. Bliss has called Minnie every thirty minutes, and has worked his way back through the list of Daphne's friends and acquaintances in an effort to establish the last known sighting.

"No one saw her yesterday at all," Bliss explains to Donaldson over another coffee. "I didn't wake her when I left for Liverpool at six, though I'm sure she was there, so she must have ..."

Bliss's words gradually trail off, and the back of the upholstered armchair takes a prisoner as he slowly slumps, letting his empty cup fall softly to the carpet. Superintendent Donaldson turns off the light, helps himself to two more chocolate cookies, locks the package in his safe, and creeps out of his office as Bliss begins to snore.

It's nearing lunchtime when Bliss is driven out of Donaldson's office by a nightmare.

"Any news of Daphne?" he asks, grabbing the first officer he sees.

The sergeant shakes his head and the nightmare continues. "Sorry, sir," he says, "but the Super is briefing a search party in the parade room in ten minutes."

More than sixty off-duty officers have volunteered to look for Daphne, and only half of them can cram into the room. A path is made for Bliss as he arrives, and Donaldson introduces him to the crowd before detailing the sparse information that is available. Daphne's description is superfluous, despite the fact that she has been retired for a couple of years; almost everyone knows her personally and, as far as is known, no other pensioners are missing.

"The woods near Ms. Lovelace's house may be a good starting place," explains Donaldson, though Bliss isn't convinced, saying, "I don't think she usually walks through there in the winter, sir."

"You're probably right, Dave," continues Donaldson, "but we've checked all the places she's known to frequent."

Places known to frequent, muses Bliss to himself, as Donaldson's briefing continues, and the jargon of the missing persons bureau sticks in his mind as he desperately tries to think of every place Daphne ever mentioned visiting.

"We can't use the chopper in these conditions," Donaldson is explaining while Bliss is deep in thought, as he tries piecing together Daphne's daily activities.

"A couple of dog teams are already out there," continues Donaldson, "but all they've sniffed out so far are motorists stranded in snow banks. I think we should start with the woods. Unless anyone has any better ideas."

"What about the river?" calls an officer from the back, and Donaldson agrees.

"Take a half-dozen men with you," he instructs, then has a general warning. "Make sure that everybody has a radio or a cellphone, and keep in constant touch. They say it's going to get much worse."

As the parade of searchers in overcoats and galoshes move off, Bliss grabs his coat and gloves. Donaldson is at the door and has other ideas.

"Not with that gammy leg, Dave," the senior officer says. "I don't want my men having to search for you as well. Anyway — I need your help to coordinate and deal with the press."

Bliss is out-ranked, albeit by an officer of another force, and he concedes with a clear conscience. "You're probably right, sir," he says, taking off his coat and setting his eyes on the media relations office.

The news editor of BBC Westchester readily takes Daphne's details, though he is quick to point out that he makes no promises as he surveys the pile of bulletins related to power outages, blocked roads, and closed schools. The reporter at the *Gazette* appears much more interested, perhaps because it will add morbidity to his extensive storm coverage. "Elderly spinster feared dead in blizzard," has more clout than "Worst snow in memory," but the possibility that Daphne could have perished is so alien to her character that Bliss simply cannot bring himself to accept it, and he spends the next hour calling all of her friends and acquaintances again to urge them to renew their efforts to find her.

The riverbank team calls in with the first bad news a little after three, a body floating in the ice-crusted river not far from the old tannery. Bliss, Donaldson, and a half-dozen other officers race to the control room to listen to the garbled radio messages as the men at the scene grapple to get a purchase on a corpse.

"It's jammed under the ice," yells one, while another asks control to send some ropes and an ambulance. "You'd better send the coroner's officer at the same time," continues the officer. "This definitely isn't a case of natural causes."

"Oh my God," Bliss exhales and is readying to make his way to the scene when one of the officers risks his neck by wading into the river and taking hold.

"Male, white, in his mid-thirties," calls the voice on the radio and Bliss almost faints in relief. Moments later, as more details come in, Bliss feels a pang of guilt that his anxiety had been assuaged at the expense of someone's mother, wife, or child, but, despite her years, it is impossible for him not to see Daphne as invincible.

As dusk falls, Donaldson delivers the second blow. "I'm calling it off for the day," he says sadly, leaving Bliss close to tears of frustration. It's barely five o'clock, but the snow is still pounding down and the city has skidded to a complete halt. "We'll never find her in the dark, Dave," continues Donaldson. "And, to be perfectly honest, I don't think it's going to make any difference how long it takes to find her now."

"I'd better get back to her place and relieve Minnie," says Bliss, keeping his voice as straight as he can.

chapter thirteen

The hollow emptiness of Daphne's house, despite the presence of Minnie and the promise of a roaring log fire, leaves Bliss shivering when he struggles out of his overcoat and borrowed Wellington boots in the hallway. "Is there a power failure?" he calls as he enters the sitting room and finds it lit by candles.

"No," says Minnie lightly as she scurries out of the kitchen to put the finishing touches to the dining table, "I just thought it would be cozier."

Bliss doesn't want cozy; the very last thing he wants is cozy; the thought of being cozy in Daphne's house when she is lying frozen to the bone in a snow drift or under the river's ice is so revolting that he is tempted to snuff the candles and douse the fire, until Minnie points out that she has had Daphne in mind and has set the table for three.

"I wouldn't want the poor old soul coming back to a chilly house with nothing on the stove," says Minnie, and Bliss has to concur, though he quickly switches on the main light and opens the curtains, hoping to send out a beacon.

Despite the fact that Bliss has lodged at Daphne's for more than six weeks, he sits on the edge of his chair and feels increasingly uncomfortable that Minnie's presence at the house will lead to an explosive encounter if Daphne returns. It is not simply that Minnie and he are alone together in the house, it's the fact that Minnie is happily bustling around in Daphne's kitchen, wearing one of Daphne's cardigans, Daphne's "Harrods" apron, and a pair of Daphne's bobble-toed slippers.

"I didn't expect to be here all day," Minnie explains quickly, at the sight of Bliss's raised eyebrows. "Or I would have come prepared with a change of clothes."

"I'm just going to have another look in Daphne's room," says Bliss, finding Minnie's Daphne-esque appearance more than a little disconcerting.

She still hasn't asked me if there is any news of Daphne, Bliss thinks as he climbs the stairs, although he can't help feeling that he is being uncharitable, and that he should be grateful to have someone to talk to. *Of course she didn't ask*, he chides himself. *You've phoned her at least twenty times today. What's the point of rubbing it in? She knows there is no news.*

Establishing the precise location and time that the subject was last known to be alive, "the starting point," is the primary goal for any detective attempting to locate a missing person; but, in Daphne's case, it doesn't seem to help. None of her friends or acquaintances has admitted seeing or speaking to her since Bliss had left her in front of the television the night before last. "I think I'll stay up a little while longer," she'd said, when he'd told her that he was going to bed. Then she had jabbed slyly, "I don't have to get up as early as you in the morning, David. I'm not going to Liverpool again tomorrow."

"Oh, Daphne," he'd sighed. "I told you you could come if you really wanted to."

But Daphne had sloughed it off. "No, David. You're probably right. I'll find something to amuse myself, don't you worry."

Had she meant it? Bliss has questioned himself a hundred times since her disappearance. Or was she so ticked off with him that she'd simply booked herself into a hotel or spa somewhere, and will pop up as innocently as a snowdrop in a few days, saying, "I would have told you I was treating myself to a little holiday, but you were in Liverpool."

She wouldn't do that, Bliss tells himself. *She wouldn't have left the kitten to starve.* However, he checks and re-checks Daphne's suitcases on top of her wardrobe until he is almost convinced that one is missing; then he finally convinces himself that it's not. Daphne's "Beatles" bag is still by her bed and it brings a lump to his throat as he recalls the last time she carried it — like a teenybopper strutting down Penny Lane — as they'd walked the streets of Liverpool.

Nothing has changed in Daphne's bedroom since he discovered her disappearance the previous night — an ancient hairless teddy still sits on her nightgown atop the pillow of the tightly made little bed; a regimented row of creams, powders, and lipsticks march across the dressing table; her toothbrush, denture cream, and eye drops line the sink. Everything is still in exactly the same spot she would have left them if she were just popping over to the butcher's or the baker's. The neatness and completeness of her personal toiletries mean only one thing to Bliss — she had not planned on vanishing. However, that conclusion leaves him little choice but to accept the worst-case scenario, and he prays that her wartime survival training had taught her to build an igloo for shelter and a fire for warmth.

The only other clue to Daphne's whereabouts may lie in her writing cabinet in the sitting room, although the thought of trawling through Daphne's personal papers with Minnie breathing down his neck adds to Bliss's anxiety. *I'll wait until she's asleep,* he thinks, as he is drawn by interesting aromas back down to the dining room.

"Would you like a drink while I serve dinner, Dave?" asks Minnie as she polishes off Daphne's sherry and reaches for the Dubonnet. Bliss is inclined to stop her, finding a certain sacrilege in raiding the missing woman's liquor cabinet, but consoles himself with the thought that he will happily buy Daphne an entire hogshead if she returns.

"I'll just have a small scotch, please," he says, but he is beginning to feel distinctly uneasy at the way that Minnie has so readily slipped into Daphne's shoes, and the liberties she is taking with her friend's provisions — almost as if she is enjoying it; almost as if she had planned for it. That troubled thought brings Bliss up with a start and he quickly questions, "When did you last see Daphne, Minnie?"

"Christmas Day," she replies crisply as she heads back to the kitchen. "When she snapped my head off every time I tried talking to you."

Bliss stiffens at the words. The possibility that he could have been the cause of a jealous spat between aging friends bothers him, but the thought that Minnie could have been involved in Daphne's disappearance is so improbable that it is hardly worth considering. Yet he does consider it; considers the evident acrimony between the two women; the swiftness with which Minnie had arrived on Daphne's doorstep in the early hours — as if she had been already dressed and expecting a call; the speed with which she has made herself at home without considering the hullabaloo that will occur if Daphne walks in. *What if she's not bothered because she knows Daphne can't walk in?* he wonders.

Samantha phones, as she has several times during the day, and breaks into Bliss's musings. "I'd come down and help," she tells her father, "but all the roads are blocked and the trains aren't running."

"I don't think there's anything you could do anyway," says Bliss, downhearted. "I don't think there's anything anyone can do now ... If only I'd taken her to Liverpool with me."

"Dad, don't blame yourself," jumps in Samantha. "And don't leap to conclusions either. She might just have gone away for a few days and forgot to mention it."

"Without her toothbrush and flannelette nightgown?" he questions, though he recalls the numerous times he'd tried to mollify petrified parents in similar situations, when their fifteen-year-olds hadn't shown up at the breakfast table. "Probably staying over with friends and forgot to phone," he'd said, and had generally been proven right. But Daphne isn't fifteen, and if she has any more friends than the ones who have been contacted, no one knows of them.

"That's the worst thing about getting old," Daphne had told him one evening, referring to everyone but herself, "their friends gradually die off until they're the only ones left."

"The bell-curve of social interaction," Bliss had mused knowingly, and wondered if he had already hit the mid-life peak and would soon start sliding down the other side while the Grim Reaper picked off his friends one at a time.

Bliss's unease at Minnie's apparent lack of reverence is further heightened by the fact that she has set the table using Daphne's finest Wedgwood and her gilt silverware. She has even buffed up the candelabra and the napkin rings and has crafted a centrepiece from maraschino cherries, a couple of tangerines, and a bunch of greenery that looks suspiciously like clippings from Daphne's perennial Christmas tree.

"I'm not sure we should be using Daphne's best stuff," murmurs Bliss, terrified that his hostess is going to walk through the door and throw a fit at him for letting Minnie take over the house, but Minnie has no such qualms and has rummaged through Daphne's fridge and freezer to concoct a four-course extravaganza.

"I'm trying to watch the weight ..." Bliss begins, using his stomach as an excuse as Minnie brings in the salmon pâté appetizer.

"I know exactly what you mean, Dave," says Minnie as she tightens her bum, sucks in her gut, and sticks out her chest. "As Shakespeare said — If you can keep your figure when all about you are losing theirs." Then she sits, closes her eyes, and puts her hands together. "May the dear Lord take care of our friend Daphne, and may she quickly return to the fold."

"Amen," echoes Bliss with a skeptical eye on the sprightly septuagenarian. "So, what do you think has happened to Daphne?" he asks conversationally as they start eating.

"She didn't take any clothes or anything with her," says Minnie, then she shakes her head. "I don't want to sound pessimistic, but in truth I only cooked enough for two. I expect she got caught in the storm."

Bliss is fishing, and he's careful to keep his hook lightly baited as he replies, "Yes. That's what I think. But where could she have been?"

"Well. You know Daphne, Dave. She could have gone anywhere."

Not without leaving a note for me and feeding the kitten, he thinks as the pheasant soup follows the salmon. But it is the fact that she had disappeared hours before the start of the storm that really concerns him, and especially the fact that Minnie doesn't seem to understand the relevance of that detail. "So," he probes, "what time did you go to bed last night, Minnie?"

"That's a saucy thing to ask, Inspector," says Minnie with a girly giggle and Bliss rips into her.

"Minnie, this is very serious. Do you know anything about Daphne's disappearance at all?"

"No. Of course not. I'm as worried about her as you are," says Minnie and she bursts into a flood of tears.

Bliss is at her side and comforting her in a flash. "Sorry," he says, realizing that in his paranoia he's probably gone overboard, and he puts his arms around her as she sobs, "Daphne is the only friend I've got."

"It's OK, Minnie," consoles Bliss. "I'm just so frustrated that I can't do anything to find her."

Superintendent Donaldson phones mid-evening with some good news. "The army is lending us two hundred men and some snowmobiles first thing tomorrow." The bad news is that another six inches of snow will be on the ground by then. "Dave, I hate to keep saying this, but if she is outside it's already far too late."

"I know," agrees Bliss, and with all the evidence pointing to her intention of returning home, he is left with little hope — although he is willing to consider anything, even the bizarre notion that she's been caught up in some Christian Fundamentalist scenario — God reaching down to pluck his favourites off the earth while disbelievers are left behind to suffer in abject misery — but sanity prevails and, as Minnie washes up, he begins phoning Daphne's friends with the news that the search will resume in the morning.

"I want you to think of anywhere she could possibly have gone," he tells each of her friends in turn, but none offers anything constructive, other than Mavis Longbottom mentioning that if she had gone to a hotel she would have needed money.

Superintendent Donaldson had thought of that. "We had someone give all the banks a bell while you were asleep in my office this morning," says Donaldson when Bliss phones back. "She hasn't taken out any cash in the last few days, and if she'd been mugged for her plastic or cheques, nothing has shown up yet."

"She would have put up a struggle," says Bliss unhesitatingly. "She would have given 'em a good going-over if she had a chance. Have we checked the hospital for any dodgy characters with gouged eyes or swollen bollocks?"

"Dave, be serious. What villain's going to admit being done-over by a raging granny?"

"Just a thought. We've got to be missing something."

"What about the time of disappearance?" asks Donaldson. "Have we got a better handle on that yet?"

The unlit fire nails down Daphne's departure to somewhere before five in the afternoon, assuming she had followed her daily routine of cleaning out the grate in the morning and making a tepee of newspaper and kindling ready for lighting at sundown.

"I think it's time to lower the flag and stoke up the fire, Chief Inspector," she would pronounce in the manner of a regimental colonel each evening as the room dimmed in the twilight.

Daphne's insistence on elevating Detective Inspector Bliss to a higher plane was based purely on his appearance. "You look like a chief inspector to me," she had told him firmly the first time they'd met, and she had never altered her opinion.

"Nothing new on that front, guv," says Bliss, answering the superintendent's question. "As far as I know she was still in her bed at six when I left for Liverpool, and she obviously planned on being home before dark or she would have left the front porch light on like she usually did."

Daphne makes the highlights of the BBC's nine o'clock news. "Today's blizzard has claimed at least six lives," says the bubbly anchor, voicing over a montage of bleak scenes. "And there is growing concern over the fate of one elderly Hampshire pensioner who has been listed as missing since the early hours," she continues, before throwing to the meteorologist who warns that the back edge of the storm is still way off the radar screen.

Elderly and pensioner are words that Bliss simply cannot associate with his Daphne, but the news anchor had given no name, no details, no description, and Bliss feels a sense of disconnection as he seriously wonders if they are talking about some other person. *In which case*, he asks himself, *precisely where is Daphne?*

With the dishes washed and put away, Minnie pours herself a shot of Daphne's brandy, settles into Daphne's favourite fireside chair and declares herself almost ready for bed — Daphne's bed.

"It's only a bed, David," Minnie complains when Bliss shakes his head, saying, "No. No. No."

"If Daphne comes back I'll be up like a shot."

"I said no, Minnie. Absolutely not."

"That's just silly," she says, struck by the illogicality of the situation, but Bliss digs in his heels.

"You are not sleeping in Daphne's bed," he says, but he knows that Minnie cannot be expected to go home. It had taken him more than half an hour to slog through the snow from the nearest main road in daylight. Minnie would never make it in the dark. "You can have my room," he tells her. "I'll stay down here. I don't expect I'll sleep much anyway."

Minnie has no choice but to agree, and Bliss is halfway up the stairs to tidy his room and remove his personal belongings when the phone rings.

"Telephone," yells Minnie, and Bliss dashes back down and virtually snatches it from her hand.

It's Mike Phillips in Vancouver, and there is a flatness in Bliss's tone which reflects his disappointment as he says, "Oh. It's you, Mike."

"Oh, shit! Did I screw up the time difference?" asks Phillips with concern. "It's not like, four in the morning there, is it?"

"No," says Bliss, then fills in the Canadian officer with the basic details of Daphne's disappearance.

"I'm sure she'll turn up all right," says Phillips, though Bliss's optimism is draining.

"I'm so worried about her I forgot to call you," says Bliss, adding, "Not good news, Mike, I'm afraid. No one is putting their hand up to a bit of backstage hanky-panky with Ruth's mother, and a guy called Geoffrey Sanderson is the only one that I haven't been able to check out. Nobody seems to know what happened to him after the North American tour ended."

Bliss had found Sanderson's last known address in Liverpool with little difficulty, but it had been his parents' house and, according to the present occupant, both of them had been dead for several years. "The old fella next door might know what happened to their kid," the young mother had told Bliss. "He's lived there forever."

The next-door neighbour had remembered Geoffrey, but not until Bliss had tested the ancient man's hearing aid for a couple of minutes, and spent another two minutes explaining that he wasn't attempting to sell the old-timer a plot in the cemetery.

"He went to America wiz the Beatles," the pensioner had said in his high-pitched Liverpudlian accent, when Bliss had finally gotten through to him.

"But where is he now?" Bliss had asked.

"I jus' told ya. He went to America wiz the Beatles."

"Yes. But that was forty years ago. What happened to him afterwards?"

"I keep telling ya. He went to America wiz the Beatles."

Bliss had tried rephrasing his question several times, but the answer was always the same, and eventually the old guy had slowly closed the door saying. "Hey, Chuck. If you ain't gonna listen to me there's nor a lotta use me talking is there?"

"I think he means that Sanderson didn't return home at the end of the tour, although I have no idea where he may be," Bliss tells Phillips. Then he asks, "What's the situation with your friend Ruth?"

"Well at least she's off the hook for murder. Her husband turned up."

"Where?"

"In the crematorium — natural causes."

"Oh, shit. Well I guess that's good — for her anyway."

Other things have been good for Ruth in recent days. Her health has continued its dramatic improvement, Mike Phillips has been a regular visitor and, to the relief of the Button teenagers, Ruth has started taking over the kitchen from their mother.

"You and your husband are so good to let me stay here," says Ruth as she makes pepperoni pizza while Trina surfs the Web searching for an escape-proof guinea pig cage. "I'll never be able to repay you."

"You don't have to," replies Trina. "Actually, it's kinda fun knowing the neighbours are all talking about me having a murderess living in the basement."

"I'm not a murderess," protests Ruth, and Trina quickly leaps to pacify her.

"I know that, Ruth. But people only hear what they want to hear, and to listen to your ex-mother-in-law anyone would think that you somehow gave Jordan cancer."

"I don't know what to do ..." whimpers Ruth, and Trina comforts her.

"You've just got to get your strength up and fight back, that's all. Hammett thinks the Crown might drop the assault charges 'cuz the surveillance tape was recorded over — 'accidentally,' the police said, but he doesn't believe them for a minute."

Ruth stops crying and her expression becomes puzzled as she looks at her friend and asks, "How do you know that?"

Trina reddens and blusters, "I don't know. Maybe you told me."

"No I did not. Hammett hasn't said anything about that. Anyway, I haven't seen him for weeks."

"Well, maybe ... Maybe Mike told me then."

"Oh, of course," says Ruth, relaxing, though adding, "I wonder why he didn't tell me?"

"Probably wants it to be a surprise," says Trina, desperately hoping that she can get to Phillips before Ruth does.

chapter fourteen

The second dawn of Daphne Lovelace's disappearance holds the promise of a brighter day. The storm has swept on across the North Sea to Scandinavia, where it will be welcomed, but it has left behind both the beauty and the beast. It has finally stopped snowing in Westchester, and the freshly fallen powder has been sculpted by the wind into a myriad of whimsical figures, but the ice demon hides its victims beneath the virginal surface, and it is only a matter of time before someone stumbles across a frozen arm protruding out of an exquisitely carved drift, and a petrified body is dug out from under an avalanche of snow.

Bliss has been testing his leg since the first light, just as the last flakes were falling and the sky was turning blue with feigned innocence. With a shovel for support he has slogged his way to the woodland at one end of Daphne's street and, as he struggles back to her house through the deep snow, a quartet of familiar figures wearily trudge in from the main road at the other end.

Peter and Blossom Jones have crammed into Mavis Longbottom's Fiat, together with Gino, to make the journey across town, but have been forced to abandon the vehicle in a drift some distance away, and they are on their last legs as they meet Bliss at Daphne's gate.

"We came to help with the search," says Blossom valiantly as Bliss lets them in, and they struggle with heavy coats, gloves, and boots while Mavis desperately dances up and down. "I'm bursting for a pee," she says as she makes a break for the stairs.

Minnie Dennon has been woken by the commotion and is emerging sleepy-eyed from Bliss's bedroom, wearing one of Daphne's nightdresses, just as Mavis hits the upstairs landing and makes a final dash for the bathroom.

"Minnie!" exclaims Mavis in disbelief and Bliss, in the hallway below, mutters, "Oh, shit!" under his breath as he ushers the others into the sitting room.

"I'm already worn out and frozen to death," admits Blossom, plunking herself beside the fire while Bliss scurries around to get them blankets and hot tea.

"You shouldn't be out in this," he admonishes — but he doesn't blame them. Leg or no leg, he has every intention of joining the hunt today and vows to himself that he will not return without Daphne. "You had all better stay here," he tells them as he tucks a rug around Blossom's legs. "There's no point in you getting lost out there as well."

"But we've got to do something," protests Blossom, as Mavis sneaks in and slyly announces, "I see you've got Minnie sleeping in your bed, David."

"Yes. And I slept down here on the couch," snaps Bliss, choking off the topic. "Now has anybody come up with any ideas to find Daphne?"

"We should hold another seance," suggests Mavis. "We could ask the spirits to find her."

"Mavis," says Bliss, pulling no punches, "this isn't a stupid party game. For all we know, Daphne could be lying out there buried in snow."

"All the more reason for a seance ..." she starts, but Bliss stomps on her.

"Seances are just silly hoaxes, Mavis."

"The spirits guided us to your man in the photo," she protests.

"Rubbish, Mavis," says Bliss as he gives her an accusatory stare. "Somebody was tapping on the table."

"How do you know?"

"Because I could feel the vibrations under my fingertips," he says and Mavis backs down a degree.

"Well, what do you suggest we do?" she asks acerbically as the phone rings.

"David?" the voice is weak, indistinct — a figment of Bliss's imagination perhaps; a vagary of the electronic airwaves.

"Daphne?" inquires Bliss disbelievingly, and the room deadens.

"Can't talk. Pick me up outside Thraxton Manor in fifteen minutes and don't tell anyone."

"Where?" Bliss asks, but the line is dead. "Daphne ..." he calls desperately. "Daphne ..."

A moment of amazed silence is exploded as a cacophony of voices gabble simultaneously, "Was that her? Was it Daph?"

"I think so," says Bliss vaguely, still trying to get his mind in gear, then the cogs click and he makes a run for the hall.

"Mavis," he yells, "I need your car. I left mine at the police station."

"But where are you going? Where is she?"

"Peter. Phone the police and tell them to hold the search ..." Bliss starts, then he changes his mind and pulls out his cellphone as he struggles into his boots. "Don't worry. I'll do it myself. Now all of you just stay here in case she calls again."

"What's happening? Is she all right? Where is she?"

Bliss ducks the questions as he heads out, shovel in hand, to beat a path to the main road and Mavis's car.

Superintendent Donaldson is briefing the early-shift police officers and the military when he takes Bliss's call. "For some reason she asked me not to tell anyone," says Bliss when the superintendent inquires as to Daphne's whereabouts, "but I'll call you as soon as I've picked her up."

Any pain in Bliss's leg is forgotten in his determination to reach Daphne as quickly as possible, and he practically runs through the deep powdery snow until he reaches the main road and Mavis's Fiat. Getting the car out of the snow bank where Mavis ditched it takes several minutes and a hefty push from a passing pedestrian, and he is already five minutes late as he hits the gas and sets the wheels spinning. But he knows the route — he had driven past the Maxwell property with Daphne a few days earlier.

"That's where Jeremy lives," she had pointed out, and he had strained to see the ancient house and stables in the distant trees, but had to be content with just a glimpse through the winter-bare hawthorn hedgerow. However, judging by the massive stone gate pillars and imposing — though rust-streaked — steel gates, he'd had no difficulty imagining the building's long-lost grandeur.

"Thraxton Manor," says the peeling sign on the gate as Bliss drives slowly past, but there is no sign of Daphne in the blinding alpine whiteness, and he is beginning to wonder if there is a second set of gates when he spots a ghostly figure gingerly rising out of the roadside ditch. Daphne, shrouded in a white bed sheet, tries to haul herself up the steep bank to the road, and Bliss slides to a halt and races to her rescue.

"Thank you, David. Thank you," she whispers through chattering teeth as he hauls her out of the snow and sees that she is shoeless.

"Hold on," he says, picking her up and carrying her in his arms to the car. "Straight to the hospital," he adds, turning the heat to maximum, but Daphne has other ideas.

"Ju ... Ju ... Just a warm bath," she stutters.

"Don't argue. You're going to the hospital," he says adamantly as he phones Donaldson to call off the search.

"Where was she?" asks Donaldson, but Bliss needs to concentrate to keep the car on the road.

"Meet me at Westchester Memorial, guv," he says as he clicks off the phone.

"Hold tight please," Bliss jokes as he expertly fish-tails the car around a snow-clogged bend, but fortunately the main road into the city has been partially plowed and he is soon able to pick up speed. Daphne is shaking so violently that he feels the car vibrating in sympathy and, in the sparse traffic, he keeps a worried eye on her, asking, "Are you all right?"

"I'm just a silly old woman," she chatters and Bliss senses in her voice that she is not talking about being lost in the storm.

"Don't worry. We'll soon have you warmed up," he says. "But, what happened?"

Daphne pulls herself together and snivels, "I feel such a fool, but it was all Minnie's fault."

Bliss takes a deep breath, hardly daring to ask. "Minnie?"

"Yes. The stupid woman said that he was Monty Maxwell's son."

"And he wasn't?"

"No."

"Who is he, then?"

"His name's Jordan Jackson."

"Westchester Hospital," announces Bliss as he pulls into the ambulance bay at the emergency department five minutes later, where Superintendent Donaldson is waiting alongside a full medical team.

"Ms. Lovelace has a touch of dehydration and hypothermia," the doctor tells them after a brief examination. "Fortunately, she's in generally good health so there shouldn't be any lasting complications, although her feet are a bit of a mess."

"When can we see her?" inquires Bliss, but he receives a non-committal shrug.

"We'll call you, but we'll probably keep her in for twenty-four hours, just to be on the safe side. How old is she, by the way?"

Bliss and Donaldson shrug in unison. "We may as well get something to eat," suggests Donaldson, tugging Bliss's arm. "They do a good breakfast in the doctor's canteen here. The black pudding with baked beans ..."

"There's a few people I should phone first," says Bliss, cutting him off; then he leaves Donaldson to order for him.

It's more than two hours before Daphne is sufficiently recovered to explain what happened, but it has taken Bliss most of that time to eat his way through the spread Donaldson laid on. However, he had used the time to inform the senior officer of Daphne's indiscretion with Monty Maxwell that had so horribly backfired.

"It's probably best if you don't let on that you know," Bliss is telling the senior officer when a young nurse announces that Daphne is up to receiving visitors.

"I thought I was a goner in that ditch," laughs Daphne as Bliss and Donaldson sit on either side of her bed, gently rubbing her still frigid hands a few minutes later.

"So, what happened, Daphne?" Donaldson asks, and Daphne explains how, with Bliss away in Liverpool for the day, she had decided to pay Jeremy Maxwell a surprise visit, but when she had shown up without warning, he had not been at home.

"I'd walked all that bloomin' way," she moans to Donaldson. "So I was buggered if I was going back home without doing a bit of cleaning up for him."

During her previous visits to the apartment above the manor's stable block, Daphne had discovered a spare door key under a flowerpot, so she had let herself in and begun tidying when a Canadian passport had caught her eye.

"I was putting a few of his clothes away in a drawer when I found his passport and was just curious to see what his photo was like," she carries on. "But when I opened it up it gave his name as Jordan Jackson."

"Are you absolutely sure it was his passport?" asks Bliss, but Daphne is in no doubt. "Oh, yes. It was his picture, all right."

"But when you first visited him did he actually say he was Jeremy Maxwell?" inquires Donaldson.

"Yes, sir. He did."

"Daphne, love, you don't have to call me 'sir,'" says Donaldson leaning over her bed. "It's Ted."

"Oh, no, sir. That wouldn't seem right. Anyway, I'm quite certain it's not Jeremy. I should have realized when I first spoke to him. He was sort of nervous — vague.

He claimed he remembered me, though I don't suppose that I had any reason to doubt him at the time. Minnie Dennon said it was him, and I was so pleased to see him again. I've often wondered what had happened to him after all these years."

"But you told me you recognized him," Bliss reminds her. "You even said that he looked like his father."

"Wishful thinking and a failing memory, David."

"There's nothing wrong with your memory," says Bliss, adding, "Don't worry, we'll find out what's going on; but where have you been for two days? We were worried sick."

Daphne had been trapped by her own inquisitiveness. No sooner had she found Jackson's passport than the scrunch of car tires on the gravel driveway had alerted her to the owner's return. Unable to face him with her new-found knowledge, she had tried taking a back way out of the upstairs apartment, but had found herself ensnared in a hayloft.

"I couldn't get down into the stables. I found the trap door, but there was no ladder," she tells them. "And I couldn't go back through the apartment because he was there."

Slender shafts of daylight penetrated the old tiled roof on Daphne's first day in the loft, and she had made a bed of hay bales while she waited for the man to leave so she could escape. But he hadn't left, and the longer she remained in hiding the more difficult it had been to think of a way out.

"'I was just looking for bats or a barn owl,' might have worked in the first ten minutes or so," she carries on, "but after that I couldn't do anything but wait. And then it started getting cold."

The blizzard had howled through the drafty loft,

forcing tendrils of snow between the cracks in the tiles, and Daphne had buried herself deep in the hay for warmth during the first night.

"I hardly slept," she admits. "The wind made such a noise that the horses were restless, and some rats kept snuffling around."

"You must've been terrified," suggests Donaldson.

"They were only rats, sir. I was so hungry I would've eaten one if I could've caught it."

"You wouldn't," Bliss protests, though guesses that, if pushed, she probably would have.

"Anyway," Daphne carries on, "I knew it was morning when I heard him outside starting one of the cars."

Not realizing that the driveway was impassable, Daphne had assumed that Maxwell, or whoever he was, was on the point of leaving, and had crept out of her hiding place to make her escape when she'd heard him returning up the stairs from the stables.

"I just grabbed a bottle of water and some bed-clothes and shot back into the loft," she explains. "Then I had to stay there all day and night again until he left this morning."

A nurse shows up to run a battery of tests and flushes Bliss and Donaldson out of Daphne's cubicle. "We're going to be a little while," she explains as she hooks up another IV bag, and Bliss gives Daphne's hand an extra squeeze.

"I'll come back this afternoon," he says. "Don't worry about a thing."

The brightness of the midday sun is deceiving as the two officers leave the hospital and feel the wintry chill.

"Have you got time for lunch?" Donaldson asks as he pulls his coat around him and hustles for his car, but Bliss shakes his head.

"No. I think I'll have a word with Mr. Jackson, or whatever his name is, first. There has to be a simple explanation."

"The Mitre Hotel's got a new chef," continues Donaldson as if he's not heard. "The venison sausages are really special. You could meet me there afterwards."

"Thanks anyway," calls Bliss, still bloated from breakfast, "but I've got a few of Daphne's friends waiting to hear what's happened. Next time, perhaps."

The occupant of the stable's apartment at Thraxton Manor has just returned home by the time Bliss drives up the freshly cleared driveway. Two of the stables' doors are open, revealing a couple of very high-priced mechanical stallions — a Ferrari and a Jaguar — while a new Range Rover idles outside the front door as the owner unloads groceries. Daphne's tracks from the stables, across the pristine field to a gap in the hedge, are so blatant that Bliss immediately seizes on them as a pretext as he flashes his police ID.

"Detective Inspector Bliss," he introduces himself to the tall, middle-aged man who is carting a box of supplies to the door. "We're looking for an escaped prisoner," he adds, not entirely untruthfully, but the man seems unconcerned.

"I haven't seen anyone."

"And you are, sir?"

"Maxwell. Jeremy Maxwell. Why?"

"Just wondered, that's all. You're not English are you?"

"Astute of you — Canadian actually."

"Is this the Maxwell estate then?" inquires Bliss as he sweeps a look around the grounds and takes in the decayed manor house together with numerous outbuildings and barns.

"Has been for the past four hundred and fifteen years, Inspector."

"I guess you're used to this weather," continues Bliss realizing that he's running out of questions and hoping to start a dialogue.

"Yep."

So much for that, thinks Bliss as he struggles for a reason to remain. "Would you mind if I had a look around?" he asks finally. "I have an interest in conversions. I'm thinking of buying an old barn myself."

"I'm a bit busy at the moment," says the man, nodding to his supplies. "Some other time, perhaps."

"Of course. Sorry to disturb you," says Bliss, turning away; then he spins back hoping to catch his quarry off balance. "I don't suppose you know someone called Jordan Jackson by any chance? I think he's Canadian."

"Sorry. Never heard of him."

As Bliss drives away, the new tenant of Thraxton Manor climbs the stairs to his apartment, puts his box of groceries on the kitchen table, and takes a very serious look at a pair of soggy women's shoes that he has dug from the snow near the apartment door. Then he checks his underwear drawer and thoughtfully balances a Canadian passport in his hand.

Daphne doesn't waste time at the hospital, and by three in the afternoon, when Bliss returns as promised, she has cajoled the doctor into releasing her.

"Whatever happened to your shoes?" Bliss asks her as he drives her home.

"I lost them in the snowdrifts outside the stables," she replies. "I'll have to go back and get them when it thaws."

"I think you'd better stay away from there — until I find out who he really is."

"You do believe me, don't you?" she asks warily and Bliss has to admit to a certain confusion.

"It's just that you seemed so positive that it was Jeremy before," he says as he checks the dashboard clock. "Maybe I'll give Mike Phillips a call and see if they've got any record of either man in Canada. It's about seven-thirty there at the moment. I'll try his cellphone as soon as we get home and get you tucked into bed."

The sun is just rising over the Rockies as the earth rolls on another day in Vancouver, but a low-pressure system has swept over the Strait of Georgia from Vancouver Island and threatens a deluge. Mike Phillips stands nude, peering out of his hotel window at the slate sky and charcoal clouds, and wishes that he could snuggle back into the giant warm bed. But duty calls, and he gently brushes his lips on an exposed forehead.

"Good morning, Ruth. I have to go to work now," he coos to the sleepy woman. "Will you be OK?"

"Mike?"

"Yes."

"Kiss me again, please."

Phillips laughs. "Anybody would think you've never been properly loved before." Then he kisses her — tenderly at first, their lips barely touching; their breaths mingling; then deeper and harder, until their tongues entwine and she reaches out to hold him.

"What are you planning for today?" he asks, inching his lips away a fraction as he softly strokes her face and peers into her eyes.

"I could think of something," she says lasciviously, and draws him back to bed.

Phillips readily slides under the sheets, saying, "I really do have to go soon."

"I know. I just wanted to give you a little something to make sure you wouldn't forget me by tonight."

"Oh, I don't think that'll happen," he says as he runs his hands over her naked body and finds her breasts.

"I'll go round to Trina's to do the laundry and cook dinner as usual," Ruth says as she gently massages him. "Don't forget: I'm supposed to be staying there as part of my bail conditions."

"Only when you're not in police custody," he says, smoothly slipping a hand between her thighs. "And at this particular moment — you are."

"Is this called fraternizing with the enemy?" she moans as she melts under his touch, then Phillips' phone rings.

"Oh, shit," mutters Phillips, and is inclined to let it go, but Ruth loses the moment.

"You might as well answer it," she whispers. "I'm not going anywhere until I've been given all my rights."

"Mike Phillips," he calls into the phone with a touch of aggravation.

"Oh, Mike. It's Dave Bliss in England. I haven't screwed up have I?"

"No," laughs Phillips, "neither of us have. What's happening, Dave? Are you having a party there?"

"Not exactly," answers Bliss, then explains Daphne's dilemma as Blossom, Mavis, and Peter help their old friend continue her warming trend with a bottle of champagne in the background. Minnie is keeping her head down over some sausage rolls in the kitchen, knowing that it's only a matter of time before Mavis blows the whistle on her unauthorized sleepover.

Prior to picking up Daphne from the hospital, Bliss had raced around replenishing the liquor cabinet and taking Minnie to the supermarket to restock the cupboards. Then she had bounced around, putting everything straight and desperately trying to get her house in order before the return of Daphne; even snapping at Peter for wanting a chocolate cookie. "They're not made on trees," she had told him crustily. "Money doesn't grow on Daphne. She's only a pensioner, same as us."

"Jeremy Maxwell," Phillips repeats as Bliss asks him to see if anything is known of the man, and the Canadian officer chews the name over as he types it into his laptop. "It's got a ring to it ... I'll check it out as soon as I get to the office," he says. "Mind you, without a date of birth or a social insurance number, it's a bit of a long shot."

The name Jordan Jackson, on the other hand, has much greater significance.

"Talk about coincidences," says Phillips slipping into the bathroom and quietly closing the door behind him. "Ruth's husband was a Jordan Jackson. Though it's a common enough name. What does he look like?"

The similarity between the description furnished by Bliss and the one given to him by Ruth are sufficiently striking to elicit a whistle from the Mountie. "If he wasn't dead, I'd say it could be him," says Phillips. "But why does she think his name's Jackson?"

"His passport," explains Bliss, then relates Daphne's story.

"I'd need more info," says Phillips. "Though, if it is the same Jackson, I'm guessing that somebody lifted his passport from the dump he was living in when he died."

"But Daphne insists that the guy in Maxwell's house is the one in the passport and, to be honest, if she says it's the same guy, I'm inclined to believe her. You've met her Mike. You know what she's like."

"Then it has to be a different character altogether. My Jackson is definitely dead. But if you can get me a date of birth or the passport number, I'll happily see what I can come up with."

"Leave it to me," says Bliss. "I'll pay him another visit. There has to be an explanation."

Thraxton Manor's new occupant appears to be out when Bliss returns just before dusk. In the absence of a bell, Bliss bangs repeatedly on the apartment's door and even tries the handle.

"Anyone home?" Bliss calls as the doorknob refuses to budge, then he stands back to toss a few pieces of gravel at the apartment's window.

"Shit," he mutters, and is on the point of leaving when he takes Daphne's standpoint. 'I've come all this bloomin' way ...'"

The flowerpot key has gone, but one of the stables is open and he slips in and searches for the trapdoor leading into the hayloft. A ladder stands against an empty horse stall and tempts him, but the thought of the owner showing up and throwing a fit sends him back to the apartment door.

"Mr. Maxwell," he tries again, calling through the letterbox, but his voice echoes hollowly up the stairs.

The ladder is his only choice and he moves it into position under the trapdoor as stealthily as possible. *This is not only stupid, it has to be illegal,* he tries telling himself as he climbs, though he knows that's not the case — not unless he's planning on murder, rape, theft, or damage — which he's not. Trespassing with intent to take a peek at a suspect passport is a statute yet to be enacted, and Bliss worries more about getting lashed with a riding crop than stung with a prison term.

The trapdoor budges easily with a shove of his shoulder and Bliss is quickly in the loft, but the sound of passing traffic startles him and he is readying to bolt back down the ladder when he spies the door to the apartment in the gloom. *In for a penny* ... he muses, and tries the handle. It's locked, and an enormous cast-iron escutcheon plate suggests that the lock is both old and substantial — though, he suspects, easy to pick with the right equipment.

The light is fading fast as Bliss exits the stables, but he has one more task before he leaves, and a few minutes later he is searching around in the snow for Daphne's shoes and doesn't notice the apparent heir to the estate ride up, his horse's hooves muffled by snow.

"Inspector — are you trespassing on my land for a reason?" calls the rider. "Don't you need a warrant or something?"

"Hot pursuit of a convicted criminal," explains Bliss as he wades out of the drift and gestures to the imprints that Daphne had cut across the grounds to the road. Then he approaches the owner and points to the stables. "I suspect that he took refuge in here during the storm, Mr. Maxwell. That's why there's only one set of tracks."

"But why are you looking here?" the rider demands. "Surely it makes sense to see where the tracks end — not where they begin."

"That's true," says Bliss, stalling momentarily. "But I wondered if he'd stolen anything — guns or weapons of any kind."

"I don't think so."

"Have you checked?"

If Bliss was hoping to worm his way into the apartment he was disappointed. "I'll be sure to phone your station if I find anything amiss, Inspector," says the rider, dismounting and leading his mount toward the stables. "Now, if you'll excuse me ..."

"Thank you, Mr. Jackson," says Bliss, with litte to lose.

The horseman turns with a growl. "It's Maxwell. I told you. I've never heard of Jackson."

"Sorry, I forgot," says Bliss, and he is left with no alternative but to retreat.

The main gates had been padlocked on his arrival and he'd been forced to abandon his car in the roadway and enter by a side gate. Now, the walk up the long driveway in the gloom of dusk is lengthened by the feeling that a pair of eyes are burning into the back of his skull, and it takes all Bliss's willpower to stop himself from turning around.

Bliss is right. The horseman does have a suspicious eye on him and watches him all the way to the gate, then he quickly tethers the horse, lets himself into the apartment and heads for the phone.

Mort, the porn merchant in Vancouver, is still in bed when his phone rings. "Yeah?" he answers.

"It's me," says the apartment dweller, and Mort tells him to hang on while he shoos his latest schoolgirl out.

"Go and do something in the bathroom. Know what I mean, luv?" he says, unsure of her name.

"What, Mort?"

"I don't f'kin' know. Whatever f'kin women spend hours doin' in there. Just f'kin git. Know what I mean?"

"What's up?" Mort demands into the phone as the fifteen-year-old sulks off into the bathroom.

"We've got a problem. The pigs are sniffing around."

"What?"

"Yeah. Some old woman has been shit-disturbing and a snoopy inspector from Scotland Yard's gotten involved somehow."

"Bollocks," says Mort. "He's way off his patch out there. Unless he's National Crime Squad."

"Can we delay for a few weeks 'til it calms down?"

"How much does the dame know?"

"Not much, or he would've gotten a search warrant. It'll probably blow over if we give it time."

"We don't have f'kin time. Maybe she could have a nasty fall — know what I mean?"

"Maybe ... But what's happening at your end? Is it all quiet now?"

"Yeah. Some screwy woman got her jugs on the front page and stirred up the law a bit, but the old doc set 'em straight with the death certificate. Jordan Jackson is just a box of ashes — know what I mean?"

"I've had a call from England about a Jordan Jackson," Phillips had told Ruth as he'd finally prepared to leave for work, and Ruth's expression had drained. "No. Don't fret," he'd continued. "It's probably someone with the same name or somebody has gotten hold of his passport. Probably stole it from his room in that apartment building."

"I'm still trying to come to terms with his death," Ruth had said with a worried mien. "I don't think I could stand another shock."

"You have nothing to worry about. It's not Jordan, I promise," Phillips had said as he'd kissed her goodbye, unaware that he had unleashed another nightmare in her mind. *What if he's not dead?* she'd asked herself. *What if he really did go to L.A. for treatment? What if he turns up cured? Oh my God — what if I lose Mike now?*

chapter fifteen

Ruth sees her world spinning out of kilter again as she waits for a bus to take her to Trina's. It's a couple of months since Jordan's disappearance and, if anything, the news of his death was a relief, even if it did occur several weeks before she actually missed him. The fact that he was no longer suffering was a comfort, so the possibility, however remote, that he may still be alive plays on her mind, and sends her into a convenience store in search of a chocolate bar.

Don't do it.
But I want one, she tells herself at the door.
You know what'll happen.
Just one, I promise.
You can't have just one. You've never had just one.
I will this time; honest.
Phone Trina and ask her, then.
She'll say no.
Don't do it then.

"A Hershey's milk chocolate bar please," says a familiar voice.

I told you not to.

"The family size, Ma'am?"

"Sure. Go for it."

Oh, no — not the family size. What an idiot. You know you can't.

"There's a special on this week, Ma'am. Three for the price of two."

"Oh, great. Yeah. Why not?"

You stupid fat cow.

"That's seven dollars, twenty-three cents, including the tax ma'am."

"I'm not sure that I've got enough," says Ruth searching the bottom of her bag.

"What about that lottery ticket ma'am?" says the assistant, spotting the ragged piece of paper in her purse. "Have you checked it? You never know, you might have won ten bucks."

"It's probably out of date," mumbles Ruth as she hands it to the young man while continuing to count pennies. "How much did you say?"

"Seven-twenty-three," he replies as he scans the ticket. Then he pales and starts to hand it back. "Sorry. I can't pay this ma'am. You'll have to go to the lottery office."

"Oh, I haven't got time for that. Just give me one bar, then."

"But ... but you've won."

"Well give me all three, but hurry, or I'll miss the bus."

"No. I mean you've really won."

"How much?" she asks with a glimmer of understanding.

"I don't think I'm supposed to say," he replies, nervously checking to see if other customers can hear.

"What are you talking about?"

"I think it's supposed to be verified at the office first."

"Look. I'm going to miss the bus in a minute," says Ruth in frustration as she begins opening the chocolate.

"You'll have to ask at the office," says the flustered assistant.

"I will if I've got time. But, like, what is it, fifty or something?"

"It's a little over five million," says the assistant cagily, adding very quickly, "but don't quote me, and don't blame me if the machine's screwed up, either. I'm only telling you what it says here."

"How much?" she says, dropping the chocolate.

Ruth leaves the bar on the floor and walks past the bus stop as the rain begins to pound down. The lottery ticket in her hand is beginning to get saturated, and she puts it back into her purse convinced that the young assistant had made a mistake.

Throw it away then, says the voice in her mind.

But what if you really have won?

Wake up, Ruth. Losers like you never win.

But he said you'd won.

Then what? asks the voice.

Then you can pay back all the money you owe. You can pay Trina — who lied about hiring Hammett and thinks that you didn't figure it out; and her husband and kids who know what you're supposed to have done and adore you anyway. Then there's Mike who's been treating you like a princess for the past few months. And Raven — if it hadn't been for her nagging you would never have bought the ticket. Even Tom, not that he deserves it after lying to the police about you, but at least you wouldn't have to worry about him popping up out of the blue with his grubby hand out.

Yeah. And the moment I walk into the lottery cen-tre the bells will sound and the whistles will blow. "Five million dollar woman," will scream the headlines and the first person on my doorstep will be Jordan's stingy mother, followed by Inspector Wilson, wanting to know why I waited nearly six months to claim a jackpot on a lottery ticket that I just happened to have bought the very day that Jordan supposedly announced that he was supposedly dying of cancer. The very day that he was last seen by anyone who knew him.

But you didn't know you'd won. You didn't even remember buying the ticket.

Isn't that just a teensy bit convenient? says the voice, thinking of Inspector Wilson's reaction. "Now you won't have to share the prize with your husband; you won't even have to repay his mother — after all, it was Jordan's debt, not yours. The old witch was quite adamant about that. 'I'm not lending you this money, young woman,' she told you. 'This money is for my son's business. I hope you understand that. If anything happens to the two of you — he will be keeping the business. And don't think you're going to get half of it either. It was his money that built it, and his money that he keeps.' And all the time you were pleading poverty, saying you couldn't afford a lawyer, you were walking around with five million in your purse."

But I didn't know.

And you think they'll believe you?

"Excuse me, are you OK?" asks a voice from outside as a grey-haired man with his poodle stops in concern.

"Oh. Yes. I'm fine," says Ruth, coming to, amazed to discover that she has walked half a mile and is standing on the beach in Stanley Park where Trina chases the ducks.

"You're getting very wet," says the man as he peers out from under his umbrella and tries to size her up;

then he has an idea. "Maybe you should take my umbrella," he says, but Ruth declines with a smile.

"I'm OK. Honest."

"I'd get you a taxi, but I haven't got enough money."

It doesn't matter. I'm a multi-millionaire, the voice in her mind is trying to tell her, but she knows he'll laugh. "I like walking in the rain," she says, shaking the water from her hair and clearing her mind; then she heads back to the bus stop calling, "Thanks anyway," over her shoulder.

"Hi Trina — sorry I'm late," Ruth calls cheerily twenty minutes later, as she lets herself in the front door and feels something furry brush against her legs.

"Don't let the rabbit ... Oh, shit."

"Sorry Trina," yells Ruth as her friend tears out the door and races down the road in full flight while drivers blare their horns and swerve to avoid her. Ahead of her, a fluffy grey creature hops for its life and eventually disappears through a fence into the woodland.

"I didn't know you had a rabbit." says Ruth, as Trina returns breathless.

"It's a stray. I was going to take it to the pound."

"Trina — that's not a stray. It's a wild rabbit."

"What! Are you sure?"

"Yeah. Quite sure. Where did it come from?"

"It was eating the guinea pig food ... Oh! Oh!" she says and dashes back through the house yelling, "I left the guinea pig out again."

As Trina dances around the back garden, Ruth smiles, puts on her apron, and starts clearing the Button household breakfast dishes just like any other day of late.

Why are you doing this, you stupid woman? You just won five million bucks.

"And pigs might fly," she says aloud.

But you have.

So what if I have? she tells herself. *Do you think Trina and her family would want me doing their dishes and washing their underwear if they knew? Do you think they'd still want me living in their basement? Do you think Mike would still trust me if he thought I'd kept it secret? Do you think it would make me happy?*

You could buy your own house.

And live in it all by myself 'til I go back to jail — all by myself.

You could treat yourself.

With candy bars and steak dinners — that's all I need.

You could treat Mike and Trina.

The question in her mind stops her halfway to the sink with a stack of cereal bowls as she thinks her way around Trina's life and her house. *What could I possibly give her?* She already has a magazine lifestyle; a beautiful home with a terrific view, a husband who loves her so much he forgives her for everything; two kids — one of each, just as it should be. She could be at the gym, skiing, or having her face done if she wanted, but she'd rather be washing old men's bums and rounding up strays.

What are you going to do?

Nothing.

You can't do nothing.

Just watch me.

"So, how was big Mike last night?" giggles Trina, giving Ruth a knowing nudge, once the guinea pig is safely back in its cage.

"You're disgusting," laughs Ruth, then tries changing the subject. "I thought you said the guinea pig was pregnant."

"False alarm ... I told you he liked you the first time I saw him looking at you."

"How do you know?"

"Well, he may be a Mountie, but I don't think that was a pistol in his pocket."

"You really are disgusting," Ruth continues laughing. "Anyway, I meant 'how do you know' the guinea pig isn't pregnant?"

Trina turns sheepish. "I took it to the vet."

"And?"

"It's a boy ... He said I overfed it, then he got cross with me 'cuz I wouldn't pay the fifty bucks for the pregnancy test. "I've told you it's not pregnant," he said, "so now you have to pay." But I said, "Of course it's not pregnant — boys don't get pregnant, but I wouldn't have the guts to charge you fifty bucks for telling you that." Anyway, in the end I gave him ten and he was really nice about it. He even gave me the name of a new vet who's much closer."

"Trina?" says Ruth, pulling her face straight once she's stopped laughing. "You don't mind me staying here do you?"

"Are you kidding? Rob and Kylie would kill me if you left." Then she gives Ruth a suspicious eye and screeches in delight. "Oh my God — you're moving in with Mike."

"No," says Ruth. "He lives in a hotel. Anyway, he's only here 'til April."

"So?"

"I can't. I'm married."

Trina's face drops and she peers deeply into her friend's eyes. "Ruth, you're not going again are you?"

"Going where?"

"Like ... You are feeling all right, aren't you?"

"Yeah. I'm fine. Why?"

"'Cuz you're not married anymore. You're a free woman again. You can sleep with anyone you want now."

"Trina," she scolds, though she adds inquisitively, "You know it's funny, but I never really thought of it like that. I just don't have that feeling of freedom that I used to have when I was single."

"That's because you never saw his body, and that witch of a woman wouldn't let you have his ashes."

"Is that all he is now — ashes?"

"I did a roast chicken like that once," laughs Trina as she scoots around getting ready for work. "I put it in the oven and forgot we were going away for the weekend." Then she stops with a thought. "Maybe you should visit Jordan's doctor — the one who issued the certificate. It'll give you a sense of closure. I'll come with you if you'd like."

"Would you?"

"Of course I will. In fact I'll call right now and get an appointment as soon as possible."

"Dr. Fitzpatrick isn't taking any new patients," the receptionist tells Trina when she tries to book an appointment, and the girl is hesitant when Trina explains the circumstances. "I'll have to ask the doctor and get back to you," she says.

Mike calls as Trina hangs up and Ruth glows as her friend hands her the phone, saying in a comically dark whisper, "It's a Mountie with a shooter in his pants for Ruth. I'm off to work. See you later."

"Oh, Trina ..." rebukes Ruth as she takes the phone.

"I just wanted to put your mind at ease over that passport," Mike Phillips tells her. "I've had a word with someone in the Immigration Department and they've got at least sixty Jordan Jacksons on their books. The passport could belong to any one of them."

David Bliss is of the same opinion when Phillips calls him back later that evening. Daphne is upstairs, safely snuggled in her own little bed, while Minnie and the remainder of the geriatric mob have cleaned up after the party and have gone home, leaving Bliss contentedly in front of the fire with a large scotch, mulling over the events of the day and contemplating how different things may have turned out.

"Thanks for checking, Mike," he says to his Canadian counterpart. "But, to be honest, I suspect Daphne might have got her knickers in a twist over nothing. There could be dozens of valid reasons why Maxwell might have someone else's passport. He might even have a man friend staying there that he doesn't want Daphne to know about — if you get my drift."

"Didn't she think it was Maxwell's photo, though?" queries Phillips.

"She did. But I'm beginning to worry about her eyesight, to be honest, and you know what passport pickies are like. I wouldn't be able to spot myself, let alone a stranger."

"OK, Dave. But I did turn up something interesting on a Jeremy Maxwell. I thought I recognized the name, though it might not be the same guy."

"What have you got?" asks Bliss, sitting up a notch.

"No convictions, but that name's cropped up a few times when we've managed to get people on the inside. In fact there is a 'locate request' out on him at the moment — though whether or not he's the same Maxwell that Daphne knows is anybody's guess."

"Interesting," says Bliss, and he promises to call if he can get any further information on the new man at the manor, adding as an afterthought, "I don't suppose you've got pictures of either of them in your files, have you?"

"No; sorry, Dave. Like I said, Maxwell is clean and nobody seems to have any photos of Jackson — not even his wife."

Dr. Fitzpatrick is another person who doesn't have any pictures of Jordan Jackson, although it took Trina's chutzpah to find that out. Margery, his receptionist, had not called her back as promised, so late that afternoon Trina had taken matters into her own hands and turned up at his office with Ruth in tow, saying, "We'll just wait here until the doctor has time to see us."

"He won't see you without an appointment," the receptionist had warned, but Trina seemed to think that he would. "We'll take that chance," she'd said, confidently plunking herself down in a comfortable chair and picking up a nine-year-old *Reader's Digest*. Ruth was less sure and had hovered nervously until Trina had whispered, "Don't worry, I've done this dozens of times. They always cave in the end."

By five forty-five the receptionist had relented as predicted, and had slotted Ruth in for a five minute consultation close to the end of the day in lieu of a no-show, but Dr. Fitzpatrick is far from happy at the visit, and sits with his arms folded at a cleared desk.

"I've told the police all I know," he says tersely, once Trina has explained the situation. "It was a straightforward case."

"Apart from the fact that no one notified his wife," digs Trina as if Ruth is not in the room.

"Not my responsibility," shrugs Fitzpatrick. "All I can tell you is that he died of cancer back in November. I assumed the funeral director would notify next of kin."

"Do you have any pictures of Mr. Jackson?" asks Trina, searching for something solid to show Ruth.

Fitzpatrick gives her an odd look, then snaps, "We don't photograph our patients, Miss."

"No, I meant X-rays or CAT scans," explains Trina. "Something that Ruth could keep as a memento."

"No, I don't ... Like I told the police, he refused treatment."

"So, you didn't prescribe any drugs at all?"

"Nothing."

"Surely you prescribed something for the pain."

Fitzpatrick shrugs. "He had his own way of dealing with it."

"He smoked medicinal marijuana," pipes up Ruth, adding credence.

"Maybe if you just showed Ruth his notes then," suggests Trina, desperately searching for some way of solidifying Jordan's demise in Ruth's mind.

"Sorry. They're confidential," Fitzpatrick says, shaking his head.

"But this is his poor wife," Trina insists, noticing that Ruth has started to cry. "What difference would it make? In any case, he's dead. He can't object."

"Sorry, I can't help you. They are destroyed once a person is deceased. Now, if you'll excuse me, I really do have to get on. Patients are waiting."

The doctor's waiting room is surprisingly empty as they leave the office, and Margery is putting on her coat.

"You closing now?" asks Trina jovially.

The young receptionist checks the clock. "Yeah. We finished ten minutes ago — good night."

"I think he was just trying to get rid of us," snivels Ruth as they make for Trina's car. "That was a complete waste of time."

"You're right," says Trina. "He was very rude. I wonder why?"

Doctor Fitzpatrick has a furrowed brow as he watches from his office window and sees the two women getting into Trina's Jetta, but he waits until Margery has called, "Good night, Doctor," and closed the office door behind her, before picking up the phone.

Trina is still puzzled as she drives away. *I'd like to know where Jordan got the Zofran pills from,* she muses to herself, and the fact that Fitzpatrick has destroyed Jordan's file has her scratching her head. "What if there's been a mix-up over the drugs and someone wants to sue?" she says to herself, then turns to Ruth to explain, "I'm sure he shouldn't have destroyed Jordan's file. I'll speak to someone about that."

"Don't cause any trouble, Trina. It's not worth it. I'm OK now that I've seen him, even if he was miserable. And I guess you're right — I am single again."

"Great," yells Trina, then she gives Ruth a sly glance. "Does that mean you want to be dropped off at Mike's place, then?"

The phone is ringing in an adjacent office as Constable Vernon McLeod of the RCMP, alias Dave the photographer at Mort's porn studio, keeps the film rolling as one of the Englishman's heavies mugs for the camera with a young actress. "Get hold of it properly," shouts Joshua, the goon, as he grabs the hesitant young woman's hand and forces it to his groin. "It won't f'kin bite ya." Then he turns to McLeod. "OK, Davey boy. Get a close up as I ..."

"Josh?" yells Mort from the adjoining room. "Get in here."

"Hang on, Mort ..."

"Now!"

"What's up, Boss?" asks Joshua as he enters and closes the door, still zipping up his fly.

Behind him, McLeod plugs an earphone into his ear and fiddles with a control on the camera while he says to the girl, "You can get dressed now."

"Where do I get paid?" she asks naively as she pulls on her panties.

The audio feed from a radio microphone, carefully buried in the wall of Mort's office, comes through as clear as the CBC in McLeod's earpiece and, as the girl dresses, he touches a button and starts a recording while pretending to adjust the bulky camera. "You only get paid when Mort sells them," he says, and the girl's face falls as he tunes into Mort complaining about Trina.

"The stupid woman has been mixing things up at the doc's now. I've just had him bleating on the phone. She just can't f'kin leave it alone."

"I thought Tom said he'd dealt with her."

"He's a useless piece of shit. I dunno why I bother with him to be honest. All he had to do was put the frighteners on her."

"He said that he had."

"Well it didn't work," shouts Mort, slamming his fist on the desk. "I mean, for chrissake, why the hell did he give the Jackson broad ten grand in the first place? He's a bloody moron."

"He didn't know about Jordan, Boss."

"He f'kin shoulda done. Jeez, anyone would think I'm runnin' a kiddies' playschool."

"What do you want me to do?"

"Tell Tom to come and see me," he spits. "But don't tell him too gently — know what I mean? I'm totally pissed off with that little creep, playing the big shot with his stupid bloody magazines." Then he stops briefly to mimic Tom in a silly voice as he simpers, "Have you seen my absolutely whopping great big f'kin boat?"

Joshua laughs as Mort carries on. "He's a lying little shit and it's time he learnt who's in charge — know what I mean?"

"Sure Mort, I'll get Dingo to give me a hand."

"Right. Not too bad, mind. I still want him in one piece so that he can do something about that Button bird — know what I mean?"

Daphne Lovelace is her usual indomitable self the morning following her ordeal, and is up at her usual hour, raking out the embers and re-laying the fire.

"I expected you to have a lie-in this morning," says Bliss as he opens the curtains and stretches in the warm rays of sunshine.

"God knows why they made all that fuss at the hospital," replies Daphne, demonstrating her fortitude by snapping some kindling. "I told them there was nothing the matter with me that a hot toddie and a warm bath wouldn't fix, but they wouldn't believe me."

"You really ought to take it easy for a few days," says Bliss, as he carts the bucket of ashes out to the garden and spies a bald spot on one side of Daphne's potted Christmas tree. "That blasted Minnie," he moans, quickly turning the damage to the wall.

"Actually, I was thinking of going back to the manor," says Daphne as he re-enters, and he shoots her down. "No you will not."

"Why not, David? Besides, he'll get suspicious if I don't show up again. Anyway, I keep telling you he's Jackson — I saw his photo in the passport. It's him for sure."

"And what if he's found your shoes?"

"Well, he won't know how they got there. In any case, he's a man. What man ever notices the shoes of a slightly older woman? At any rate, what could he possibly do to me?"

Tom Burton in Vancouver is definitely having a "lie-in" this morning, but he has no such worries about what could happen to him — he already knows. Joshua and Dingo had shown up just after supper and bounced him from one end of his grotty basement to the other like a ping-pong ball as they'd rammed home Mort's message. Tom's new wide-screen television, his DVD player, his computer, and every stick of furniture he possessed had managed to get in his way as he had been flung back and forth by Mort's two gorillas.

"Mort wants you to sort out the Button broad properly," Joshua had said, lifting Tom's head off the bloodstained carpet by his hair, once the damage had been done. "And he's ticked off with all your f'kin B.S., so be a good man and stop pissing him about or you might get hurt real bad."

Tom hasn't moved from the floor all night, and knows that he needs a doctor, but Dingo had ripped his phone off the wall and trampled it to pieces as soon as they had arrived. "Just in case you get any silly ideas," the goon had said.

Trina Button, on the other hand, does have a phone — a payphone in the foyer of the Pacific Mall — and she too has a doctor in mind when she puts on a husky tone to call the Health Ministry's accounts department, where her prayers are answered.

"I'm new here," says Candace, the clerk, when Trina claims that she doesn't recognize the young woman's voice.

"Oh. Hi, Candace," continues Trina sounding forlorn. "I'm Margery Woods calling from Dr. Fitzpatrick's office; Dr. William Fitzpatrick on Hastings. Look I'm in a lot of trouble and I really, really need your help. Don't tell anyone for Christ's sake, but I think I've totally screwed up this time and I'm gonna get fired."

"Oh my gosh. What have you done?" asks Candace, clearly feeling for her.

"I think I've totally over-billed the insurance company on one of our patients," Trina whimpers and goes on to give Jordan's particulars before saying. "I won't go to jail, will I? I mean, it was an accident — honest. You won't call the police, will you?"

"No. Stop worrying. I can sort it out. Let me just check his records."

"No record at all?" exclaims Trina in disbelief a few minutes later when Candace gives her the news. "It's worse than I thought, then. Are you absolutely certain?"

"Yes. Quite sure. According to this, Jordan Jackson hasn't visited a doctor in more than five years, so you're in the clear. Just submit the correct bill now and no one will ever know the difference. My lips are sealed."

"Oh, Candace. You're fantastic. Thanks so much," warbles Trina, more puzzled than ever as she puts down the phone and heads back to her car without noticing that Dingo is on her tail.

Mort's black BMW idles silently in the parking lot as Dingo peels off from Trina, slips into the back seat and reports.

"I didn't hear much, Mort, but I think she's on to Fitzpatrick."

"Fuck. Who was she talking to?"

"Someone called Candy I think, but I couldn't hear much. Though she definitely said Jackson's name."

Jackson is also on Daphne's mind the following morning as Bliss drops her at the gates of Thraxton Manor.

"I don't agree with this at all," he tells her for the nth time, but she blanks him out.

"I've got your cellphone, David, and I'll call as soon as I'm ready to be picked up."

"Don't forget what I said. Just press '1' then 'send' for the police station if there is any problem. Are you sure you don't want me to come in with you?"

"Good grief, no. That really would make him suspicious."

"Are you quite certain about this?" he tries for a final time.

"David. Did I ever tell you about the time that I talked my way into the Russian Embassy in Cairo and slipped out the back with a defecting East German scientist?"

"You didn't ..." he begins, but capitulates. "All right, you win. Just make sure you call. I'll be waiting."

Daphne is nonchalant as she jauntily strolls through the gate and up the driveway, humming Ringo's "Act Naturally" to herself. The spotlight of springtime has rallied against winter's final fling, and the speed of the thaw has been remarkable. It's only been three days since the blizzard, yet the early risers are already pushing up through the grass. Swathes of snowdrops and yellow crocuses line the approach to the old manor with abandoned profusion, while ribbons of snow, sheltering under hedges and in ditches, still frame the surrounding green fields in white.

Maxwell, a.k.a. Jackson, is stiff as he meets Daphne at the apartment's front door, and he doesn't soften as she climbs the stairs ahead of him, prattling on about the lovely sunshine and how it's so nice to have gotten out again after being forced to stay inside since the storm. "I do hope you managed all right without me," she is saying as she walks into the kitchen and finds her missing shoes sitting accusingly on the table.

"Oh. You found my shoes," she cries in delight. "You clever man. I wondered if I would ever see them again. They're one of my most comfortable pairs. Wherever did you find them?"

"They were in the grounds," he says dryly.

"Oh dear. They must've dropped from my bag the day before the storm when I came and you were out. It was such a lovely day, so I walked around the garden. I remember when your dad ..."

"Well, I'm not my father," he butts in harshly. "So in future I'd rather you didn't just wander around when I'm not here. Anyway, how could you have gotten home without your shoes?"

Daphne ignores the coldness and pushes ahead with the script she's already practiced in her mind as she picks up the shoes. "These are my working shoes. I always wear walking shoes to get here — you must've noticed. These must have fallen out of my bag when I sat on the lawn."

"They were under the snow."

"That would be right, Jeremy," she says slipping them in her bag with ease and pulling out her duster and furniture polish. "It was the day before the big storm. Thank you ever so much. I'm really quite fond of them."

But the apartment dweller has an edge to his voice as he takes hold of the spray can, saying, "Look, Daphne ..."

"Daffodil ... Remember, Jeremy? When you were a little boy, you always called me Auntie Daffodil."

"Yes, precisely," he says. "But I'm not a boy now and I can manage perfectly well, so, to be honest, I really don't think you should come anymore."

Daphne picks up a smile as she takes the can back and boldly sprays the table. "Oh, I don't mind ..."

"Well I do," shouts the occupant as he grabs the can and throws it into the garbage. "Now just leave me alone you old bat, and don't come back."

"Jeremy would never have spoken to me like that," Daphne bitches ten minutes later as she relates the experience to Bliss when he picks her up near the manor's gates. "Monty would have wrung his neck."

"But that was forty years ago," he reminds her as they drive away.

"People don't change that much, David," she says, still full of umbrage. "He was a nice boy then, and he would be a nice man today. He is definitely not my little Jeremy."

"Never mind," says Bliss. "How about lunch at the Mitre Hotel to cheer you up? My treat."

"I'd like that, David," she says, perking up; then she adds mischievously, "The food's quite good there now that Mavis has retired."

"By the way," he says as he drives into the city, "speaking of Mavis, I've had another phone call from the newspaper guy in Liverpool."

Once Bliss had dropped Daphne off close to the gates of Thraxton Manor, he had raced back to the house and had been dancing around the phone awaiting her call, when the features-editor of the *Merseyside Mail* had called.

"I'm just doing a follow up," the familiar voice had said. "Would you happen to know if Ms. Lovelace managed to track down all the people in the Beatles' photo?"

"Yes, thanks. Apart from someone called Geoffrey Sanderson, I believe," Bliss had answered, hoping to end it there.

"So Mrs. Longbottom is still planning the reunion then?"

"Oh yes. I think so," he'd replied, wishing Daphne were home to do the lying.

"OK. Well we'll run the photo and a little blurb asking if anyone knows the whereabouts of Geoffrey. Can you tell me anything else about him?"

"Not really. He'd be in his sixties — probably — and his old next door neighbour thought he might have stayed in Canada after the tour."

"Oh, that's interesting," the editor had said. "If we don't turn up anything here, I'll have a word with a Canadian reporter I know. See if we can get something rolling out there."

"This is very good of you."

"Not really. Good human-interest stories with happy endings aren't that easy to come by. Who knows, we might even be able to get Sir Paul or Ringo to attend — now that would be a scoop."

"Daphne Lovelace, OBE," Bliss had said to the air once he'd put the phone down. "You are going to be in big trouble with Mavis Longbottom."

"Oh, you are an old worrywart," Daphne laughs, once Bliss has recounted the gist of the call and they arrive at the Mitre. "How on earth is Mavis ever going to find out?"

Superintendent Donaldson has also chosen the Mitre for lunch and is thrilled to see that Daphne has fully recovered. "This is on me," he insists as they wait in the lounge bar to order.

"I told you the food had picked up," says the senior officer as the three of them choose the day's special of steak and oyster pudding, with asparagus spears and creamed spinach, followed by Bramley apple crumble and custard.

"You were lucky to get sausage and mash before," sneers Daphne, then she outlines the details of her recent visit to the manor, saying to Donaldson, "You've got to arrest him, Superintendent. He's a charlatan."

"Daphne, my dear," replies Donaldson with a kindly hand on her arm. "To be perfectly honest, I'm not sure I can do anything at all. I'd never persuade the Magistrate to give me a search warrant because you thought you saw a dodgy passport when you were trespassing in someone's apartment."

"But he's claiming to be Jeremy Maxwell," she complains bitterly.

"He can claim to be George III if he wants, Daphne. As long as he's not doing it with intent to defraud."

"But he's living on the Maxwell estate."

"So you're going to have to dig up the real Maxwell to swear on the Good Book that he's been diddled out of his inheritance by an impostor; otherwise, I don't see what I can do."

"We could run both the names through the computer to see if there's anything known," suggests Bliss, and Donaldson quickly agrees.

"OK, Dave. Stop by the station once you've dropped Daphne off at home after lunch and we'll have a look."

Lunch at the Mitre had been everything that Donaldson claimed it would be. However, he is still rounding it off with a cup of tea and a handful of chocolate digestive cookies when Bliss shows up to check the criminal records at three.

"Would you like a biscuit, Dave?" offers Donaldson, as Bliss spells out the names, but he shakes his head, laughing. "You'll explode one of these days, sir."

"Ah, but I'll explode happy, David," he replies, then goes on to say that without full names and dates of birth it may be very difficult to get a match on either of the two men.

"I realize that," says Bliss, well used to the problems of information overload, and, after the computer has spent a few seconds in electronic thought, he's proven correct. Nearly a thousand Jeremy Maxwells and over five-hundred Jordan Jacksons have somehow found their way into the archives over the past thirty years, and separating out the inhabitant of Thraxton Manor proves impossible.

"It might be easier if we had a photo," says Bliss, and Donaldson has an idea.

"I'll send one of our surveillance guys out to snap a mug shot of him," the senior officer says, adding, "but only because it's Daphne Lovelace saying it. I sometimes wonder how we manage without her still around."

"Thank you, sir," says Bliss. "I'm sure that will make her happy. And I can send a copy to my contact in Vancouver to see if they can ID him."

chapter sixteen

The temptation to tell Ruth that the doctor had lied about treating Jordan leaves Trina Button with a major headache — if Fitzpatrick hadn't seen Jordan since September, if ever, why had he signed a death certificate? Answers may lie in the box of Zofran pills found in Jordan's room, Trina suspects, and she is on the trail of the pharmacist who sold them. She had wheedled the box out of Sergeant Brougham, despite the fact that the officer had gotten his mind entrenched in prosecution mode, and was still trying to claim that they were material evidence in a murder case.

"And precisely whose murder are you talking about in particular?" Trina had demanded of Brougham, as she'd challenged him in the foyer of the police station, then she'd openly switched on her mini tape recorder and defiantly held it under his nose as she awaited a response.

"Turn that off," he'd ordered, trying to snatch the tiny machine, but she had spun away and adroitly dropped it down the front of her nurse's uniform, shouting loudly to the desk clerk, "Sergeant Brougham is assaulting me. I want to lay charges."

All heads had swivelled their way and Brougham had backed off faster than if he'd been stung. "I'm not going to touch you as long as you turn it off," he'd angrily protested, but Trina had kept up her vociferous tirade.

"Sergeant Brougham is now attempting to blackmail me," she had ranted, attracting the attention of several members of the public and a passing policewoman.

"Just turn it off, damn you."

"Sergeant Brougham is now swearing at me."

"I'll throttle you ..."

"Sergeant Brougham has just threatened to kill me. I have it on tape. Call the police."

"Shut up, you stupid woman. This is a police station."

"He's swearing at me again."

"I'll arrest you if you don't stop it."

"I am now being unlawfully arrested by Sergeant Brougham ..." she had yelled at the top of her voice and had slapped her wrists together and held them up in front of his face.

"All right, all right. You can take the damn pills."

The first pharmacist to whom Trina had shown the box had clearly been disinterested. "I have no idea where they came from," he'd told her. "And without the label you'll never find out." But the white-coated man in a second drugstore has other ideas.

"You're in luck," he says as he turns the small box in his hand, "Zofran aren't usually sold in blister-packs. You probably won't find more than a couple of places in Vancouver who sell them like this. Here," he says, reaching under the counter for a typed list of all the pharmacies in the area, "all you need is a phone."

It takes Trina an hour to check all the drugstores on the list, and she discovers that the pharmacist had been correct. Assuming that the Zofran were purchased in the Vancouver area, there were only two possible sources, both miles apart, but they will have to wait — she has patients to take care of, and she needs a coffee.

Trina Button may be banned from the Corner Coffee Shoppe, but she still peeks nostalgically in the windows as she passes. The cream cakes and cholesterol dreams are back, but the customers are not, and the café has slid downhill since Ruth's flab-fighting days.

Cindy is still there, standing on a table to wipe the dust off a lampshade, and she gives Trina a brave smile and a nervous thumbs-up. Dave, the bum-pinching telephone engineer, seems to be the only customer, and he lies back in his chair pretending to read the morning paper as he tries to see up Cindy's skirt and snatch a glimpse of her panties. There could be a few other diners keeping out of the spotlight in the back, but Trina doesn't notice them as she gives Cindy a wave and walks on.

The crossworders have now set up shop permanently in Donut Delight, following an abortive return to their old haunt in January, when Gwenda Jackson had harassed them away by constantly bleating about people stretching coffees and stealing pencils from the cash desk. It's mid-morning; Darcey, Maureen, and Matt have only a couple of intractable clues left when Trina barges in.

"'QINDARKA' — 74-down," she says without even checking the clue.

"How do you know?" demands Darcey.

"It's the only eight-letter word in the English language that begins with a Q which isn't followed by a U," she says, as if it's the sort of thing everyone knows.

"Hi Trina," calls Raven as the lanky woman brings a tray of donuts from the kitchen. "How's Ruth?"

"She's much better," answers Trina, then she queries, "Are you working here now, Raven?"

Raven puts down her tray and wanders over. "I've had to give up being a channel," she admits with a drawn face. "Serethusa's let me down so much that I don't trust her anymore. I mean, look what I did to Ruth. She was so happy when I told her that Jordan would be all right, then he turned up on the other side."

"Yeah. And you were wrong about my accident as well," reminds Trina.

"I said 'bus' ... Oh, never mind. Do you want a coffee?"

"Yeah. To go, please. If I don't get a move-on I'll be up to my neck in exploding colostomy bags."

"Trina!" rebukes Darcey as she looks up from the puzzle. "This is a café you know."

"Cobblers," says Trina, pointing to 72-across, then she grabs her coffee and makes for the door.

Raven's parting admonition to Trina to "Watch out for traffic," comes just in time as she steps onto the narrow sidewalk and feels the wind blast as Tom's sun-blistered Toyota skims by her. "Hey!" Trina yells, almost dropping her coffee in alarm, but the conman's mind is mired in concern, and he doesn't notice her.

Tom is headed for an appointment with his boss, and a few minutes later he finds a space and hobbles across a parking lot toward Mort, who is sitting in his car overlooking the port, while smiling wryly at the approaching figure. Tom has licked his wounds for a day or so, and he crawls painfully into the BMW's front passenger seat in submission, saying, "Josh said you wanted to see me, Mort?"

Mort says nothing and lets the tension build as he stares ahead to watch a slab-sided leviathan of a ship being loaded with containers.

"D'ye know how I got this?" Mort snorts eventually, sticking the stump of his right arm in Tom's face. "'Cos I screwed up bad. Now," he adds menacingly, "unless you want this to happen to you, you'd better stop that Button bitch from asking anymore questions — know what I mean?"

"Yeah, but ..."

"I mean," Mort carries on as if Tom hasn't spoken, "look at it from my point of view, Tom. You give Jackson's bit of slack my ten grand, she gives it to her old man, and he gives it back to me. I mean — what sort of f'kin business is that? Know what I mean?"

"But I didn't know he owed you the money, Mort; honest," whines Tom. "She told me he was dying."

"He wuz, you f'kin prat. He wuz dying. He wuz dying to get away from her, the fat cow, and his bitching mother, and he wuz supposed to pay me to make him die — know what I mean?"

"You didn't tell me ..." Tom starts but Mort holds up his amputated arm in warning.

"See that?" says Mort, using the stump to point at a container rig entering the dock area, and they watch as the huge truck is manoeuvred alongside the berthed ship in the port below them.

"Yeah," says Tom.

"That container is stuffed chock-full of the finest British Columbian product that money can buy — know what I mean?"

"Yeah, Mort."

"Good. Well there's another twenty just like that one. And the last f'kin thing I need is for any nosy stupid bitch to make waves with the law — know what I mean?"

"Yeah, but ..."

"Good. So, how are you gonna stop the Button woman from lousing up my entire f'kin organization?"

It is mid-afternoon by the time Trina has finished her rounds, and she is completely unaware of the danger she is facing as she heads off to interrogate the pharmacists at the two potential drugstores. Tom is on the tail of her Volkswagen in his beat-up Toyota, but he's still smarting from his previous confrontation with her, so he has devised what he believes to be a safer approach, and once he is certain that she is headed away from her home, he spins back.

Trina's house appears deserted as Tom drives by, then he parks around the block while he writes a note with a felt-tipped pen on a ragged piece of paper.

Trina's driveway is clear when Tom returns on foot a few minutes later, but he thinks of himself as a pro, so he also checks the garage, and even scrutinizes the neighbours' windows for signs of life, before pulling on a pair of surgical gloves and slipping around the side of the house.

Ruth is in Trina's kitchen, with its spectacular garden outlook, and is preparing dinner for the Buttons — oyster paella for the adults; spaghetti Bolognese for the teens, but she has other plans for herself; Mike Phillips is taking her out to dinner — again.

"I've got something very serious I want to ask you," he had said when he'd phoned earlier, and her heart had momentarily skipped, though something in his tone suggested that it wasn't necessarily good news.

Ruth sniffs and licks at the tears dribbling down her cheeks as she chops onions for the pasta sauce, then, when she looks up to wipe her eyes, she catches a movement in the garden through the mist of tears. "What the hell ..." she starts, and stares in disbelief as Tom takes a final furtive look around before grabbing the guinea pig out of its cage.

"That's Tom ..." she muses, then she dashes for the phone as something solid slams into the wooden back door and makes her jump.

It has taken Trina nearly an hour to find one of the pharmacies that may have sold Zofran in blister-packs, and she has just managed to beat a slow-footed pickup driver into a parking space when her cell-phone rings.

"Trina Button ..." she starts, but is cut off by Ruth's wail.

"Trina," she screams. "It's me. You've got to come home now."

"But I'm ..."

"Now Trina, please," she cries. "Tom's trying to break in."

"Oh, man!" Trina moans, then yells, "I'll call the police," as she steps on the gas and dings the fender of a parked car. "Stupid place to park," she screams, as she scorches away with one hand on the wheel and the other on her phone, dialling 911.

The police arrive first, and Ruth still has a carving knife in her hand as she answers the front door to a couple of uniformed officers with guns drawn.

"Mrs. Button?" queries one of the officers, trying to look past her into the hallway.

"No, I'm Ruth Jackson," explains Ruth, but doesn't realize that the guns are trained on her.

"Put the weapon down, ma'am," says one of the officers, a lumpy female.

"It's just a kitchen knife ..." Ruth starts, but the woman isn't listening and keeps up the pressure.

"I said 'Put the weapon down.' This is your last chance."

"OK, OK," says Ruth, but she's frozen with fear and doesn't move.

"Intruder is armed with a knife," the male officer calls into his radio, and Ruth goes cold as she relives the recent past.

"Please don't shoot," she pleads as the guns hold steady. "You've got it wrong. I didn't kill my husband."

"Put the weapon down now," spits the female officer. "Put it down."

"But I haven't ..."

"Put it down," yells the man, and the knife clatters onto the ceramic tiles at Ruth's feet.

"Good. Now step away from the weapon and put your hands on your head."

Trina's arrival brings a degree of sanity to the situation as she skids her Jetta to a halt with the aid of the parked police cruiser, and she runs up the driveway shouting, "Police brutality! Don't shoot. Don't shoot. You've got the wrong man."

"Oh, for chrissake. Not you again!" exclaims the female, recognizing Trina from her imbroglio with Sergeant Brougham earlier in the day, and Trina whips out her tape recorder and presses 'Record.'

"I think he's gone," Ruth tells them shakily after Trina has smoothed things over. "I would have gone after him, but he looked so fierce."

"Did you recognize him ma'am?" asks the female officer as she guides Ruth back to the kitchen.

"Yes. He's Tom something-or-other. Inspector Wilson knows his name."

"Inspector Wilson?" queries the officer and Ruth regrets saying it as she finds herself explaining her recent spell of incarceration.

"And you think this is revenge for cutting his throat?" asks the male officer skeptically, but Ruth is absolutely positive.

"I knew he'd track me down eventually."

"So, did he take anything?" asks the woman constable, moving on, and Ruth points to the empty cage in the garden. "Just the guinea pig."

But Ruth is wrong. Tom hasn't stolen the furry little creature. It is still there, in the back garden, though not in its cage. It is now skewered by the slender blade of a stiletto and pinioned to the back door, where it hangs lifeless, like a child's stuffed toy on a coat hook. Tom's warning note is pinned against the door by the poor creature's body.

"Oh my God," keens Ruth at the find, and Trina rushes to comfort her.

"Buddy has been watching too many *Godfather* movies," says the constable as he prepares to withdraw the blade.

"Wait a minute," yells Trina, letting go of Ruth to grab the policeman's hand. "He moved."

"I don't think so," says the officer as an unmarked cruiser screeches to a halt in the street and Mike Phillips comes running.

"Are you all right, Ruth?" Phillips says as he bundles the crying woman into his arms, but Trina won't release the uniformed officer's arm, shouting, "I think he's still alive. Call a vet."

"It's dead. It's got a knife sticking ..." begins the constable, but Trina pulls rank and rounds on him. "Constable, I'm personally acquainted with your Sergeant Brougham. Now call a vet before I tell him what a jerk you are."

"Sorry, ma'am," says the officer. "But I'll get into trouble ..."

"DS Phillips, RCMP," says the Mountie stepping forward. "Call for a vet, officer. I'll take responsibility."

"Right Sergeant. If you say so," he says and, as he radios his station, Mike Phillips carefully extracts the blade and releases the crucified animal while Trina begins mouth-to-mouth resuscitation.

"You're joking ..." laughs the constable, but he gets a black look from Phillips as Trina delicately massages the tiny body while gently blowing. Then she stops and shrieks, "Yes!" as she feels a tiny organ bumping away under her fingertips. "His heart's still beating," she yells, heading for the kitchen. "Quick. Put the oven on, Ruth."

"What?" exclaims the officer.

"We might need to warm him up."

By the time a vet arrives, the little animal has pulled itself together without the need of heat, and is frantically scooting around the kitchen floor.

"It's a miracle," says the smart young vet as she lifts the plucky little rodent and carefully examines him on the kitchen table. "The knife must have missed all the vital organs. I'll have to take him for an X-ray and observation, but he seems fine."

Trina laughs in relief, but Ruth's mind is clouded by the thought of Tom's misspelled threat, scrawled in a pretty shade of salmon. "YOU'VE BIN WARNED. YOUR NEXT," says the note, now in an evidence bag in the constable's hand, and Ruth turns to Trina.

"I ought to find somewhere else to live. I've caused you so much trouble."

"What are you talking about?"

"It's me he's after, Trina. It's me who owes him the money."

"Not after this you don't," says the constable, flourishing the note. "Uttering a death threat should keep him locked up for quite awhile."

"Maybe I should take Ruth on a little vacation for a few days, just until he's caught," suggests Phillips, and Trina sees a twinkle in his eye.

"You'll have to take my kids as well," she teases as she gives Ruth a cheeky nudge. "They'll starve to death without her."

"First, we're going to dinner," says Phillips as he hands Ruth her purse, but she turns to her friend.

"I haven't finished cooking ..."

"Get out of here," laughs Trina, bundling her toward the basement apartment. "Go and gussy yourself up for the nice man while I make him a coffee. And hurry up."

The restaurant Phillips has selected for dinner is a ritzy Japanese diner just off the waterfront, and they sit waiting for their soup while watching the water-busses buzz back and forth across the harbour.

"You remember I said I wanted to ask you something," says Phillips with a serious mien, and Ruth confesses that she had forgotten amidst the afternoon's brouhaha.

"This isn't going to be easy ..." Phillips carries on, as if to himself, leaving Ruth wondering if he is about to propose.

Oh, God. This is too soon, she says to herself. *Jordan's only been gone a couple of months.*

Three and a half months, contradicts another voice. *Remember the date on the death certificate.*

"The fact is, Ruth," Phillips starts hesitantly, "that I need to talk to you about your mother."

"My mother?"

Tough luck, says the voice, but inwardly she lets out a sigh. Not that she wouldn't love to marry him, it is simply that she is still burdened by Jordan, and the visit to Dr. Fitzpatrick hadn't helped, even if she had told Trina that it had.

"What about my mother?" she wants to know and Phillips puts on his policeman's mantle as he explains that his detachment is looking into the disappearance of a number of women from Vancouver's streets.

"You said that she just vanished," he reminds her, then swears her to secrecy before admitting that a serial killer could be at work. "Wouldn't you like to know what happened to her?" he asks, but she starts to shake her head, saying, "She wasn't a good mother ..." But it's a line that has run its course and she knows it. "It's been more than twenty years, Mike. I don't know what to think anymore. I suppose I was always angry with her for running off and leaving me."

"But what if she didn't run off? What if someone had killed her and that's why she never came back?" he asks as gently as he is able.

"It never occurred to me," she admits, and her mother's character begins to change in her mind when Phillips questions, "Did she physically abuse you?"

"Never ... Not really. Sometimes she'd be mad at me because it was hard to find somewhere to stay with a kid. But I guess I should be grateful that she always tried and didn't just dump me in a home or leave me on someone's doorstep. She always managed, somehow."

"What do you remember about her?"

"I've blocked her out for years, to be honest, but I was thinking of her when I was arrested; wondering if she'd ever been in that same cell. I think that was the worst thing about being inside, Mike. Thinking that my mother might have been stripped and shackled just like me; thinking that when she'd come home covered in bruises that she may have got them the same way that I did. And she didn't do anything wrong either — not unless trying to stay alive is wrong."

"There are some people who would say that what she was doing was wrong," he says, carefully distancing himself from the accusation.

"Mike, I know what she did," says Ruth. "She was a hooker, but what else could she do to survive? She didn't have much education, and her people had nothing. So she sold the only thing she had."

"Her people?" Phillips questions.

"Coast Salish First Nations," explains Ruth, flooring Phillips.

"She was a Native?" he breathes in total surprise.

"Yes, Mike. And so am I — well, part Native. Don't say you didn't notice."

"But I didn't," he protests. "It never occurred to me."

Ruth takes a moment to peer questioningly into his eyes before warily asking. "Does it make a difference, now that you know?"

Mike Phillips may be able to plug his tears, but he can't cover the crack in his voice as he lovingly takes her hands. "I fell in love with a woman, Ruth, not a colour or a race. I fell in love with you."

"Thank you," she says, gripping his hands. "Though God knows why you would feel that way — knowing what you do."

"All I know is that you are a wonderful person who doesn't deserve all the crap that's been thrown at you, and I'll do my best to make up for it."

Ruth smiles through tears of gratitude as their meal arrives, then asks, "What can I do about my mother?"

"We have an idea where she could be, Ruth. Would you give us a small blood sample, so that we can test for DNA?"

"Yes," says Ruth, unhesitatingly. "Of course I will."

It is already dawn in Westchester, England, when Mike Phillips takes Ruth back to his hotel in Vancouver and guides her upstairs to his room. And, on the other side of the world, a man rides out of the stable yard at Thraxton Manor unaware that a telephoto lens is tracking him as he gallops off across the field toward the barns.

"It's the best I could do, sir," says the photographer an hour later as he drops the fuzzy photographs on Donaldson's desk. "I hope it's the right guy. He moved so quickly that I had a job to get a good focus."

"I don't know," admits Donaldson, "I've never seen him." Then he takes a closer look. "What's happening in the background? Do you know?"

A bevy of workmen fixing up the old barns have been caught in the photographer's lens, though he had been so focussed on the galloping horseman that he hadn't noticed.

"It looks as though they're doing the old place up," continues Donaldson, peering deeper. "I've got a feeling Ms. Lovelace mentioned that he had plans for the place. Anyway, I'm sure she'll recognize him easily enough. Thanks, Bob."

Daphne has no doubts when Donaldson lays out the photos on her dining room table a little later. "That's him, sir. That's the impostor. Are you going to arrest him?"

"I don't think we have any evidence that he's done anything wrong, Daphne," protests Donaldson. "He denied being Jackson when Dave asked him. Plus, he happens to own a fair chunk of Westchester real estate."

"Successful villains don't live in Council houses, Superintendent. You should know that," she chides lightly.

"But Daphne," Donaldson remonstrates, "you've absolutely no reason to say that he's a villain."

"After the way he spoke to me," she complains with resentment, "and the way he just tossed my furniture polish in the bin — that was a brand new aerosol, Superintendent. And it wasn't one of those cheapie things from ValueSpot either; they don't last two minutes. 'This is for Thraxton Manor,' I told the Mr. Benson in the hardware store, 'I only want the very best.' And Jackson, or whatever his name is, just ripped it out of my hand and chucked it in the bin. Honest people don't do things like that."

"It's not exactly the most heinous crime we've had this year, Daphne," mutters Donaldson, but she is determined to press her point.

"It may not be much to you, but six pounds is six pounds. And I still say he's a crook."

"What do you plan to do with the photo now, Dave?" Donaldson asks Bliss, hoping to change the subject, but Daphne rises to make a point.

"I think I need a soothing cup of tea," she says, crossly. "I assume you'll stay for some Keemun, Superintendent?"

"How could I resist," says the officer, seizing an opportunity to placate her. "The tea at the station hasn't been the same since you left."

Daphne hesitates for a moment with the idea of volunteering to take back her old job at the police station, but thinks better of it. "Young women today have never been taught to make tea properly, that's the problem," she says, heading for the kitchen.

"I'll email the picture to my contact in Vancouver later this afternoon, says Bliss as he takes a look at the time. "It's still the middle of the night there. Mike Phillips knows Jackson's wife. She'll be able to clear this up."

"Good. So, how much longer are you staying? I

was just thinking that you've never had the pleasure of Mrs. Donaldson's Sunday roast, have you?"

"Thanks, but I should be getting back," says Bliss. "I was actually going last week until all this blew up, but I'll probably stay for a few more days, just to make sure that Daphne's all right."

"I can manage perfectly well on my own, David," Daphne yells irritably from the kitchen. "My hearing is fine, and it's not my fault if people won't believe what I saw with my own eyes."

"Daphne," calls Donaldson. "I'm not doubting you for a moment. I just don't have sufficient evidence to get a warrant."

"He stole my polish," she carries on as she brings in the tea, though she knows that won't get her far.

"I'll give you the money for that," says Bliss. "Anyway, lets just wait and see what Mrs. Jackson has to say about her husband, all right?"

Lunchtime brings further news on the Jackson case. Daphne is in the kitchen defrosting the last of the turkey soup when Bliss takes another call from the *Merseyside Mail* office.

"Dave," gushes the editor, "I've got some brilliant news for Ms. Lovelace. We may have found Sanderson."

"Really?"

"Yes. She was right. He didn't come back after the sixty-four tour."

"Where is he?"

"Well, I got a paper in Canada, *The Globe and Mail*, to run the picture with a story, and someone spotted him. Apparently he used to live in Vancouver."

"Used to?"

"About ten years ago, the woman said, but she moved away, so she doesn't know if he's still there. I'm going to ask a Vancouver paper to run the story next, but I've a feeling we're getting close. Could you let Mrs. Longbottom know?"

Bliss puts down the phone, calling to Daphne. "You'd better start working on Mavis. I think the Beatles reunion is getting closer."

"What's that about, David?" asks Daphne poking her head into the room.

"Wouldn't it be weird if he lives right around the corner from Ruth," Bliss carries on, once he's given Daphne the details. "I mean, you read about these kind of things in the papers and you never quite believe them — adopted twins who've lived next door to each other for fifty years and never knew; that kind of thing."

Daphne is equally overjoyed. "Maybe we should have a drink to celebrate," she says opening the liquor cabinet. "The sun is just about over the yardarm."

"Whoa!" exclaims Bliss. "Why are we getting so excited? Aren't we forgetting something?"

"What?"

"We have no idea if Sanderson is Ruth's father. Her mother might have made up the whole story. And even if she did tell her the truth, what's the chance that it was Geoffrey Sanderson with the mop-top haircut and a guitar case doing a backstage bonk while George was out front being screamed at?"

"Oh, David. You are a wag," laughs Daphne, but she takes the point. "How are you going to find out?" she asks.

"I was hoping you'd have some ideas. I'm stumped."

"Well, I think you've done magnificently so far David, but if I could make a suggestion, I was reading the other day about a private investigator who did the old switcheroo with a chap's beer glass in a pub to get his DNA off the saliva. Now it may be the sort of thing that only happens in novels, but it sounded genuine enough."

"It sounds a bit iffy to me," replies Bliss. "Though I suppose it might work. But they've got to find him first. Mike will probably be able to help, but let's wait and see what he has to say about the man at the manor first."

Mike Phillips and Ruth Jackson had more than sleep on their minds when they had gone to bed the previous night and, in consequence, are late rising.

"I'll have to get a move-on," muses Phillips as he plugs in his computer to check for messages, but Ruth's mind is still on Trina's guinea pig.

"I would never have forgiven myself if the poor thing had died," she is saying as he pulls up his emails and finds the photograph from Bliss. "What's the matter?" she asks, realizing that her lover has suddenly gone quiet.

Phillips takes a deep breath. "You remember I told you that a Canadian named Jordan Jackson had turned up in England?"

"Yeah. You said not to worry. Why?"

"Well. A friend of mine has sent a photo, and he wants to know if you recognize him."

Mike Phillips may be feeling nervous as he prepares to open the photo attached to the email message, but Ruth is backing up faster than a lion-trainer with a smashed chair.

"What if it's him? What if I'm still married?"

"Ruth, you've got a copy of his death certificate."

"Signed by a doctor a month before he died," she reminds him.

"You don't have to look at it if you don't want," Phillips tells her as he closely examines the picture evolving on screen.

"Tell me it's not him, Mike. Please tell me it's not him."

"I never saw him," admits Phillips. "He'd gone before I arrived. But he could be about the right age."

Curiosity draws Ruth closer until she finds herself peering at the screen, and Phillips watches her face for a clue.

"Is it him?" asks Phillips, heart-in-mouth at her puzzled expression.

"It could be," she says vaguely, but she is clearly indecisive. "Possibly."

"You're not sure?"

"I can't remember what he looked like," she finally admits in frustration and takes off for the bathroom saying, "What about Trina? She'll know."

"It's probably psychosomatic," suggests Trina when Phillips phones for her email address. "Ruth's tried so hard to blot him out of her memory that she's forgotten what he looks like."

"See if you recognize him." says Phillips as he forwards a copy, then he hangs on the phone while Trina opens her email.

"Well?" he asks.

Trina studies the picture carefully but is still non-committal, "It could be, but I haven't seen him for six months, and I didn't know him very well before that."

"I'm surprised Ruth isn't more certain," he says closing his screen as the horseman disappears.

"There might be another problem, Mike."

"What?"

"Oh, come on. Wake up, man. She never loved him. She loves you to pieces, and the last thing she wants now is for him to pop back up and ruin the best thing that's ever happened to her."

Phillips' face is somewhere between puzzlement and glee. "Is that true?" he asks, and Trina scoffs in amazement.

"Men! If they spent more time looking at a woman's face and less time ogling her tits, they might have a better idea what was going on in her mind."

"Hey!" exclaims Phillips, though he doesn't try arguing the point as Trina continues, "You said you were going to take her away for a break. Why not take her to England and confront him? Neither of you are going to be completely happy until you're sure."

chapter seventeen

Superintendent Donaldson has had a touch of indigestion ever since lunch — an allergic reaction, he suspects, to the second heaped portion of spotted dick pudding with custard, but he also has had a gut feeling that he has too lightly dismissed Daphne's assertions about the new tenant on his beat. The fact that Daphne had never been wrong about a case during her twelve-year tenure at Westchester police station, albeit as the cleaning lady, eases neither his stomach nor his mind, and he finds himself taking a more critical view of Thraxton Manor before driving back to see her in the late afternoon sunshine.

"I thought I'd just take a peek," Donaldson tells Bliss and Daphne as she hands him a cup of Keemun.

"Biscuit?" she offers, and Donaldson takes four of the chocolate ones to settle his stomach.

"Anyway, the place is absolutely crawling with workmen," he continues. "And it looks as though he is having the fences repaired and surveillance cameras put up on the gates."

"He's certainly touchy about trespassers," admits Bliss, recalling his second visit to the estate, when he'd had his head bitten off.

"Did he give you any idea of his intentions?" Donaldson asks, turning to Daphne.

"I thought you weren't interested," says Daphne, being deliberately snotty. "I thought you said he wasn't a heinous criminal."

"Daphne, I said we had no evidence that he had done anything wrong, but I must admit, it does seem a little strange."

Feeling vindicated, Daphne puts down her teapot and relents, saying, "He told me that he was going to do the old place up, and that he had plans for the out-buildings. But he didn't say what."

The phone rings. It's Mike Phillips for Bliss.

"Mrs. Jackson couldn't positively ID him from the photo," Phillips says. "So I thought I might bring her over for a few days to give her chance to get up-close and personal."

"Wow!" exclaims Bliss. "The RCMP must have money to burn."

"Are you kidding?" laughs Phillips. "This is coming out of my wages."

"I don't have room for any more guests, David," worries Daphne once Bliss has informed her and Donaldson.

"They'll have to stay at the Mitre," says Bliss. "I remember it being quite cozy when I stayed there once, and it wasn't terribly expensive."

"This is getting interesting," says Donaldson, helping himself to two more cookies. "Maybe I should try to get an undercover man in there. With so many workmen coming and going it shouldn't be too difficult."

"Hang on, sir," cautions Bliss. "Nothing has changed. We only have Daphne's suspicion that he's up to no good, and now we're not even sure that he is an impostor."

"David ..." spits Daphne, angrily. "I thought you were on my side."

"I just think it makes sense to wait until Mrs. Jackson takes a gander at him, that's all. Then we'll know for sure. Mike says they'll be over in a day or so."

DS Phillips' plan for a quick hop over the Atlantic comes unglued almost immediately when he tells Ruth about it.

"Would you like that?" Phillips asks her as he hangs up on Bliss. "Spring in merry old England. We could do the sights, and we might even see the Queen."

"I'd love it. After all, I am half English — as far as I know," replies Ruth, but her face tells an entirely different story, and she grips the chair with white knuckles.

"What's the matter?" asks Phillips, spotting the distress.

"I can't. I'm not allowed to leave the country while I'm on bail. Anyway, I don't have a passport. People like me don't usually get very far."

"Stop that this instant," snaps Phillips. "I don't want to hear that kind of nonsense ever again." Then he takes her into his arms and hugs her warmly, saying positively, "Leave it to me. I'll sort something out. We are going to England."

Mike Phillips' departure leaves a vacuum in the hotel room once he's gone to work, and Ruth finds the walls being sucked in around her until she can stand the pressure no longer and escapes onto the balcony.

The warm spring sunshine glares off the snow-blanketed peaks, but it fails to lift Ruth's claustrophobia as she finds herself hemmed in by the ring of mountains; mountains that she has never crossed. Beyond them, she knows, are the wide open prairies rolling from Alberta through Saskatchewan to Manitoba, and after that, the lakes and forests that stretch all the way from Ontario to the islands that edge the Atlantic Ocean. But for Ruth Jackson, née Ruth Crowfoot, of the Coast Salish First Nation, the Rockies are as much a hurdle as a heritage.

"I can't do it," she muses aloud, as she watches a plane from Vancouver International Airport rising like a gull on the wind as it circles to gain height before slipping eastward over the peaks. "I'm trapped here. I can't fly."

The persistent ringing of the room's telephone draws her away from the balcony and she grabs the receiver, expecting it to be Phillips.

"Ruth, it's me," says Trina, then she laughs. "Kylie and Rob are threatening to leave home."

"Why?" asks Ruth.

"OK, tell me I'm stupid if you like, but ... Do you put bananas in your Bolognese sauce?"

"Oh. Trina," laughs Ruth, then her tone darkens. "Mike wants me to go to England with him."

"I know," gushes Trina. "Aren't you the lucky one?"

"I'm scared."

"What do you mean? Scared of what?"

Of flying; of leaving here; of what I might find in England; of strange people in a strange country; of strange customs and food, she thinks, though she says only, "I'm scared of having to give up Mike."

"Why would you have to give up Mike?" Trina demands, but she knows the answer; she knows that when Ruth had stood next to Jordan, repeating, "For richer, for poorer; in sickness and in health; 'til death do us part," she had meant every word, and going back on any of those promises now, whatever the provocation, may be difficult — if not impossible — for someone who has vowed to atone for her mother's immorality.

"Don't worry," carries on Trina. "I don't expect it's him."

"Him," murmurs Ruth distractedly, as she tries unsuccessfully to come up with an image of Jordan in her mind. "I'm not sure if I would know him anymore," she carries on, honestly.

"Good," says Trina. "After what he's done, if it is him, he doesn't deserve to be remembered. Now why don't I pick you up in ten minutes and we'll discuss this England thing over a coffee?"

Trina's driving is all over the place as usual, and it takes Ruth a few minutes to realize that they are headed in the general direction of her old home. "We're not going back to the Coffee Shoppe are we?" she asks in sudden panic.

"You can't avoid the past forever," says Trina, though she adds reassuringly, "No, we're not going back there. I thought we would visit Raven and some other people who've missed you."

"Do you think Jordan misses me?"

"Ruth ..." says Trina, looking her friend deep in the eyes and letting God take the wheel. "Jordan is dead. You have the certificate."

"The really strange thing is that I don't hate him," carries on Ruth, her mind as wayward as Trina's driving.

"But lack of hatred isn't love, nor is it the opposite of love," says Trina, then questions herself out loud. "Where the hell did that come from?"

"*Reader's Digest* or *Chicken Soup* for somebody-or-other's soul," suggests Ruth. "But I know what you mean."

Ruth's reception in Donut Delight is embarrassingly effusive as Darcey spots her and shrieks to the others, "Look everyone. It's Ruth. It's Ruth."

The entire crossword gang — and half a dozen other ex-patrons of the Corner Coffee Shoppe — rush to hug her, and she wilts under the deluge in the doorway as Trina keeps up the pressure from behind.

"Wow. Look at you," enthuses Matt as he holds her at arm's-length and eyes her appreciatively.

"Don't turn sideways or we'll miss you," teases Maureen, and Ruth obligingly spins to show off her svelte figure as she jokes, "Don't take your envy out on me, Maureen Daniels."

Raven is the last to appear, and she is altogether repentant as she brings a couple of cappuccinos to the table, saying to Ruth, "I'm really, really sorry about Jordan. I've given all that channelling stuff up now." Though she smarts a little when Ruth replies, "Don't blame yourself, Raven. I didn't believe you anyway."

"When are you coming back?" is a question on everyone's lips, though the answer "Never," sticks in Ruth's throat.

"The old café isn't the same without you," says Darcey. "We never go near the place now."

"I bet she'll have to close soon, the way it's going," adds Matt, though any smugness that Ruth may feel is well hidden as she responds, "That would be a shame."

"I'm still worried what Tom might do," admits Ruth, once she is sitting alone with Trina over their coffees.

"He's just a piece of dirt," spits Trina. "Just do what I did. Let him know that you're not scared of him." Then she checks her watch and leaps from her seat. "Shit! I've forgotten to clean up Mrs. Hewitt's morning barf," she says, then she gives Ruth a reassuring smile. "Just be careful where you go, that's all;

though he won't try anything in a busy place, and if he does, just knee him in the balls."

"I already tried that," says Ruth, "but he came back again."

"Here, catch." says Trina, taking a cellphone from her medical bag and throwing it to Ruth. "It's Kylie's. I confiscated it."

"Why?"

"Boys," scoffs Trina. "Her last bill cost me a fortune. Do me a favour, will you?"

"Of course."

"If any boy calls, tell him she moved to Yellowknife."

Trina is half out the door when she pauses in thought, then rushes back to Ruth with her hand in her purse. "Here," she says, slipping a fifty dollar bill into Ruth's palm. "Pay for the coffees and treat yourself with the change."

"Trina. You can't ..." protests Ruth, but the home care nurse has gone.

"It's on the house," says Raven with a confused look a few seconds later as Ruth attempts to foot the bill. "I told Trina."

The sun may still be shining as Ruth makes her way back to the city centre, but she hardly notices as she wanders down Georgia Street to the duck ponds in Stanley Park, her mind in turmoil over Mike's proposal.

Is it fear of flying or fear of facing the future? she wonders to herself as she approaches the water and finds a familiar figure tossing crusts to the birds.

"What a gorgeous day," says the grey-haired man with the poodle, now minus his umbrella, and his accent causes Ruth to stop and ask, "Are you English?"

"Many moons ago, lass," he replies with a smile, and he hands her some bread. "Here. I'll keep the gulls busy if you look after the ducks."

"Thanks," she laughs, then finds herself saying, "I'm going to England soon," as she aims for the mallards and the other mergansers.

"Give my regards to the old place," says the man, and Ruth promises that she will.

So, you are going then, she says to herself once the bread has gone and she's left the elderly man to his birds. But the answer is still elusive as she worries about the cost.

Have you forgotten?

What?

The lottery ticket.

And what will Mike think of that now? she laughs sardonically to herself. *It's not like I haven't had plenty of chances to tell him.*

Say that you've only just found out.

Lie? Is that what you're suggesting? You want me to lie to Mike?

It won't hurt. He'll never know.

OK, work with me on this, she tells herself as she pulls the crumpled lottery ticket from her purse and stares thoughtfully out over the ocean to the distant islands. *A recently arrested daughter of a hooker is now a liar as well.*

So why not just toss it in the sea if you feel that way?

But I owe so much, she reflects, and tries telling herself that she could ask Trina to collect the lottery prize for her.

And you don't think that would make you look guilty?

Who would know? Only Trina — and the kid in the convenience store who told me I'd won. But he won't remember me from Eve.

And you think Trina could keep it a secret? Forget it. She'd be in Donut Delight filling-in the crossword with "JACKPOT" in seconds. In any case, the lottery corporation and the press will make a big deal of some-one winning so much. How would she explain to Rick and the children, not to mention her family and friends, that she didn't actually win anything. They'll all be browsing car lots, real estate agents, and fashion maga-zines, and if she tells them the truth, someone will blab.

Kylie's cellphone breaks into Ruth's deliberations. It's Phillips.

"Mike?" she queries in surprise.

"Trina gave me the number," he explains, before asking, "Where are you? I'll pick you up. I need you to sign some papers."

The speed of the following events has Ruth in such a whirl that she can't get her mind to stay still long enough to explain to Phillips that she is terrified of fly-ing to England and, minutes later, she finds herself sign-ing a hastily prepared application — to amend her bail conditions and enable her to leave the country — in front of a Supreme Court judge in his chambers.

"Approved," says the robed god, affixing the offi-cial stamp while peering over the rims of his glasses with smiling eyes. And, as he adds his signature with-out even reading the application request, Ruth realizes that a certain detective sergeant has already greased the right wheels.

"Next stop, the passport office," says Phillips, bundling Ruth back into his car with an eye on his watch. "We should just make it."

"But when are we going?" Ruth asks fearfully and is rocked back in her seat as Phillips replies, "Tonight, of course. Our suitcases are in the trunk and the tickets are at the airport ready for pickup."

"Tonight ..." she echoes.

Ruth's mind is still trying to catch up to her legs an hour later as she and Mike Phillips walk toward the British Airways check-in desk at Vancouver International. The hurriedly issued emergency passport in her hand is the only hard evidence that she is not dreaming, and she grips it so fiercely that it is damp and creased.

Another surprise awaits Ruth at the check-in desk, where Trina Button is causing a minor disturbance. Trina, herself a last-minute passenger on the overnight flight to London, is railroading the well-groomed clerk into seating Ruth and Phillips alongside her in first class.

"Are there a couple of vacant seats in first class? That's all I'm asking. Is that a difficult question, young man?"

"No madam, it's not. There are seats, but I'm sorry, I am not authorized to upgrade passengers from economy."

"OK," says Trina lightly, seemingly quitting, then she whips out her tape recorder and shoves it in front of his face, demanding, "What's your name, please?"

"W ... W ... Why do want that?" he stammers nervously, while looking around to catch the eye of a security guard.

"Just so that we know who to sue if she dies."

"Dies?"

Trina slowly drops the tape recorder and leans forward, whispering truthfully, "Ms. Jackson has severe heart problems. That's why I'm travelling with her. But if she's in economy and I can't get to her in time ..."

"Oh dear. Should she be travelling then?"

Trina pulls the young man closer and makes a play of checking that she's not being overheard as she says, "She may look as fit as a fiddle, but her heart has no more than a day or so, unless she gets the right treatment. England is the only place in the world that it's available right now."

"Gosh," gulps the young man as he consults the first class plan and earmarks two fully reclining seats. "Just bring them to me and promise that you won't tell anyone else, will you?" he says.

"How on earth did you manage that?" asks Phillips in awe a few minutes later, once he and Ruth have been upgraded and processed.

"I just showed him my tape recorder, Sergeant," shrugs Trina with an innocent grin, "and he absolutely insisted."

"Sounds like extortion to me," laughs Phillips, but Ruth is still dumbfounded over her friend's presence.

"Are you sure you told me you were going to visit friends in London?" she asks vaguely, and Trina takes her arm and guides her toward the washroom in the first class lounge, saying, "You've got a lot on your mind at the moment, Ruth. You probably forgot. But what a coincidence, eh?"

The opulence of the washroom, with its onyx basins, gold fittings, and starched linen hand towels, has Ruth ready to bolt. "Wow," she breathes, "Are we allowed in here?"

"Of course we are," says Trina, adding, "Don't be fooled, Ruth. Most of the crap that goes down these toilets stinks a lot worse than ours, if you get my drift."

"This is how I would imagine a bathroom in heaven," says Ruth, as she washes her hands and luxuriates in the softness and scent of the ten-dollar soap, then she turns worriedly to Trina. "Did you really tell me that you were going to England?"

"All right," confesses Trina. "I lied. The truth is that I'm terrified that if you discover that it is Jordan, you'll make the biggest, most stupid mistake of your life. He's no good Ruth — he never was."

"He married me when everyone told him not to," replies Ruth as if it were something for which Jordan should have been decorated.

"Maybe he married you *because* everyone told him not to. Have you ever considered that? As painful as it may be, have you ever thought that the main reason he married you might have been to piss off his mother?"

"She always hated me," admits Ruth.

"What she hated most is the fact that her dearly beloved son chose a brown-skinned girl when he could have picked a nice white one."

"Is it that obvious?" Ruth asks as she closely examines her face in the mirror.

"No. I just thought you had a great tan when I first knew you."

"But he stayed with me, even after we lost the baby," Ruth asserts, still trying to defend him, and Trina looks up to peer questioningly into her eyes through the looking glass. "Was he really with you, Ruth? Where was his mind?"

Ruth knows what Trina is getting at, and can't hold her friend's gaze as she recalls the numerous times she'd complained about Jordan spending his nights glued to the inflated boobs of a bimbo in a porno magazine, or slumped in front of a sex site on the Internet with his hand in his pants.

"He said he loved me," she says lamely, and catches Trina's incredulous look as she adds, "I just assumed all men were like that."

"You should sit by the window," Trina tells Ruth as

the stewardess leads them to their seats on the 747, but Ruth is unsure.

"I don't think I can look," she says nervously, and Phillips gives her hand a reassuring squeeze. "You'll be fine."

Ruth's fear falls away as quickly as the earth, and she is mesmerized by the city's golden lights as Vancouver drops behind them and they soar like an eagle in an updraft, rising high over the majestic escarpment of the Rocky Mountains, and heading northeast toward Hudson's Bay and the Arctic ocean.

"It's fabulous," muses Ruth, encompassing the experience — the service, the food, and, above all, her new found sense of freedom. "It's not scary at all, is it?" she says, once she has acclimatized, and Trina trots out another gem. "It's just like marriage, Ruth — exciting as heck when it takes off, but afterwards all you do is sleep, watch television, and go to the john. And, if you're lucky, you don't crash."

"Thank you for that comforting thought," says Phillips sourly as the stewardess turns his seat into a bed.

"Right. Set your watches ahead," instructs Trina, as she prepares to snuggle down in her recliner. "It's already six in the morning in England."

The new sun is still below the horizon at their destination, but the time is fast approaching when there will be sufficient twilight for David Bliss to do an early morning reconnoitre at Thraxton Manor to mollify Daphne, and to pave the way for the arrival of the Canadian contingent.

"I'm sure he's up to monkey business," Daphne had asserted the previous evening after Superintendent Donaldson had left. "Maybe you should try taking another look at the place. If anyone can figure out what he's up to, it's you, David."

"I'll see if I can sneak in while he's still asleep," he had told her as he had set his alarm for an early awakening, though he had no idea what he was expecting to find.

"Do be careful, David," Daphne tells him as she pours him a second cup of tea while he waits for the first rays of dawn. "He seemed a nasty piece of work to me."

"I'm not planning on meeting him this time," says Bliss as he adds milk. "I just want to get the lay of the land."

A tethered goat in an adjacent field bleats a warning at Bliss's arrival, and a couple of deer, together with a hare and half-dozen rabbits, scamper away from the hedgerow where they have been feasting on the fresh shoots. Bliss parks the car some way from the manor's gates and uses his binoculars to spy on the estate through the lightly-leafed hedges as he walks the quiet road along the perimeter. Then, as dawn breaks and a brightly-plumed cock pheasant screeches in alarm at his approach, the sun's slanted rays glint on the shiny steel of new fence posts, and he spies workmen emerging from a number of caravans set up on the site. "So much for Donaldson's idea of sending in a mole with the work crews," he says to himself as he watches the men preparing their equipment.

The manor's giant main gates are still closed, and Bliss is heading for the side gate when an approaching vehicle causes him to veer off and carry on along the road. The vehicle, a tractor-trailer carting a forty-foot shipping container, waits at the entranceway until a powerful whirring sound hums through the still morning air and, as the huge gates slowly open, the truck sweeps through into the estate and heads for the out-buildings behind the stables. Bliss is momentarily tempt-ed to try to slip through the gateway in the vehicle's wake, but he's deterred by the eagle-eye of a surveillance camera on the top of one of the entrance pillars, and the beam of a powerful floodlight from the other.

Returning to his car with no clearer picture of how Ruth will be able to get a view of the suspect, Bliss is preparing to pull away when the truck reappears — minus its load — heads out the gateway, and makes for the main road.

I wonder if the driver knows anything? Bliss won-ders, and fifteen minutes later he finds out as he buddies up to the man over bacon, eggs, and fried bread in a greasy truck-stop café.

"What a' ya hauling then, mate?" asks Bliss con-versationally as he starts into his breakfast alongside the man.

"Plywood from Canada. What about you?"

"Bloody 'ell, ,mate, that's a long way to drive," jokes Bliss as he ignores the question.

The driver laughs, "Nah. I only take it from the docks to the old manor."

"Thraxton Manor?" prods Bliss with a mouthful of egg.

"D'ya know the place?"

"Yeah. What the bloody 'ell do they do with it there, then?"

"Buggered if I know. I ain't paid to ask questions. I just drops it off."

"Do they get a lot?"

"I brings one up from Southampton most nights. Then sometimes I take an empty back with me."

"Huh," snorts Bliss. "Seems a funny place for a warehouse."

"No. They've got machines and such for cuttin' it up," he says, then gives Bliss a critical stare. "So what d'ye do then?"

"Bit o' this. Bit o' that," Bliss replies as he quickly tidies his plate and leaves, calling, "Thanks, mate. See ya," over his shoulder.

Superintendent Donaldson is just reversing into his spot as Bliss pulls into the police station parking lot a short while later.

"I thought you'd like to know that my Canadian guy is arriving this morning to take a peek at 'Matey' up at the manor, sir," says Bliss as he greets the senior officer.

"Christ. That was quick," replies Donaldson.

"They're eight hours behind us. Makes all the difference," says Bliss before telling the superintendent about the plywood shipments. "It seems fair enough," continues Bliss. "He's a Canadian, whatever his name is, and he's importing Canadian plywood."

"Great. Well, we'll just have to wait and see what the woman says about him. But you're in luck this morning. I'm trying out a new place for breakfast. It's just opened on Monk Street."

"I've already had a bite ..." doesn't get Bliss very far as Donaldson catches his arm. "Come on, Dave. You've been here three months and I've only managed to get you for one breakfast. What kind of host does that make me, eh?"

"So when are you leaving?" Donaldson wants to know, once he's ignored Bliss's plea of "I couldn't possibly ..." and ordered two He-Man specials at the counter of the Gay Friars restaurant.

"Later today, probably," answers Bliss. "Mike Phillips should arrive with the woman at lunchtime and, once she's had a chance to ID the bloke at the manor, I said I'd take them back to London and show them the sights."

"How's Daphne feel about you leaving?"

"Not happy, but I've got to get back to work before I'm accused of swinging the leg."

"I'll excuse the pun," laughs Donaldson, softy tapping Bliss's injured thigh as he carries on. "I think she's going to miss having you around."

"She's funny," laughs Bliss fondly. "Ever since last night, when she heard the Canadians were coming, she's been rummaging through the attic for a Paul Anka LP and a Maple Leaf flag that she got signed by Pierre Trudeau at the Beatles concert in Montreal. And she's planning today's reception as if she's expecting a royal visitor.

"I'll have to use Canadian salmon and Canadian cheddar in the sandwiches, David," she had said as she'd made her shopping list. "And I suppose I should make a dessert using maple syrup."

"Maybe they'd prefer something typically British for a change," Bliss had gently suggested, but it had merely drawn a flippant rebuke.

"I could do tripe and onions, jellied eels, or haggis," she had said with a straight face. "Though I noticed that the butcher had some chitterlings in his window yesterday — that's boiled pigs' intestines, David. Which do you think they might like?"

"I think they'll like the salmon and cheese," he had laughed, and left her in charge of the remaining arrangements.

By the time that Bliss eats his way out of the Gay Friar, the British Airways flight from Vancouver has taxied to a halt at Heathrow, and Ruth's eyes are everywhere as she walks through the terminal attempting to see through the chimera. The ground feels solid enough; the strange accents of the immigration and customs officers sound genuinely English; the posters and billboards advertising alien products are all well conceived, yet she knows that this isn't happening — although she would be the first to admit that whoever concocted the illusion has done a stellar job.

"How are you feeling, Ruth?" asks Phillips, noticing her perplexity, and she wants to ask, *How did they do this?* but realizes that it's a stupid question.

"I still can't believe it," she says. "I'd ask you to pinch me, but this dream is so real that I'd probably feel it."

"You're not dreaming," says Trina. "Look, there's a 'bobby' over there."

"Don't ..." yells Phillips a fraction too late to stop Trina rushing up to the helmeted policeman as she pulls out her camera.

"Sorry, officer," says Phillips as he grabs Trina's arm and starts to drag her away.

"I don't mind, sir," says the constable. "I'm used to it."

"Great," says Trina, breaking free, and she quickly pushes Ruth into place so that she can get a group shot.

"I used to go out with a copper," Trina tells Ruth and Phillips as they walk away.

"Where?" asks Ruth.

"In London," Trina answers matter-of-factly. "I was a student here in my crazy days. I lived in a shoe-box overlooking Piccadilly Circus."

"I didn't know that," declares Ruth.

"I even lived in Moscow for awhile. Though I've forgotten most of my Russian," she adds, then she spots the sign for the railway station and heads them in that direction.

"Why not take the train to Westchester," Bliss had suggested to Phillips when he had called the previous day. "Then I can drive us up to London and show you around."

"Thanks," Phillips had replied, grateful that he wouldn't have to get his mind in gear for driving on the left; but as they stand in line for train tickets, he is beginning to wonder if it might not be quicker to rent a car. The line has been at a standstill for several minutes as the front man, an enormous Russian, battles with a belligerent booking clerk who is determined not to comprehend the foreign visitor. Despite the aspersions Trina has cast over her linguistic ability, she finally loses patience and steps in, saying, "He wants three return tickets to Westminster Abbey. Two adults and a child, please." Then she turns to the new arrival and carries on chatting as cordially as if they were long lost friends.

"What were you saying?" asks Ruth in awe as they make their way down the escalator to the platform, with the Russian and his wife and daughter in their wake, and Trina sloughs it off. "I've no idea, but he seemed to understand."

Ruth is mesmerized by the sights as the Heathrow Express zooms them into the heart of London, and she stands on the banks of the Thames pointing out the Houses of Parliament and London's giant Ferris wheel, saying, "Oh my God. I can't believe it, Mike."

The locals say "Gob-smacked," according to Trina, and she smiles at the happy couple as they gape at London's famous skyline, and she prays that the black spectre just over the horizon will turn out to be nothing more than a harmless will-o'-the-wisp.

The high-speed train from London to Westchester rockets along at over two hundred kilometres per hour, while Tudor hamlets with thatched cottages and Victorian towns with neat rows of brick-red houses fly past the windows.

"The cars are so cute," says Ruth, watching the traffic as they run alongside a road for a few moments.

"They look like little ducklings zipping along to catch up their mother."

The spring sunshine has swept away all but the very deepest drifts of snow, and the fields and hedgerows are bursting with fresh green growth. An ordinarily lazy river rushes with melt-water, snatching and tearing at the branches of a weeping willow as it trails its slender tentacles in the torrent, while another tree, a small oak, has succumbed to the urge and is riding the barrage all the way to the sea. Meadows of spring flowers splash past the windows in smudges of yellow and white, until the lowlands give way to the chalk downs, where the winter wheat has had the weight lifted off its back by the thaw, and is now spurting skyward in a verdant rush to the summer's harvest.

"Are you nervous?" Phillips asks Ruth as the train starts to descend into Westchester, and all the joy drains from her face as she suddenly remembers the purpose of their visit.

"Is it true that if you travel fast enough, you go back in time?" she asks, and Phillips nods. "I've heard that. Why?"

"I guess that's what I'm doing."

"The past is the only thing that prevents you from grasping the future," says Trina, sounding grandiose as she quotes from *Reader's Digest* again.

"I feel like I did when Mom disappeared," admits Ruth. "Part of me wanted her to come home, but most of me didn't."

A familiar smiling face greets Mike Phillips at Westchester station's platform barrier, and Ruth puts on a brave face as Bliss shakes her hand.

"We've brought a friend," says Phillips, and sees Bliss's puzzlement as he looks along the near deserted platform. "She's just sorting out a little problem," he adds, pointing to Trina who is now crossing the foot-bridge to the opposite platform with a family in tow.

Trina has finally hit the jackpot as a saviour of strays and has scored a hat trick. While she had been making her way to the end of the carriage, readying to disembark in Westchester, she had been aghast at the sight of the Russian man, together with his wife and daughter, rising from nearby seats and preparing to leave the train with her.

"Westchinster?" the man had asked in pidgin English as he'd pointed to the "Westchester" signboard, and Trina's face had fallen, knowing that, at Heathrow air-port, when she had said "Just follow us" in broken Russian, she had meant only as far as the station platform.

"At least she's not taking them to the pound," laughs Phillips while they wait for Trina to guide the confused family to the correct platform for their return to London. Then he looks around, asking, "Where's Daphne?"

"She's probably lining up a ceremonial guard of neighbours for you to inspect," says Bliss with a smirk. "Although knowing Daphne, it wouldn't surprise me if we get back to find the Regimental Band of the Royal Marines marching up and down the street playing the 'Maple Leaf Rag.'"

"I know someone like that," laughs Phillips, giving a nod in Trina's direction.

Ruth's nervous silence is palpable as they wait at the gate for Trina, and her striking ebony eyes dart back and forth as if she's expecting to be attacked.

"So when do we meet the man in the manor?" asks Phillips, knowing that someone will eventually have to bring up the thorny topic.

"We'll have lunch first, so that we can discuss tac-tics," suggests Bliss, though he knows that he has no plans other than a brazen frontal attack on the manor's main gate. "Daphne's laying out quite a spread in your honour," he carries on, as he picks up Ruth's suitcase at the sight of Trina running along the platform toward them.

Daphne has called upon reinforcements to help with the preparations. Mavis and Minnie are scuttling around doing all the menial tasks, while she puts the finishing flourish on her pyramids of salmon and cheese sandwiches by adding a handful of miniature Canadian flags flying from toothpicks. A flask of rye whisky and several bottles of Canada Dry ginger ale stand on the sideboard and, over a large pan of boiling water in the kitchen, steams her *pièce de résistance*. Adding a distinctly Canadian twist to a traditional English favourite, she has made a gigantic maple syrup suet pudding, which she will serve with lashings of homemade creamy custard.

Superintendent Donaldson, in full regalia, pulls up at the house just as the visitors arrive, and leads the charge on the dining room. Trina quickly migrates to the kitchen, offering to help, and finds a soulmate in Daphne.

"What a brilliant young woman — and we even spoke in Russian," Daphne tells Bliss, as everyone except Ruth digs in to the sandwiches a short while later.

"You speak Russian?" says Bliss without a hint of skepticism.

"I've forgotten most of it," Daphne admits modestly, "but Trina and I did quite well, considering. It's so nice to talk to someone from another country; you can learn so much. I simply had no idea that Canadians put bananas in more or less everything."

Ruth has found a corner and sits as glumly as a convict awaiting sentence, while the others try not to let her depression drag them down.

"I know it's Jordan. I always knew he wasn't dead," Ruth moans to Donaldson when he gets too close, "but no one believed me."

"We'll soon know for sure," says the superintendent, and Bliss suggests that it is time for her to bite the bullet.

"Are you ready, Ruth?" he says as he holds out her coat. "I'll drop you at the gates, but you and Mike will have to walk up the drive."

"Aren't you coming with us, Dave?" asks Phillips, but Bliss shakes his head. "I think I'm *persona non grata*. He'd probably come after me with a shotgun."

"But what's Jordan doing there?" Ruth questions, having finally accepted the inexorableness of the situation.

"Plywood," replies Bliss; then he tells them of his morning's chat with the truck driver.

"I didn't think he knew much about wood," claims Ruth, but she doesn't push the point, realizing that there are a lot of things she doesn't know about her husband. Then she asks, "What does he look like now?"

Mike Phillips watches her expression closely as Bliss describes the man at the manor. "He's tall, about my height, distinguished looking — like a politician; he's got blue eyes, and his hair is just turning at the temples. If you had a photograph, I'd soon tell you."

"There aren't any photographs," says Phillips, though Ruth is more honest as she admits that Jordan had destroyed them all.

"You might have a problem getting in ..." starts Bliss, then pauses, realizing that there is no delicate way to tell Ruth that her husband might turn her away. "If he sees you on the security camera he might not open the gate," he continues, but Daphne has an idea, and she quickly trots upstairs and returns with an enormous wide-brimmed straw hat. "He'll never see you under this," she says plopping it onto Ruth's head.

"I just hope the wind doesn't get under it," laughs Bliss, as Ruth uses both hands to balance it, and he's almost waiting for Daphne to explain how she'd last used it as a parachute to fly a Bulgarian dissident to freedom across the Iron Curtain, or some such spine-tingling escapade, when she confesses that she'd never worn it.

"You'd better stay here and keep Daphne company, Trina," suggests Phillips, fearing her presence at the manor could inflame a potentially volatile situation, and the nurse pulls him to one side, whispering harshly. "If it is him, Mike — you drag her out of there by her hair if you have to."

The main gates to Thraxton Manor are closed as Bliss drops off Phillips and Ruth, telling them that he will be watching from a parking spot further along the road.

"You'll have to use the side gate," Bliss tells them as he leaves, but as they approach, a snarling bull mastiff throws himself at the fence and Phillips is forced to use the telephone attached to the gate pillar.

"I'm Sergeant Mike Phillips of the RCMP. I heard a fellow Canuck was in the neighbourhood," he says cheerily in response to the gruff, "Yep."

The remote-controlled surveillance camera swivels their way and Phillips hisses, "Keep your head down," to Ruth. A silent whistle stops the huge dog mid-bark and sends it running back to the house, and an electronic "click" announces that the gate is now unlocked.

"Just walk straight up the drive to the stables. Someone will be with you in a few minutes," commands the voice, and Ruth starts backing away, saying, "I'm gonna throw up."

Phillips grabs her, slots her through the gate, and hustles her out of the view of the camera as she heaves up her breakfast, while at the top of the driveway inside the stable apartment, the occupant is looking at his watch and praying that Mort will answer the phone despite the earliness of the hour in Vancouver.

"What?" yells Mort.

"What the hell's going on, Mort?"

"What's the f'kin time? An' I told you — no names on the phone. You never know who's listening — know what I mean?"

"I've got a pig from Canada at the door, says he was just passing by."

"I dunno," says Mort, still trying to get his mind straight. One of my shit-heads got hauled in by the fuzz for drillin' a hole in a kiddie's guinea pig, but he doesn't know nuvving. In fact, he's so f'kin useless that he's gonna have to go — know what I mean?"

"What do you think I should do, then?"

"You'd better see what he wants or he might get ideas and blab to the bill."

As Mort puts down the phone, a teenager's hand exploring his groin reminds him that he's not alone in the bed.

"What was that about, Mort?" says the young woman and Mort grabs her hair and roughly drags her face up to his. "You didn't hear anything, right?"

"Mort. You're hurting ..."

"Say it. Nuvving. You didn't hear f'kin nuvving, right?"

"I didn't hear nothing, Mort."

"Good," he says, but he keeps a hold on her hair and slams her face to his groin, adding, "Now be a good girl and you won't get hurt."

"Jeremy Maxwell," says the occupant of the Thraxton estate a few seconds later as he opens the front door with his hand outstretched and a welcoming smile. "Do come up, Sergeant." Then he turns and leads his visitors up the stairs.

chapter eighteen

The apartment-dweller's slow Canadian drawl sinks Ruth. On a day when she has been surrounded by the staccato of rapid English, the voice of the man at the door has an all-too-familiar ring, and she vacillates between running and grabbing onto Phillips for support.

"Come on up," repeats the voice, ascending the stairs ahead of them, and Ruth inches up the hat rim expecting the worst, then her eyes dance with delight, and she is so excited that she can hardly get the words out as she tugs furiously at Phillips arm and whispers in his ear. "It's not Jordan."

"Are you sure?"

"Absolutely. I've never seen him before. He must be Maxwell."

"Everything all right, Sergeant?" asks their host as he reaches the top and turns.

"Yes, as a matter of fact. Everything is just great, Mr. Maxwell," replies Phillips.

Daphne and Trina are still swapping recipes in the kitchen when Minnie spies the smiling group walking back up the garden path half an hour later, and with a shriek of delight, she rushes to open the door so that she might give Ruth a congratulatory hug, followed by one for Bliss, as if he had in some way been responsible for placing the right man in the manor.

Trina is so overjoyed at the news that she kickboxes her way around Daphne's dining table, whooping, "Yes! Yes! Yes!" and Minnie invites herself to root through Daphne's liquor cabinet, saying, "We ought to have champagne." Daphne, on the other hand, is less enthusiastic, protesting that she simply can't believe that she had could have been so wrong.

"I was so sure that little Jeremy was going to turn out nicely," she says, as the weight of additional guilt bears down on her.

"Well ... He's definitely not Jordan Jackson, Daphne. So he has to be Jeremy Maxwell," explains Phillips, but Daphne is far from convinced, asking, "Then why did he have the other man's passport?"

"He could have found it. Maybe he bought the chest of drawers second-hand and it was already in there."

"It might be years out of date, and somebody simply chucked it away," suggests Bliss.

"I don't suppose we'll ever know," continues Phillips. "We can't ask him outright without admitting that somebody's been snooping."

"But why was he so horrid to me?" whines Daphne. "He was such a well-mannered little boy."

"Daphne ..." says Bliss, taking her to one side, as Ruth finds her appetite and digs in to the salmon sandwiches, leaving the rest of the guests to polish off the maple syrup pudding. "Have you considered the possibility that over the years he's discovered more about his father's relationship with you than you might want him to know?"

Daphne pales. "And you think he blames me?"

"Everybody else did — or so you said."

"They did, David. Believe me, they did."

"Well ... As he grew up he was bound to be curious about the fate of his parents. There must have been a time when he realized that the Nile wasn't as heavenly as he thought it was. Anyway, from what you told me of his grouchy aunt in Canada, it sounds as if she was probably the sort of woman who'd go out of her way to blacken you if she could."

"That still doesn't give him the right to bin my polish," Daphne pouts, unwilling to admit defeat.

"To listen to you talk, anyone would think she'd raised him to be a mass murderer," says Bliss in exasperation.

"Well, something awful must have happened for him to have turned out like that. She must have poisoned his mind."

"Daphne," Bliss reminds her firmly, "it was just a can of spray polish."

"There's no smoke without fire, David. You know that," she persists, though Bliss can't help feeling that mountains and molehills might produce a more apt maxim.

Daphne's offer of suet pudding is declined by Ruth, who pats her now-shapely midriff, saying, "I really mustn't, Daphne. But thank you anyway. You've been very kind."

"Oh, don't mention it — absolutely nothing at all," she twitters. "I'm really quite thrilled for you, though I must admit that in a way I was hoping that it was your husband at the manor."

"Well I'm glad it wasn't," says Phillips, as he steps in to put an arm around Ruth's waist, adding to her, "And I've got another surprise for you — if you can take it."

The welter of strange experiences in the past twenty-four hours have been so unreal to Ruth that nothing would surprise her anymore, and she looks around the table at the kindly group of smiling foreigners as she stands in the dining room of an aging British agent, wondering why God has decided to turn her world upside down. Then a voice deep inside suggests that maybe he's turned it right side up.

"Well," queries Phillips, "can you take another surprise?"

"Sorry," says Ruth unfreezing herself. "Of course, Mike. What is it?"

Mike Phillips has had the surprise in his pocket for a couple of days, but he's been holding back, fearful that Jordan Jackson could still be alive. But now, with his mind at ease, he announces that he's been granted a further three months' secondment in Vancouver.

"Well, kiss him for chrissake," says Trina, giving Ruth a nudge.

"So what cases have you got on the go at present?" asks Bliss, once Phillips has disentangled himself from his fans.

"I've been working the biker gangs, mainly: drugs, extortion, and porn," he answers, adding, "But we're beginning to think we've got a serial killer on the loose."

"They're always tricky. What's the MO?"

"Hookers and addicts; easy targets — usual thing. No one misses them for weeks or months, if ever, and the trail's stone cold before we even start."

"Any suspects?"

"Not at the moment. He's probably some sort of religious nutbar claiming he's cleaning up the world for God."

"We've had a few of those — that's what the Yorkshire ripper reckoned he was doing."

"Our problem is that he's suddenly gone quiet. It's been more than four months since the last case, but some of them stretch back twenty years or more. Even Ruth's mother might have been one. By the way, any news on her father?"

Bliss laughs, and is in the process of recounting some of Daphne's little pretexts that had finally led them to isolating Geoffrey Sanderson, when, by a fortuitous fluke, the editor of the *Merseyside Mail* phones with news.

"We think we've found Sanderson," he tells Bliss excitedly.

"Where?"

"He's still in Vancouver, apparently. The local paper ran the photo this morning and they've had several calls."

"That's great."

"By the way. Is Mrs. Longbottom planning the reunion for Liverpool or Westchester?"

The temptation to hand the phone to Mavis, saying, "It's for you," is fleeting, though nonetheless amusing, but Bliss thinks better of it and stalls for time as he asks, "Has Sanderson actually been approached in person? Only, it's a fairly common name."

"Not unless one of the informants told him. I think the Vancouver paper is holding off in the hope that they can fly Mrs. Longbottom over to get a mushy front-page photo. You know the sort of thing: 'Old friends reunited after forty years.'"

Daphne is looking quizzically in Bliss's direction and he's seriously tempted to call her over and tell her to deal with it, but she appears so disheartened about her misreading of Maxwell that he carries on stalling. "I expect she'll need to confirm that it is the right man first. Have you got an address for him?"

"That was good timing," says Bliss handing Phillips the Vancouver address on a Post-It Note. "Sanderson is the only possibility, although he's a long shot, and I've no idea how you can persuade him to put his hand up to doing the nasty with Ruth's mother all those years ago."

"I'll just have to ask him, I suppose."

"Daphne thinks you should pinch his beer and check the glass for DNA."

"I suspect that's illegal, Dave," says Phillips. "Though I might be willing to give it a try if all else fails."

"What about Ruth? Will she give a sample?"

"She already has," Phillips says, then explains the circumstances surrounding the disappearance of Ruth's mother, and the difficulty of finding human remains in the British Columbian wilderness. "There's a whole lot of back-country in the mountains, Dave. You should come and visit sometime. But if he's stashing bodies up there, the wolves and coyotes won't leave much that can be identified. The best we might do is DNA from a few bone fragments or a few scattered teeth."

"Good luck," says Bliss.

"I guess it's time we were heading back to London," says Phillips as the excitement of the day wears down, but Daphne has one last surprise.

"Wait a minute," she yells, with a sudden thought, and she dashes out to the rear garden and into the coalhouse tacked onto the back of the house. Thirty seconds later she reappears, smothered in coal dust, triumphantly carrying a dilapidated and dusty cardboard box which she places on the kitchen table with as much reverence as if it contains the crown jewels.

"Paul Anka," she beams, as she opens the box and withdraws the warped and cracked remains of a forty-year-old LP, then her face falls as she says, "Oh, dear. I guess he's seen better days."

Trina and Ruth share the back seat of Bliss's car with a couple of suitcases that wouldn't fit in the trunk as they prepare to leave. Minnie has already kissed David Bliss goodbye twice without complaint from Daphne, so she tries a third time.

"Time we were getting off, Minnie," says Bliss as he ducks aside, fearing that Daphne might explode, but Daphne is still sulking over her misjudgment of Maxwell's identity and doesn't seem to notice.

"You just keep out of mischief or I'll have to come back," Bliss tells her as he gives her a warm hug, then she pulls away in thought. "Wait a minute," she yells, regaining some of her bounce, and she rushes back to the house and reappears with the giant hat that Ruth had worn to the manor.

"Here ... Keep it as a memento," Daphne says, stuffing it in the window to Ruth, and, for opposite reasons, both women have tears in their eyes.

"It seems so funny that someone would actually be happy that their husband is dead," says Daphne as she waves the car away, but Mavis doesn't find it at all unusual, telling her, "You've never been married, Daphne, that's your trouble."

In any case, Jordan Jackson isn't dead. A point demonstrated a few minutes later when Mort gets another early-morning call in Vancouver.

"It's me," says Jackson, and Mort uses his stump to shove a girl off his bed, hissing, "Get out," as he spits into the phone. "Jordan, what the fuck do you want?"

"I wanna come back, Mort."

"Well you can't can ya?"

"I want my ID back," bleats Jackson.

"Have you got the ten grand?"

"I already paid."

"Yeah ... with me own money. What d'ye f'kin take me for?"

"But I didn't know where she got it from."

"That's your problem, Jordan," he shouts. "Ten grand or you can stay there and rot." Then he slams down the phone and yells to the bathroom, "Oy. Get back in here, slut. You ain't finished yet."

chapter nineteen

The David Bliss sightseeing tour of London had taken in much more than the castles, palaces, and cathedrals over the following two days, but Ruth Crowfoot — formerly Jackson — and Mike Phillips had spent most of their time gawking at each other, rather than the sites of infamous events and notorious murders. The historic horrors of The Tower of London, Whitechapel, and the gruesome Black Museum at New Scotland Yard, had rounded off the trip in something of a rose-tinted blur for the happy couple and, as Bliss drops them at the airport, Mike Phillips promises that they'll stay for a week next time and pay more attention.

Trina Button is no longer with them. Having declared that she would be knee-deep in doo-doo if she left her patients a moment longer, she had headed straight back to Vancouver the day after their arrival.

"I guess that means we'll have to fly back with the jolly old riff-raff," Phillips had said to Ruth in an

English accent, but she hadn't cared, replying, "I'd sit on the wing as long as I'm with you."

"You could always use Daphne's hat as a parachute if anything goes wrong," Bliss laughs as he sees his guests through check-in at Heathrow, then, as he waves the homebound Canucks through security, his cellphone rings. It's a panic-voiced Minnie Dennon in Westchester.

"David. You've got to come back right away. Daphne's gone missing again."

"What?"

"I left my gloves round there the other afternoon and when I went back this morning she'd gone."

"She's probably out shopping."

"The milk is still on the doorstep, David," says Minnie, her voice loaded with meaning, and Bliss comprehends immediately as he counts the number of times Daphne had told him that the milkman always delivers before six in the morning, usually adding, "He knows I can't do a thing until I have my morning cuppa."

"But it's barely eleven," says Bliss, checking his watch. "Maybe she went to visit someone in a hurry. Have you asked the neighbours?"

"David," insists Minnie, "the milk is on the doorstep."

"Maybe she forgot to take it in," he tries finally, though he knows it's not at all likely; knows that, as spontaneous as Daphne may be in certain areas of her life, only matters of State would deter her from an early morning cup of Keemun with fresh milk.

"OK, I'm on my way," Bliss says, as he makes a run for the parking garage. "And I'll call Superintendent Donaldson."

Donaldson is having a mid-morning snack in the canteen to keep him going until lunchtime, and is just sitting down with a plate of buttered toast with strawberry jam and cream when Bliss phones.

"Have you got any clues?" asks Donaldson, once Bliss has filled him in.

"You might get someone to have a word with Maxwell up at the manor," suggests Bliss, devoid of other ideas, but the superintendent is skeptical.

"Surely, she wouldn't have gone back there?"

"She might ..." starts Bliss then carries on to explain that he wonders if it was guilt that drove her to offer to help clean Maxwell's apartment in the first place. "She seems to blame herself for turning him into a villain."

"Whatever gives her the idea that he's a villain?"

"Oh. She was really narked about her furniture polish, guv. 'That's theft, Chief Inspector,' she told me, as if she expected me to arrest him. But now she knows he really is Monty Maxwell's son, my guess is that she'll try to put matters right with him, though it's difficult to believe she would have stayed overnight."

"Do you reckon she's in any danger?"

"Good grief, no. I can't imagine anyone wanting to hurt her."

"Dave. We are talking about the son of a murderer, here," Donaldson reminds him, but Bliss isn't buying it. "If she is there, she'll have him eating out of her hand. You know what she's like when she turns on the charm."

Nothing could be further from the truth. Daphne Lovelace is certainly at Thraxton Manor, but she doesn't have charm on her mind, nor is the occupant of Thraxton Manor eating out of her hand, although the bull mastiff on guard duty certainly has been. In fact, he has eaten so much that he will happily snooze until noon, given the chance. The large bag of chuck steak that Daphne had brought with her had greased her way into the grounds, though the fact that the big dog had been introduced to her on her previous visits had helped.

Daphne is pinned down in a foxhole just inside the cover of the trees surrounding the old house, where she has been since the early dawn, monitoring the comings and goings of workers unloading the shipping containers stacked behind the stables. Her lookout post, a natural hollow inside a clump of alder bushes, is equipped with a flask of steaming Keemun and a hot water bottle for staving off the early morning chill, and she has a couple of flashlights and a camera in an old canvas shopping bag at her feet. She's well camouflaged, in a drab olive coat, old brown hiking boots, and a rattan hat interwoven with sprigs of greenery clipped from her garden, and she is peering through a pair of binoculars that hang around her neck.

From her concealment, Daphne is timing each operation as two men inside the container manhandle a skid of plywood onto the tines of a forklift which, in turn, manoeuvres it into one or the other of the enormous barns before returning. She is trying to gauge the best moment to make a dash for the manor's outbuildings without being seen, but she has a problem. Before she can slip into the stables and back into the apartment through the hayloft to search out Jackson's passport or other incriminating material, she has to wait until her quarry has left; something that he doesn't seem to be in a hurry to do.

David Bliss, on the other hand, is in such a hurry that he has twice triggered radar speed cameras as he races to Westchester, and he calls Donaldson again hoping for good news.

"I'm just arriving at the manor," says the superintendent, once Bliss is patched through to the senior officer's radio, "although I'm damned if I know what to say Maxwell. He must be getting ticked off with people turning up on his doorstep unannounced."

A Scotland Yard inspector, an RCMP sergeant, and now the local superintendent have all beaten the same path within the past week or so, and alarm bells are ringing off the wall in the apartment above the stables when Donaldson announces himself at the gate. But the voice on the entry phone is more guarded than aggravated as the new lord of the manor says, "Just drive straight up to the stables, Superintendent. I'll meet you at the door."

The giant gates whirr open and Superintendent Donaldson motors slowly up the driveway as he takes a good look around. Work on unloading the container stops briefly as the men eye the newcomer, while Daphne spots the familiar figure through her binoculars and muses, "Damnation," under her breath.

"Sorry — I haven't seen her for a week or more," says the apartment-dweller as he greets Donaldson. "What makes you think she'd be here?"

"Just from what she said to a friend, Mr. Maxwell. Apparently there was some sort of misunderstanding over some furniture polish."

"Yes, of course. I've still got it upstairs. Perhaps you'd give it back to her. Would you mind? I felt bad about what happened. I guess I was just having a bad day."

"Don't worry," laughs Donaldson. "I don't think she intends pressing charges."

"Hang on then," says the man and he rushes up the stairs to the apartment two at a time, returning with Daphne's aerosol can in seconds. "Tell her, 'sorry,'" he says as he hands it over.

"Delighted to," says Donaldson, then he spots a couple of heavies patrolling the perimeter fence and queries, "You seem to have quite a bit of security for a woodworking shop, Mr. Maxwell."

"We're pretty isolated out here, Superintendent. In any case — have you bought any wood recently?"

"Yes. I know what you mean," says Donaldson. "I paid ten quid for a bit of shelving the other day."

"If you ever need the odd sheet of plywood, give me a call and we'll fix you up."

"Thanks, Mr. Maxwell," says Donaldson, as he gets into his car and throws the can of polish on the rear seat, "I might take you up on that." Then he pauses with an afterthought as he looks around the estate. "I don't suppose Ms. Lovelace would have gone into any of the barns for any reason? Only, she can be very inquisitive at times."

"You've seen my security, Superintendent. What do you think?"

"Good point," says Donaldson, adding, "Just give us a call if she's shows up."

"There's no sign of her at the manor," Donaldson tells Bliss when he phones him back a few minutes later. "And Maxwell seems a pretty decent bloke. He even gave me her polish back."

"Well, I didn't get a good feel about him," admits Bliss. "Don't you have a tame Magistrate who'll give us a search warrant?"

"Dave, there isn't a shred of evidence that she is there. Maxwell is going to be on the phone to the Chief Constable if we don't stop pestering him."

"I hear you, sir, though I'm buggered if I know where else she might have gone. I'll be at her place in about ten minutes; maybe I'll find some clues."

Daphne had watched Donaldson's car drive out the gate, breathed a huge sigh of relief, and has just started pouring herself the last of the tea when the scene in front of her takes a dramatic change. A dozen or more men pour out of the barns and buildings and race toward the stables, along with the unloaders and security guards, and, just when she is thinking that it might be a good opportunity to stretch and exercise away some of her cramps, the men fan out in all directions, clearly intent on finding something — or someone.

"What on earth could they be looking for?" Daphne questions to herself as she sees two men with shotguns headed her way.

Inspector Bliss and Superintendent Donaldson arrive simultaneously at Daphne's to find Minnie sitting disconsolately on the doorstep.

"She's gone for good this time. I know it," snivels Minnie.

"Rubbish," says Bliss slumping down beside her and putting his arm around her shoulders.

"Well, where could she be?" Minnie carries on. "I've phoned everyone. No one has seen her."

"Have you been inside ..." Bliss starts, then lightning strikes. "Shit!" he exclaims, leaping up. "I bet she's still in bed. I bet she's sick and couldn't get up to take the milk off the doorstep this morning."

"That never occurred me," says Donaldson, as Bliss starts checking the windows to find a crack.

"Me neither," admits Bliss, giving Minnie an accusatory stare. "Someone convinced me that she'd done a bunk."

"I wish I'd made a copy of her door key now," says Bliss a few minutes later, when both the front and back windows have failed to yield. "Brick through the window it is then," he adds, but Donaldson grabs his arm.

"Hold on, Dave. If she's like most oldies I bet there's a key under a rock or a flowerpot. It doesn't make any difference how many times we warn 'em not to."

"Maybe under the Christmas tree," muses Bliss, and he can't help noticing that the little fir tree growing in its pot by the back door has developed a second bald spot as he tilts it to look underneath.

"Bingo!" Donaldson exclaims, and a few seconds later they are inside calling, "Daphne ... Daphne ... Where are you?"

The momentary elation of finding the key soon turns to disappointment once the entire house has been searched.

"Talk about déjà vu," says Bliss as he counts suitcases, then he stops in thought. "Sir," he calls, and Donaldson barrels into Daphne's bedroom as Bliss points to the bed, "Look. She hasn't made it since she last slept in it."

"Meaning?"

"She must have left very early this morning. She would never leave her bed unmade all day." Then he checks her alarm clock. "I knew it — five a.m."

"But where could she go at that time?" asks Minnie. "There're no busses."

"She must have walked," replies Bliss, heading back down the stairs to the sitting room and pointing out that the partially burnt logs and ash in the fire grate tell the same story as the milk on the doorstep.

"This means she left really early for sure," says Bliss as he prods the lifeless fire. Missie Rouge begging by the refrigerator door offers another clue. "And she must have planned on returning this morning, or she would have fed the cat."

"I've put out a missing person report to the men on the ground. Maybe I should call the dog teams back in to try and track her."

"The only place I can think of is the manor," says Bliss.

"But I've spoken to Maxwell," insists Donaldson. "She hasn't been seen there since the episode with the furniture polish."

Superintendent Donaldson's statement is no longer true. While in her day Daphne Lovelace might have slipped stealthily away into the woodland, or even tried to take them out with a knife or a hastily fashioned garrotte, she had been no match for the armed guards who had roughly hauled her out of her trench and marched her to the stables with her arms behind her back.

"Oh, for chrissake. That's all I need," says the man at the top of the stairs as Daphne is forced inside. "Bring her up and tell the men to get back to work."

"Maybe we should think this out over lunch," suggests Donaldson, with an eye on his stomach, as Bliss escorts him back to his car outside Daphne's. "Unless you've got any other plans, of course."

Bliss is just about to say that he had intended visiting the force's doctor to get signed back to work, when his eye is caught by Daphne's can of polish on Donaldson's rear seat.

"Hey, guv. Did you say that Maxwell handed that polish to you?"

"Yes."

"Great. Would you get it checked for his dabs, please?"

"Sure, but why?"

"Look, I know Ruth reckoned that Maxwell definitely wasn't her husband, but I'm just beginning to wonder if she lied, and Daphne was right all along."

"Why would she lie about that?"

"I bet the last thing she really wanted was to find that her husband was still alive, judging by the way that Mike dotes on her. And Mike told me that he'd never seen Jackson before, so he wouldn't have known who he was talking to."

"Dave," says Donaldson with a kindly hand on Bliss's shoulder, "don't you think you might be taking this Maxwell thing a bit far?"

"No, sir, I don't. Daphne is certain that he's an impostor, and, to be perfectly honest, I don't think I've ever known her to misjudge anyone."

"And if there are prints?"

"We can send them to Mike Phillips. He'll be back in Vancouver by this evening. Who knows, either Maxwell or Jackson could be on file in Canada."

"Well, I don't suppose it'll do any harm," says Donaldson, relenting. "Though I doubt it will do any good either. If she is there at the manor, I'd bet my pension that he doesn't know it."

It would not be a good day for Donaldson to back a horse, and he could never picture the scene above the stables at Thraxton Manor as the diminutive Daphne, looking like an ad for a shelter for the homeless, clutches her sprouted hat in one hand and her tattered old shopping bag in the other, while Maxwell leans over her, demanding, "Who knows you're here?"

"Lots of people: Minnie Dennon, Mavis Longbottom ... She used to be the cook at ..."

"Shuddup you stupid old bat. Why the fuck couldn't you have left me alone?"

"You should have your mouth washed out with soap ..."

"Shuddup! Shuddup!"

"Temper, temper, Jeremy."

"I said shuddup!" he screams, and slaps her sharply across the face.

Daphne takes a second to compose herself before softly saying, "I suppose you're proud of that, Jeremy."

"Shuddup or I'll do it again."

"Do you smack little children about as well?"

"I warned you ..." he starts, and the second slap sends Daphne sprawling.

"The game's up Jeremy," she says calmly, from the floor. "Why do you think Inspector Bliss from the Yard and Sergeant Phillips gave you a visit? Just a friendly social call? Or perhaps they wondered what you were up to shipping that funny smelling plywood all the way from Vancouver."

"Shuddup ... Shuddup ... Shuddup."

The afternoon drags slower than the wait for a heart transplant for Bliss. He's toured the city a couple of times, and checked the hospital; the neighbours have rallied and searched their gardens again; Donaldson has sent a few uniformed constables to quiz the locals and search the woods at the end of Daphne's street; and Mavis Longbottom has ditched Gino and shows up with a different man.

"I was never quite sure if Gino was asleep or dead most of the time," she explains as the lanky George unwinds himself from her little car and stands awaiting an introduction.

And you think this one looks alive? muses Bliss to himself as he watches the dour six-footer with slumped shoulders staring at the ground.

"I could ask the army to help again," Donaldson had half-heartedly suggested mid-afternoon, "but I haven't a clue where to tell them to search. Plus, I'll look like an idiot if she comes waltzing back again like she did last time."

A reporter from the *Westchester Gazette* shows up a little after four and asks for a recent photo. Without the weather to worry about, the pressman is scratching for work, although he loses interest somewhat when he learns that Daphne's disappearances are becoming habitual. "Let me know if she's not back by tonight," he tells Bliss.

By five in the afternoon, with no sign of Daphne and only an hour or so until sundown, Bliss is beginning to fear the worst and thinks he is headed for a nervous breakdown.

Across the world in Vancouver it is the other end of the day, and with the morning sun just a few degrees above the Rockies, it's time for Trina Button to pull off another scam on Candace at the Health Ministry, before the greenhorn clerk has a chance to get the sleep out of her ears.

During all the excitement over the England trip, Trina had put aside the box of Zofran, but the question, "To whom were they prescribed?" had bugged her for two days until she had found the relevant pharmacy. Then she had used her nurse's uniform and a saucy smile to twist the pharmacist's arm until he'd admitted that the serial number stamped on the torn label showed they had belonged to a cancer patient named Peter Healy.

"Who's his doctor?" Trina had inquired as she'd peeked over the man's shoulder at the store's computer terminal.

"Dr. Fitzpatrick," he'd replied, and the alarm bells in Trina's mind had rung all night until the phone lines to the Health Ministry opened in the morning.

"Hi Candace. It's me, Margery Woods," Trina says from a payphone when she finally gets through the computerized messaging maze at nine-fifteen. "You remember ... from Dr. Fitzpatrick's office?"

"Oh, Margery," says Candace in resignation. "What have you done this time?"

"I pushed the wrong button and totally deleted a patient," replies Trina bouncily. "One minute he was there, and the next minute — poof! He was gone."

"No worries, Margery. I can sort that out."

"Candace, dear, are you ever going to stop saving my life? Maybe I could take you out to the theatre, or dinner ..."

"Don't worry about it," laughs Candace. "What's the patient's name?"

"Peter Healy," Trina says, then reads off the date of birth and Personal Health Number that she had finagled out of the pharmacist.

"That's interesting," muses Candace, and Trina holds her breath while the girl complains about the uselessness of the system before asking confusedly, "Are you sure that name's right, Margery?"

"I think so," replies Trina. "Like I said, I just 'poofed' him into thin air, but what's the matter?"

"It looks like you 'poofed' him permanently."

"Oh my God. He's not dead, is he?"

"No. But he should be. According to this, he hasn't had any treatment since early November."

"I've probably screwed up his records. You know what I'm like."

"But he's got AIDS and cancer."

"Maybe he transferred to another practice," suggests Trina, but Candace has already checked.

"No. He had his last hospital treatment on the fourth of November and Dr. Fitzpatrick prescribed

Zofran on the sixth, and that's the very last entry."

"I probably made a boo-boo," laughs Trina, but Candace fails to see the funny side and her tone darkens.

"Margery, this is serious. I'm going to have to report this. Mr. Healy could be dead for all we know. This just isn't good enough."

"Does that mean I can't take you out to dinner, then?" says Trina with a crack in her voice as she feigns the sniffle of a tear.

"Please don't cry, Margery."

"Sorry, Candace. It's just that I feel that I've lost a really good friend," says Trina, barely able to control the tears, and her snivels start the other girl off.

"I feel the same way, Margery," sobs Candace. "But I don't know what else to do."

"What if I really, really, really promised to be more careful in future, Candy sweetheart."

"I don't know ..." wails the clerk.

"I'll never, ever, screw up again, Guide's honour," bawls Trina, giving herself a salute, and Candace starts to break.

"If you promise ..."

"Thank you. Thank you," cries Trina. "You're wonderful, Candace." Then she pushes her luck. "Oh, there's just one more little thing. Just so that I can get my records straight. What was his address?"

"You'd better write it down," says the girl as she pulls up a screen, and Trina readies herself with a lipstick, but the row of cherries have already clinked into place in her mind, and she is not in the least surprised when Candace replies, "One-four-six-five Newport Avenue, apartment twenty-four."

While Candace in the Health Ministry might have been a walk in the park for the home care nurse, the elderly curmudgeon in the Department of Vital Statistics is less of a pushover when Trina phones asking for information about Peter Healy's apparent death.

"Sorry, Madam. But the rules don't allow me to give details of deceased persons over the phone," the woman says, starkly.

"I'm not asking for details of a deceased person," says Trina sweetly. "I'm simply asking you to confirm that he isn't deceased. Now, is that against the rules?"

"Probably."

"Well, is it?"

"I'm not sure."

"Would you please find out? By the way, perhaps I should advise you that I am recording this conversation."

The line dies briefly before a blast of muzak nearly takes off Trina's ear.

"Sorry. Was that too loud, dear?" says the woman when she comes back on line five minutes later.

"No, I was enjoying it," says Trina, truthfully. "So, can you tell me?"

"I suppose so," snaps the woman, and she hands over the information as if it is coming out of her own pocket. "No record of any Peter Healy in the past year."

"There," says Trina in her nurse's voice, "That didn't hurt one little bit, did it?"

Daphne is back in the hayloft above the stables at Thraxton Manor, but this time she is firmly tied to a solid beam that hasn't shifted an inch in more than four hundred years, and nothing a little old lady does is going to change that. Her arms feel as if they have been broken, her fingers are numb from the bindings on her wrists, and her mouth tastes like a dirty dish-cloth.

"Sorry about this, me old duck," Liam, one of the security guards, had said as he'd prepared a length of broad duct tape to gag her. "I don't wanna do this, but you're such a wily old bird — we can't have you flying off when we ain't looking now, can we?"

"Oh, no; it's quite all right young man. You needn't apologize. I do understand," Daphne had replied, but her apparent empathy had failed to soften him.

Trina Button, in Vancouver, is equally unyielding as she pays the smelly superintendent at 1465 Newport Avenue another visit, and sees a flicker of recognition in his face when she asks about Peter Healy.

"Never heard of him," lies the stinky sixty-year-old as he tries to shut the door in her face. But Trina knows different, and she launches herself against the door with a flying drop kick that sends the paunchy little man crashing back into his apartment.

"Sorry," says Trina, attempting to lift him by his right ear lobe while firmly planting a stiletto heel on his hand, "but I happen to know that he was here. So, unless you want me to rip off my clothes and scream rape, you'd better start talking."

"I don't ..." starts the little man, but Trina fiercely wrenches at his ear, yelling, "One more lie, and I scream."

"He'll kill me," he mumbles and Trina begins to screech.

"All right. All right," yells the old man. "Quit it, will ya?"

"So," she says, keeping up the pressure on his ear, "tell me why you lied about Jordan Jackson. Tell me about Peter Healy."

"They just give me the names, lady. Like I told you before, it ain't healthy asking questions around here."

"Who gives you the names?"

The momentary delay in answering causes the superintendent considerable pain as Trina's free foot slams into his groin.

"Ow, bitch."

"Shall I do it again," she questions sweetly, "or are you going to tell me?"

"OK. Lay off. I'll tell you, I'll tell you."

When Trina leaves the building ten minutes later to fetch a bandage for his hand and pain killers for his groin from her medical kit in the car, she has extracted more than enough details from the superintendent for Mike Phillips to work on when he gets back from England, although she still plans to squeeze the scruffy little man for the name of the organization's "Mr. Big."

The superintendent plays dead when she gets back with the pills, and Trina's threats to batter down the door won't make him budge. He has crawled into his bedroom, barricaded himself in, and is on the phone, adding to Mort's woes.

"She's figured it out, Mort," he bleats as he lays on his bed trying to rub life back into his testicles. "She's blown the doc's story, and she even knows that Jackson ain't dead."

Trina stuffs a handful of Tylenols into the superintendent's mailbox in the lobby on her way out, then tries piecing together her new-found knowledge as she drives off to visit her first patient.

"It is so simple," she says to herself, realizing that it wouldn't be difficult among Vancouver's legions of street people to find one who was on his last legs who bore a passing resemblance to Jordan. The promise of a bed more comfortable than the sidewalk, a steady supply of dope, and a little bit of cash for dependants, would have been all it took. After all, Healy was dying anyway. And when he was too far-gone to recover, or even care, he was carted off to the hospital and signed in as Jordan Jackson. Dr. Fitzpatrick is conveniently on hand to confirm his identity and condition and, as the body is trundled away by the undertaker, the good doctor puts his signature on a death certificate bearing the name of Jordan Artemus Jackson.

"I bet half the people in that dump are just waiting to die," she tells herself with a backward glance. "Just waiting for someone else to step into their shoes, miraculously recover, then walk away a new man, with a valid driver's license, a passport, and a clean slate."

Tom Burton is also a new man, and he walks out of the remand centre absolutely determined to go straight, when Joshua and Dingo drive up in the black BMW. "Hi Tom," calls Dingo jovially from the passenger seat. "Mort sent us to give you a ride."

"I'll walk," says Burton, having finally decided that his life as a villain's pimp is not worth the aggravation, but Dingo's door starts to open.

"That's not very friendly, Tom," says Dingo, slamming Tom against a wall. "Especially as it was him who fixed your bail. He gets upset if people turn him down."

"He'll have to be upset then. You'd better tell him that I can't work for him anymore."

"You're gonna have to tell him yourself," says Dingo, as he opens the rear door with one hand and flings in the unfortunate man with the other.

Mort is in his office behind the porn studio, but he's not expecting to see Tom — ever again — nor is he expecting a buzz on the outside door's entry-phone.

"Shit!" he exclaims when he checks the surveillance monitor and sees a figure nervously searching around as if he's on the lam.

"Come up," yells Mort viciously as he releases the door lock, and he walks through the studio to the landing. "Well, well, well," carries on Mort sarcastically as the familiar figure climbs the stairs. "If it isn't my poor little f'kin cousin Jordan."

"Hi Jeremy ..." starts Jackson airily as he reaches the top, but Mort turns on him with a snarl.

"I've told you before. Don't call me that."

"It's your name."

"Do you reckon I should be proud of that, eh? D'ye think I should go 'round sayin' I'm Jeremy Maxwell, son of Monty? You know ... the bloke who blew his wife away and topped himself?"

"I know what your father did. That's all I ever heard from you when we were kids. 'My dad's a murderer,' you used to say to frighten me and the other kids, like it was some sort of achievement."

"Scared you though, didn't it?" laughs Maxwell as he heads back through the studio with Jackson in tow. "'I'm Mort — short for mortuary,' I used to say in a creepy voice, and you'd hide under the f'kin bed for a week."

"It wasn't funny, Jeremy ..."

"Will you stop calling me that?"

In England, Daphne Lovelace is having the same problem with John Waghorn, as he checks on her in the hayloft and takes the tape off her mouth to give her some water.

"Why are you doing this to me, Jeremy?" she asks him when she's moistened her lips.

"Oh, for chrissake, cut that out. You know damn

well that I'm not Maxwell. You nosed through my stuff and found my passport."

"Jordan Jackson," muses Daphne, confusedly.

"So?"

"Well ... Why didn't your wife recognize you?"

"Wife? What are you talking about? What wife?"

"She came the other day with Sergeant Phillips from Vancouver."

"I thought she was his wife ..." he starts, then spits, "Oh, shit!" and shouts through to the apartment. "Liam. Get in here and tape her up before I forget my manners and kick her teeth in."

"Sure, boss," says Liam, and the lord of the manor heads for the phone.

"Mort," he calls as soon as the Vancouverite answers. "We've got a huge problem." But Mort has his own problems with his little cousin and yells, "I'll call you back," as he slams the phone down.

"So what d'ye want?" Maxwell says, turning on Ruth's husband.

"You owe me," says Jackson. "If my mother hadn't taken you in you would've been in an orphanage."

"Your f'kin mother — the old witch," spits Maxwell. "She treated me like scum from the day I got here. Just 'cos my dad shot my mum then topped himself. I didn't ask him to do it."

"It wasn't my fault," complains Jackson, but Maxwell turns on his younger cousin, mimicking with a sneer. "It weren't my fault ... Nuvvin was ever your fault, was it? Oh, no. I got blamed for everything, didn't I? You made sure of that, didn't you? You were just like a snitchin' little brother, always dropping me in it — and how come you always got everything and I didn't, eh?"

"You oughta be grateful she put a roof over your head after what your dad did to her sister."

"Grateful for what? Grateful she didn't kill me? She wanted to. I could see it in her eyes when she was belting me ... Here's another one for my big sister."

"She wasn't that bad."

"You don't know the half of it. You were still shitting in your diapers when she was beating the crap out of me every night, just so I wouldn't forget what my old man did. When did she ever smack you around, eh?"

"She did, sometimes."

"Yeah, right. What'd'ye want anyway?"

"I wanna come back."

"You can't. Jordan Jackson is in England. We can't have two Jordan Jacksons running around. Someone might get suspicious."

"You sold my passport?" says Jackson in surprise.

"Well you didn't f'kin pay for Healy's did ya? I have costs Jordan: the apartment, drugs, doctors, undertakers, cremation ... Ten grand for a clean ID is a poxin' bargain, but you gave me my own money."

"That was Tom's fault."

"Yeah, well, he won't be doin' it again, that's for sure," snaps back Mort with meaning as he attempts to lead Jackson to the door, saying, "You'll just have to get used to being Healy."

But Jackson digs in his heels. "Aren't you forgetting something, Jeremy?"

"What, Jordan?" spits Maxwell menacingly.

"I know what you're doing. How many people are running around with fake IDs, Jeremy? What's the going rate for a ton of pot? Who's been wasting hookers? I could go to the cops and spill everything. I haven't done anything illegal. Changing names and going on holiday for a few months ain't a crime. They can't touch me."

"Aren't you forgetting something as well?" responds Mort as his hand goes into his pocket.

"What's that, Jeremy?"

Mort pulls out a handgun, saying, "I think you forgot that you're supposed to be dead, Jordan."

The hidden microphone in the wall of Mort's office picks up the crack of the gunshot that chokes off Jordan's final shriek, and transmits it to the digital recorder built into Vern McLeod's camera. McLeod isn't there to hear it, but he will later, when he shows up for work.

Jeremy Maxwell's phone starts ringing again and he steps over Jackson's body to answer it. "What now?" he screams, recognizing the English number.

"We've caught some old granny snooping," says Waghorn worriedly.

"So?"

"She's figured out that I'm not the rightful heir."

"God! Do I have to do everything? Just get rid of her then — know what I mean?"

Waghorn's reluctance to eliminate Daphne comes through in his hesitation and Maxwell questions, "Is that a problem?"

"She's, like, a hundred and fifty."

"Who the hell is she?"

"I dunno. Daphne somebody-or-other."

"Not Daphne Lovelace?" queries Mort.

"What did she call herself?" muses the man in the manor. "Auntie Daffodil or something like that."

The silence could be a break in the transatlantic service and, fearing that he's been disconnected, Waghorn queries, "Are you still there?"

"Yeah."

"D'ye know her?"

"Yeah. She kinda killed my parents. Christ, I thought she'd have been dead years ago."

"What do you mean, 'killed your parents'?"

"Long story. I should hate her I s'pose, but I don't. She was a damn sight better than the woman who brought me up."

"Oh, Christ. Well, what d'ye want me to do with her?"

"What does she know?"

"Everything. She may be a hundred and fifty but she's got all her marbles. I reckon she'd cottoned on that I wasn't you the moment she saw me, then she found Jackson's passport and just kept coming back until she figured out the rest."

Maxwell takes a glance down at his cousin's spread-eagle body, before saying, "Sometimes we just have to say goodbye to the ones we love — know what I mean, John? Just do me a favour ... make it quick — nothing messy, OK?"

chapter twenty

By nightfall, David Bliss is beginning to despair at ever seeing his sprightly old friend again. Minnie has re-colonized Daphne's domain and is putting the finishing touches to a shepherd's pie, telling Bliss that he has to keep up his strength. *For what?* he wonders, as he switches on the light and listlessly puts a match to the fire. The extent of his powerlessness is wearing, and he questions whether or not he has missed an obvious clue. He has driven past Thraxton Manor a dozen times — pausing to scour the fields and buildings through his binoculars; he has walked the High Street quizzing every little old lady he could get to stop; he's checked the hospital twice; and he's pored over Daphne's wardrobe trying to work out what she might have been wearing.

"I don't know what else I can do," he deliberates, more to himself than Minnie, but she puts her head around the kitchen door, saying, "Stop getting yourself in a tizzy, Dave. She'll be back." Then, just as she goes on to say, "I made an extra big pie because Mr. Donaldson is coming over," the superintendent's car rolls up.

"We've sent those prints to Sergeant Phillips," Donaldson affirms, before Bliss has a chance to ask.

"Great," says Bliss, then checks his watch. "It's about a ten hour flight — then he'll have to get home. It'll be midnight here at the earliest before he gets them."

"I could've gone through official channels, but it would've taken a week," explains Donaldson, adding, "Do I smell shepherd's pie?"

It's lunchtime in Vancouver, and Trina is back on Jordan's trail as she seeks out the crematorium where the benefactor of his new persona was fired. Even in her calmest of moments there would have been a good chance that she may have taken the wrong entrance — it's clearly marked, "Undertakers' vehicles only," but in her haste, she flies up the service road, skids around a corner of the building, and bumps solidly into the back of Mort Maxwell's BMW as his two henchman wait to make a very special double delivery.

"Oy. Stupid bitch," yells Dingo as he steams out of the car and heads for Trina.

"Oops. Sorry," laughs Trina, leaning out of the Jetta's window. "It's probably only a scratch."

Then a look of recognition comes over Dingo's face, and he spins and slinks back with his head down.

"I said I was sorry," calls Trina, climbing out to inspect the damage, but Dingo is already in the front passenger seat and the car is driving away.

"I need your name for the insurance," she yells after the departing BMW, just as a white-coated attendant appears at the unloading bay with a gurney.

"They've gone," says Trina, and she sees a look of fright on the man's face.

"Oh ... Right," he says, and races back inside.

"What's going on ..." starts Trina, then the final cog drops into place and she dashes back to her car with the BMW's license plate number on her lips.

"Mort," yells Dingo into his cellphone as he and Joshua drive away. "That Button bitch showed up just as we were making the delivery."

"Shit! Did she see anything?"

"Don't think so, but she's smacked the car."

"She's gotta go, Dingo. She's worked out the whole deal. But for chrissake be discreet — know what I mean?"

"Mort, the effin trunk is already full. What do you expect us to with another one?"

"Just do it."

Trina spots Maxwell's car the moment she hits the main road, but her plan to follow it takes an immediate twist when the BMW detours through a corner gas station and comes out behind her.

"Two can play at that game," she mutters, and she does a sudden double U-turn in the face of oncoming traffic, ending up on their tail again.

"What the ..." howls Joshua, as Trina sticks to his rear bumper like a wasp on a child.

"Shake her off," yells Dingo, but they're boxed in with traffic.

Trina is enjoying the ride as she nudges the rear of the BMW, while yelling excitedly to her husband on the phone. "Rick. Don't argue. Just get the kids out of the house." Then she calls back in a panic, shrieking, "Don't forget to take the guinea pig."

"Inspector Wilson, please," Trina hollers into the phone next, driving one-handed as she repeatedly taps the BMW's rear.

"Get rid of her," shouts Dingo as the little Volkswagen slams into their trunk again and again.

"It's Trina Button," she yells, when Wilson answers. "Granville Street Bridge. There's going to be an accident."

"What?"

"Hang on," she shrieks, as the BMW suddenly lurches to a halt and she is slammed into its rear by the car behind her. The trunk of the BMW pops open on impact and, if Trina's airbag had deployed as it should have, she wouldn't have seen the scrunched bodies of Jordan and Tom, nor would she have seen Dingo and Joshua furiously advancing on her.

"They're packing heat," Trina yells into the phone, hoping that she's got the correct lingo, as Dingo shoots-out her side window, while Joshua tries to slam his trunk.

"Get out," screams Dingo. "Get out." But a dozen cellphones are calling 911 as stalled motorists stare agog at the bodies in the trunk, and Joshua panics.

"Dingo, Dingo," he yells, leaving the trunk open, jumping back into the driver's seat, and starting to drive away.

"Hey! Wait for me ..." bellows Dingo, racing after him.

"Too late again," Trina tells Wilson as she shakes glass out of hair and picks up her phone, "I'm surprised you ever catch anyone." Then, just as he's readying to boil, she gives him a description of Maxwell's musclemen, the BMW's plate number, and details of its gruesome cargo.

Dinner at Daphne's was a solemn affair. Bliss had hard-ly touched the shepherd's pie, though Donaldson had thought it only polite to clean out the dish, and Minnie had admitted that she was beginning to feel concerned.

"It's the not knowing that's the worst," bemoans Minnie as she pours three large scotches.

"I'm going back to the manor," asserts Bliss as it nears ten o'clock, his tone dissuading Donaldson from protesting. "I'm bloody sure she's there."

"I can't stop you, Dave," says the senior officer, though he's grateful that he's not Bliss's superior and won't be responsible if the quest goes to hell. "Just don't let Maxwell catch you trespassing, for God's sake."

"He can't do anything about it though, can he," explains Bliss. "Since when is simple trespass a crime?"

"I'm not worried about him prosecuting. I'm more worried about his heavies. Anyway, how do you propose getting past the cameras and security?"

"I'll hitch a ride with a mate of mine first thing in the morning, if you'll help — though I'll need some sleep first."

Sleep is the last thing on John Waghorn's mind at Thraxton Manor, as he paces in front of his goons, yelling, "Call yourselves security? She's a hundred an' fifty years old, for chrissakes. And that stinking dog of yours. What was he doing when she got in — licking his balls?"

"Sorry John," says Liam, the Irishman. "He kinda got attached to the old biddy."

Waghorn snorts in disbelief. "Some guard dog ... So what happens now? What's the deal with the cops? They obviously think she's here. Do they need warrants or what? Can we buy off a judge?"

"Maybe in London, but not here, John. I reckon it'll be a dawn raid," says Marky, Liam's cockney partner. "I reckon they'll turn up mob-handed with the artillery, hoping to catch us in our pits."

"Well, what the hell are we gonna do with her?" yells Waghorn.

"I dunno for Jesus' sake," sighs Liam. "The ground's too bloody soggy to dig."

"The floor in the barn still ain't finished," suggests Marky, but Waghorn rounds on him, "You think they won't notice a big patch of wet concrete?"

"They ain't gonna be happy 'til they've found her," moans Liam.

"Let's give her to 'em then," says Marky with an idea.

"Oh, yeah. So she can drop us all in it?"

"No, John. Once they've got a body they'll stop looking. All we gotta do is ditch the old crumbly on the road somewhere, then run her over with the Range Rover a couple of times. That thing weighs a bloody ton. She'll hardly feel it, and the filth will put it down to a drunk driver and back off."

"Hey, that just might work," muses Waghorn, brightening. "Though you'd have to make sure she's properly waxed. One peep out of her and we're screwed."

"Yeah. Of course."

"Hang on," says Waghorn while he plays the idea through his mind, checking for flaws, before pronouncing, "OK. It's a go. Just be damn sure that you don't leave a trace. Make sure that she's got her bag and everything, and for chrissakes remember to take the stuff off her hands and mouth."

"Of course, John."

"And don't damage the f'kin Rover, and wash it off properly before you bring it back. I don't want them finding her blood and guts all over the place. And make sure there aren't any of her prints anywhere either."

Five minutes later, the floodlight over the manor's entranceway bursts into life, the gates slowly open, and the Range Rover drives out. The two men in the front are pros, and are equipped with ski masks, surgical gloves, and treadless shoes, while a selection of weapons are at hand, concealed on clips under the dashboard for ease of access. Behind the vehicle's rear seat, bundled under a blanket, and still securely tied, is Daphne Lovelace, OBE.

Ruth and Mike Phillips arrive back at the sergeant's hotel minutes before four in the afternoon — nearly midnight in England — and find Trina pacing the foyer with Sergeant Brougham.

"I've got to talk to you right away," bubbles Trina as she escorts them toward the elevator while handing Phillips an opened envelope. "It's a message from Dave Bliss," she carries on chattily. "He says 'Hi,' and says you've got to check your email as soon as you get in ... Oh, and he says Daphne's gone again."

"You opened my mail?" Phillips queries in astonishment, taking out the receptionist's hand-written message.

"Of course I did. It might've been important ... Oh, nearly forgot — Dave says 'Hi' to Ruth, as well."

"Thanks, Trina," says Ruth with a smile, though Phillips looks less pleased, stopping abruptly to ask, "Why is Sergeant Brougham here?"

"Protection," Trina boasts proudly. "The mob is trying to kill me."

"I'll fill you in upstairs, Mike," says Brougham.

Mike Phillips fires up his computer the moment he hits his room, while Brougham outlines Trina's escapades. Trina has taken Ruth to the hotel's restaurant for tea, and has theatrically checked for mobsters around each corner and even under the table, elatedly explaining to Ruth, "There's probably a price on my head," before confiding to her friend that, after a spell as Mrs. Peter Healy, she is now finally a free woman.

It only takes Phillips a few seconds to pull up the fingerprints from England and forward them to his detachment from his email. A couple of minutes later he is on the phone to Bliss in a serious panic.

"Dave. You've got a real nasty situation ... the prints you sent — if it's the man in the manor — he isn't Maxwell. His name's John Waghorn."

"And he is?" asks Bliss.

Phillips takes a breath. "Keep this under your hat, Dave, but he's the prime suspect in our serial killer case."

"What? Are you certain?"

"Yeah. He slipped off our radar about four months ago, just about the time that Maxwell showed up at your end, I guess. We had an 'all ports' watch out for him, but no one reported him leaving the country."

"Because he was travelling as Jordan Jackson," says Bliss, piecing the scenario together, and reaching the place where Daphne had been several weeks ago. "But why didn't he use Maxwell's name?"

"He couldn't. I checked Waghorn's file. He's a buddy of, wait for it, a nasty little shit-rat named Mort Maxwell. English, born 1958, a.k.a. Morty Maxwell. Real name — you guessed it — Jeremy Maxwell. I knew that I recognized the name. He's seriously naughty — convictions going back to the seventies. Maxwell can't move a muscle without it setting off an alarm."

So much for Daphne thinking he would turn out straight, thinks Bliss, asking, "What's his form?"

"Drugs, laundering, assault. His cover is a back-street porn studio. We've got a man in there. I'll try to contact him before he goes in this evening — see what else we can get. And Trina has just spotted two of his goons riding around with a couple of stiffs in the trunk."

"Trust Trina," says Bliss. "But what have you got on our man here?"

"Nothing solid — not enough for an arrest warrant. Anyway, what's happening there? What's this about Daphne?"

Bliss catches Donaldson just before the senior officer goes to bed, and a few minutes later a couple of patrol cars speed to take up static positions close to the manor's gates while a third tours the surrounding area, but they are fractionally too late. The Range Rover has returned and the gates are closing behind it.

"Well," demands Waghorn, meeting the vehicle at the stables, "did it go all right?"

Liam is shuffling his feet while Marky, the driver, taps the steering wheel and stares at the floor.

"What's going on?" demands Waghorn, and Marky speaks up.

"We finds a real quiet road and this Irish pillock unties her and gets her gag off. Then he gives her her handbag and the bloody old bat takes out a little bag of chocolate f'kin biscuits and gives 'em to him, sayin' 'Here. You look like a nice young man. You 'ave 'em 'cuz I won't need 'em where I'm goin'.' And the next thing — he's bawling his f'kin eyes out."

"So? Why didn't you drop her, for chrissake?"

"John ... Like, she's an old lady, you know ..."

"Oh, what a pair of wussies. Give me the keys, for chrissakes. Do I have to do everything around here?"

Waghorn is back at the stables in less than five minutes, and is dragging Daphne out of the Rover's trunk, shouting for Liam and Marky to help.

"What's up, boss," says Liam. "You didn't fall for the biscuits, did you?"

"Shuddup, for chrissakes. The bloody place is crawling with cops. Get everyone together, we've got a lot of work to do."

Cops are also on the move in Vancouver. Cruisers from all over the city are converging on the black BMW as it speeds south toward the US border. The flapping trunk lid catches the attention of every passed motorist, and cellphone calls jam the emergency switchboards of half a dozen police districts, as drivers and passengers alike recoil in horror at the ghastly sight.

Jeremy Maxwell, alias Mort, is desperately cleaning out his safe when Dave, his trusty cameraman, shows up for work with half a dozen well-armed friends. And the one-handed Englishman is still pleading both ignorance and innocence when Dave morphs into Constable Vern McLeod, takes the concealed digital recorder from his camera, plugs it into a speaker, and turns up the volume.

It's a little before five a.m. in Westchester, when Minnie Dennon bustles around Daphne's kitchen making tea for Bliss. She's wearing Daphne's cardigan and slippers again, but Bliss is too preoccupied to notice, as he daubs his face and hands with black shoe polish and struggles into the black overalls that one of Donaldson's officers had delivered to Daphne's doorstep overnight.

Donaldson sends a car for Bliss at five-fifteen and greets him at a roadblock about a mile from Thraxton Manor.

"We thought this would be the best place for it,"

says Donaldson, sweeping his hand around the collection of officers and vehicles while checking Bliss over. "Here's a radio — just squawk and we'll come running." Then he queries, "Are you carrying?"

"No, guv," says Bliss. "I didn't plan on doing this today."

"Here, take this," says Donaldson handing him a loaded police special.

Bliss hefts the piece meditatively for a second. "You realize that you'll be writing reports 'til the day you get your pension if I have to use it."

"Don't worry about it, Dave. I could retire tomorrow if I wanted."

The driver of the truck, on his way from the docks with yet another container bound for the manor, is on schedule until he comes around a bend and is surprised to find a commercial vehicle inspection team at a police roadblock.

"Just a routine stop, driver," says Donaldson, climbing up to the cab. "Can I see your driver's and carrier's licenses, please?"

"Sure. You blokes are out early this mornin', aren't you?"

"We're going fishing," muses Donaldson. "Early birds and all that," before asking, "What's your destination, driver?"

"Thraxton Manor — I got a load of plywood."

"We won't keep you long," carries on Donaldson as he gives a nod to a group of officers, and four of them move in to inspect the tires and brakes.

Bliss also gets the nod, and he's shielded by a posse of officers as he crouches low to scuttle under the container, where he crawls on top of a substantial girder and clings on, thinking that he's lucky it's not far to the manor.

The whirr from the manor's big gates is lost amidst the thunder of the giant truck's engine a few minutes later, but Bliss knows he is inside the Maxwell estate as soon as the vehicle starts bouncing along the rutted gravel driveway, threatening to throw him off the girder.

The workshops and barns are dark and silent as the vehicle comes to a halt, and Bliss is just about to slip quietly from underneath the trailer when Liam approaches with his dog.

"There's an empty to go back," the Irishman calls to the driver as his mastiff tries to pull him under the container. "Get outa there," he yells, yanking on the animal's collar, while the driver protests, "No one told me about a return."

Liam shrugs. "Not my fault, mate."

Bliss stealthily drops from under the container as Liam wanders away, and, in seconds, he is slipping into the dark stables.

"Nice horsey," he whispers, as the stallion under the hayloft's trapdoor snorts restlessly. *Now what?* Bliss asks himself, knowing that his last encounter with the equine kingdom was at the age of nine, riding a holiday donkey on the beach in Brighton — and even that had landed him in the Red Cross tent with a scraped knee.

Liam's guard dog has Bliss's scent, yet the Irishman keeps him on a tight rein, shouting, "Shuddup. It's only a horse," as he concentrates on making sure that the driver doesn't leave without taking the container. But the whinnying horse is both a blessing and a curse as Bliss stumbles around in the murky corners of the stable, feeling for a bag of feed, or some rope. He finds the feed first and tips a pile onto the ground outside the animal's stall before opening the door.

The hayloft's trapdoor creaks open a few minutes

later, just as the truck drives away, with Liam and his dog alongside the driver in the cab.

"I ain't s'posed to take passengers," the driver had complained when Liam had stated his intentions, but the look in the Irishman's eyes had been enough to persuade him.

"Daphne?" whispers Bliss into the darkness of the hayloft, and he switches on his flashlight, fearful of what he may find. But there is no sign of Daphne, although his light glints on something in the hay.

"Keemun ... I knew it," he muses, once he's unscrewed the stopper of the stainless steel vacuum flask, then he throws caution to the wind, pulls out his gun, flicks off the safety, and crashes through the door into the apartment.

"Waghorn ... Armed police. Come out with your hands up," he shouts to the room, but nothing happens.

"Waghorn, I know you're in here," he yells, dashing frantically from room to room, breaking all the rules, building himself up to shoot first and sort out the mess later. "Waghorn. Come out."

It only takes Bliss a minute or so — just long enough for the truck to drive out of the gates and head for the Southampton Road — before he catches on, and shrieks into his radio, "Stop the lorry. Stop the lorry. Armed men in the container."

There is also a very large stash of marijuana, and one gutsy old lady lying bound and gagged on the floor, as Donaldson finds out a few minutes later when he throws open the container's doors, shouting, "Armed police. Put down your weapons."

"They wouldn't have lasted two minutes in the war," Daphne tells Bliss a short while later, after he has helped her out of the container. "'Here. Have my chokky bickies,' I said, and the big soft Irish twerp just burst into tears."

"Oh, Daphne," laughs Bliss, close to tears himself as he hugs her.

"Is Missie Rouge all right?" she asks as he holds her.

"Minnie's feeding her at the moment, but I think she's getting used to being abandoned," he says as he pulls out his cellphone and calls Phillips in Vancouver.

Inspector Wilson takes Bliss's call. Sergeant Phillips is in the midst of interviewing Monty Maxwell's son, who is boasting, "I ain't done nuvvin. You can't nail me — know what I mean?"

"We already did, Jeremy," says Phillips confidently. "We got you on tape blowing your cousin away."

"He was already dead."

"Won't wash," says Phillips shaking his head. "Plus, Dingo isn't too happy about taking the full rap for wasting Tom Burton."

With a whisper in Phillips' ear, Wilson steps in. "Good news, Jeremy — though not so good for you, I'm afraid. We've just busted your entire operation in England, and John Waghorn's singing your name."

"All I do is the porn. And that ain't illegal," persists Maxwell. "I just gave him the flicks and if he liked what he saw, then we'd fix him up."

"And he'd bump 'em off."

Maxwell shrugs. "When do I get my lawyer?"

"We know what you were doing Jeremy," carries on Phillips as if he hasn't heard. "Your friend who runs the crematorium tells us that you've kept him pretty busy for years."

"You can't pin that on me. It was Waghorn, the perv. He'd get carried away — string 'em up too tight, get a bit rough, pump 'em full of dope, smack 'em around a bit too hard. I mean, they were all scrubbers and druggies. They were used to it. It's a rough trade."

"They weren't used to dying, though."

"Hey. Happens — know what I mean?"

"So, when it happened, you and your boys would clean up his mess?"

"Prove it."

"We will. So, why did Waghorn leave the country?"

"The heat was on."

"So you sold him your cousin's ID."

"So what? Snitchy f'kin Jordan didn't need it."

"He certainly doesn't now," admits Phillips.

"Back to the hospital with you," says Bliss as he helps Daphne into a police car.

"Not bloody likely," she replies haughtily. "There's nothing wrong with me that a good drop of vintage brandy won't cure. Come on, David. Take me back to the manor. I know where he keeps his stash."

"Daphne — you can't do that. It's theft," he says, as he jumps in beside her.

"Are you joking, David? After what he did to me?"

Superintendent Donaldson greets them outside the stables as he turns a small corner of broken plywood over in his hands.

"How did you know it was drugs?" Donaldson inquires of Daphne as they drive up.

"Elementary, my dear Superintendent," replies Daphne, in a Holmesian tone. "It was the way that they unloaded it that got me thinking. All the stacks from the back of the container were taken to that old barn over there, where nothing was happening, but all the others went into the barn that had been renovated. 'Why are they different?' I asked myself, 'They look the same.'"

"Because they have a different filling in the middle of the sandwich," says Donaldson as he splits apart the layers.

"Precisely, Superintendent. A thin sheet of highly compressed grass — I think that's what it's called today — between cedar veneers."

"And you could smell it?" Donaldson queries in surprise.

"No," laughs Daphne. "All I could smell was the cedar and the glue, but I knew he was up to no good and called his bluff."

"I still don't know why you didn't trust him."

"If you must know, Superintendent, I simply couldn't see any man with an appreciation for wood throwing a can of the most expensive wax polish into the rubbish bin."

"Daphne Lovelace, you are a genius," says Bliss, though he is still puzzled over how she had gotten into the estate.

"I'll show you," she says, starting to rise. Then she gives him a scowl as he puts out his hand to help. "I can manage, David."

A sea of white wood-anemones scattered with little bouquets of sunny primroses and vibrant splashes of violets greet the three of them as they make their way into the copse behind the ruins of the old manor.

"We used to play here before the war," says Daphne, as she leads them along an overgrown path for a few hundred feet. Then she stops. "See anything?" But neither Donaldson nor Bliss catches on.

"Over there," she points with a nod to a low grassy hillock, but it is only when they are right on top of it that they see and old wooden door set deep into the side of the mound.

"It's a tunnel," says Daphne, pulling her flashlight out of her old canvas bag; seconds later they are inside a limestone cavern last used as a D-Day ammunition dump in World War II. "It comes out in the basement of the old church," she explains, her voice echoing as she ushers them through the long, narrow gallery. "It was pretty scary coming in here after all those years, but at least I didn't have to worry about East German border guards popping up and blowing my head off."

"Waghorn nearly did, though," Bliss reminds her, and she stops to upbraid him with a reproachful look. "You should have listened to me, David. I told you something wasn't right about him."

epilogue

It's almost a year since Jordan Jackson went home knowing that he was about to rip out his wife's heart with his tale of woe, but he could never have imagined that all he might do was cut out those parts that were rotten. Under the tutelage of Trina Button, and the kindness of others, Ruth Crowfoot is now a trendy thirty-something who has spent her summer days feeding the ducks in Stanley Park, and the evenings and nights feeding her lover.

Mike Phillips has won a permanent transfer to Canada's Pacific coast, and, across the Atlantic in London, David Bliss is back at work, his leg fully healed, when Daphne Lovelace phones.

"Did you get one as well, David?" she wants to know, and Bliss catches on immediately.

"I guess you mean the wedding invitation — yes. Are you going?"

"Naturally. September in Vancouver sounds wonderful. You are coming, aren't you?"

"Well, I'm fairly busy ..." teases Bliss, then he relents. "Yes. Of course I am. Mike's asked me to be his best man. It's a funny time of day, though. Eleven in the morning?"

"That's what I thought. Maybe that's the way they do it over there — after all, they do drive on the wrong side of the road and eat banana omelettes for breakfast."

"September the ninth," muses Bliss as he pores over the invitation in front of him. "I've got a feeling that's about the time when all that baloney started with her husband."

September the ninth in Vancouver starts propitiously enough, with a brilliantly clear blue sky, and a fresh frosting of snow on the highest peaks. But at street level, where the summer's sun still warms the patrons on the patios of the city's myriad coffee shops, Daphne Lovelace is taking her new hat for a walk and is headed to the seafront along with Bliss.

"You don't think it's too green, do you, David?" she worries, as she clamps the feathery creation to her head against the soft ocean breeze.

"It looks sort of blue to me," replies Bliss perplexedly, and receives a snort of disdain.

"Hah. Men!"

Trina Button is experiencing similar feelings about her husband as she puts the finishing touches on the banquet table in her expansive dining room.

"Who says you can't have banana cream pies at a wedding?" she demands, and Rick backs off. "Whatever you say, dear."

Ruth Crowfoot has no such disharmony with the men in her life, and she stands checking out her nicely-shaped figure in the mirrored walls of Trina's bathroom, wondering when her world will finally stop spinning and she'll wake up.

"Fifteen minutes to makeup, Ms. Ruth," yells Trina, tapping on the door, and Ruth laughs — like she does every day — like she has done every day since March, when Jordan had finally been put to rest, and Mike Phillips had taken her by the hand and walked her to a neat little apartment building overlooking the harbour at False Creek.

A small dog had started yapping as Phillips had rung the bell, and the owner had calmed it as he'd opened the door.

"Mr. Sanderson? Geoffrey Sanderson?" Phillips had asked, as the grey-haired man's little poodle had rushed out to greet Ruth.

"That's right," the old Liverpudlian had replied cagily, then his face had lit up at the sight of Ruth. "Oh, hello, lass. We feed the ducks together don't we?"

"Can we come in for a moment?" Phillips had continued, well aware that neither Ruth nor the other man had any idea what was happening, and Sanderson had happily stepped aside.

"Of course you can. Come in; come in. I don't very often get visitors."

"This is Ruth Crowfoot. I think you knew her mother once — at the Beatles' concert at Empire Stadium," Phillips had said as they'd sat in Sanderson's tidy little apartment.

Phillips had felt Ruth's pulse quicken under his fingertips, and he'd sensed her questioning look, but he had kept his gaze on Sanderson and watched as the aging man's face had slowly warmed with the memory.

"Do you mean Nellie?" he had queried, and Ruth had nodded in a daze.

"Yes. She called herself Nellie."

"I looked everywhere for your mother, lass," he had carried on, giving Ruth's arm a gentle pat. "She was a lovely woman, lovely colour — like a nice piece of mahogany. And her eyes were pitch black — not unlike yours. I even left the boys in the lurch for the rest of the tour. I mean, Vancouver's a beautiful place and all that — I might have stayed anyway. But it was your mother who kept me here."

"But she said she met someone called George."

"Aye, lass. I used to tell all the girls that. Used to fancy meself with a guitar, I did. 'Course I weren't no good, not like George himself, but I could strum a tune or two, and I prob'ly dreamt that one day he'd not turn up and I could've stepped in for him."

"Nellie had a baby, Geoffrey," Phillips had chimed in gently, noticing that Ruth had clammed up and was biting back tears.

"Did she?" he'd replied. "She never told me. Not that it would have mattered. I would have loved to have had some kids, but it didn't turn out that way."

Ruth's lips had puckered and, as tears had streamed down her face, she had timidly asked, "Can I come and feed the ducks with you again ... Dad?"

"You knew Geoffrey was my father, didn't you?" Ruth had questioned a few days later when she'd got her mind straight.

"I had a pretty good idea, yes," Phillips had replied.

"But how did you know?"

"It's a secret," he had said, knowing that Geoffrey Sanderson would never remember the scruffy man in a baseball cap who had sat next to him one lunchtime while he was enjoying a small beer outside a waterfront tavern.

"OK," yells Trina playfully at her bathroom door, "I'm coming in to put your face on. Ready or not."

The door opens and Ruth stands in front of her, still in her dressing gown, with her eyes full.

"Christ. Are you ever going to stop crying?" laughs Trina. "What is it now?"

"Why are you so good to me, Trina?" snivels Ruth.

"Oh, I'm just the same with guinea pigs," replies Trina, then she leads Ruth to the bedroom, saying, "Come on, girl. We don't want to keep the guests waiting."

But Ruth is still skeptical that anyone other than Trina and her family will show up, worrying that her second wedding will be no better attended than her first. However, things are different this time — Trina has made sure of that. The Corner Coffee Shoppe has been closed for several months, and is up for sale, but Trina has managed to track down most of the old customers, and Ruth's side of the wedding chapel is bursting. Darcey, Maureen, and Matt — the crossword gang — have all brought partners; Cindy has brought Dave Smith, the telephone engineer, and spends most of the time flapping her engagement ring under noses.

"I thought you said he pinched your bum?" says Raven as she takes a peek.

"I never said I didn't want him to," protests Cindy.

Robyn from the candle shop and several of the other business owners have closed their doors for a few hours, and Trina has drummed up most of her kick boxing class, together with Erica from the cancer support group.

Inspector Wilson, Sergeant Brougham and many of Phillips' colleagues round out the congregation, though Hammer Hammett, Ruth's lawyer, sends his regrets.

"His only regret is that he didn't get a fat cheque because the police dropped all the charges," Trina had said when she'd opened his response. Geoffrey Sanderson looks and feels like a king as he walks his only daughter up the aisle with Maid of Honour Trina Button tripping along behind. But if Sanderson is a king, Ruth is the beautiful princess, and her charming prince waits at the altar with stars in his eyes.

"Have you got the ring, Dave?" Mike Phillips mutters from the corner of his mouth for the tenth time, and Bliss instinctively checks his pocket again.

"Yes. Stop worrying, Mike. Ruth doesn't want a ring, she only wants you."

"Everyone back to my place," yells Trina as soon as the officiator has said, "You may kiss the bride." She has a very special surprise waiting in a backyard marquee, and can't wait to see Ruth's face.

The Bootles, a tribute band with a Ringo look-alike on drums and a couple of wig-wearing kids on guitars, are apparently waiting for the fourth member as the guests grab glasses of champagne and crowd in. "Where's George?" asks "Paul" and, on cue, Ruth's father takes to the stage and picks up the guitar, saying into the microphone, "This is for the most beautiful woman in the world. My daughter, Ruth." Then the band begins and he sings sweetly, "Is there anybody going to listen to my story. All about the girl who came to stay ..."

"Ah girl. Girl," choruses the rest of the band, together with most of the audience, and Geoffrey Sanderson's lifelong dream comes true.

The applause is deafening when Geoffrey takes a bow, and the "real" George Harrison feigns reluctance in taking over from him for a few seconds until Geoffrey is embraced by his daughter and has to leave the stage.

"I've been practicing that for months," beams Geoffrey as Ruth melts all over him.

Trina has long-since given up on repairing her protege's makeup, so she just dabs at Ruth's face with a napkin as the Bootles strike up "All My Loving," quickly followed by "And I Love Her."

"When I'm Sixty-Four" is playing in the background as Ruth Phillips finally plucks up the courage to deal with the cloud on her horizon, and she walks her husband out of the tent into Trina's garden, asking, "Do you really love me, Mike?"

"You know I do. I've loved you from the moment I first saw you."

"And you never doubted me, did you?"

Something in her tone bothers Phillips. He wants to say, "Never," but he holds back, querying, "Should I have doubted you?"

If the band is playing, "Listen. Do you want to know a secret," Phillips doesn't hear, as he focuses worriedly on his wife.

"What would you do if I said I've kept something from you?"

"Nothing could change the way I feel about you, Ruth," he answers, then tries to kiss her.

"Wait a minute," she says. "Can I make a speech?"

"I think Dave's supposed to go first but ... Hey, it's your day."

With the audience stilled, Ruth stands at the microphone holding the bead bag that her mother had stolen for her as she says, "I've always thought that this was the only thing that my mother ever gave me, but now I know that she gave me the most important thing in life, the only thing she had to give — love." Then tears trickle down her cheeks as she weeps, "I'm sorry that I was never able to thank her. I just hope she can hear me."

"She can hear you," says Raven, her faith in Serethusa vindicated. "And she wishes you luck."

"Thank her for me," says Ruth through the tears as a dapper sixty-year-old man with a large hooked nose and dark glasses slips unnoticed into the back of the tent.

"I owe so much to so many of you," Ruth carries on, once she's straightened her voice, and she has Jordan Jackson, his abusive mother, and Tom Burton on her mind when she adds, "All my life I only ever met people who wanted something in return; who always took more than they gave. But in the last year I've realized that not everyone is like that."

Behind her, Ringo's double turns on a keyboard and quietly plays "With a Little Help from My Friends," and the newcomer at the back sings along softly, as Ruth goes on to say, "I know some of you are wondering why I chose today to marry Mike. Well, tomorrow is the anniversary of the day that my first husband decided to leave me, and it's also the day that Raven told me that it was my special day." She stops to wipe her eyes, and her hands shake as she opens her bead bag for a tissue, but then she takes out an envelope and hands it to Mike, saying. "I've been holding on to this for nearly a year. At first I was terrified that it made me look guilty, then I was terrified that Trina would stop being my friend if she thought I didn't need her, then I was terrified that you would stop loving me if you found out. Now I've got a father, a husband, and lots of friends; I've got everything I want, so it doesn't matter anymore. You can throw it away if you want."

"What is it?" he questions as he opens the envelope, joking, "That's married life for you. She gets a gold ring and all I get ... is an old lottery ticket."

A yell of delight comes from the floor as Raven screeches, "She was right! Serethusa was right! It *was* your day."

"How much?" asks Phillips, slowly catching on.

"Five million dollars," says Ruth sheepishly and the tent erupts in noise as the Bootles start back up with "Baby, You're a Rich Man."

"There is something else," says Ruth, holding on tightly to her husband while she looks tenderly into her father's eyes. "You're finally going to be a grandpa, Dad."

"I don't know if I can take all this," Phillips is saying, as Trina joyously waves her tape recorder in his face.

"Well, Mike. What's it like being married to a millionaire?"

"Wait a minute," says Phillips, taking hold of the machine, "There's no cassette in here."

"What cassette?" asks Trina in puzzlement. "Nobody said anything about a cassette. I just thought it recorded."

The band has switched to "All You Need Is Love," and Daphne Lovelace is bopping her way around the dance floor with David Bliss.

"I'm not really surprised that Jeremy went bad after what happened to his parents," says Daphne, her face showing the hurt of knowing that, in a way, she bore some responsibility. And she has a tear in her eye as she goes on, "Mind you, if he'd been brought up by someone who loved him it would have made all the difference. I mean, look at Ruth. What sort of start did she have? But she's dead right, all she really needed was love."

"Who's that over there?" queries Bliss as he spots the strange man in dark glasses having a quiet word with Mike, Ruth, and her father at the side of the stage.

"Where?" inquires Daphne as she struggles for height, but she only catches a glimpse before it's too late; with a handshake and a hug he has gone.

"It was just a very old friend," Geoffrey Sanderson tells Bliss a few minutes later as he and Daphne congratulate him, but he has more than an ordinary twinkle in his eye when Daphne muses, "He looked a bit like Ringo to me."

Cindy is one of the first to congratulate Ruth on her win, but Ruth points to her husband. "It's up to Mike to decide. He's got until tomorrow afternoon at five. Maybe he'll just want to keep things the way they are."

"It's only that the Coffee Shoppe went broke," carries on Cindy, not wanting to hear. "You could buy it back cheap."

"I could," says Ruth, as if she's unsure, then she laughs, "but I'd need someone reliable to run it for me."

Raven has tears of joy as she hugs and kisses Ruth. "Serethusa was right all along," she cries. "She told me there was nothing wrong with Jordan, and she was absolutely right about you. It really was your day."

"Yeah, but what about my accident?" Trina butts in, still waving her tape recorder.

"Bus!" screams Raven. "I said a bus — not a crazy kid on a bike. Bus! Bus! Bus! ..."

The End